High Praise for DENNIS JONES's
THE HOUSE OF THE PANDRAGORE

"Well put-together and consistently entertaining."
Locus

"Intriguing and engrossing . . . does not follow the
obvious path . . . Dennis Jones has a refreshing
respect for genuine virtue, but a solid understanding
that when goodness is pitted against relentless evil
there is no guarantee that good will prevail."
Robin Hobb, author of *The Farseer Trilogy*

"I picked it up after dinner and read through to the
end at 12:15 a.m.
That I don't often do."
Ann McCaffrey, *New York Times* bestselling author

"Strong male and female protagonists, a vivid assort-
ment of villains, and a satisfying conclusion that
leaves room for sequels."
Library Journal

"Plays fairer with the reader than some more famous
serial works of high fantasy."
Publishers Weekly

"In the tradition of Terry Goodkind . . . [It] will thrill
even the most jaded reader of epic fantasy adventure."
Realms of Fantasy

Also by Dennis Jones

THE STONE AND THE MAIDEN:
BOOK ONE OF THE HOUSE OF THE PANDRAGORE

BOOK TWO OF THE HOUSE OF THE PANDRAGORE

THE MASK
AND THE
SORCERESS

DENNIS JONES

An Imprint of HarperCollins*Publishers*

EOS
An Imprint of HarperCollins*Publishers*
10 East 53rd Street
New York, New York 10022-5299

Copyright © 2001 by Dennis Jones
ISBN: 0-380-80619-3
www.eosbooks.com

Published by arrangement with HarperCollins Publishers Ltd., Canada.

First Eos paperback printing: March 2002
First Eos hardcover printing: April 2001

Eos Trademark Reg. U.S. Pat. Off. and in Other Countries, Marca Registrada, Hecho en U.S.A.
HarperCollins ® is a trademark of HarperCollins Publishers Inc.

Printed in the U.S.A.

10 9 8 7 6 5 4 3 2 1

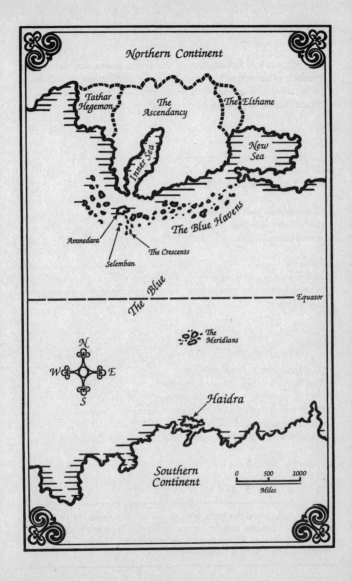

THE MASK
AND THE
SORCERESS

I

THE BLUE HAVENS

1

THEATANA AND HER GUARDS WALKED ALONG THE LA-
goon's beach toward the rising sun. The slanting light turned
the fine-grained quartz sand at her feet from white to rose,
and brushed the lagoon's ripples with molten copper. As
usual, the lagoon was calm; separated from the open sea by
its barrier reef, it remained placid even when the ocean was
in an angry mood.

The four guards trailed a score of paces behind her, which
was their habit during her morning walks. Occasionally
Theatana wondered what they would do if she threw off her
clothes, ran into the water, and began to swim for the reef.
She would never reach its distant dark line, of course; the
reef was a long way out, and she wasn't a strong swimmer.
But would the guards spear her when she was a few yards
from shore or, obeying some secret order not to interfere
with her suicide, would they simply watch her swim away
until she sank?

The question was no more than an idle fancy. Theatana
had no intention of killing herself, for her death would
merely relieve the minds of those who had exiled her to this
utterly remote island of Selemban. As long as she lived she
could at least burden her enemies' days with flashes of
worry. It was little enough, but she had been on Selemban
for a long time, and she no longer hoped for any greater revenge.

She halted to gaze at the distant sea beyond the reef. She
wore a thin white dalmatica that fell almost to her sandaled
feet, and with it an overmantle of yellow linen. Though the

3

cloth was rich, no jewelry glinted at her throat nor on her fingers or wrists. Her hair was black and cut short about her shoulders, and in it were fine strands of gray, for she was at the later edge of childbearing age. Her hands bore no marks of toil, and neither harsh weather nor strong sunlight had marred her golden skin. Though her face was still fit to turn men's heads, she had never borne children, and her slender figure showed it. Her eyes were the color of indigo, or the deep sea beyond the reef.

She scanned the horizon. She did so even knowing she would see nothing but the sea and the morning sky. The supply ship wasn't due for twenty days, and in any case it always approached from the other side of the island. Then it sailed round the island's western tip to gain the shelter of the small harbor inside the reef. The harbor itself was out of sight beyond a low ridge of white stone, in the direction from which she had come.

Theatana glanced back toward the ridge. On its crest, and inland behind the beach, grew tall fretwork palms. She was vaguely aware that people on other islands harvested their bark for its intricate natural embossing, and made artifacts from it to send to the mainland far to the north. No such people lived on Selemban. Here there were only Theatana, her guards, the guard commander, and the deaf-mute eunuch who cooked for all of them. In her first years on Selemban she had sometimes diverted herself by pretending they were her household, and that she was a ruler again. But the fantasy was too disheartening, and she eventually, bitterly, gave it up. She had been a prisoner for all her adult life, and no intensity of imagination could obscure her fate. She had missed almost everything of her life, and even now, after so many years, she could not really accept its ruin. Sometimes she lay awake in the hours before the dawn and silently wept for her loss.

She noticed a movement among the distant palm trunks on the ridge. The guards stirred and looked at it. Theatana said nothing to them, for they knew nothing of her language and she loathed speaking theirs, though she'd learned a good deal of it during her exile here. They were dark-skinned

Mixtun islanders, in leather and iron armor and carrying short stabbing swords at their belts. Each wore a thick braid of hair that snaked from beneath his helmet and hung swaying at his back. The one in charge of her escort—she had no idea of his name, for all the guards except the commander were changed every month—grunted, and gestured at her to go toward the ridge and the man now hurrying toward them. Theatana stared hard at the Mixtun, and he made a furtive warding sign with his least finger and his thumb.

But his gesture against her supposed evil meant nothing; the guards would still force her compliance if she did not go willingly. Accepting necessity, she turned and began to walk at a languid pace toward the still-distant figure. By the man's helmet crest and smudge of black beard she could tell that it was Tabar, the Mixtun guard commandant.

Suddenly her pulse quickened as she realized the oddity of his behavior. Why was he wearing a helmet? Normally he went bareheaded because of the heat, as did the guards. More peculiar still, why was he coming for her himself, instead of sending one of his men? He was a rigorous jailer, and scrupulously kept his distance from his captive. He spoke to her only when it was essential for him to do so. This suited Theatana perfectly; he was a stupid, narrow man.

Perhaps, she thought suddenly, it was her death warrant and her death that he brought. Would he hasten his steps like this, for such a purpose?

No, that's not it. He'd cut my head off from behind, without warning, so I'd have no chance to curse him. And after this long, it's not likely there's been such an order.

What was his hurry, then? Was she to be moved? Out of the twenty-five years of her captivity, she had been on Selemban for eleven of them, eleven years on an island two miles long and half a mile wide. She knew every stone and bush of the place. Still, it was better than the tower in the Numera, the old fortress at the center of the Fountain Palace in faraway Captala Nea. On Selemban she could see horizons. She supposed she was well treated, in comparison to what they could have done to her. Books and writing materials were allowed, and the food and wine were good.

But where would they move her that was more secure than this? All the other habitable islands of the vast archipelago called the Blue Havens lay well to the north of this fleck of stone. To the south of Selemban lay nothing but a scatter of tiny, unpeopled islets, and beyond those stretched only the boundless realm of the deep ocean, the Blue itself. They could move her no farther in that direction; if there were other lands over that distant, hard-edged horizon, as some of the old stories said there were, no one knew how to reach them.

Perhaps it's death after all. I'll curse him well before I go.

Tabar had almost reached her, and she stopped to let him approach. He was a dark brown sinewy man, black-eyed and militarily experienced, some years older than she. She had contemplated seducing him into getting her off the island, but some intuition had warned her this would be useless. She had nothing to offer him but her body, and he was too severe a man to fall into that trap. Gold might have done it, she thought, but for this precise reason she was allowed to possess not so much as a plain silver ring.

"What is it?" she asked coldly. "May I not even walk without disturbance?"

Tabar saluted. "My lady, there is a sail rounding the island from the north. You must come back to the compound."

"Why? The supply ship is merely early."

He looked uneasy. "You are not allowed outside your quarters when there is a ship in the harbor, my lady. You know that."

"A stupid regulation. Am I likely to secrete myself in the hold, with your dirty savages watching me?"

"I must insist."

They would drag her, an indignity, if she did not comply. "Very well. Get on with you, then."

He led the way back toward the ridge. He tried to hurry her, but she went slowly in order to annoy him. Consequently, a considerable time passed before they reached the ridge's stony base and began climbing, and as they topped its crest the sun was already well above the horizon.

Tabar stopped short, and swore in Mixtun.

Theatana also stopped. From the ridge she could see down to the small harbor and to the nearby walled compound that contained Tabar's residence, the guards' barracks, and her private quarters. A stack of thick palm logs lay near the compound gate, waiting to be cut into firewood, and a skein of pale blue smoke rose from the chimney of the compound's service building, where the kitchen was. No boats were moored in the harbor, but just outside it floated a ship, her sails luminous in the morning light.

Theatana stared at it. This could not be the supply vessel, arriving early. It looked wrong; in fact it did not look like any ship she had ever seen. It had three masts, rather than the customary one or two, and on both the foremast and aftermast were triangular sails striped with bands of green and white. The mainmast carried a tall, narrow sail, this one rectangular and the color of pale sand. The black hull was lean and low, with a sharp bow and a raised afterdeck that jutted out over the stern.

And gliding around the stern from the ship's far side, heading fast toward the harbor mouth, was a boat packed with gray-clad rowers.

Tabar swore again and seized her arm. A moment later he was dragging her downhill at a run, toward the fort. As she ran she watched the progress of the boat. It was coming fast, and the fort's gate was still distant. Tabar made her run faster. She was not used to hard exercise, and a stitch pierced her side.

They were nearing the gate when the strange boat grounded a few yards offshore. Even as it stopped, its crew shipped their oars and began leaping into the shallows to splash toward the sandy beach. Theatana felt a stab of shock. They were huge men, clad in gray armor, bearing swords at their waists and carrying long spears and round red shields painted with a big-eyed gray bird like an owl. And they weren't Mixtuns. Their skin was too pale, some wore beards, and the beards were yellow-gold in the morning light. Theatana had never seen anyone with a yellow beard.

Now she and Tabar were close to the compound's narrow entrance, her guards pelting alongside to form a line between her and the onrushing strangers. There were about thirty of the attackers, yelling what sounded like battle cries, but in no tongue Theatana had ever heard. The stitch in her side was almost unbearable, but she forced herself to keep running.

The raiders had reached shore just a little too late. Theatana rounded the stack of palm logs and staggered with Tabar and her guards into the compound. She heard the gate crash shut behind her and the rumble of the bar being drawn. Several more moments passed while she stood doubled over, gasping for breath. Then, from the gate's far side, came harsh laughter and a loud hammering. The yellow-beards must have been right on her heels, and now were knocking derisively on the gate as if for admittance.

Tabar gave her a shake. "Did you summon them? Are they here to free you? Who are they?"

She straightened painfully, still breathing hard. "Don't be a fool. Was I trying to run *to* them? And have you ever seen men who looked like that? I haven't."

He seemed to believe her. "My lady, you have to go to your quarters."

"What for?"

"Your own protection."

"What use will that be if they get in? There are three of them to every man of yours. And more on that ship."

"Nevertheless. Please, my lady."

The ten Mixtuns of her guard were crouching on the wall-walk above. One peered over the wall, then leaped back as a spear hurtled into the air, narrowly missing him. Deep, raucous laughter rose from outside.

She shrugged and crossed the courtyard to the door to her quarters. Tabar came with her.

"What do you want?" she asked, standing on the threshold. "Are you going to lock me in?"

"Yes, my lady. I have orders."

She looked into his eyes, and narrowed hers. "And if they kill you all and set fire to the place? Am I to burn to death for your orders?"

He hesitated. "Very well. But bar the inner door."

"I have no bar on my side, or had you forgotten?" She bared her sharp white teeth at him. "Again, your orders."

He capitulated. "Go in, my lady. But stay there, or I will lock you up after all."

Theatana turned on her heel, marched through the doorway, and thrust home the heavy plank door. Inside was an anteroom, its walls plastered plain white, with a rush mat on the floor. She went through the inner doorway into her sitting room, which was sparsely furnished and lit from high up by narrow windows set into the plastered walls. The windows were unglazed but were barred; even if they hadn't been, they were too narrow for her slender frame.

Through the openings she heard yells and a sudden, heavy *boom*. The yellow-bearded men had found a palm log to use as a battering ram. She wondered how long it would take them to get through the gate, or over the wall. The top of the parapet was only twice a man's height.

What would happen to her then?

She knew the immediate answer. They were clearly raiders, and they were men, and she was a woman. But if they didn't kill her afterward, if they just gave her a little time—

I've been a prisoner for twenty-five years.

The gate boomed again, then a third time. Much shouting and yelling, cut through by a scream. She heard a sharp crack, then more yells, and clangs of steel on steel. Had they gotten in already? The gate must have been weaker than it looked.

She turned and walked swiftly into the small room where her bed was. It was a massive wooden platform with a down mattress on it, and an embroidered coverlet. With some difficulty, bracing her feet against the join of wall and floor, she started working the platform away from its usual position. It had never occurred to Tabar or her previous warder that she might be stronger than she appeared, and the searches of her quarters had never included moving the bed. The wood grated and squealed as she inched it across the uneven flagstones, but there was now such a deafening clamor from outside that no one would hear her, much less pay attention.

Finally, the platform was two handbreadths from its normal place. She scrabbled at the small square flagstone the movement had revealed, and with pain stabbing at the quick beneath her fingernails, she pried the stone from its mortar bed. Beneath the stone was a cavity, and in the cavity lay a short, curved blade with a rough wooden handle. It was a stripping knife, of the sort the islanders used to peel bark from the trunks of fretwork palms. She'd found it almost buried in the sand three years ago, while she was sitting on the beach, and had been deft enough to conceal it in the sleeve of her overmantle and smuggle it back to her quarters. It wasn't intended for fighting, but she'd realized that it would make a vicious close-in weapon. The blade was orange and pitted with rust, but as she had carefully ground its edge on a bit of stone she'd seen the razor gleam of metal appear. The sharpened knife had lain under the flagstone ever since.

She took it from its hiding place and slipped it into her sash beneath her overmantle, well around to her left side where it wouldn't show. Then she heaved the bed back into position and returned to the sitting room. The clangor of weaponry outside was even louder. A man screamed in agony.

She peered into the anteroom. Her heart pounded. *What now?*

She was still standing there when the courtyard door flew open and banged against the anteroom wall. Tabar staggered through it, his left forearm agleam with blood. Right after him came a raider. The man didn't have a spear, but his sword was out, and crimson. Between the cheek pieces of his domed helmet his mouth was snarling, his teeth bared above the rim of his shield. Tabar spun to face him just in time, and their swords hammered edge to edge, like the din of a forge. Theatana could see past Tabar and the raider, into the courtyard. Knots of men struggled and flailed at each other. She took three steps closer to Tabar's heaving back.

Without warning, a Mixtun fell through the courtyard door into the anteroom. He had taken a blade in the throat and was dying. He rolled across the flagstones, kicking and gurgling, and knocked the raider's feet from under him. The man yelled and went down, falling backward beneath his shield. Tabar pounced, ramming one booted foot onto the shield to keep the raider prone, and deflected a clumsy sword stroke from the fallen man.

Theatana yanked the stripping knife from her mantle. As Tabar's blade came up, poised to drive into the raider's face, she slashed the Mixtun across the back of a bare knee. The knife cut deep, parting tendon and muscle like shears through flax. His leg unstrung, Tabar shrieked, toppled sideways, and rolled onto his back. His appalled and disbelieving gaze met hers, and he seemed to have forgotten he was clutching his sword.

The raider was struggling to his feet. Quick, she had to be quick. She couldn't get at Tabar's throat; his armor protected it. Theatana bent over him, drew a quick little breath through parted lips, and drove the knife deep into his eye socket.

2

ILARION SAW THE BODIES FIRST.

He spotted them shortly after *Ascendancy Maid* sailed into the lagoon and just as she was swinging her bow toward the harbor mouth. Startled, but unwilling to believe that the dark shapes at the foot of the compound's wall were indeed corpses, he pulled the spyglass from his belt and snapped it open. The gentle sway of the ship's foredeck beneath his seaboots made the lens wander, but after a few moments he captured the two men in his field of view. Dark-skinned, naked except for breechclouts, they lay by the compound's gate in the late-afternoon sunlight. They were clearly dead, for small blue salt-hawks and a few gulls pecked and flapped around their heads and bellies.

Ilarion swept the glass across the foreshore below the compound. No boats were drawn up on the beach. Except for the white-and-azure flutter of the scavenging birds, he saw no sign of life. The sunlight lay like a clear molten glaze over sea and land; at this hour of the tropical afternoon, it made even the sea breeze sultry. Ilarion found the heat oppressive, for both sides of his family came from the temperate zones; his mother was born in the lowlands by the Inner Sea, and his father in the lofty, mountainous plateau of the Elthame. Ilarion had his father's dark bronze hair, as well as a highlander's height and straight nose, but his deep blue eyes and the hint of gold in his skin betrayed his mother's race.

From the port rail, the leadsman called out, "Depth two and a half," and pulled up his sounding line for another heave. *Ascendancy Maid* was now bearing down on the harbor mouth, picking her way carefully through the shallows. She was a two-masted artema, a long-distance dispatch vessel some eighty feet from stem to stern. Her big square mainsail was now brailed up to its yardarm, and her smaller guide-sail on its slanted foremast was set to catch the onshore breeze. At her masthead floated the banner of the Ascendancy, a golden sun disk with wheat garlands on a green ground.

Ilarion lowered the spyglass and turned around. As was routine when *Ascendancy Maid* approached a foreign landing, the dozen soldiers of her fighting complement waited near the ship's boat, under the eye of their peltarch. For this voyage, Ilarion had handpicked both the officer and the men; they were all elite marines, Paladine guardsmen trained in sea combat.

"Ethon!" he called to the peltarch. "A word with you."

Ethon approached and saluted. He was a little younger than Ilarion and an excellent line officer. He had served last year in the amphibious campaign against the pirate nests of the southwest Inner Sea, a campaign Ilarion had commanded.

"My lord?" he said.

"Someone or something has killed people onshore. Treat the landing as hostile."

A gleam of anticipation lit the peltarch's eyes. "Yes, sir. A fight?"

"Possibly. Carry on."

As Ethon returned to his men, Ilarion hurried aft to the raised stern deck, where Captain Batilicus kept a watchful eye on the Mixtun pilot hired to navigate them through these foreign waters.

"My lord?" Batilicus asked, seeing Ilarion's face as Ilarion came up the steps of the deck ladder.

"Something's wrong ashore. I saw bodies. Would you be so good as to slow us down while I speak with Prince Lashgar."

Batilicus shouted, and two sailors hauled on the guide-sail until it spilled its wind. Ilarion went aft to the stern rail and waved at the ship that followed his own. Unlike *Ascendancy Maid*, the prince's vessel was a fighting craft, a long, narrow hemiolia of seventy-six oars, painted in the bright patterns of yellows, crimsons, and greens the islanders loved. Her nameboards, fixed to her hull on each side of her prow, proclaimed her to be *Scourge*, and at her masthead floated a white-and-blue ensign displaying the moon disk of Ammedara. She was moving under shortened mainsail, though her oarsmen were at the ready if she needed help to make her anchorage.

Scourge approached quickly; in light winds she was faster than *Ascendancy Maid*, though in heavy weather she would need to run for shelter long before the artema did. *Ascendancy Maid*, if her seams were tight and her hatches well battened down, was twin to a corked bottle and could ride a stormswept sea for weeks. Yet, like all ships of the Ascendancy and the Blue Havens, she would still be blown wherever the gale sent her. Ilarion was convinced that ships could be built to be less prey to the weather. The search for ideas about how to do this was one reason he was on this state visit to the islands.

The other reason for his journey was much less congenial. It involved Aunt Theatana, long exiled to the island of Selemban that lay ahead of the artema's bow. Or she *had* been exiled there; on the evidence of the bodies by the compound gate, she might well be dead. Ilarion much preferred to believe she was. He did not want to think about what might happen if Theatana had escaped. Or worse, if she had escaped with the help of unidentified allies.

Aunt Theatana: the bad seed of the family. Much worse than bad, in fact. When Ilarion was a boy she had been *mad* Aunt Theatana as well, though she had recovered her wits, or appeared to, around the time he was fourteen. Shortly thereafter she'd been sent into distant exile in the islands. He was twenty-five now, so she'd been here for over a decade. Six months ago she wrote to his mother to ask for books that were available only in the Ascendancy, and those books were now in a wooden chest below in his cabin. Ilarion was here to deliver them, and to assess his aunt's health and state of mind. Though Theatana would never be released from her imprisonment, his mother could never bring herself to ignore her half sister entirely.

"Be very careful when you're in your aunt's presence," his father had told him the day he sailed. "She's a Dascaris, and despite her evil reputation she can charm fish out of the water if she cares to. Even your grandfather Archates Dascaris could do that, though he usually chose to be unpleasant. And if you want to know the power of the Dascarid charm, well, you've seen the effect your mother has on people."

"I know. Everyone wants to please her."

"Yes. House Dascaris bore two kinds of fruit, the sweet and the bitter, and your mother's the sweet. But make no mistake about it, Theatana is the other kind, no matter how she presents herself. She's got the savagery and the hunger for power that was the blot on the Dascaris family, and you'd better remember that when you see her, and her cunning as well. As soon as you let her know who you are, she'll try to convince you that she's harmless, remorseful, and deserving of your sympathy. Don't be taken in by it."

"I won't. You've told me enough about her."

"Be sure you keep it in mind. And in the name of the All-father, don't ever be alone with her, don't eat anything she offers you, and don't turn your back to her. She'd kill you if she could, because of who you are, and because of what your death would do to me and to your mother."

"Even if it meant her own death?"

"Possibly. As far as I can tell, she lives for revenge. If she can get that, she may not care about dying."

But, Ilarion thought as he watched *Scourge* draw near, *Aunt Theatana may already be dead.*

His father would be relieved if she were, though he had never outright demanded her death. That was because Ilarion's mother would never have agreed to it; it was well-known that she didn't want the blood of her half sister on her hands. Occasionally Ilarion wondered how he would feel if Katheri, his own sister, hated him as deeply as Theatana hated their mother. Luckily, Katheri was nothing like their aunt or their grandfather. He, however, had not been quite so fortunate.

He pushed the disagreeable thought away and returned his attention to the present. *Scourge* now lay twenty yards astern, her pace matching *Ascendancy Maid*'s. Ilarion saw Lashgar making his way to the hemiolia's foredeck. The wiry dark figure leaned over the warship's prow and called, in the musical island tongue, "What's the matter?"

Ilarion said in Mixtun, "There are bodies by the compound gate. I see no movement; I think they're all dead."

Lashgar cursed vividly and briefly, then called an order over his shoulder. His twenty Mixtun marines, who had been sitting amidships, got to their feet. Their gilded helmets and blue-enameled body armor proclaimed their special status: guardsmen to the family of Jaladar II, King of Ammedara. Lashgar was the king's son, and two years younger than Ilarion.

"Let *Scourge* pass you and make land first," Lashgar called. "It's slack tide—we'll go in on oars and run her onshore."

"Do you want my men?"

"Yes, if you're willing. But your ship can't get onto the beach the way *Scourge* can. Can your men come over if we lie alongside you?"

"Of course. We'll hop across. Give me a moment to arm."

"All right. I'll do the same."

Ilarion hurried aft to his cabin. By the time he emerged, wearing mail tunic and helmet and carrying sword and shield, *Scourge* was already abeam of the artema. Ilarion got up on the rail, where he steadied himself by grabbing the mainmast's starboard backstay. His Paladines got ready to follow him.

"Don't fall in," Lashgar warned. "There are sharks in these lagoons."

"We'll try not to." Ilarion knew little about sharks, for the Inner Sea of his homeland was free of the predators, except near the straits that joined it to the Blue. He did know enough about them to avoid an encounter, and took a somewhat firmer grasp on the backstay.

Scourge and *Ascendancy Maid* closed until a foot of water separated them and he could step over the gap onto the war-ship's rail. Lashgar seized his arm and steadied him as he jumped down to the deck. His Paladines followed, in a rumble of hobnailed sandals on decking.

"Welcome aboard," the prince said as he released his grip. He grinned, displaying the silver inlays in his teeth. Unlike his marines, he wore the light seaman's armor of the islands—a red quilted cuirass over a brown-and-white tunic and a simple iron helmet—and carried a crescent shield and a battle-ax. His face was a narrow triangle, with a tapering chin accentuated by his close-trimmed, pointed beard. Ilarion still found beards a little unusual. Except for priests, Ascendancy men went clean-shaven, but every male in the Blue Havens grew a vigorous black beard as soon as he was old enough to produce one. Lashgar was very proud of his, and trimmed it almost daily.

Ilarion acknowledged the greeting with a quick nod as his eyes scanned the shore. The hemiolia swung away from the artema. As soon as *Scourge* was well clear of the other vessel, her shipmaster yelled orders, and her rowers slid their oars into position. A timing drum thudded, the crew picked up the beat, and the oar blades bit the waves in quick bright splashes. *Scourge* rode only half as deep in the water as *Ascendancy Maid*, so her master wasn't bothering to take soundings, though he did have a lookout up at the masthead.

"Do you think we'll get a fight?" Lashgar's narrow dark face was intent. He shaded his eyes with the flat of his hand and squinted shoreward.

"I'm beginning to think we won't. It looks deserted."

"It does." Lashgar's voice took on an edge of worry. "My father . . . he'll be very distressed. We were supposed to keep your aunt secure and alive."

"She may still be here," Ilarion said, more to spare Lashgar's feelings than because he believed it. He used his spy-glass to scan the beach for a keel's furrow. "There's no sign of a boat having come ashore. If one did, it was at lower tide. I see a lot of footprints, though."

"My father put ten men here to guard her," Lashgar said tersely. "The prints may be theirs."

Ilarion lowered the glass. Lashgar was likely wishing that his father had not offered the island as a place of exile for Theatana, though up till now it had seemed a good idea. On Selemban she was far from the Ascendancy's shores, far from anyone who might profit from aiding her, and Jaladar of Ammedara knew from personal experience how dangerous this woman could be. Ilarion's parents, who were also among Jaladar's oldest friends, had known they could trust him to keep her guarded and harmless.

What in the name of the Allfather could have happened? he thought. *There are no pirates in these waters, not since Jaladar burned them out of their nests. And what petty ruler in the Havens would bother to rescue my aunt and provoke Jaladar's fury?*

The answers would come, perhaps. Ilarion shoved the spyglass into his belt and waited while *Scourge* closed steadily on the white sand beach. In a few moments he heard a shouted order from the stern, and the hemiolia's oars rumbled inboard. Moments later the vessel slowed suddenly; she'd grounded. The slim hull ran on a few more paces as the keel bit into the sand, and then the vessel stopped, her ram barely submerged.

"Follow me," Lashgar said to his marines. He unbuckled his sword belt, held the weapon and its scabbard over his head to keep it from getting wet, and dropped from the warship's foredeck rails into the thigh-deep water. Ilarion did the same, with the Mixtun troops and his own Paladines following, and they all splashed ashore. The water was so warm that Ilarion barely felt it against his skin.

"The gate's been smashed in," he said as they halted at the tide line.

"I see," Lashgar said furiously. "Pirates. I'll have their guts on a gibbet." He turned to the captain of marines. "Alaco, take your men and see if there's anyone in there."

Ilarion told Ethon to hold the Paladines in reserve, and Alaco ordered his men into a spear hedge and started them toward the gate. At their approach the scavenging gulls and salt-hawks rose shrieking from the corpses, and flew away. Ilarion and Lashgar went over to the wall to inspect the bodies, their eye sockets pecked clean by the birds. But they were clearly Mixtuns, by their dark skin and the single thick braid of black hair each wore. The raiders had looted the dead men's armor and weapons, and they wore nothing but bloodstained white breechclouts. Even the fine silver wire that the island soldiers used to bind their braids had been ripped away.

"It happened yesterday or the day before," Lashgar said after a few moments. "The birds have been at them for a while. I'd make it two days ago."

Ilarion nodded, gazing down at the bodies. Just a few nights past, these men would likely have counted off another day of their service on the island, calculated how many days were left, would have grumbled at the isolation and the boredom. They had not known that their fates moved toward them from across the midsummer sea. The knowledge saddened him.

"Spears, by the look of it," he said. "Very exact spearmen, too. Not much hacking and slashing. One thrust to do for that man, two for the other."

He knew about wounds and about death in battle, for he had inflicted both, and had twice narrowly escaped dying. He had fought against steppe nomads trying to penetrate the passes of the Great North Wall, against a Tathar border lord who decided to ignore the peace treaty between the Ascendancy and the Tathar Hegemon, and last summer had led a dromon squadron to root out a pirate haven in the southwest of the Inner Sea. But he knew his battles hadn't been vast ones, not, for instance, like the Ascendancy's catastrophic defeat at Thorn River back in his father's day, when the War of the Chain was beginning. By that standard his battles were little more than skirmishes.

"You should be glad they're small," his father had told him when he commented on it. "The Ascendancy had a hundred years of border fighting under the Dascarids, along with a dozen civil wars and rebellions. Too many of those battles were big ones. No one wants those days to come again. We're still recovering, even after a generation."

Since the previous winter solstice, however, the Ascen-

dancy had known nothing but peace from the Marches to the
Inner Sea. Ilarion finally had his opportunity to sail *Ascendancy Maid* to the islands, as he had wanted to do since she
was built. He had been to Ammedara five years before, when
he accompanied his parents on what was supposed to be a
state visit but was really an excuse for Key and Mandine to
spend a month with Jaladar, their old friend and comrade-in-
arms. For their part, Ilarion and Lashgar had sailed the islands and hunted in the mountain forests of Ammedara.
They had also drunk a lot of wine together, and Lashgar
knew some uncommonly pretty dancers and drum girls. But
on this second visit, Ilarion was at the center of the state occasion. Hunting and wine were present in moderation and
drum girls not at all.

And the visit was not, he told himself glumly, turning out
at all well. If Theatana had escaped, Jaladar was ultimately
responsible. The friendship between him and Ilarion's parents could become strained unless he and Lashgar somehow
got her back. And Theatana might just possibly be a threat
in herself, though Ilarion couldn't imagine precisely how;
she had no allies or friends, much less armies, fleets, lands,
or wealth. And as for her rumored sorcery, if she were truly
skilled, she'd have long since used her craft to free herself.

Maybe she's dead, he thought. *But even if she is, we won't
know it for sure if we don't find her body. We'll have to
search the island. And if we don't find her, where has she
gone and with whom?*

Alaco came back alone and saluted. "There's no one alive
here, my lord prince. Commandant Tabar is dead, and I
counted eight more soldiers inside, in addition to the pair
here. And there is a dead eunuch in the kitchen."

"That's all of them, then. Looted, I suppose?"

"Yes, my lord. Whoever it was, they cleaned out the armory, as well as stripping the bodies. There's not a weapon
left in the place. They picked the storerooms bare, also."

Lashgar yanked angrily at his beard. "Like hawks on a
fish head. Curse them, whoever they are."

Ilarion felt a wash of disappointment and anger. Now
they'd have to search the island and hope to find Theatana

either dead or in hiding. He glanced up at the sun. It was declining toward the west, but several hours remained before dark. *Ascendancy Maid* had dropped anchor in the harbor's center, and her crew was furling her guide-sail and securing the main. She'd be safe enough there, even with the Paladines busy ashore.

Lashgar might have overheard his thoughts. "Time to start looking for your aunt, I think. It will take till sundown to cover all the ground."

They found no trace of her, living or dead. By late dusk the marines and the ships' crews were all back at the harbor beach, where they lit fires to cook a sailor's meal of barley porridge, dried lentils, and salt fish. Ten rowers had been left out of the search to bury the dead; the corpses now rested in a deep grave well inland so that their ghosts would be less likely to trouble the living.

Ilarion and Lashgar sat on a palm log placed on the sand a little apart from the men. They had finished eating and held cups of rough shipboard wine. In the west the sky glowed with sullen russet and copper, and a dark blue reef of cloud lay along the horizon.

"I can't fathom it," Lashgar said morosely. "My father has spies in the other princedoms, as you well may imagine, and he tells me most of what goes on there. There's been no whiff of a rescue attempt. Which is not to say there was none. But what would anyone have to gain by freeing her? Your aunt has no claim on the diadem of the Ascendancy, and no one would follow her in a rebellion even if she did. Your house is too much loved, and even if it were not, she has too dire a reputation. Not just treachery, but—" Lashgar looked around, and made a warding sign. "The other thing, also."

"I know." Ilarion glanced inland. The gravesite was distant, and its rough cairn of stones was already invisible in the deepening blue-gray of dusk. Even so, the newly dead made uneasy company. He would have been less uneasy if Theatana Dascaris had been among them.

His aunt had an evil reputation, as Lashgar had suggested.

It was not merely that she had usurped the throne of the Ascendancy from Ilarion's mother Mandine, and had slaughtered hundreds of innocents to secure her grip on power. Much worse, she had ultimately tried to betray the Ascendancy itself to the sorcerer Erkai. It was Erkai's ghastly talisman that had given its name to the War of the Chain, in which the Ascendancy had fought for its survival against him and his allies, the Tathar hordes from the west.

Also entwined with her treachery was Theatana's dabbling in the Black Craft, the forbidden sorcery that needed a death to work even its simplest spells. She had always had a taste for the darkness, and it was well known that people who took up the Craft did not easily lay it down again. If freedom offered Theatana a chance to develop her arts, she would inevitably seize it without hesitation.

But Ilarion knew that his parents were most uneasy about her because she had, for a short time, submitted herself to Erkai's will, and that submission might have entailed more than mere obedience. According to the Perpetua Orissi, the high priestess who probed Theatana after her capture, there was a taint in her, a taint of something foul. What that taint might grow into, if Theatana were ever permitted to nurture it with the Craft, not even Orissi could tell. But the warning was clear: Theatana must never be free.

And now she was.

"Father cleared out the pirates in Ammedaran waters," Lashgar was saying. "There are still some in the far eastern islands, but we make sure they don't dare come here. Maybe some backwater baron from Nevali's princedom has taken it into his thick head to go raiding, in spite of the treaty. But somebody like that wouldn't take on a fortified place, not one with a detachment of regulars to defend it."

"Whoever it was," Ilarion said, "I'll have to go looking for them. I have to find out if she's alive or dead." He wondered if Theatana could have advanced her command of the Craft enough, even in captivity, to procure a rescue. It seemed unlikely.

Lashgar dug at the sand with the heel of his seaboot. "I'm coming with you. And it'd be better if we made the search in

Scourge. If the men who took your aunt are in a warship, and they likely are, I don't think your artema will catch them. I'd like to send *Ascendancy Maid* back to Ammedara, with a message to have my father call out the fleet. You should send a dispatch home about what's happened, too." He took a deep breath, let it out. "But if the ship that took your aunt is in the islands or on the Blue, we'll find it."

"All right." But it was a little late for such promises. The Blue was boundless, and myriad islands lay across it. How could Jaladar have been so careless? A hundred men should have guarded Theatana, not ten.

We'll never find her.

Ilarion looked down at his hands and saw that they shook. The nape of his neck seemed to quiver, as if the tendons there vibrated like harp strings; his lips felt numb.

Stop. Stop it, this moment.

He recognized the old enemy, the fury that fortunately seldom woke in him, but which nevertheless lurked always in his depths. Though he was almost entirely his father's son, the Dascaris blood flowed in him, too, and with it had come some of his grandfather Archates' temperament. It manifested itself in upheavals of towering, murderous rage when strain and apprehension harried him, and some fool blundered and he had to put the blunder to rights.

He thought: *You've cost men their lives because you couldn't master yourself. Stop this, now.*

His remorse seemed to cool his fury, but he knew it was not really doing so. He knew he was calming down only because what had happened was not quite enough to put him over the edge.

"I don't blame you if you're furious," Lashgar muttered. Years ago, in the Fountain Palace, he'd once seen Ilarion in a Dascarid rage. That anger was not at Lashgar, and Ilarion had shamefacedly apologized for his conduct afterward, but it was clear from Lashgar's sidelong glance that he remembered it. "My house had a responsibility to your house," he added glumly, "and we failed in it."

Ilarion said, lying, "I'm not angry. I'm only worried. No one could have expected this." Now that he was thinking clearly again, he realized it was true. Given Theatana's isolation and friendlessness, even ten men should have been enough to prevent her escape. Who could have predicted that someone would come to Selemban and release her?

His maternal grandfather would have answered: *Jaladar probably did it, you imbecile.* For Archates had lived in endless foreboding and anxiety, suspecting conspiracy everywhere and in everyone. Ilarion dreaded discovering this flaw of distrust in his own nature along with his weakness of anger, and when he found himself suspicious of someone's intentions he became uneasy. Consequently he usually gave people the benefit of the doubt, even when the evidence of their behavior and his better judgment suggested he should not. He fretted over this but did it anyway.

But, he told himself, what he was really furious about was the misfortune of Theatana's disappearance. He didn't want to be angry at Lashgar, for he liked the Mixtun prince immensely. Their friendship had begun when Lashgar was thirteen; Jaladar had sent him to the Fountain Palace in Captala Nea for a year, to perfect his education, and the prince had become the younger brother Ilarion didn't have. He had helped teach Lashgar the Logomenon, the common tongue of the Ascendancy, and from him learned fluent Mixtun. Between them they perpetrated a good deal of mischief, and when Lashgar returned to the islands, Ilarion missed him sorely.

But the bond between Ilarion's family and Lashgar's was older than either of the sons. Lashgar's father had met Ilarion's parents twenty-six years ago, when Jaladar was a mercenary in the Ascendancy's Paladine Guard. He had allied himself to the young Key Mec Brander and Mandine Dascaris, and fought beside them in the War of the Chain. In those days Jaladar was an exile. Now he was almost sixty and the ruler of Ammedara, the largest and most powerful of the island realms of the Blue Havens. He had been king there for over twenty years, having returned after the war to lead a successful uprising against the tyrant who had earlier driven him out. The bond between Jaladar and Ilarion's parents remained close, though Jaladar was king of a dozen islands while they were the Dynast and the Dynastessa, rulers of the vast and ancient mainland commonwealth called the Ascendancy.

Likewise, Ilarion and Lashgar had always ignored the difference in their backgrounds. Ilarion might be the Luminessos, next in line to the Ascendancy's throne, and Lashgar a mere crown prince of the islands, but they were both heirs to ruling houses. On that footing they considered themselves equal.

"More wine?" Lashgar asked, holding up the jug. Of the sunset only a faded streak of pale orange remained. The tropical dusk was brief, not like the lingering twilights of the north.

"Yes, please," Ilarion said, holding out his cup. As Lashgar poured, he went on, "You're right about sending *Ascendancy Maid* to Ammedara and going on in *Scourge*. I'll bring my Paladines with us—if we catch these people, we'll have a fight on our hands." He paused, thinking about where they might have gone, then said, "There are no inhabited islands south of us, are there?"

"No. There are just some bits of rock with a palm or two and sometimes a spring. We call them the Ends of Earth. They were pirate hides, back when there were pirates. If you sail due east, there's another scatter of islets a day's sail away, the Crescents. Beyond those you'd need another day with a good following wind, to reach Nevali's islands. In short there's not much out here—the Crescents to the east, the Ends of Earth to the south, and due west of us there's no land at all."

"Where would raiders go first, do you think?"

"Not north. There's too much shipping, and our naval patrols as well. Not west, since there's nothing there. The wind's been blowing mostly eastward the last two days, so we'll try that."

"Will your shipmaster agree?" Ilarion asked. It could be dangerous for warships to undertake long sea passages far from land; if they were blown too far from shore, the limited food and water they carried would not keep their crews alive long enough to regain a safe harbor.

"He won't like it, but he must. We have a responsibility in this." Lashgar stroked his beard, then asked, "How dangerous could she become, if we didn't find her?"

"I don't know. I wish I did."

"She couldn't get at the Great Sorcery, could she? Isn't it true that no one can do that without dying?"

Ilarion needed a moment to realize that Lashgar meant the Deep Magic, as it was called in the Ascendancy. That power made even the most virulent spell of the Black Craft seem a child's conjuring trick, for it reached beyond the world, into the raw energies of creation and chaos. It could crack mountains, and it had. Seventeen centuries ago it destroyed the Old Dominion, the ancient civilization to which the Ascendancy was the successor.

After that catastrophe, Athanais, the last of the White Diviners, had set a spell called the Ban to lock the Deep Magic away from the meddling ambitions of humankind. The Ban killed anyone who tried to wield that terrible power, and for countless years it went unchallenged, until the Deep Magic itself was almost forgotten. Then the sorcerer Erkai the Chain, whom everyone believed to be long dead, had reappeared.

Erkai believed he knew how to break the Ban and survive to use the sorcery it guarded. But in the end, Ilarion's mother and father destroyed him even as he made the great attempt; indeed, Ilarion himself was present at Erkai's defeat on the Hill of Remembrance, being then in his mother's womb.

No one else had witnessed Erkai's destruction except Theatana, and what she experienced on the Hill had inflicted years of madness on her. After she recovered from her dementia she had never told anyone its cause, at least as far as Ilarion knew. He had only seen her twice in his life, once when he was eight and again when he was fifteen. The earlier glimpse was from a narrow window above the Upper Yard of the Numera, the fortress-citadel within the Fountain Palace; she had been taking exercise. She was a tall, slender woman, he remembered, and even to his young eyes very beautiful, despite her prison pallor.

The second time was more memorable. It was the night

she was sent into exile, and Ilarion was with his father in the palace grounds when the torches came down the hill from the Numera. Theatana was among them, beautiful as ever, ringed in steel by an escort of the Paladine Guard. They didn't let her stop, but she had seen Key and his son, and she cried out, "The slut's husband and the slut's brat! You call yourself a Tessarid, you barbarian mongrel, but your house found the diadem in the bed of a Dascaris! You are no ruler, nor ever will be!"

His father had shrugged and turned away. The Tessarids, after all, had governed the Ascendancy long before House Dascaris did. Until Ilarion's birth, Key had been the last descendant of the earlier dynasty. His line had been concealed in the eastern highlands for a hundred years, until he emerged in the War of the Chain and married Mandine Dascaris, thereby uniting the two houses and restoring House Tessaris to the throne. From that marriage had come Ilarion and Katheri, titled in the ancient manner the Luminessos and the Luminessa. The succession, at least, was secure.

As for the Ban, it had stood against Erkai's sorcery and killed him. Or so almost everyone believed, Lashgar among them.

The belief was wrong.

A very few people, including Ilarion, knew the truth: Erkai did indeed break the Ban. Athanais's ancient spell had not withstood him, for Erkai was twice-born, having died and returned to life through the blackest art of the Black Craft. Even the White Diviner's fierce sorcery could not strike down one who had already died, and it was not the Ban but rather Key and Mandine who destroyed him, in the nick of time, in the instant of his victory. But Ilarion's parents were no sorcerers; an enigmatic power other than the Ban had flowed through them to bring about his ruin.

They had told Ilarion all this when he reached his majority; as the Ascendancy's eventual ruler, he must know that the Ban no longer protected the world from the likes of Erkai. They also said that Theatana might know that Erkai had succeeded, though they'd never been sure she did. What she might do with this knowledge, if she ever got loose, and given the taint that lurked in her, was an open question. But neither she nor anyone else knew the arts of calling up the Deep Magic, and Ilarion did not see how she could pose much threat from that direction.

As for Lashgar, he didn't know about the fall of the Ban, although his father did. But Jaladar would have to pick the occasion to tell him, if at all; it was not Ilarion's place. Feeling a little uncomfortable about his prevarication, he said:

"Even if she were willing to risk dying to use the power, she wouldn't know how to go about it. Whatever Erkai knew, he didn't communicate it to her. We'd have seen the results by now, if he had."

"I suppose so." Lashgar fingered his beard. "How *did* your mother and father defeat him, anyway? He killed many people, but he didn't kill them. Or couldn't. Nobody seems to know how they did it, exactly. I've asked Father, and he says it was the grace of the Lord and the Lady."

"Maybe it was," Ilarion said, reluctantly prevaricating again. He was aware that his parents had destroyed Erkai by finding and using something called the Signata, but only the few people who knew about the Ban also knew this. There was an obscure legend about the Signata: it was said to be the place that contained all places, and the moment that contained all moments. When he pressed his mother for more information, she'd only said:

"It destroyed Erkai by turning his evil back on him. But there was more to it than that. When it acted, it took us somewhere else. It was . . . I can't describe it. It was beyond thought or speech. It was something like perfect knowledge, but that's not it, either." She'd paused, then added, "I was carrying you at the time. When you were little, I was a bit concerned that the experience might have affected you. Fortunately, it appears it didn't."

So he now knew the most secret history of the War of the Chain: Erkai being twice-born, and thus defeating the Ban. But still . . . he could not rid himself of the notion that his parents had not told him quite *everything*. He trusted them to provide all the knowledge he needed to rule well, so what they'd left out must be something deeply private and personal. It would be unseemly to pry, so despite his curiosity he had never done so.

Lashgar shifted uncomfortably on the palm log. "Anyway, none of this answers the real question. Who took your aunt, and how do we get her back?"

Relieved that Lashgar had lost interest in his parents' supposedly sorcerous doings, Ilarion answered, "That is indeed the problem."

There was a long silence, underlain by the murmur of men's voices. Lashgar looked out to sea, into the south. Finally, he said, "What do you suppose is out there? Way out, where our ships don't go? Does the Blue go on forever?"

"Who knows? Maybe there's land, but it's so distant no one could ever find it."

Far to the southeast, a dim light flickered on the rim of the sea, then vanished. Ilarion watched for it, but the pale illumination did not reappear. "I think there's some weather out there," he muttered.

"Probably only a squall," Lashgar told him, and yawned. "The summer storms are what you really want to worry about. They come up in a hurry this far south—there was one a few days ago, and another a while before that. But nothing's sure on the Blue. We might have perfect weather for the next month."

"Pray for neither squalls nor storms," Ilarion said. "If we're going to find my aunt, we're going to need all the clear sailing we can get."

3

DAWN WAS FLOODING THE HORIZON WITH SCARLET LIGHT
when the two ships slipped out of the harbor into the lagoon.
They maneuvered carefully, for the passage was tortuous
and in places none too deep, especially for *Ascendancy
Maid*.

Finally, they reached blue water, and the two vessels prepared to part company. Ilarion watched from *Scourge*'s afterdeck while the artema swung her bow away from him,
and as *Ascendancy Maid*'s deckhands prepared to loose her
mainsail, he felt a twinge of homesickness. He had not only
paid for her, he had also helped design and build her in the
naval shipyard in faraway Captala Nea. Over the shipwrights' conservative grumblings he had sharpened the lines
of her bow and stern; the refinement had increased her
speed, just as he had hoped it would. At the beginning of the
summer he had sailed her out of Captala's naval harbor, and
since then she had carried him faithfully in good weather
and bad, through the Inner Sea and out to the islands of the
Blue. He knew every creak of her timbers, her scents of
hemp and tar and wet wood; she was his home. In *Scourge*
he was a visitor, a welcome one, but a visitor nonetheless.

Ascendancy Maid shook out her mainsail to the wind.
Painted in green and gold on its white linen was a pandragore, the ancient winged serpent that his parents had
made the family emblem of the Tessarids. Ilarion himself
wore a seal ring with the pandragore badge cut into its
square emerald; his father had given it to him when he came
of age. Key owned a similar ring, but its emerald was oval,

and the jewel was much, much older. It had once belonged to the first Ilarion, the heir of the Tessarid lineage that ruled the Ascendancy before House Dascaris took the throne a hundred years before.

That earlier Ilarion never wore the diadem. He died mysteriously when he was twenty-two, likely poisoned by the man who succeeded to power in his place. That was Rabanes, first Dynast of the House of the Dascarids. Knowing that, Key and Mandine had named their son after the murdered heir, so that one day an Ilarion would wear the diadem after all: a kind of belated justice.

As *Ascendancy Maid* diminished in the distance, *Scourge*'s helmsman turned the warship's bronze ram to the east. The west wind was a fresh and vigorous one, which would make her master happy; no warship captain used his rowers when he could sail. The wind would also hurry *Ascendancy Maid* to Ammedara, for which Ilarion was thankful. The sooner their search was reinforced by the Ammedaran fleet, the better.

Scourge's deckhands let out her sail and sheeted it home. The wind's direction had decided the first step of the hunt for Theatana: They would run eastward until they reached the string of islets named the Crescents, a day's sail away. If they found no one there, and if the wind cooperated, they'd swing back to the southwest to investigate the outermost atolls, the ones Lashgar had called the Ends of Earth.

The sun rose, changing the copper and indigo of dawn to the hot azure and gold of morning. *Scourge* had the wind at her back, and she raced through the waves with sheets of foam curling from her ram. Every so often she plunged into a deeper trough, thumped into the green afterslope of the next wave, and hurled plumes of spray into the air as she rose to its crest.

In the exhilaration of *Scourge*'s speed, Ilarion was almost able to put aside his worry about Theatana. This was what he loved best: a graceful ship, a favoring wind, and the deep ocean. He had always loved the sea in a way that neither of his parents did, nor any of his friends at home in Captala. It made him restless; he ached to see what was beyond it, as if a thing he longed for but could not name might await him beyond its blue and empty horizons. He had never been so happy as in the last few months, as he wandered down to the Havens from the Inner Sea.

But he could not wander all his life. Someday he would be Dynast, and his footloose days would be over. What lay beyond the horizons of the Blue would then be sealed away from him forever. This sometimes made him gloomy, though he didn't really believe he would ever find the object of his yearning, no matter how far he sailed.

Just now, though, he had to find Theatana. Shipmaster Mardo had posted a lookout at the swaying masthead, and twice Ilarion climbed to the main yard, where he used the spyglass to sweep the rim of the sea. But he saw no sails, for *Scourge* was well south of the shipping lanes that stitched the inhabited islands together.

The day warmed as the hours passed, and by late morning it was already very hot. At noon the crew and the soldiers ate in shifts, taking a meal of hard ship's biscuit, dried stockfish, and water purified with vinegary wine. Ilarion, Lashgar, and Mardo had theirs on the afterdeck, standing with their backs braced against the windward rail. Mardo was in middle age, with a graying beard and thick gray eyebrows, and meaty forearms corded with muscle. He was a taciturn man at best and Ilarion's presence almost silenced him. Like his crew, he wore a linen seaman's jerkin the color of old straw, and a pair of coarse hempen breeches. He went barefoot, unlike Ilarion and Lashgar, and his only marks of rank were the thin gold torque about his throat and the dagger sheathed at his belt. If he was unhappy at taking *Scourge* so far out of sight of the main islands, he did not show it.

Also on the afterdeck was the helmsman, swaying to the pull of the tiller, his eyes shifting constantly from the sail to the horizon to the compass stand, then beginning the circuit again. As Ilarion chewed a mouthful of flinty biscuit he watched the helmsman and pondered the compass. He'd always wondered who had first rubbed a lodestone across an iron needle and then discovered that this needle, if properly suspended, would always align itself north and south. The effect smacked of magic, except that anyone could produce it if he had the stone and a sliver of soft iron. It required no spells to make it work, seeming to be some natural virtue that transferred itself to the metal by the act of friction. The islanders had used the needles from time out of mind, and as far as anyone knew were the first seamen to make compasses. The instrument was less commonly employed by the Ascendancy mariners of the Inner Sea, who sailed from headland to headland and were rarely out of sight of familiar seamarks. But anyone who navigated the Blue used a compass, not only the islanders but the deep-water traders of the Ascendancy's southern coast.

They had been talking during their meal about the antipiracy campaign that Ilarion had led in the Inner Sea, but the conversation had trailed off. Then Lashgar said, "By the way, you've gotten your accent perfectly, just in these last few days. Anybody would think Mixtun was your native tongue. How do you do it? I still speak your Logomenon like an outlander."

"I don't know," Ilarion confessed. "I have an ear, I suppose. If I hear a language long enough . . . it just comes."

"Does Katheri have the same talent?"

"No. Mother doesn't have it, either. But Father's side of the family has always been very good at languages."

"How many *do* you speak now?"

"Well, the Logomenon of course, and Mixtun, and the Haema, since that's my father's birth tongue, and a bit of the steppe language, and pretty good Tathar."

Lashgar shook his head glumly. "A scholar, as well as a soldier and seaman."

"Not really. I don't work at it. It just happens."

"That makes you even more annoying." Lashgar glanced up at the wind telltale, a white pennon on the port backstay. "Look, the breeze is shifting."

"It's veering a bit to the north, my lord," Mardo said, as he straightened from peering at the compass. "It has been for two turns of the glass."

Lashgar frowned. Ilarion asked, "How long till we reach the Crescents?"

Mardo went to the rail and tossed a chip of biscuit into the sea. He watched the dun fleck glide sternward, studied the angle of the wave crests, then said, "If the wind holds where it is now, we'll raise them about the seventh hour and make shore about sunset."

"So we can start to search in the morning," Ilarion said. "Good."

Mardo studied the northeastern horizon, then glanced up at the sun. "Weather permitting, my lord."

"Weather?" Ilarion asked, remembering the distant lightning flash he'd seen last night.

"Yes, my lord. The dawn was too red. We may have squalls by midnight."

"But there won't be anything worse than that," Lashgar said. "Will there?"

"It'd be uncommon, my lord Prince, after the two big blows we got earlier this month." Mardo pursed his lips. "But there are usually salt-hawks out here, and I've seen none since midmorning. I think we might get a bit of wind."

Ilarion looked around. Mardo was right. The darting blue birds, which had earlier skimmed back and forth across *Scourge*'s wake with every appearance of enjoyment, had vanished without his noticing it. "It's just as well we'll make land by sundown, then," he observed.

"Yes, my lord."

The afternoon wore on. The rowers sat on their benches or on the main deck, where they busied themselves carving intricate designs onto wafers of bone or wood. The Mixtun and the Ascendancy marines tended to doze although a few tried to play dice, not very successfully, on the slanted planking. The seamen mended ropes or stitched sailcloth; two worked with the ship's carpenter to recaulk a leaky deck seam. The helmsman watched the compass, the sail, and the sea, and from time to time Mardo tossed a chip overboard to estimate *Scourge*'s speed. The four deck lookouts scanned the horizon, and the fifth did the same from the masthead. From time to time the deck officer replaced them with fresh men.

By midafternoon the wind had veered even more, so that

it was blowing almost directly out of the north. Despite its heat it had taken on a heavy, damp feel, and though the sky was still cloudless, the air smelled of rain. *Scourge*'s speed had dropped by half, since she no longer had the wind from well astern. It appeared less and less likely that they'd reach the Crescents by dark.

Lashgar and Ilarion stood with Mardo at the afterdeck's port rail and watched the sky and the set of the waves. These, like the wind, had shifted until they, too, were coming from the north, and were running in a confused and angry chop. *Scourge* began rolling so much that the deck officer called the masthead lookout down from his perch, and Mardo put two men on the tiller. Ilarion hadn't spent enough time in the islands to experience everything their weather could do, but he knew that the sea and wind conditions were making both Mardo and Lashgar uneasy. This didn't bode well; Lashgar was a good seaman, and the shipmaster was among the most experienced in the Ammedaran fleet.

Scourge took a hard gust of wind on her sail and heeled sharply to port. Several rowers yelled in alarm. The deck's heave caught the two steersmen off-balance, and their weight threw the tiller hard over. For a few moments the ship was out of control, with Mardo bellowing orders. The steersmen caught her just as her bow slammed into a wave; timber met sea with a tremendous crash, and *Scourge*'s decking shuddered. Ilarion held hard to the rail to keep from being pitched onto the midships deck, and wished he were aboard *Ascendancy Maid*; she would behave far better in these conditions than the hemiolia.

"My lord Prince," Mardo said, as *Scourge* shook herself and bravely recovered from her heel, "we can't go on like this. She'll roll her mast out of her if it gets much worse. We have to ease her off the wind."

"We'll be heading south by east," Lashgar objected.

"Can't be helped, my lord. Better to lose some miles than the mast."

"You're right. Ease her, then."

Mardo called an order. The steersmen, with relief written

clearly on their faces, let *Scourge*'s bow swing away from the wind. The hemiolia picked up speed, and her thrashing eased. But now they were heading southeast, angling away from the Crescents, and moreover were being driven into the empty depths of the Blue. The islanders would accept this when they had to; plenty of their fishing vessels and freighters got blown well to the south, then made their way back to land when the wind changed. But a warship could not endure many days without a landfall. Out here, *Scourge* and her crew were far more vulnerable than a fishing boat or cargo carrier.

Mardo tossed another chip of wood. It moved aft very quickly. Ilarion estimated they were doing a good ten knots. If the wind blew from the north for more than three days, they might never see land again. The sky was hazing over, and though the day was still bright, the sun wore a halo of dull gold.

"We must lie a-hull, my lord," Mardo called. In the wind's hiss and roar he had to shout to be heard. "We must get the sail down and a sea anchor out."

"Yes. Give the orders," Lashgar shouted back.

They brought down the heavy main yard, the deckhands and crew struggling to control its ponderous swings. Finally, the mainsail was brailed up tight, and the yard was on deck and lashed down. Then they secured one end of a long, heavy cable to the forward anchor bitts and let the free end of the cable pay out over the hemiolia's bow. As the cable slid into the sea its drag through the water began to swing *Scourge* up into the wind.

"Be ready when she's beam-on to the seas, my lords," Mardo shouted. "She'll want to roll."

As the hemiolia came broadside to the crests, a huge green wave surged down on her. She heeled far to starboard, hesitated, and began to rise to its rush. Ilarion found himself looking down into a valley of emerald water. Then the wave crest passed under the warship's keel and she lurched wildly to port. The steersmen heaved frantically at the tiller, and she steadied. Then the wave had scudded past, and the pull of the trailing cable was drawing *Scourge*'s head well up to the wind.

They were not done yet; the mast had to come down to reduce their speed and their rolling still more. The ship's gyrations made the timber seem evilly alive; it swayed and swooped as though it wanted to throw itself overboard, or smash a hole through *Scourge*'s flank and sink her. Eerily, with the waves and the wind at almost gale force, the sunlight remained hot and bright, although it was hazed with a sickly greenish yellow hue. Ilarion had never seen anything like this on the Inner Sea, whose storms were black with cloud and laced with sheets of driving rain. Here, the almost-clear sky seemed to promise a quick passing of the gale, but he sensed that the promise was false. There was more threat in this baleful light than in a wall of purple cloud seamed with lightning.

They finally wrestled the mast to the deck and secured it in its cradle, then rigged lifelines between the fore and after rails. Ilarion and Lashgar hauled themselves on one of these up to the stern deck. Mardo had ordered the tiller lashed amidships, and *Scourge* now pitched and rolled at the mercy of the wind and waves, with only the sea anchor keeping her head to the wind. It was impossible to stay on one's feet without holding fast to some support.

On the northeast horizon a pale gray line appeared. The others had seen it, too; it thickened even as Ilarion watched. "Line squalls?" he shouted to Mardo.

The wind dropped suddenly, as if cut off by a closing door. Ilarion heard a distant, steady thunder, as of a myriad iron cartwheels running over stone.

"No," the shipmaster answered, and there was a shake in his voice. "It's a storm. A bad one. A white norther."

Cold stole along Ilarion's veins. Lashgar had told him of these gales, the dread of the island mariners. And the only people who knew they were out here, and why, were far away aboard *Ascendancy Maid*. Would the artema herself survive, to carry the news of their whereabouts to Ammedara?

That was in the laps of the Lady and the Allfather. "What can we do?" he asked.

Mardo gave a harsh laugh. "Lash ourselves to the ship, my lord. And pray."

4

ILARION DRAGGED HIMSELF HALFWAY THROUGH THE AFTER-deck's tiny hatch and flinched as the gale hit him. The wind seemed solid, a club that battered his face and chest, and spray lashed his skin like a flail. But even that was better than the darkness belowdecks, the stench of vomit and fear, and the moans of men injured by the ship's wild tossing.

He made sure the length of rope was still coiled around his waist, then pulled himself the rest of the way on deck. It was a painful struggle, for his fingers and wrists were cramped and knotted from hours of clutching at handholds, and he was badly bruised from being thrown against the rowing benches. But at last he emerged completely from the hatch and paused to cling to its rim, while he squinted against the whip of the rain. Mardo had emerged before him and was inching along the safety line toward the thick upright of the compass stand.

Ilarion slammed the hatch closed and decided not to follow the shipmaster. He used his rope to lash himself to the afterdeck rail, and then, secured to the precarious safety of the ship, he turned his face from the wind and peered into the gloom. The norther blew unabated; it lashed the ocean into white streamers of foam, ripped the foam from the waves, and spat it through the air. Rain hissed in flat sheets across the wave crests.

While he lay below deck he had lost track of time. But now he saw that the sky was no longer black, but the color of dark gray ash, and he could discern the ragged shapes of storm clouds racing down the wind. *Scourge* must have been

38

driving before the gale for fifteen or sixteen hours, though it seemed much longer, and their ordeal was far from over. According to Lashgar a norther never blew for less than a full day, and could last for as many as five. Ilarion did not believe that they could survive even two days of this, and living through five would be impossible. The wind was too strong, the waves it drove too enormous. Revealed now by the quarter-light, the huge graybeards loomed so vast that Ilarion almost wished for night to come again to hide them. Towering into the furious sky, scarred with foam, they marched relentlessly out of the murk; *Scourge* rose to each crest, hesitated, and plummeted sickeningly into the following trough. Then she would shake herself and heave her bow up to endure the next onslaught. But no such lightly built vessel could withstand such battering for days on end. She wouldn't sink, for warships of her type carried little ballast; instead she would break up and disintegrate into a litter of smashed timbers and drowning men. Ilarion was a good swimmer, but he knew he wouldn't survive long in this frenzied sea.

He turned to look forward. He had to close his eyes to slits against the wind, but even so he saw enough to appall him. Last evening, as night fell, there had been at least twenty men on the main deck, clinging to safety lines. They had refused to take shelter with the others below, for fear the hemiolia would capsize and drown them in her black insides. Now all were gone, swept away during the hours of darkness, their shrieks drowned in the wind's scream. He had heard nothing when they went.

The hatch opened again and Lashgar put his head through it. He had dark circles under his eyes and a gash on his left cheekbone. Ilarion reached down and helped him onto the deck. The prince secured himself to the rail and looked hopelessly around.

"We've lost them," Ilarion yelled to him. "The men up here."

Lashgar's mouth moved as he cursed, his words swallowed by the rushing wind. Sickened by the deaths of so many, he slumped against the rail.

A few feet away, Mardo was tied to the compass stand and was staring out past the ship's stern. Last night he had remained on *Scourge*'s afterdeck until darkness fell. Only when the waves began to board her had he come below, bringing the compass so it would not be wrenched from its fastenings and washed into oblivion. But with the ship so wet and pitching, they couldn't get a lamp lit belowdecks, so they went all night without a compass reading. Only with dawn, and with the hatch open a crack to admit some light, was Mardo able to check their drift. The news was bad. The wind was now out of the east-northeast, driving them far off course and toward the Ends of Earth. They might already have been swept past those scattered islands, out into the oblivion of the Blue, with no hope of return.

"I'm not going back down," Lashgar yelled. "Now it's light, I'd rather know what's happening."

Ilarion nodded. He was cold, drenched, and shaking with exhaustion, but that was still better than the squalid pit below. The two men sat with their backs to the wind, clutching the rail stanchions, while *Scourge* endlessly heaved and endlessly rolled. The light slowly grew until it was a dim luminosity hemmed in above by speeding cloud and bounded at the horizon by thick murk. Rain came in gusts, mixed with wind-driven spray. Ilarion's thoughts became blurred, flickering in and out of focus. Odd images and sensations came and went: the rose gardens of the Fountain Palace, a faint music of citterns and water drums as if from a distant festival.

A voice brought him back. Mardo had shouted something. He was looking downwind, in the direction of their drift. As the ship slid over a crest, the shipmaster struck the side of his head with his fist, and gave a long bellow of wordless rage.

Ilarion felt his stomach clench. "What?" he screamed at the shipmaster. "What's there?"

"Breakers! It's rocks! Anchors! Set the anchors!"

Scourge was lifting to another crest. Ilarion looked past her stern and saw, far off where the murk began, a pale, undulating wall. But this was no wind-driven foam, for even as he watched, a jagged rampart of boiling white hurled itself toward the clouds. The gale ripped its summit to rags, and then the wall sank back into the spindrift-laden sea. Instants later it rose again, and Ilarion knew it for the doom of seamen: a line of breakers on a lee shore, with a gale driving them down upon it. They could not possibly claw off under sail; even if they could raise the mast and sling the main yard, no sailcloth could survive this wind. The anchors were their only hope. Anchors might hold the ship off the rocks, if they could be released, if the flukes would bite on the seabed, if the cables did not part.

Mardo had released himself from his lashings and was dragging himself toward the hatch. He reached it, flung it open, and screamed at his crew to come on deck.

They'd need every hand they could get to manage the anchors. With stiff fingers Ilarion yanked his dagger from his belt and sawed his safety lashing through, then knotted the ends together and wrapped the line around his waist. Lashgar did the same, and together the two men staggered to their feet and followed Mardo. Traversing the deck was like trying to walk on the waves themselves; the terrifying rush upward, the breathless poise at the crest, then the sickening lurch as *Scourge* plunged into the trough beyond. Merely hanging on took so much strength that Ilarion feared it would be impossible to get the anchors out at all.

By the time they got forward, a few of *Scourge*'s crewmen had scrambled out of the bow hatch, had tied themselves to the anchor windlass, and were struggling with the first of the two main anchor hawsers. Ilarion and Lashgar joined them, also securing themselves to the windlass supports. The cables were braided hemp and the thickness of Ilarion's forearm; hauling them was like fighting an enormous serpent. Priceless minutes passed while they wrestled the hawsers foot by foot onto the heaving, waveswept foredeck, and by the time both cables were shackled to their anchors and clear to run, the breaker's terrible foaming wall was much, much nearer. *Scourge* was drifting fast toward it, but Ilarion could not yet tell whether the combers were crashing onto an isolated reef or striking part of some larger landmass. Beyond the roaring white barrier was only mist and murk.

"Loose away!" Mardo yelled, and deckhands hacked through sodden lashings. Freed, the anchors dropped from their supporting beams and plunged into the sea, their cables flying over the side after them. Ilarion clung to the windlass and prayed. A wave sluiced knee-deep over the deck and drained away. The cables raced out, yard after yard of hemp plunging into the sea. More men were risking the deck now, as word spread that *Scourge* was on a lee shore. They held to the lifelines and peered at the breakers flying skyward in skeins and banners of spray.

Ilarion watched the flying cables. Suddenly the port hawser stopped running out. An instant later the other halted; both anchors had found bottom. Ilarion willed the flukes to dig into the seabed, to catch under a ledge of stone, to fix the ship to this frail refuge beyond the rocks.

The cables tightened, drew taut, became rigid as iron bars. A vast wave bore down on *Scourge* and she rose to it. The cables strained and hummed as she climbed, the wave dragging her bow deeper as her buoyancy fought with the pull of the hawsers.

She reached the wave's crest. As it passed under her she lurched, and instantly the starboard cable went slack. Ilarion watched breathlessly for the line to tighten again, to show that the anchor had found a new bite on the seabed.

It did not. For a moment he still hoped, then realized with despair that the cable had snapped.

Scourge was already skidding left as she swung to her port anchor. Another wave swept her up, and when she was almost at its crest she lurched again. Even through the howl of the wind Ilarion heard the *crack* from underwater as the second cable parted, and in the next instant a thirty-foot whip of thick hemp flailed inboard. Its raw end slashed across Mardo's face, flayed his features from his skull in a bloody spray, and flicked him overboard. Without even a shriek, he was gone in the hissing sea.

"*Man overboard!*" Lashgar yelled, but there was nothing anyone could do. The ship, dragging her useless cables, surged toward the rocks. Ilarion watched in astonishment as his death approached. In battle his skill and courage stood between him and a blade's edge, but here no skill or courage was enough. Here he was helpless. Part of him was terribly afraid, but another, innermost part was profoundly saddened. He hadn't been given time to do everything. He wasn't finished.

In the name of the Lord Allfather and Our Lady Mother, let me live.

Around him men were wailing in terror, and Lashgar's lips moved in prayer. The rest of the crew was on deck now, and Ilarion saw Ethon and his Paladine guardsmen clinging to the safety lines. Then a crest picked *Scourge* up and drove her toward the reefs. From high on the wave Ilarion looked across a trough of spume-streaked water to a ridge of black granite gnawed by the boiling sea. Beyond the reef line ran furious surf; beyond that was something dark and motionless that might be land. He knew it was a refuge he would never reach.

Unless, he thought, *unless a wave carries her over the rocks. If she can only reach the other side—*

"Get ready to swim," he screamed at Lashgar, who clung to the windlass at his side. "If we can get over the reef, we might make it." He yanked off his seaboots and made sure his dagger was secure in its sheath; Lashgar did the same. The ship raced down into the trough, and the next huge comber lifted her. They were almost on the rocks. This was the wave that would dash them to pieces on the stone, or carry them over it.

Men wailed and howled. *Scourge*, caught at the leading edge of the wave's crest, hurtled toward the reef. She was almost on the stone. But the wave was still carrying her high. She might yet leap the wall. Ilarion caught his breath, took it deeper, held it.

For an instant he thought she would ride above the rocks, but the wave curled and broke and drove her ahead of it onto the reef. From deep within her belly came a grinding crash as her keel snapped and her planks shattered. Instantly she was no longer a ship but a seething mass of timbers, sailcloth, tangling rope, and drowning men.

The impact threw Ilarion against the windlass. He clung

to its wooden bulk as an avalanche of water fell on him and carried him down into blackness. He sensed vaguely that he was still lashed to the ship and being dragged along with it, but he was deep underwater, and the sea would not let him go. And he was running out of air; no, he had already run out. In a moment he would breathe water, and die.

A slow and powerful force struck him from beneath and bore him upward. Faint light beat across his eyelids, became brighter, and suddenly his head burst above the sea. All around was roaring water, and he was still submerged to his chest, but under him was a hard surface.

He realized dazedly that he was still lashed to the windlass, which jutted from a fragment of *Scourge*'s foredeck. The wave had torn the decking from her hull and driven it like a raft clear over the reef. The windlass protruded from the foam, and he saw that only he, Lashgar, and a seaman still clung to it. He pulled himself to the windlass drum and hung on.

They were inside the reef now, in a maelstrom of thrashing waves. Pressed down by the weight of the three men, the raft barely floated, and the waves swept across it without check. Savage currents dragged at Ilarion; though he had survived the reef, he could still drown in the whirlpools and surges on its inner side. He saw men struggling in the chaos not far away, but the waters swallowed them even as he watched. A handful of others clung to broken timbers, and he thought for a moment that Ethon was among them, but in the gloom he couldn't be sure. Ahead he saw a ragged shoreline, where the sea beat in clouds of spray. But no hope lay there; the shore was a black cliff, with gaps here and there where the breakers surged into narrow gorges.

Lashgar yelled, his shout almost carried away by the wind. Ilarion looked around. Just beyond the reef, looming out of the murk like a mountain range, reared a monstrous wave. It would engulf them as if they did not exist. Struck dumb, alone with his fate, he could only watch as it rolled toward him.

The reef vanished beneath it, and in an instant the long slope of water had reached the raft, lifting it as a fire would lift a scrap of ash. Spindrift and spray hid the world. They were rising at a tremendous speed, flying headlong toward the cliff. He waited for its shadow to loom from the mist and crush him.

But it did not. A roar of water beat in his ears; the raft stopped climbing and a wall of stone rushed past. Then, abruptly, the roar diminished and the raft almost fell out from under him. He clung to the windlass drum with the last of his strength and heard Lashgar yelling, but couldn't make out the words. Then the raft was whirling dizzily with foam waist-deep over its planks. The spinning slowed, almost stopped, and the air began to clear a little. The wind still howled, but the crash of breaking surf was muted and distant. Unable to believe he still lived, Ilarion shook water from his eyes and peered around. Lashgar was still with him, but the seaman who had shared their refuge was gone.

As he got his bearings, he realized that the cliffs behind the reef had actually been the seaward side of a great curving wall of rock. Some of the gorges he had seen in its face were narrow channels leading through it, and not far away was the opening of one such cleft. The huge wave had carried the raft through this gap, instead of dashing it to fragments against the cliff outside, and now it floated almost calmly on a stretch of gray, choppy water. High overhead the wind still screamed, but here in the shelter of the rock wall it was only eddying gusts. Other fragments of *Scourge* drifted here and there, but Ilarion couldn't tell if any survivors still clung to them.

He peered around them in the gloom and realized that they were drifting in a narrow sound between the cliff wall and an island that lay in the wall's shelter. All he could see of the island was a gravelly shore that ascended to a long rocky ridge, which bore a thin cover of stunted scrub and bush. The current and the gusts were carrying the raft toward the shore.

Lashgar croaked, "We're alive."

"Yes," Ilarion agreed weakly. "Thank the Allfather and the Lady." The current had already carried the raft to within a hundred feet of the shore, where low waves broke in a gentle surf on its gravel strand. Landing would be almost easy. He was shivering, although the water was far from cold, and he silently thanked the Allfather for the warmth of the tropic seas. In the harsh waters of the north, he and Lashgar would already be dying of exposure.

A weak hail came from his right. He looked and saw a floating timber and a man's head by it. The man was holding to the timber. His voice was familiar.

"Ethon?" Ilarion called back, his voice cracking, "can you make it to shore?"

"My lord, I don't know. I think my legs are broken."

They had spoken in the Logomenon, and Lashgar asked, "Is he hurt?"

"Broken legs. We'll have to help him get in." It was clear that the raft was soon going to ground on the shingle. "Stay there," he called to Ethon. "We're drifting in. I'll come for you."

He heard a second weak call, then a third. Like Ethon, other survivors were clinging to scraps of wreckage washed through the channel into the shelter of the cliff wall. Only five. So few.

"We've lost almost everyone," said Lashgar, his voice desolate.

Ilarion summoned his strength, and said, "I'll test the depth." He found his sheath knife, cut the rope that still lashed him to the windlass drum, and slid into the water while keeping a tight grip on the splintered planks. His foot easily touched bottom. Even when a wave passed, his head and shoulders remained above water.

"It's shallow. Let's get off this thing. But bring the ropes. We'll need them."

They left the raft and made their way through the surf to the land. The wind still blew in sharp gusts, but the rain had stopped. By then Ethon had also drifted close to the beach, and they waded back into the surf to retrieve him. His face was stark with pain, but except for a single whimper as his left foot caught on a stone, he didn't cry out. As they laid him on the rough shingle, Lashgar said, "I see two others. I'd better find out what shape they're in."

He stumbled away along the gravel. Like Ilarion, he'd taken off his seaboots, and only shin-high linen hose protected both men's feet from the rough gravel. Ethon had not even that; he'd come out of the sea barefoot, wearing only soldier's breeches and tunic. He lay outstretched, eyes closed, a pallor on his skin.

Very carefully, Ilarion used his dagger to cut away the breeches. What he saw made him wince. Both the peltarch's legs were broken below the knees; the right lay at an awkward angle, and raw bone jutted through the skin of the left. Blood pulsed slowly in the edges of the wound.

"My lord?" the peltarch said, his voice barely audible in the wind.

"Ethon, yes, your legs are broken. But we'll splint them—there's rope and plenty of wood. It won't be long till you're healed as good as new."

The officer gasped as a wave of pain hit him. Then he said, "Yes, my lord. Thank you."

But Ethon needed not only splints; he needed food and warmth and good water. That was what they all needed, and the sooner the better. Warmth might be easy; if they could find dry wood, and moss or lichen for tinder, they could at least have a fire. There were flints in the beach gravel, and Ilarion had the steel of his dagger. But water and food were another matter.

How long till we're rescued? He knew the safety of the island was an illusion. It could only be one of the Ends of Earth, one speck among scores of tiny, uninhabited islets spread over hundreds of miles of the Blue. No one would guess they'd been wrecked on one of them. Assuming *Ascendancy Maid* had weathered the norther, Captain Batilicus would report in Ammedara that *Scourge* had been bound for the Crescents. Time would pass before it became clear that she was missing. An organized search might not begin for ten to twenty days, and it would begin in the wrong place. Months might pass before a ship came anywhere near this islet.

In the meantime, they would have to survive. But most of the islands of the Ends of Earth had no water, according to Lashgar. Vegetation grew on this one, but that didn't mean it had a spring. If a rescue ship ever reached here, its crew might find nothing but human bones picked clean by salt-hawks and gulls. Rain alone wouldn't be enough to save them.

He looked up. Lashgar and a second man, one of the hemiolia's crew, were approaching along the beach. They supported a third figure between them. Ilarion recognized the third as Arino, *Scourge*'s deck officer.

They reached him and lowered Arino to the shingle. He appeared to be barely conscious. "Broken ribs," Lashgar said. "Hurt inside, too. His breathing bubbles."

A pierced lung. Arino wouldn't last long. Ilarion scanned the eddying waters of the sound, where patches of wreckage tossed and spun, and looked for a head or a desperate, waving arm. He saw none. Out of some 140 men who had set out for the Crescents a day ago, only he and the other four survived. No one else had made it alive through the narrow passage in the cliff wall.

The wind on his soaked clothing made him shiver. "We've got to find shelter," he said. "It might be better over on the far side of the island, out of the wind."

Lashgar nodded. "We'll have to shift them one at a time. We should look for a place, first."

"Yes." He didn't want to stop moving, for fear he'd be unable to start again. "I'll go."

"We'll both go." Lashgar turned to the seaman. "Mersis, stay with the others."

They set off up the slope. Above the beach the ground cover was wiry cordgrass, overgrown in places with the spiny subtropical scrub called leffa. There were a few spindly fretwork palms whose fronds had been half–stripped away by the storm. Closer to the island's summit grew patches of sea-grape, but the fruits were still green on the vines and inedible. Ilarion watched for any sign of a spring or a brook, but saw none. If they did find one, and could also find thorns to make hooks, they might survive on water and fish. The salvaged ropes, unraveled, would provide fishing line.

And if we don't survive? Ilarion thought. *What then, at home?*

He was years from ascending to the throne, but already he had been carefully trained for rulership. His sister Katheri had also been schooled in it, but she was by nature an artist and something of a dreamer. She would try to rule well, but she was a gentle soul and even now, twenty-five years after the War of the Chain, the Ascendancy still needed a stronger hand than Katheri would be likely to give it.

As for Ammedara, the prince's death would be a disaster. There were nobles in the realm whose ambitions reached higher than baronies, and if Lashgar's father died without an heir, there would be civil war again. The peace and abundance that the king had brought to Ammedara would be ruined.

Enough, Ilarion told himself sharply. *We're not dead yet.*

The wind grew as they climbed out of the shelter of the sound, and by the time they had stumbled almost to the ridge's summit it was shrieking and clawing at them. As they reached the top, it gusted as if trying to hurl them over the crest. Lashgar staggered and cried out. Ilarion, heart pounding, caught his arm and dragged him back. They clung to the spiny branches of the leffa and stared appalled at what lay before them.

There was no more island. They stood at the very brink of a cliff, and at its foot boiled the sea.

5

THEATANA SAT IN HER ACCUSTOMED PLACE, ON THE CENTER thwart of the boat that the raiders carried on their ship's main deck. She had been free for six days, and they had been sailing southwest all that time, gliding away from the Blue Havens and away from the shores of the Ascendancy. After a quarter century of imprisonment and exile, she was at last beyond the reach of the Fountain Palace. Mandine and the Tessaris mongrel who called himself Dynast could no longer rearrange her existence with a few words.

The sun was dipping toward afternoon's end. *Six whole days.* she thought as she watched the green-and-white sails of the alien vessel drive her across the green and white sea. *I wonder what my bitch half sister will say when she finds out I'm gone. I'd like to be a moth on the wall of the Dynasteon when she gets the news. I wish I could have sent Tabar's head along with it.*

Theatana closed her eyes and savored again her memory of slaughtering him. She had brought death to many, but until that day on the island when she stabbed Tabar through the eye, she had never killed a man herself. The act had proven to be her salvation, though as she stood before the golden-haired barbarian with the bloody knife in her hands, she had not known what he would do with her. She had saved his life, and that might save hers, but it might not protect her from rape or enslavement.

Never taking his blue eyes from her, the barbarian had regained his feet. His expression was unreadable. Theatana shrugged, and tossed the knife onto the tiles beside Tabar's body. Outside, the racket of the fighting ebbed away. Theatana had no doubt who had won.

In the stillness, she and the blond raider watched each other. After several moments, the man spoke. It might have been a question. Then he glanced down at Tabar's corpse, and a look of something like chagrin crossed his face. Theatana drew herself up then, and said, though she knew the words would mean nothing to him, "I am Theatana Dascaris, of the House of the Dascarids, and you owe me a life."

His eyes narrowed, as if he might have guessed the sense of what she told him. He yelled something, and another raider appeared at the courtyard doorway. They exchanged a few words. Then the man she had saved sheathed his sword, stepped forward, and took her arm. She tensed, then willed herself to relax. Violation might be less painful if she were relaxed.

But he didn't paw at her clothing. Instead, he spoke again to the other man, gesturing at Theatana as he did so. The words sounded emphatic, final. The other looked her up and down in surprise, then disappointment, but he nodded and bowed to her captor. Then he turned and left.

I'm to be reserved for this one alone, she thought. *But at least he seems to be their leader.*

Then, to her amazement, he released her arm and waved at the courtyard doorway. She needed several moments to realize that she was free to go. Then she remembered that she'd heard of codes of honor among barbarians. Even the Tathars, brutal as they were, sometimes cleaved to them. If you saved a life, the person you saved had to protect you from harm, if he could. At the least, he could not harm you himself.

So she was safe for the moment. Not quite sure where she was going, Theatana walked through the doorway into the courtyard. The raiders had begun to loot the place, but none of them approached her though they watched her pass. She ignored them and left the compound by the shattered gate.

Down on the sand at the water's edge was the boat. She sloshed through a few inches of rising tide to reach its bow, then climbed aboard and waited to see what would happen.

The barbarians' leader came down to the shore a few minutes later but did not appear surprised to find her there. She'd killed her jailer and she was on an island; where else would she go?

Still, she knew that saving his life might not guarantee a refuge aboard his ship when he and his war band departed. He might deem it sufficient repayment that he hadn't raped her or slit her throat.

You owe me a life. She willed her desire into his mind. *Take me with you.*

He had studied her for a while, his gaze moving over her face and over her body. He was plainly intrigued by her appearance, and Theatana realized that he found her exotic. Wherever it was he came from, women there did not look like her.

He was just as strange to her. She remembered staring defiantly back at him, taking in the strange golden hair and foreign beard, the outlandish blue eyes that slanted a little upward above the high cheekbones. She realized as she gazed that she was at least a decade older than he was. But she knew he'd want her despite that, and not just because he had been at sea for too long. None of the Dascarids showed much of their ages in the face or figure. With her black hair and golden skin, she was probably unlike any woman he'd ever had, and she knew enough of males to know that they liked variety. She wondered wryly what he'd think when he discovered that, at her age, she had never known a man.

Suddenly he had laughed, pointed at himself, and said, "Kayonu."

Theatana blinked in surprise, then elation. He appeared to be introducing himself, a good sign. "Theatana," she answered.

An instant later she was cursing herself inwardly for telling him her real name. But he had already turned from her and was shouting at his men, who were lumbering down to the foreshore with sacks of flour, wine kegs, skeins of dried fruit, Mixtun weapons, and everything else movable. Theatana calmed herself, gathered her overmantle closer about her, and settled down on the boat's thwart. The raiders loaded as much as they could into it, and not long after that she was on the barbarian ship with Kayonu, while his men went back for another cargo of looted supplies and military gear. They were obviously formidable warriors; half a dozen had taken wounds, but none had been killed.

The ship had sailed from the island at midday, with Theatana on board, and that was the beginning of her freedom.

Her position on the ship was ambiguous. She was neither crew nor passenger; nor, apparently, did she belong to Kayonu in the sense of being a female possession. She suspected that, in saving his life, she had made herself something like his liegeman, a person under his protection though also under his command. However, that command apparently did not extend to ordering her into his hammock with him. Nor had he come creeping through the night to take her, though her own hammock was slung near his, beneath the afterdeck where he and his officers slept. As for his men, they were obviously intrigued by her appearance, but her standing with their captain seemed to put her off-limits. When she bathed herself in a recess of the sleeping quarters they gave her privacy, and there was no surreptitious pawing when she went about on the deck.

She wasn't muscular enough to help work the ship, but Kayonu had made it clear that she should help with the cooking, which was done in a pottery stove set on a brick hearth under the foredeck. Theatana had never cooked anything in her life. She had been enraged when he took her down to the galley and gestured at the pots, but she knew better than to show it. After noting the insult for later reference, she quickly learned to make unleavened bread, to boil porridge, and to stew salt meat and dried fish with desiccated white beans. Before the crew ate her concoctions she usually spat secretly into the pots. It was her own saliva, so the seasoning hardly mattered to her.

She would find out more about where she stood as she learned their tongue. She'd been incensed when Kayonu began telling her the names of things and obviously expecting her to remember them. It was almost as bad as ordering her to cook. What right had he to ask a Dynastessa to dirty her mouth with anything but the pure Logomenon? If anyone were going to learn a new language, it should be him.

But on further reflection she suppressed her fury. If their destination was Kayonu's homeland, nobody there would speak her language. She might be at a fatal disadvantage if she couldn't understand people or be understood by them. So, grinding her teeth a little, she had begun to learn. Among the first facts she gleaned was that Kayonu's race called themselves the Rasenna, and referred to their language by a similar term that she translated as *Rasennan*.

The learning went more slowly than she liked, but her memory had always been good, and during her years in prison she had taught herself to concentrate and to hear everything. She knew the words for basic objects now and also essential verbs like "go," "come," "eat," "drink." Though she was a long way from being fluent, she knew that fluency would come in time. To help it along, she forced herself to think in their language as much as she could. The result was a barbarous mixture of the Logomenon and Rasennan, but it was a beginning.

Just as this ship, deep in the vastness of the Blue, was a beginning. Here in its boat, with the sunlight of freedom lying warm on her face, she was safe: The sword of the Tessarids no longer lay at her neck.

Her neck. Theatana touched herself there, where the pulse beat in her throat, and for an instant a terrifying flash of her old madness returned: the cut of the noose into her soft flesh, her windpipe closing as her struggles tightened the rope, the heat on her legs as she fouled herself. She shuddered and bit savagely down on her lower lip, using the pain to help the moment pass. Such flashes were rare, but when they did come, they shook her as little else did.

The real horror of those old visions had been that she never quite *died*. Instead of falling into the arms of blackness and silence, she would find herself again on the scaffold in the Penitential Yard. She would look up from the courtyard's depths, and see herself watching from the window, cheeks flushed, lips parted, waiting for the executioner to begin. Sometimes the sequence would repeat itself a dozen times before it relented. Then she would realize she was no longer in the grip of the madness but in her tower room in the Numera, with a padded stick in her jaws and her arms and legs in restraints. She would have asked her half sister for a real death, except that in dying she'd lose any chance to inflict a terrible revenge on Mandine, and on the people Mandine loved most.

In a way, though, the madness had been her ally. After some years she discovered that she could stave it off for an interval by her will, helped along by mental exercises she devised to clear her mind of thought. As she trained her mind further, the intervals of respite lengthened. Ten years after Mandine put her into the Numera, she had learned how to divert the onset so that she was almost free of the attacks. After the eleventh year they stopped completely. It was possible that the sorcery that caused the madness had simply dissipated with time, but Theatana preferred to believe that she had defeated it through her own mental self-discipline. Whatever the truth of the matter, she was no longer the green girl she'd been when she seized the throne. If she could travel back to that time of twenty-five years ago, she would slap her younger self across the room for her self-indulgence and lack of cunning.

Theatana's mouth twisted. When all was said and done, Mandine was to blame for her madness, no matter how much she denied it. Mandine had used some dark sorcery against her, that day on the Hill of Remembrance, the day Erkai was destroyed. And after Erkai's fall she had kept Theatana alive, the better to gloat over her half sister's pain.

During the long years before Theatana's exile in the islands, Mandine sometimes came to the tower room in the Numera. She pretended not to exult, but Theatana knew the exultation was there; how could it not be? Even more ridiculously, she insisted that the madness wasn't of her doing, and expected Theatana to believe her. Supposedly it had come from a power she would not name and no longer controlled, a power of some strange justice that set Theatana in the place of her victims so she could know their suffering.

Victims? Theatana called them traitors. They were people

who had tried to drag her from the throne even before Mandine came back to Captala. They deserved to die for lifting a hand against her—she, a Dynastessa of the House of the Dascarids. Anyway, there hadn't been all that many executions, a few score at most, and the majority of those executed were commoners. Equally, if she had liked to watch them being hanged in the Penitential Yard of the Numera, what was the harm in that? At least she didn't avert her eyes from the consequences of her acts, as her half sister did.

She still didn't know what curse Mandine had called down on her that day on the Hill, nor did she know how Mandine and her barbarian lover had defeated Erkai. She remembered nothing between the roaring moment of Erkai's destruction and the first onset of the madness, when she ran wailing through the gardens below the Hill's shattered summit, with a phantom noose about her neck. But she did remember what Erkai achieved just before Mandine and the barbarian struck him down. He had done the impossible: He had broken Athanais's ancient spell, had called on the Deep Magic and seized it, and the Ban hadn't killed him. Instead of dying, he had made himself a thanaturge.

Thanaturge. Deathmaker, in the common tongue. They were deadly evil, or considered so in the ancient world. They were sorcerers, beings of dread who knew how to draw on the Deep Magic, and they did as they pleased with their power, regarding no law. For that the White Diviners had fought and destroyed them twenty centuries ago. Three hundred years after that war, Athanais the White Diviner set the Ban, and since then the Deep Magic had slept, slept until Erkai the Chain woke it at last, and then for a brief time the first thanaturge in two thousand years had trod the earth.

Theatana knew that Mandine and her barbarian must have found some fearsome artifact of the White Diviners; no other weapon could have brought him down. But as far as she could tell, they never used the thing again. Anyone with that sort of power would employ it, so it must have been destroyed in destroying Erkai; Theatana knew, from her researches of twenty-five years ago, that this was sometimes the fate of sorcerous devices once used.

But its fate hardly mattered. What did matter was this: The Ban had been broken. That knowledge was extremely dangerous, as Mandine and her husband would be vividly aware. Almost nothing of the ancient disciplines and instruments of the Deep Magic survived, but Erkai had obviously discovered enough of them to challenge the Ban. If its destruction were known, men and women of a certain inquisitive cast of mind would soon be searching for ways of resurrecting the ancient lore, and some of them might eventually succeed. The longer the secret remained a secret, from the point of view of the Fountain Palace, the better. Theatana agreed with her half sister in this, if in little else. And though Mandine might suspect that Theatana knew about Erkai's victory over the Ban, Theatana had been very careful never to betray this knowledge. If she ever did get her freedom back, possession of the secret might serve her well.

At the moment she did not see how it would. The time would come, though; she was curiously certain of it. In the meantime, she had a language to learn.

She stretched, took a deep breath of the sea air, and leaned comfortably against the sun-warmed side of the boat. She usually sat there when she was practicing how to say things. Questions in Rasennan were tricky to form. Instead of using special words to show they were asking something, they altered the pitch of the voice and changed the word order. She wanted to ask how many days' sail it was to their final destination, but she hadn't managed it yet. There was a particular lilt and phrase . . . what was it?

It wouldn't come, and her mouth tightened in frustration. Her ignorance was sometimes enough to drive her wild. All she knew of the Rasenna was that they came from somewhere far away to the south and were returning there, taking her with them. She knew they'd come to the Blue Havens to trade and raid, for Selemban wasn't the only island they'd been on. She knew this because Mixtun goods and tools almost filled the hold, though by the roughness of the items they were from the outer islands, rather than from the richer and more civilized parts of the Havens like Ammedara. But

Kayonu was obviously satisfied with his cargo, whether he'd won it by fighting or barter, and was heading home with both it and the news of the alien lands he'd found.

Theatana glanced toward the ship's bow. Kayonu was up there on the raised foredeck, dressed in the Rasennan seaman's garb of belted brown smock, loose breeches, and bare feet. He was shading his eyes with his hand and scanning the sea, looking for something. When she first saw him at it, she'd believed he sought land, but that wasn't it. He studied all points of the horizon, which could only mean he was searching for another vessel, or vessels. Allies or enemies? The sea's emptiness seemed to trouble him, so Theatana suspected he had friends out on the Blue somewhere but couldn't find them. Or maybe he was worrying about the weather. A long, high swell had been rolling out of the northeast for almost four days, as if there were some very bad winds far astern, but the horizon in that direction had shown no more than a dull greenish haze. This morning the haze had not appeared, leaving the rim of the sea clear and blue.

Kayonu shifted his gaze to the lee side of the ship. The Rasenna didn't seem to know about spyglasses, though they did know about glass—Kayonu owned a drinking vessel of the stuff, thick and greenish, which he seemed to prize. Theatana was a little puzzled at this gap in their knowledge, especially because the ship was superb. Theatana had never been much interested in naval matters, but even she could see that this vessel was faster and more nimble than anything the Ascendancy built. It was also strong, and Kayonu seemed to have absolutely no qualms about setting off into the depths of the Blue with it. The Rasenna also knew about compasses, which likely accounted for some of his confidence. Kayonu's instrument was in a bronze case and had a lid of some transparent membrane, so that he could see the pointer while it remained shielded from the wind. He was a barbarian, and only just human as far as she was concerned, but it was clear that his people were clever creatures. That cleverness, Theatana believed, was something she should be ready to use.

As for that, she should be ready to use anything at all that came to her hand, or to her mind. It was bad enough that she didn't know where the ship was going; it was worse not to know what company she might fall into when it arrived. Kayonu and his men treated her as well as she could expect, allowing for the fact that they were savages, but if she left Kayonu's protection, what then? She had no power and no wealth; nothing but her body, her wits, and her relentless will.

If only, she thought, *I'd had some way to study the Black Craft while I was in prison. But what a foolish idea that would have been, really. Even if one is free, working the Craft is a capital offense. But they were so frightened I might be up to something! They sent that priestess to see me time after time, to test me and make sure I wasn't at it somehow.*

Her mouth tightened again as she remembered: Orissi the Perpetua, the high priestess of the Two, arriving from Temple Mount to inspect her like some possible carrier of a plague. Using her dry fingers to touch Theatana's forehead, but not just her forehead, touching her inwardly, feeling about in her mind. Theatana had fought savagely at first, but when her guards started putting restraints on her she gave it up and submitted because she knew she must. Orissi's words still floated through her mind, like a bad smell in a corridor.

Daughter, you've been tainted by Erkai. It happened when you submitted to his will and let him into the city. Look inward and find the taint, so that you and I together can cleanse it.

I don't know what you're talking about, you old fool.

And it was true. She didn't know, and it wasn't for want of looking. She had delved tirelessly within herself, searching for the wisp of Erkai the Perpetua said inhabited her, but found nothing. He had been ripped away from her. She had lusted for him and needed him, and together they might have ruled not only the Ascendancy but the world. He had understood her, and she him.

And her half sister Mandine had destroyed him, in league with her barbarous lover. She had ruined Theatana's womanhood, as she had also ruined Theatana's childhood and youth: Mandine, always the more lovely sister, the more sparkling, the clever one, the one who would be Dynastessa, the one everybody loved. Even their father, cold and sour as he was, had preferred Mandine to her. Mandine's mother had died young, and too bad, but so had Theatana's; Theatana didn't remember her, didn't know if she had loved her only daughter at all. Indeed no one had ever loved Theatana, not truly. She had dreamed that Erkai might come to care for her, but Mandine put an end to that hope forever. Because of Mandine she had been torn from him, like skin flayed from living flesh, and Mandine had carefully salted that never-healing wound with the suffering of perpetual imprisonment.

Fury and hatred swept through her as she sat in the boat, hatred so fierce that her sight blackened and her blood roared in her ears. She had passed hardly a lucid hour of her imprisonment without savage dreams of revenge, but this attack made those cravings seem no more than indolent fantasy. This was a black whirlwind that might rise from the sea and carry her to far-off Captala, where she would drag her enemies shrieking from the Fountain Palace and inflict on them agonies of unspeakable invention.

Slowly the fit receded. It had shaken her, and she wondered, with a moment's tremor, if she were about to enter a new realm of madness. But the sick dread that had always preceded the earlier attacks wasn't there. Instead she felt a delightful quiver in her midriff, as if she were about to be given some marvelous, unexpected gift.

What's this? she thought.

Outside her the world seemed no different. The green-and-white sails still bellied in the slanting golden light of late afternoon, and the sea still rolled green and white and blue. But she sensed that she had changed subtly within. It was as if a part of her had awakened after a long, long sleep. She felt it uncoiling in her, deep as the marrow in her bones.

What's this?

Something like instinct made Theatana close her eyes and look within, as Orissi the Perpetua had long ago urged her to do. In the darkness, the feeling of something wakening in her was very powerful. But her first impression had been wrong; it was not part of *her* nature, but some other's. No words could describe it: It was most like another awareness enveloped in her own. At the same time it seemed as if it were gently folding into her, like a thick purple wine trickled from a goblet into pure water, tendrils of sumptuous color suffusing into mists of pink and rose. She wondered if she ought to be frightened, and in a corner of her mind she was astounded that she was not, for nothing like this had ever happened to her. She had never even realized that such a thing was possible.

What are you? What are you doing to me?

But suddenly she recognized the thing. It was astonishing that she hadn't known it instantly; perhaps that was because she had given up hope so long ago.

It was like Erkai, but not fully him, for Erkai was dead. But it was his taste, a taste of that rich, dark sweetness she remembered, the taste of the Black Craft, of his relentless will, and of his power.

Orissi was right. It was there, sure enough, though she called it a taint. Taint? To me it is the savor of life.

But what could have awakened it, to glide into her so naturally and smoothly, into the profound welcome she had so long and so unknowingly prepared for it?

Cold amusement filled her. *Of course, how obvious, if only I'd looked.*

She had killed Tabar. It was as if her jailer's blood had moistened and fertilized the dry seed within her, and days later it had sprouted. The tiny remnant of Erkai had lain hidden in her depths for a quarter century, like a spell written invisibly in a book. And that remnant must have partaken of the nature of the Black Craft, whose spells needed a killing to awaken them, for she had given it Tabar's death, and it had awakened.

Now, in the crimson dimness behind her eyelids, she strove to comprehend it. What powers could it give her, what sensibilities, what perceptions?

Part of his essence had found its way into hers; that knowledge might give her a place to begin, if she could determine how he'd accomplished it.

She remembered how it had been before they met in the flesh, when she would stand on Captala's towers and look down at his tent in the camp of the besieging Tathars. Often he sat in front of it, distant but unmistakable, as if he had awaited her arrival. And she remembered feeling that he somehow *knew* her, that they touched, although she had never in her life been closer to him than this space of two bowshots.

Did his awareness seek out mine, touch my thought, and I didn't realize it? Was that among his abilities? And has it passed into me, with this trace of him?

The tendrils coiled in her; a sense, perhaps, of assent.

So maybe I have the same ability; perhaps it did enter me with his essence. I'll test the possibility, why not? Just to see what happens.

But whom should I use for the test? Not Kayonu. The captain should have his wits about him, and if I succeed, I don't know what the effects might be. Use some unimportant, stupid man.

Theatana opened her eyes and looked across the boat's bow, past the mainmast. A Rasennan seaman squatted at the foot of the ladder leading up to the foredeck. He was splicing rope, eyes down and intent on his work, oblivious to the woman staring at him.

Summoning every power of concentration and will, Theatana thrust her awareness toward him with such unthinking force that she nearly fainted. For an instant she sensed the trace of Erkai seething inside her; then an excruciating pain shot through her head, as if a bludgeon were clubbing at her skull from the inside, and she almost toppled into the boat's bilge. But she never took her gaze from the seaman, and in the instant the pain was at its worst she sensed an awareness not her own. It was like a low satisfied murmur, the mind of someone content at a minor task on a sunlit afternoon.

The moment passed, and she slumped on the thwart, suddenly nauseated, sweating, and weak with exhaustion. Then she saw the seaman lift his head sharply and look over one shoulder, then the other, as if someone had touched or called him from behind. Theatana instantly gave all her apparent attention to the sea, but watched him from the corner of her eye. Seeing no one, he frowned, glanced at her, then returned to his task.

For all her hope that her test would succeed, she was stunned that it had. It was as if she'd had a wonderful dream of power, and had just awoken to discover that it had come true.

Unless it had been her imagination. But she rejected the idea instantly. The sense of another had been too strong, too clear, not at all imaginary—she'd never felt anything like it in her life. She'd done something she'd never thought possible; she'd touched a man's awareness, and from a distance. Even Orissi the Perpetua, who had the exceedingly rare talent of probing another consciousness, needed physical contact to do so.

So the trace of Erkai she bore was no mere token of his existence; it was in fact a seed of sorcery. How powerful that sorcery might be, she had yet to discover fully. But at the moment she was recovering only slowly from her nausea and exhaustion, and the mere thought of exerting her newfound ability brought a wave of crushing weariness. It was clear that what she'd just done could not be swiftly repeated.

A movement from the foredeck ladder drew her gaze. Kayonu climbed down to the main deck, then came aft, his brow furrowed. She hoped he'd pass her by, but he didn't. He stopped and said something, and she caught the word for *ship* and *comrade-in-arms* and some others she didn't understand. Kayonu saw her perplexity, then made whistling noises and waved his hands with exaggerated wavelike motions. He was imitating a storm. So: A storm might have caught a ship that had friends in it, and he was worried.

Theatana didn't care about his friends or his worries. She wanted him to leave her alone, so she could recover from her weariness. She smiled a little, and said in the Logomenon, "I hope they all drown. And you, too, just as soon as I'm off your stinking ship. Now go away, you stupid savage, and leave me be."

He smiled in return and went on toward the afterdeck. Theatana promptly dismissed him from her thoughts; he was unimportant. What was important was that she carried Erkai's seed within her, a seed that she could nurture and feed until it grew into a soaring tree. It would bear marvelous fruit, ripe for her feasting.

The image pleased her. She chuckled and thought: *But I'll be sure to share the harvest with everyone, and I don't believe they'll like its taste nearly as much as I will.*

6

ETHON DIED ON THE MORNING OF THEIR FOURTH DAY ON
the island.

Ilarion was returning from another fruitless egg-hunting
expedition when he saw Lashgar approaching from the direction of their camp. The prince's face was glum.

"Is it Ethon?" Ilarion asked as he came up. Lashgar was
not yet gaunt, but he had never carried much extra flesh, and
his delicate cheekbones were beginning to stretch the skin.

"Yes. He's calling out for you."

It won't be long, Ilarion thought. *Those smashed legs are
going to kill him.* Ethon's would be the second death since
they'd come ashore. Arino had died the night after they
landed. He was buried farther down the beach with three
more of *Scourge*'s crew, whose drowned bodies had washed
in with the tide.

The day was already bright and hot as they headed for the
camp. From the hillside they could see much of the island, a
rough crescent of stone about a mile long and a quarter of
that across. The pebble beach where they had landed was on
the inner curve of the crescent; from there, the land climbed
in a long slope that ended abruptly at the sheer precipice that
formed the island's south side. Beyond the beach was a long,
narrow sound that stretched in from the open sea. On the
sound's far side rose the wall of rock, with the cleft through
which their raft had been carried. No other land was in sight.

"Did you catch anything?" Ilarion asked, brushing sweat
from his eyes. In spite of his grief for Ethon, his hunger was
too savage to ignore. Fishing was keeping them alive, but

65

barely. So far their makeshift thorn hooks, baited with grubs dug from the soil, had caught only five tiny pintara and three wafer-thin moonfish. On the island itself there was nothing to eat. The terrain was rugged, cut by shallow ravines and sprinkled with boulders, and little but scrub palms, ironthorn trees, and leffa grew in the thin soil. Mercifully, however, they'd found three springs.

"Not yet. Mersis and I were down on shore until Ethon called us. Mersis is with him now."

Ilarion was feeling light-headed by the time they neared the camp, which was near the best of the water sources. It consisted of a thatched lean-to in a stand of stunted fretwork palms, a fire pit, some beds made of the less prickly undergrowth, and a small clutter of salvaged boards, timbers, and sailcloth that had drifted ashore from *Scourge*'s wreck.

Mersis, who had been kneeling beside Ethon's pallet in the lean-to's shade, got up as they trudged into the camp. He looked glum and made a negative gesture that said, *There's no help for him now*.

Ilarion went down on one knee at Ethon's shoulder. The peltarch's face was grayish yellow; his eyes were closed, and he was breathing in quick, shallow gasps. His infected leg was uncovered, and the skin was swollen and splotched with purple and black.

"He fell asleep a little while ago, my lord," Mersis whispered. "He spoke some, before then."

I should let him sleep, Ilarion thought, but then the man's eyelids flickered and he half opened his eyes. "I'm here, Ethon," Ilarion said softly.

"My lord. Thank you. I wanted to see you to ask . . ."

He bit his lower lip very hard, holding back the pain. "Hold on, Ethon," Ilarion said. "You'll see home again."

The officer managed to shake his head. "No, my lord, I won't. We both know it."

There was no point in pretending; Ethon deserved better than that. Ilarion nodded.

"But please," the young man gasped. "Please, my lord, tell my father and mother I died thinking of them. And if you could come to the family tomb when they do my rites of remembrance . . . it will ease their grief, if they know you thought that well of me."

"I swear it, Ethon," Ilarion said softly. "As I am the Luminessos. I'll tell them, and I'll be there."

"Thank you, my lord." He fell silent a moment, then whispered, "Can you build up the fire? I'm cold."

He closed his eyes, and his breathing softened but remained as quick. He had slipped into unconsciousness again.

"I hope I go in a hurry when I go," Lashgar muttered at Ilarion's elbow. "This is no death for anyone."

Ilarion fed the fire as Ethon had asked. The driftwood had dried in the days since the storm and burned without smoke. After he had a good blaze going, Ilarion moved to sit on a flat stone near his officer. Mersis returned to his fishing, and Lashgar went with him. Ilarion watched them wade thigh-deep into the water, then cast their lines again and again, but without luck. Mersis had talked of making a net from unraveled rope, but they didn't have enough rope. Perhaps, if they could get out to the reef, they might find some remaining from *Scourge*'s wreck.

The hours passed as the sun climbed toward its zenith. Ethon did not fully wake again, but whispered of thirst in his sleep. From time to time, Ilarion soaked a rag of sailcloth in the spring and squeezed the cloth between the man's lips. Down on the beach the fishing did not go well; neither Mersis nor Lashgar caught anything for all their efforts. Ilarion knew he should help them, but he could not leave Ethon. Ethon was his officer, and he knew how he would feel if he awoke sick and dying, on an alien shore, and found that he was alone.

It was just midday when Ethon suddenly took a deep, ragged breath, then released it. Ilarion waited for him to breathe again, but he did not.

With his right palm on Ethon's searing forehead, Ilarion said the soldier's death prayer to the Allfather Protector. When he had finished, he wiped the perspiration from the man's cooling skin, gently arranged the limbs, and drew the sailcloth over the dead face. Then he left the camp and

walked down the shore toward the others. Coiling his useless fishing line around his forearm, Lashgar waded out of
the shallows to meet him.

"He's gone?"

"He's gone."

The prince's mouth worked a little. "Curse it. I'm sorry.
The last of your men. He was a good soldier, wasn't he?"

"Yes. Very good."

"I'm not sure of your rites. But I'll help with anything I
can."

"We should do it now," Ilarion said. "We're not getting any
stronger, and it's too hot to leave him above ground for long."

"All right."

They carried Ethon along the shore to the place where the
others had their cairn, and buried him there. Ilarion performed the rituals over him, and burned a wreath of cordgrass on the stones. He should have made the wreath from
bittersweet, but he hadn't been able to find any on the island;
it was a northern plant.

Weariness overtook him after it was done. Mersis stumbled back to the camp to rest, but Ilarion and Lashgar remained at the grave. Ilarion sat on a stone next to the prince
and tried to summon enough energy to get his fishing line
and try to catch something. He wondered dully why the fish
were so scarce around this island. The lack of fish meant few
seabirds, and those few nested on the cliffs, well out of reach
of starving castaways.

"Are you angry with my father?" Lashgar asked suddenly.

"What? No, of course not. Why do you think that?"

"It's . . . well, Theatana got away from him, and that's why
we're here. And I know you've got a temper sometimes. You
were very angry, for a while at least, the other night on Selemban."

Ilarion rubbed his face with both palms. His skin gritted
with sweat-salt under his five days' beard. "Yes, I was. But
it's— Lashgar, it's worse than a temper, when it gets hold of
me, which it didn't the other night, thank the Allfather."

"Ah," Lashgar said, eyeing him thoughtfully. "I think I
saw it once in Captala, when we were boys."

"Yes. I remember that, too. Anyway, my grandfather Archates had the weakness, I'm told. It's a kind of fury that takes over the mind. I've tried to learn to control it, but I don't know how successful I've been."

"So long as you don't do any harm, though—"

"But I have," Ilarion said wretchedly. "Over two score of my soldiers would still be alive, except that I lost my temper." He wondered why he was confessing this. He didn't need to. Perhaps it was because he was likely to die before long.

"Oh, I see." Lashgar frowned, puzzled. "Well, no, in fact I don't."

"It was three years ago on the North March. I was in command of a cavalry detachment, fighting steppe nomads, a big ten-clan raid. Nothing went right for a month—weather bad, running fights all the time, no sleep, short of supplies and horses. Finally, we got a good hold of the raiders, then one of my peltarchs made a stupid mistake and they slipped away."

"And you lost your temper."

"Yes. It was getting dark, and I went after them with only forty men. I knew better, knew they'd ambush us, but I was blind with fury. And they did ambush us. Half of us got away, the other half didn't. Twenty-three men dead because I lost my temper."

"But you've led men in battle. You have to give orders, and men die because of them—"

"That's different. What I did was stupid and *unnecessary*." Ilarion laughed without humor. "Then I did something as bad, or worse."

"What?"

"We had a dozen prisoners. Four were women—some of them ride as scouts because they're light on a horse and fast. I was still in a rage when we got back to camp. I ordered all the prisoners hanged."

"Oh," Lashgar said, "I see. The women, too?"

"The women, too, the Honored Lady forgive me. The only thing that saved them, and me, was that my officers delayed it long enough for me to come to my senses. I countermanded the order."

Lashgar exhaled slowly. "And the other nomads, in the end?"

"Oh, we finally slapped them around enough so they went home. I sent the prisoners after them and told them if they ever came back, I *would* hang them. But when I got back to Captala I had to tell my father what happened. He never hit me in my life, but that time I thought he might. He said if I lost my temper badly enough to make me act like a savage, I had no business being Dynast, and if I didn't learn to control it, he'd give Katheri the diadem."

"But you *have* learned," Lashgar said. "Haven't you?"

"I don't know. I haven't been tried like that since. It troubles me."

The two friends lapsed into silence. Then, abruptly, the prince sat up straight, and said, "Listen!"

"What?" Ilarion heard only the familiar noise of the wind blowing gently down the sound, its faint hiss sounding from the palms and the ironthorns. Waves broke quietly on the shore.

"There," Lashgar said, between the fall of two waves.

Ilarion tilted his head. *Had* there been something? Like a shout, followed by another voice calling in reply?

A minute passed, and it didn't come again. "Stupid of me," Lashgar said. "I'm hearing things."

"But I thought I heard it, too. It came from the east." Ilarion felt a jab of hope that got him to his feet. "We'd better go over to the end of the island and look. It might be a ship."

Lashgar gave a bitter laugh. "Already? At home they won't even know we're missing."

"You said fishermen sometimes come this far south. Come on."

They walked along the shore, their bare feet crunching on the round pebbles. The wind strengthened a little and soon made enough noise in the palms to blot out any repetition of the mysterious voice, if it had been a voice. The hope that had dragged Ilarion to his feet faded away, leaving him weak and dispirited.

They passed below the camp. Mersis appeared to be asleep and did not follow them. After a while they neared the eastern tip of the island. High above them, a flat-topped ridge of stone cut the sky before dropping sheer to the sea at the land's end, a natural causeway leading nowhere.

"Do you hear anything yet?" the prince asked. "I still don't."

"We haven't checked the other side of the ridge. There's that scrap of beach down there, remember, where the cliffs have fallen away? Maybe somebody's on it."

Lashgar gave a tired shrug. "Maybe. Let's go up top then, and have a look."

They trudged upward through the undergrowth, slowly gaining height as they approached the causeway at the top of the ridge. Ilarion, sweating, wondered why he had been so foolish as to waste his and Lashgar's strength on this futile venture.

The wind dropped for a few moments, and in one of those moments they heard a voice.

"I *heard* it!" Lashgar exclaimed. "Did you?"

"Yes," Ilarion said. He broke into a run, stumbling over rocks and thrusting himself through nets of spiny underbrush. Lashgar followed, breath rasping. They reached the causeway. On its far side was a steep slope, not quite a cliff, and at the foot of the slope was a small crescent of beach. The sea was calm, and a line of low surf broke in white ribbons along the shore. They stopped, wheezing, gazing down at the sea, bereft of words.

Just beyond the surf, where the water deepened, was a ship.

"A *ship*," Lashgar gasped. "A *ship*, thank the Sea Lord. We're going home!"

"So we are," Ilarion said, laughing with relief. But even as he stared at the vessel, perplexity leavened his exultation. She didn't resemble any type he'd seen before. She was noticeably bigger than *Ascendancy Maid*, had three masts, and was clearly a seagoing craft. On her foremast was a long slanting yard, which carried a big triangular sail striped with narrow bands of red and white. Men were lowering the yard in preparation for taking in the sail. The canvas on her main- and mizzenmasts was already furled.

A man on the ship's afterdeck saw them, pointed, and shouted to someone else. He was a long way away, and the words were too faint to understand. It had been a freak of the wind that had allowed Lashgar to hear the voices earlier; the island and the cliffs opposite it must have funneled the noise to his ears.

"What in the name of all that's sacred are they doing here?" Lashgar said. "Did they see the smoke from our fire?"

"I didn't think there was that much smoke. Maybe they're looking for water or game."

"Yes, maybe."

Ilarion studied the exotic-looking ship. A few of the biggest Ascendancy grain freighters were equipped with three masts, but those vessels were square-rigged from stem to stern. This one's main yard seemed to be intended for a square sail, but judging from the shape of her foresail and the slant of her mizzen yard, she carried triangles of canvas everywhere else. Ilarion had never seen such a rig.

Lashgar was waving at the ship. No one waved back, but the pace of her crew's movements looked purposeful. The men seemed to be wearing hoods of some pale golden cloth. Lashgar stopped waving.

"Which part of the Havens does she come from?" Ilarion asked.

"What?" Lashgar looked at him in surprise. "None, as far as I know. I thought she was some kind of Ascendancy ship."

A prickle ran over Ilarion's skin. "She's not."

"What, then? Tathar?"

Ilarion snorted. "Tathars can barely make rafts. She *must* be from the islands."

"I tell you, she isn't. I know every type in the Havens, and that's not one of them. We don't use three masts, and we don't make the afterdeck jut out past the rudder post that way."

"They aren't wearing hoods," Ilarion said. "I thought they were, but they aren't. That's their hair. It's yellow, like gold."

Lashgar squinted. "What? I thought they had head scarves on. Nobody has golden hair. Unless the Tathars—"

"Theirs is silver or gray, never yellow. Does anybody in the Havens color their hair?"

"Not that way. What about in the Ascendancy?"

"Not there, either."

Some of the yellow-haired men were rigging a hoist, and Ilarion realized they were getting ready to lower a small boat that was tucked onto the main deck. He felt a wash of relief, and said, "Well, whoever they are, it seems they're not planning to leave us here."

"Or they're coming ashore to rob us." In spite of his words, the prince laughed with relief. "It will hardly be worth their trouble."

"Hardly. Come on, let's go down."

Lashgar was about to follow him, but stopped. "Wait. They might be slavers. There's a few of the jungly princes in the eastern Havens who buy slaves. And you told me the Tathars use them."

Ilarion, already on the slope, looked back at him. "If they are, our families will ransom us. Anyway, what choice have we got? They already know we're here, and they're our only way off this piece of rock. We're between the sword and the wall."

Lashgar grunted a reluctant agreement and followed. The two men worked gingerly down the steep slope, holding tufts of cordgrass to keep themselves from a breakneck slide to the beach. By the time they were halfway down, the strangers had swung their boat into the water and its crew was aboard and rowing for the shore. It was a small boat, manned only by six rowers and one steersman, but even so the speed with which they'd embarked was impressive. Wherever they came from, they were superb seamen.

As Ilarion jumped onto the coarse sand of the beach, the craft was only a dozen yards beyond the low surf. Now he saw that the silver-gray clothing of its rowers was actually armor, and that their strangely colored hair had vanished under domed helmets. On their backs were slung round shields, painted with the insignia of a helmeted warrior's head. The steersman was holding a spear whose slender blade glinted dully in the sun.

They expertly maneuvered the boat through the surf. The little craft had a rough look to it, as though it had been built in a hurry from whatever lay to hand, and its planks were the pale yellow of raw wood. But the mother ship didn't give an impression of crudeness, and Ilarion wondered briefly if the boat might be a replacement for a better craft that had somewhere come to grief.

He squinted at the three-master, wishing for his spyglass that now lay somewhere in the depths of the sea. The vessel's rail was sparsely lined with watching men.

"How many people do you count out there?" he said. "If that's all she has aboard, plus the seven in the boat, it's not many for a ship that size."

Lashgar counted under his breath. "Fourteen, I think. Add a few we can't see. No more than twenty-five."

"Those yards are big. It'd take eight men to raise one in a hurry."

"Eight at least. She's shorthanded, for certain." Lashgar nibbled his lower lip doubtfully. "Do you think we ought to let them know who we are? Given *where* we are? My father has enemies."

"They may not speak our language, but if they do . . . I think we'd better be careful. We should let them know we can pay well for a passage home, but you'd better not be Jaladar's son. Who are you?"

"Ah—all right, I'm Sirdan of Uleim. That'll offend no one. What about you?"

"Theron Carmanas. We'll have to tell Mersis—"

He broke off. The boat was sweeping in to shore some twenty yards away. She skidded as a breaker picked her up and slued her to port, but the steersman straightened her adroitly. A moment later he shouted an order and the rowers brought their oars in with a rumble and thump. The two men nearest the bow leaped overboard into thigh-deep foam, then scrambled ashore with their shields and swords at the ready. There they halted to watch Ilarion and Lashgar, while the remaining rowers disembarked and hauled their craft onto the beach. As soon as it was well grounded, the steersman ran lightly from thwart to thwart up to the bow, used his spear shaft as a vaulting pole, and jumped dry-shod to land.

The seven men stalked forward with the steersman in the lead. All except for him had now drawn their blades, and Lashgar muttered uneasily. Ilarion did not reach for his dagger; against a spear and six swords it would be useless, anyway.

The men continued to advance until they were ten paces distant. Then they stopped, and Ilarion slowly let his breath out.

Everyone stood motionless while the strangers looked the two castaways up and down. The steersman hadn't bothered to unsling his shield from his back. He was a hand taller than Ilarion and had green eyes, something Ilarion had never seen. Neither had he seen anyone with yellow hair; it escaped in fronds from beneath the cheek pieces of the man's helmet. His upper lip was clean-shaven, but his cheeks and chin were covered by a thick gold beard trimmed to a blunted point. Above the beard his sunburned face was uncomely; some long-healed disease had pitted the skin of his forehead, and some past fight or mishap had flattened his nose and pushed it off center. But even in its ugliness his face wore an authority Ilarion recognized: It was the mask of command.

Ilarion opened his hands and held them up, palms outward, to the strangers. Lashgar did the same. The leader's eyes narrowed, and he gestured toward the dagger Ilarion wore at his belt. Ilarion drew the weapon and tossed it to the sand. The leader gave a curt order, and his men sheathed their swords.

"That's no island language," Lashgar said. "Have you ever heard it before?"

"No. Nowhere."

The leader spoke. It seemed a question, and Ilarion said, in the Logomenon, "We're wrecked naval officers of noble blood." He repeated the words in Tathar, Haema, and less fluently in the steppe-nomad tongue. He saw no sign of comprehension. After a puzzled silence, the leader spoke to one of his men, who tried what might be other languages. The sounds meant nothing to Ilarion.

"I don't think they're from anywhere around here," Lashgar observed uneasily.

The leader walked up to them. His ugly face was weather-beaten, and he looked about ten years older than Ilarion. His men were more youthful, three appearing to be roughly Lashgar's age.

The man reached out and fingered the sleeve of Ilarion's tunic. Despite its wear and tear the linen still showed its quality. It was not a fabric an ordinary seaman would wear, and the expression on the stranger's face showed that he knew it. He stooped, picked up Ilarion's dagger, and inspected the weapon. The tapered blade was the finest patterned steel the Ascendancy could make, and the pommel and guard were inlaid with gold and set with snake-eye sapphires. The gems glittered in the sunlight, and the yellow-haired men muttered in surprise or greed, or both.

Well, Ilarion thought, *either he's got an idea of my rank, or he thinks I'm a thief. I hope he enjoys having it at his belt.*

But the man didn't take the weapon. Instead, he held it out hilt-first, and Ilarion realized he was returning it. Taken aback, he accepted the dagger, and said, "Thank you."

He was about to sheathe it, when some instinct warned him that he might find a better use for the thing. He bowed slightly and offered the hilt of the weapon. The stranger grinned, gave a bellow of a laugh, and accepted it. He pushed it into his sword belt, and in return handed Ilarion his own belt knife. It was a workmanlike dagger of gray iron, with a yellowing bone hilt and a guard made of bronze.

The golden-haired man thumped his mailed chest. "Rook." He appeared to be introducing himself. He gazed expectantly at Ilarion.

"Do we need to use those silly false names?" Lashgar muttered. "Our real ones won't mean a thing to him."

"I suppose you're right." Ilarion pointed at himself, and said, "Ilarion." He pointed at Lashgar, and said, "Lashgar."

"Ilarion, Lashgar," said Rook. He waved expansively at his men, then banged his chest again. "Rasenna."

"Rasenna?" Ilarion asked.

"*Isti.*" The word for yes, perhaps. "Rasenna."

Lashgar said, "Is that what they call themselves? I've never heard of a race called that."

"Neither have I," Ilarion answered. He indicated himself and the prince, and said, "Mixtun."

"Mixtun?" asked Rook.

"*Isti.*"

"You're not Mixtun," Lashgar objected. "You're the wrong colors."

"He doesn't know that. I'm trying to keep things simple."

Rook cupped a hand, raised it to his mouth, and made drinking motions. Then he waved at the slope behind the beach, and said, "Ashwa."

"They need water." Ilarion pretended to stuff food into his mouth, chewed, swallowed, then tapped his chest. "Bread."

Rook pointed at the slope. "Ashwa." Then he pointed at the ship. "Bread, *isti.*"

He was a quick study. "They'll take us aboard and feed us if we show them where they can get water." Ilarion's stomach clenched painfully at the prospect.

"Then let's show them, for pity's sake."

Ilarion knelt and drew a map in the sand, including the two entrances to the sound, and using sign language to indicate the spring by the camp. Then he drew two stick figures to indicate himself and Lashgar, and a third to show the presence of Mersis. Rook understood, for when Ilarion ventured, "*Isti?*" he held up three fingers, and said, "Mixtun."

When the map was finished, Rook studied it for a moment, then issued brief commands. His crew headed for the boat. The Rasennan leader started after them, gesturing brusquely for Ilarion and Lashgar to accompany him.

"What makes him think he can order us around?" Lashgar muttered in annoyance.

"He doesn't know who we are, and he's got the swords. If we have to take his orders to get home, at least we'll get there. Come on."

They followed Rook and clambered into the boat's stern with him. The crew pushed off and rowed vigorously through the surf. Once they were beyond the breaking water,

Rook turned the boat's prow east, instead of heading for the ship.

"What's he doing?" Lashgar said plaintively.

"I think he's making a reconnaissance around to the camp. He's taking us along so he can kill us if we've led him into an ambush."

"That's a cheering thought. But there's no one here but us and Mersis."

"He doesn't know that. For all he knows, there's a hostile naval squadron in the sound."

"Curse it," Lashgar muttered. "I wanted to eat."

As they passed Rook's ship—it was anchored, Ilarion now saw—the Rasennan bellowed instructions or information at the men aboard. Excitement mounted in Ilarion as he studied the craft. He'd come to the islands looking for ideas that the shipwrights of the Ascendancy could use, and perhaps, in the alien vessel, he had found them. He could pay Rook lavishly to take her to the naval shipyards of Captala, and there she could be examined and copied.

Rook settled down to steer around the island's tip, toward the entrance to the sound. Ilarion was almost happy despite his hunger. They'd been rescued. They were not going to die on the island. All he had to do was get Rook to understand that he'd be well paid for taking them to Ammedara. From there he would continue the search for Theatana, and send word to Captala of her escape—

Great Allfather, I haven't been thinking.

"Lashgar."

"What?"

Don't say her name, just in case they've heard it. "My aunt. Someone took her. Maybe these men."

Even with the wind he heard the hiss of the prince's indrawn breath. "Yes. Pirates. It must have been them. My father will—"

"Govern your voice. The man steering is no fool."

Lashgar softened his tone. "They're freebooters and pillagers. My father will hang them from Manacle Gate."

"If it *was* them." But who else could it have been? Rook and his crew were no simple merchant sailors. They knew the sea and knew it well, but their armor and weapons belonged to men whose trade was war. Men like these could have taken on the Ammedaran soldiers who guarded Theatana, and won handily.

"If they're freebooters," he said, "it's going to be hard to persuade them to go anywhere near civilization. Except to raid it, and it looks to me as if they've lost too many men to make that comfortable. They may be on their way home, wherever home is."

"I know. What are we going to do?"

"Think," Ilarion said, and thought.

He had to assume the worst: that these Rasenna, as they called themselves, had raided Ammedaran territory and taken his aunt and slaughtered her guards. That being true, Rook would hardly agree to return to those waters, where hostile naval forces might be stirred up and looking for him. Promises of a rich reward, however, might persuade him to go elsewhere in the islands, or even to the Ascendancy—assuming Ilarion could communicate the promise, and assuming Rook believed it. Ilarion was far from sure that Rook would.

And Theatana? If she were still alive and aboard the ship, and given the habits of pirates everywhere, she was almost certainly Rook's bedmate. Ilarion reflected that she might well prefer this to being transported to the Ascendancy and imprisoned again. She'd do whatever she could to avoid that fate, and he'd have to guard his back if they walked the same deck. But a freebooter like Rook wouldn't lose a chance at a rich reward merely to please a woman. If he were expecting one, he'd sail for the Ascendancy no matter how Theatana reacted.

"What do you think?" Lashgar asked.

"I'll try to get him to take us to islands outside Ammedaran waters, or failing that, to the Ascendancy." Ilarion glanced at Rook. "If *she's* on the ship, so much the better, but if she isn't, your father will start looking for her as soon as *Ascendancy Maid* reaches Ammedara. The alarm will be raised without us."

"But my father will soon be looking for us, as well as for

your aunt," Lashgar pointed out. "If we go straight to the Ascendancy, he's going to spend at least two months believing
I'm dead."

"I know. I'm sorry. I can't think of anything else."

"But *will* this Rook take us there? If he's really freed your
aunt, well, she's a convicted traitor. Helping her would be a
capital offense in the Ascendancy, wouldn't it?"

"Yes, but he doesn't know what he's done, if he does have
her. Anyway, I'd intervene. He saved our lives."

Lashgar gave an angry grunt. "That doesn't mean he
won't slit our throats tomorrow morning."

"I know, but look, we have to take a step at a time. The
main thing is to get home in one piece."

"Yes, I know."

Suddenly too weary to speak, they fell silent. The
Rasenna rowed tirelessly, and the mouth of the sound approached. When Ilarion looked back, he saw that the ship
had weighed anchor and was slowly following them under a
small sail secured to her forestay. Rook saw him looking,
and said, with obvious pride, "*Statira*."

That must be the name of the ship, or it was their word for
a ship. "*Statira*," Ilarion repeated, and added, "A beautiful
name."

Now they were entering the sound, and Rook concen-
trated on his steering. In a short while they reached the camp
and went ashore. Mersis was still asleep when they arrived,
and gave a strangled yell of terror when he woke to find
himself surrounded by armored giants with yellow hair.

"Don't worry, Mersis," Lashgar said. "We're heading for
home. I hope."

When the Rasenna had quenched their thirst at the spring,
it seemed as good a time as any to tell Rook where they
wanted to go; he was in a jovial mood because of finding the
water. Ilarion found a patch of bare sand where he could
draw a map. Rook watched with interest as he used a series
of dots to sketch the Ends of Earth, and indicated that that
was where they now were. Rook nodded, and said, "*Isti.
Harappo*."

The second word meant either *island* or *I understand*.

Ilarion drew a longer arc of dots above the Ends of Earth, to show a stretch of the Blue Havens. Then he glanced at Rook. The Rasennan pursed his lips, then shrugged.

He's not about to let on where he's been, Ilarion thought. *That suggests he doesn't think it wise to go back. Very well, we won't insist.*

He moved to the other side of the sand patch and drew the largest oblong the space allowed, well separated from the dots of the Blue Havens: *A big land.* Then he pointed to himself, then to the oblong, then north. Rook watched impassively. Ilarion bent again and drew a crude ship with three masts, beside the dot representing the island they were now on. He pointed at the Rasennan leader, then at the ship.

"*Harappo*," said Rook. *I understand.*

The other Rasenna had watched the proceedings with growing interest. Now the persuasion had to begin. Ilarion drew a line from the ship to the large blob, then drew another three-masted ship there, then erased the original. *Sail to the big land.*

"*Harappo*," said Rook again. He grinned, then shrugged. He drew Ilarion's dagger, tapped the largest sapphire on its hilt, then made a cup of his two palms.

Lashgar gave a humorless laugh. "An expensive passage."

"It's a lower price than staying here." Ilarion smiled broadly and pointed at the jewel. Then he went to the edge of the sand patch, picked a double handful of stones and gravel, and dumped it on the oblong. He did it again, then again, and again. He kept the pile growing until he thought he'd made his point, and straightened up. The Rasennan sailors were gazing at it wide-eyed, as though they saw the glitter of gems in the rough stones. Rook's face was shuttered, his expression opaque. He looked up from the pile, and his green eyes stared into Ilarion's, measuring him. Ilarion waited.

"*Nas*," Rook said. *No.* He pointed, but not to the north. "*Statira, Rook.*"

"He doesn't believe me," Ilarion said furiously. "He's sailing south. Curse him to the Waste." His voice had risen. Rook watched him, eyes narrowed, and his hand was resting

lightly on the hilt of his sword. Ilarion took two long
breaths, fighting his anger and his blighted hope.

"My lord?" Mersis sounded bewildered. "What are they
all saying? Where are we going?"

"Well, *I'm* not going anywhere but to the Havens or the
mainland," Lashgar said, and sat down on the ground. He
stared defiantly up at Rook. The Rasennan made a harsh
sound in his throat, bunched his fist, and took a step forward.

"*Nas,*" Ilarion said quickly. Rook paused, waiting.

"For pity's sake don't do that," Ilarion said. "It won't
help. If they want you as crew, they'll knock you out and
drag you aboard. If they don't want you, they'll leave you
here to die."

"You're going? You'll take their orders? You're the Luminessos!"

"I want to be a live Luminessos. If I can do it, so can you."

Lashgar slowly got to his feet. He smiled at Rook, and
said, "I'll hang you all, one day."

Weariness and despair washed through Ilarion. He had
done his best, and it wasn't enough. He'd wished often
enough to sail beyond the horizons, far into the mystery of
the Blue, but he had never imagined that it would happen.
Much less that it would happen like this.

Be careful what you seek from the Lord and Lady, murmured a voice in the deeps of his mind. *They might give it to
you.*

II

THE RASENNA

7

AT HIGH NOON ON THE LAST DAY OF THE MONTH OF MIDdle Spring, the forces of the Protectress Elyssa stormed Rumach Hold.

The Hold's surprised defenders put up little resistance. Neither they nor their leader Aratu had expected the First Levy of the Protectress's army to come upon them so soon, with the spring sowing barely finished in the lowlands. Consequently they were sadly unprepared for either siege or assault, and were outnumbered by fifteen to one into the bargain. The main gate and the outer walls fell a little after midday, whereupon most of Aratu's surviving men threw down their weapons; only his sworn retainers fought to the end, around their lord, on the topmost floor of the citadel's lookout tower.

The Protectress had just ridden in through the Hold's main gateway when an excited junior officer brought word that Aratu had been taken alive. She kept all expression from her face, but felt an inward grimace of displeasure as she halted her gelding. She must now deal with Aratu personally, an unwelcome prospect.

The young officer—he was a second-rank captain named Lyalo—fidgeted as he waited for her orders. Elyssa pulled her helmet off and shook her head to loosen her hair. It was cut short and hung in a smooth curve along the line of her jaw and the nape of her neck, like a second helmet of pale gold. In the gold were darker streaks, where sweat had trickled. She always perspired under armor, even up here in the mountains, where winds swept up the gorges from the sea.

"Have him brought out here," she told the officer. He quickly turned to go, and she said, "Second-Captain Lyalo."

He turned back, frightened at what he had done. In his excitement he had turned away before she dismissed him.

"Yes, Protectress?" She heard the alarm in his voice.

"You were first through the gate, weren't you?"

He looked very slightly less worried. "Yes, Protectress."

"Well done. You'll get a gate-crown for it. Now go and have the rebel brought to me."

He scurried away. A gust of wind blew in through the open gateway, and she turned her face to it, savoring its coolness on her forehead and cheeks. Beyond the gate and the level space before it, the mountain track sloped steeply away, heading down to the foothills and the lowlands. From this height she could see miles into the distance, along the coastal plain with its scattered patches of forest and its swaths of dark earth, plowed for planting. Farther down the coast, lost in a blue haze, lay the peninsula where brooding, ruined Charunna stood, the city of tombs. Hidden also in the haze, on the seashore just beyond the ancient city, were the white walls and russet-tiled roofs of Dymie, her capital.

But even from this height she could not see as far as the other shoreline, a hundred miles to the south. There lay the mainland, the lost realm her ancestors called the Great Garden, the ruined dominions of the Rasenna.

She and her people were the surviving fragment of that realm. Here on the island of Haidra its light still burned, in the capitals of Dymie and Kanesh, in their temples and in their palace libraries, in the smaller cities and towns of the interior and the coasts. But it was a dim and guttering flame, lighting only a faded tapestry of the old splendor. The Great Garden of the Rasenna had shrunk to an island three hundred miles long and eighty wide, adrift at the edge of the known world.

So much lost, she thought. *Here am I, the Protectress Elyssa Velianas, leading a thousand men against a tumbledown tower defended by threescore rebels, and we call it war. My ancestors would weep with shame.*

She leaned on the pommel of her saddle and looked

around the Hold's courtyard. She had left half her soldiers to rest in the spring sunlight outside the fortifications, but the remainder were within the walls to guard against any counterattack by Aratu's clansmen. As for his captured warriors, they had been shackled to one another and were sitting in a disconsolate huddle in an angle of the courtyard walls. Some forty had survived of the original sixty. No wonder they had lost their nerve at the sight of a thousand heavy infantry, the full strength of the First Levy of Dymie, tramping up the rough mountain track toward their ramshackle stronghold. Fortunately for them they'd had the time and the sense to send their women and children into the high pastures before the attack. Rasennan soldiers seldom raped, out of fear of the Green Lady's anger, but after a storming there was always a danger that the victors would get out of control. That was more likely in a situation like this, when the defeated were mountain tribesmen and the victors came from the lowlands. Though both the lowlanders and the mountain clans were of the same Rasenna blood, the former considered the latter to be not much better than thieves and brigands.

Near the captives was the gate to the hold's inner citadel, where Aratu had made his last stand. Elyssa's soldiers had already looted the place of its more portable valuables, which had been collected outside the gate for distribution according to rank. However, she had ordered that the provisions, furniture, and kitchen equipment be left untouched. She'd have to garrison the Hold until she could find a Warden of steadier loyalty to replace Aratu, and the place couldn't be stripped bare.

Larth Tetnias appeared in the citadel gateway and strode down the ramp toward her. The thousands of tiny plates of his armor glittered like fish scales in the sunlight. He was still wearing his helmet but half its rank crest of black-and-white eagle feathers had been sheared away by somebody's sword.

The sight disturbed her a little, for it reminded her that Larth was getting too old to indulge his taste for close combat. He was in his late fifties and had been her father's chief military leader and counselor, the Pronoyar of the Army. He had continued serving her after her father's death, when Haidra was partitioned between her and her brother Tirsun and she went to rule in Dymie. She was very glad Larth had decided to accompany her those eight years ago, for she had needed him. She still did, and he should not be throwing himself needlessly at the enemy.

"You have Aratu?" she asked. "Second-Captain Lyalo said so."

"We have him. Lyalo's bringing him out to you now." Larth took his helmet off. There were broad silver streaks in the pale yellow of his hair, and his bald spot, polished where the helmet lining rubbed, gleamed in the sunlight. He hadn't shaved since the First Levy marched from Dymie and his flat cheeks glistened with pale stubble. He turned the helmet in his hands, inspecting the ruined rank crest. "Look what he did to this. He is a very good swordsman."

Elyssa said, "I wish you wouldn't . . . *participate*. At least not so much."

"I can't help it, Protectress." Larth grinned. "After all these years, you should know that."

"Yes. But what would I do if I lost you?"

"Lead the army yourself. You can do it."

She knew it was true. She had worked hard to secure the loyalty of her officers and the respect of her soldiers. She had to; there had been no outright war on Haidra for two generations, but the island was not always peaceful. The hill tribes had to be kept docile and made to pay their yearly tribute; there were occasional probing attacks by the Hazannu mainlanders, which needed to be discouraged by punitive expeditions that could be turned into useful slave raids; and early in her rule a backcountry noble had tried to set up his own Protectorate. So from time to time the army marched, and she marched with it. When her men slept on the ground, so did she, and she ate their coarse bread with them and drank their sour, vinegary wine without grimacing. That she was beautiful could have been a liability, but she had turned it into an asset. Most of the younger men of the army were half in love with her.

But I'm *not so young anymore,* Elyssa reminded herself. *I'm twenty-six. Women on Haidra don't reach twenty-six without a husband. Most have borne half a dozen children by my age. Even priestesses marry and bear sons and daughters.*

It wasn't that she lacked suitors. Auvas Seitithi, the most powerful and richest aristocrat of her Protectorate, was among those who wanted to marry her. But she didn't want him. In fact, she could barely tolerate his company.

For so long I found no one whose touch I craved. Now— What am I going to do? Why couldn't it be simple for me?

She tried to push the worry from her and succeeded as well as she ever did. But it remained, a distant softness in the back of her mind and a pain under her breastbone. Neither it nor its cause was going to go away.

A trooper had brought the pronoyar's chestnut stallion, and Larth mounted to sit beside her. He said, "Are we to take him back to Dymie for execution, or kill him here?"

She was spared answering by the sight of Lyalo and two of her men coming out of the citadel gateway. Between the soldiers was Aratu, his arms bound behind him. A purple bruise stained his forehead, but he appeared otherwise unhurt. He needed no dragging, but walked defiantly upright. They'd taken his armor, and he wore only a sleeveless, knee-length tunic of dun wool.

Elyssa stared down at him as they brought him before her. Despite the dirt and the savage bruise she knew his face, for he had come to Dymie two years ago to swear loyalty to her, to be confirmed as the new Warden of Rumach, after his father the old Warden died. She thought he would be about twenty-two. In the late winter just past, he had rebelled against his oath and led some two hundred of his clansmen in a series of raids into the farmlands and villages at the foot of the mountains. Worse, he'd called on the other clan leaders to join him in a general revolt against her rule.

Aratu looked up at her. She had forgotten how handsome he was. He was broad-shouldered, narrow in the waist, and his face had the wild elegance that only the upland aristocrats possessed. But it was his eyes that jolted her. They were perfectly clear and unconcerned, though he must know that he was going to die.

"What have you to say for yourself?" she asked, hearing her voice grate like dry stones sliding.

"Nothing," he said, in the lilting upland accents. "I am forsworn."

So he admitted it and his men had heard him, which gave her the legal right to execute him. She felt relief at this, but it was mixed with anger. If he had known what he was doing, why had he done it?

"Why did you rebel?" she asked.

Aratu grimaced. "A man came to us here. He said that the warriors of the upland clans should not be ruled by a woman, by which he meant yourself, Protectress. He said it displeased the God, who was the master of all women, master even of the Green Lady."

Elyssa heard Larth mutter a charm against blasphemy. This was the barbarian belief of the mainland, of the Hazannu invaders who had taken over the lands of the Great Garden after it fell.

"Didn't your clan priestess have something to say about all this?" she asked, though she knew the woman might well have held her tongue. The hill tribes were less tied to the Lady's worship than were the farmers of the lowlands, and their priestesses wielded much less influence. The men of the clans normally directed their prayers to the Lady's consort, the Firebringer, rather than to the Goddess. For them, putting a male deity first would be a short step, though their wives might make them suffer for it.

Aratu said, "She told us we were fools to listen to him, Protectress. He answered that no woman would dare call us fools after we'd won. So we sent her away to the pastures and listened to him in spite of her."

"Who was this man? Where did he come from?"

"He said he was once a priest of the Firebringer in Kanesh, but he went to the mainland to live among the Hazannu tribes. He learned there that our Firebringer was an aspect of their Storm God, and that the God should rule on Haidra, not the Lady. He said that if I rebelled, all the mountain clans would join me and we would defeat you and rule in Dymie, with the God's blessing."

"You know this is not only rebellion, but blasphemy. Why did you listen?"

"The priest gave us proof that he was the God's messenger."

A chill ran along Elyssa's skin. "What proof?"

"He sacrificed to the God, using a spring lamb he bought from us, and as he did that he tranced himself. And then . . ." Aratu swallowed, as if his throat had dried. "Then he showed us the future in the fire. He showed us feasting in Dymie."

"So he was a sorcerer," she said, her voice cold. "Go on."

"We see few sorcerers here," Aratu said, "but we know that some are benign, and this one seemed kindly enough. Anyway, when he showed us celebrating in Dymie he was calm, as if he were master of the visions. But then he began to sweat and shake with fear. And suddenly we were all afraid, so afraid that some of my men pissed themselves. The fear came out of the fire."

"What did you see?" Elyssa asked. "*What?*"

"The end of Haidra. The island opened, and darkness ate it. The priest, I mean the sorcerer, screamed, and the fire almost went out and the fear went with it, mostly, but he screamed on for a while and so did some of my men. After we stopped, we swilled wine to make ourselves forget, but he told us not to, because we should remember what the God would do if we disobeyed."

"He was quick-witted, at least," Larth said wryly. "Or maybe he believed it himself. Where's he gone, do you know?"

"He's dead, my lord. I think he was too frightened to sleep that night. He went outside in the dark, which was foolish, and fell down the West Flank. We found his body the next day. We were still frightened, also. So we did what we thought the God wanted us to do, and took up arms against the Protectress."

There was a long silence. Finally, Elyssa said, "But you failed. The clans did not join you. The sorcerer's message was false."

"I know that now, Protectress. He must have been mad. But he did not *seem* mad when he spoke of the God."

Elyssa resisted an urge to reach down and strike him in the face. "Had you lost your wits?" she demanded furiously. "It was all lying sorcery, sorcery of the Foul Road. That was what he wanted your lamb for; it wasn't a sacrifice; it had nothing to do with any god; it was the offering he needed to walk the Road. And the fear that came out of the fire—that has the Poisoner's taint. You are an ignorant man, not to know that."

"Yes, Protectress," he said humbly.

She glanced at Larth. The pronoyar's pale eyebrows were drawn together in speculation.

"A word with you outside," she said harshly. To Lyalo she said, "Keep the rebel here until I come back. He is not to be harmed."

The two of them rode through the gateway, ducking to clear the low granite lintel. Outside was a level space of dusty ground, where soldiers rested near the stacks of loot. With them were the cavalry troopers that scouted for the army's advance and also provided Elyssa with a mounted escort. The men were in a good mood, and they cheered her as she left the gateway. She waved to them. Then she and Larth rode a little way out of their hearing and stopped. The sun lay warm on her hair.

"This shoe is of my brother's stitching," she said, "unless I'm much mistaken."

Larth nodded. "I think you're not mistaken at all. The Protector is stirring up trouble against you in the mountain clans again, this time with the mainlanders' God. That's cheaper than spending coin."

"And harder to find the paymaster." Elyssa stroked her horse's neck, pondering. Haidra was divided roughly in two by a mountain chain; on the west lay her Protectorate of Dymie and on the east, the Protectorate of Kanesh. The latter was the domain of her brother Tirsun, who was a year younger than she. Their father had ordered the division of the island into the two Protectorates before he died, and such was the old man's force of character that everyone, nobles and commoners alike, had agreed to it. Even Tirsun had at first seemed content with the arrangement; he had, after all, received the richer half, with three silver mines instead of two, and the only decent gold seam. And the city of Kanesh was the traditional capital, more populous and more strongly fortified than Dymie, and with a better harbor.

But she had known ever since her father's death that Tirsun wanted all Haidra for himself. To want anything less would have been quite unlike him, or unlike what he'd become since his illness. He'd contracted it when he was sixteen, the year before their father died. He fell down one day, complaining of pains in his head, and then a fever took him.

Even before the fever he had been a headstrong, temperamental person, capricious in his likes and dislikes, but intelligent and with an artistic turn of thought; when he was at his best, Elyssa had enjoyed his wit and conversation. But his willful temperament clashed badly with their father's, and Tirsun had suffered severe if intermittent beatings all through his childhood and adolescence. Still, until the illness, he seemed to have no particular evil in his nature—at least, no more than humanity usually had.

The fever was so virulent that the physicians said Tirsun's mind might be affected even if he did not die. But he did recover, and for the first month he seemed normal, if oddly quiet. Then the changes began. He flew into terrible rages when his whims were denied, and a new streak of savagery appeared. He mercilessly beat and even bit his slaves and servants, and one female slave had died in circumstances of a peculiar eroticism. After their father died and he became Protector of Kanesh, his new nature blossomed: capricious, vain, extravagant, untrustworthy, greedy, and cruel.

Yet no one could deny that her brother was also highly cultivated. He loved both luxury and beauty, and despite his avarice was ready to pay well for them. He was an openhanded patron of sculptors, painters, and poets, and his rebuilt palace on the Citadel Stone in Kanesh had become famous for its works of art and its comfort. It was a far cry from Elyssa's residence in Dymie, which was austere, old-fashioned, and a little shabby around the edges.

Perversely, Tirsun also cared about his reputation among the people he ruled. He paid for better water supplies in several of his Protectorate's cities, supported vast new irrigation works, and of late had encouraged trade and some remarkable shipbuilding. But Elyssa knew it was his vanity that moved him to do such things, rather than any real concern for his people. He had always liked to be praised for benevolence and generosity, deserved or not, and she also knew how he craved a magnificent reputation that would preserve his memory down the centuries. He itched to be known as Tirsun Velianas the Great; that was really what all his munificence was for. And to achieve that reputation he needed all Haidra, or thought he did.

Larth was saying something. Elyssa recollected herself, and asked, "What?"

"I hope the Protector doesn't become *too* interested in the mainlanders' God of Storms," Larth repeated. He chose his words carefully, for he was speaking of her kin.

Elyssa gave him a swift look. "How so?"

"Well, it's one thing if your brother uses the Hazannu God to stir up trouble for us. It'll be another if he tries to pull down the Green Lady's altars and images and erect ones for"—Larth spat over his horse's withers—"for the barbarians' God."

"He's not that foolish. Anyway, no one has pulled down any altars yet, as far as I know."

"So far this is true. But you *do* know what I'm talking about."

She did. Ever since the ruin of the Great Garden three centuries ago, people had worried that the catastrophe might have befallen the Rasenna because their Green Lady was not strong enough to turn it aside. Elyssa refused to listen to such blasphemy; she was a Daughter, a consecrated priestess of the Lady, and devoted to the Lady's worship. She took some comfort from the fact that the old religion of the Garden was still alive on Haidra, and that Daughters like her remained the chief intercessors between the Goddess and humankind. She was also proud of her Daughterhood; priestesses came from all stations of Haidran life, but few girls of the nobility endured the difficult training in the rites, as Elyssa had done. She'd been required to undergo the training, of course, being a female of the ruling line, but she'd never thought of shirking the responsibility.

Nevertheless, she recognized that the decay of the old faith had slowly made people ripe for a new one, and if Tirsun were drawn to the Hazannu storm deity, he was not alone. She knew that several of her own nobles—men, all of them—had erected private shrines to the Hazannu God, and that many in her brother's Protectorate of Kanesh had done the same. But no one had protested, for the worshipers still believed enough in the Lady to treat the God of Storms as an aspect of her consort, the Firebringer. The Firebringer was lord of the sun, who at the end of each day entered the Lady as her husband, and each morning was reborn from her womb as her child. By identifying him with the Hazannu God, people escaped sacrilege and also secured, or so they hoped, the favor of a powerful male deity as well as the blessings of the Lady.

What worried Elyssa was that influential men in both Kanesh and Dymie might start believing, as the Hazannu believed, that the male divinity should rule the female. From there it would be a short step to deciding that a woman's rule in the Protectorate of Dymie was an offense to the God and should be ended. Tirsun, even if he didn't hold this belief himself, would find it a useful weapon to turn against her. Elyssa was fairly sure that the dead Hazannu sorcerer, who had apparently conjured rather more than he'd expected, was an aspect of this weapon.

"I don't want to execute Aratu," she said to Larth. "He was out of his depth. He won't make that mistake again."

Larth grunted angrily. "Perhaps not. But he led those men into taking up swords against your rule. And the farmers and villagers down there at the foot of the mountain won't thank you for showing him mercy. They lost their stock, some of them were slaughtered, and many had their roofs burned over their heads. They want Aratu's neck stretched and his men in the mines and quarries."

"He could pay the blood-price, if he can find it, and be exiled."

"Protectress, he also broke his oath. He admitted that himself. It's a bad precedent to let oaths be broken, and the breaking paid off in silver. And even if you let Aratu do that, he'd still owe his forfeit to the Lady. And she'd collect it in *her* own coin."

"Yes," Elyssa said. "I know."

"Better to take him down to Dymie and make an example of him. It'd discourage others who might be thinking the same thoughts."

"Yes," she said again. "I know." It sickened her that the whole pointless business had happened at all. If only Aratu had listened to the clan Daughter . . . She jerked on her gelding's reins, surprising the horse so that it snorted and danced, and rode back toward the gate. Larth followed in silence.

In the courtyard, Aratu stood impassively between his guards. She told Larth to pick a garrison to remain in the Hold, so they could start putting the place to rights. He grunted agreement, swung off his horse, and headed up the ramp to the citadel gate.

She waited till he was gone. Then, from her saddle high above Aratu, she said, "You're a rebel. You will be taken to Dymie. There you will be tried for treason and oath-breaking."

He took a long breath, let it out. "And when I'm found guilty?"

"You will be hanged in Old Square."

"And my men?"

"They will go to the mines."

He winced, very slightly. "Spare them, Protectress. They followed me. I'm to blame, not them."

Fury scalded her, fury not only at his rebellion but for the way he had thrown his life away. "What of the burned villages and farms and the dead you left there?" she snapped. "Did you do all this yourself? Be glad your men will not dangle alongside you. And if the other clans had joined you, it would have been far worse. Is that what you wanted? To devastate half of our island?"

He hung his head. "No, Protectress."

To Lyalo she said, "Keep him separate from his men until we leave. Give him food and wine if he wants them. Take him away."

"Wait," Aratu said, looking up at her.

"What?" She hoped he was not going to beg, for she had thought better of him than that.

"I'm of high blood," he said. "I've been a ruler. Let me die here in my own lands, as a nobleman. I don't want to be hanged in Dymie before commoners, like a common brigand."

Elyssa almost said, *But you acted like one*, but held her tongue. She understood, even in her anger, how he felt.

But she could not do what he wanted. "Noblemen," she said, "even oath-breakers, must be tried. I cannot execute you out of hand. You have to come to Dymie, and endure what you must."

"No," he said, and looked into her eyes. "There's another way, and you know it." He paused, took a breath, let it out. "I call on the Green Lady's justice. I broke the oath that I took in the Lady's name. I owe her a death. And I know you are her Daughter, a consecrated priestess. Send me to the Green Lady, here and now."

An invisible fist punched Elyssa under her breastbone. For long moments she could hardly breathe. Lyalo was staring wide-eyed at Aratu.

"What?" she asked at last. "You want me to—"

"You know the law. Any Daughter of the Lady can do it. You cannot refuse me."

He was right, she couldn't. "But you must be tried," she protested weakly.

He stared at her, green eyes clear and certain. "You cannot refuse me. Help me make peace with her now, or the Poisoner will take me, and I will suffer in the Everlasting."

There was no way out. But how could she do what he wanted? She had never done it. She knew of no living Daughter who had. To kill in battle, though she'd never done that either, was an act she could understand; in battle a soldier's blood was up, and other soldiers were trying to kill him. But what Aratu asked her to do was different. It was cold.

"When?" she asked him, still only half-believing that this was what he wanted.

"Now."

"Where is the altar?"

"Beneath the citadel. All you need is there. We didn't destroy anything of the Lady's, even though the priest said we should."

It would be a crypt shrine, the kind that made her feel as if she were buried alive and suffocating. She tried to ignore the flutter under her breastbone, and answered, "You are intent on this?"

"Yes. I call on the Lady to witness my desire."

To prevaricate further would be close to impiety. She said, "I will do what you demand."

"Thank you, Protectress." He seemed relieved and happy, as though she were granting him life instead of death. "Let me go to my men and tell them. I don't want them to think of me shamed in a public square."

"Yes. Lyalo, see to it."

They moved away from her. She was watching Aratu speak quietly to the other prisoners when Larth rejoined her. Frowning, he asked, "What's he up to now?"

She told him. Larth didn't respond at first. Then he muttered, "He's getting off lightly."

"I'm not," Elyssa said, her voice sharp.

The pronoyar mumbled an apology. As Aratu took final leave of his men, Larth asked, "Where is it to be done?"

"He says there's a shrine under the citadel. Will you come with me?"

He grimaced. "Protectress, I—yes, very well."

Elyssa dismounted. She felt light-headed and nauseated, possibly because she hadn't eaten since dawn. But the thought of food, given what she was about to do, sickened her. She ordered Lyalo to release Aratu from his bonds, for he had to approach the altar willingly.

She would have gone to the shrine with only the doomed man and Larth, but the pronoyar insisted on the two soldiers to guard her. Everyone in the courtyard now knew what was to happen, and a nervous mutter followed them as they went up the ramp into the citadel. The building's stone walls still held the chill of winter, and the deserted main floor was lit only by sunlight falling through the narrow doorway behind them. Larth shouted for a torch, and a soldier brought one. The oily flame did little to dispel the gloom.

A second doorway beckoned to a deeper space within the citadel. Aratu walked through it, Elyssa and the others following. Beyond was a storage magazine, its huge clay jars looming shadowy in the orange light. To Elyssa they looked like monstrous fat men with loathsome appetites.

"Here," Aratu said. In the end wall of the magazine, a narrow opening showed the top of a flight of stairs. Without hesitation, he started down them. Elyssa descended next, Larth coming behind her with the torch and the guards. Their footsteps echoed in the dark well.

At the stair's foot was a low chamber, some twelve paces by ten. Elyssa could just stand upright in it but the men had to stoop. She saw immediately that this was a very, very old shrine, far older than the citadel above it. No trace of paint remained on its walls, which were covered with worn, stylized carvings of humans and beasts, interspersed with sets of concentric circles and the sickle of the moon. In the chamber's center was a smoothly cut granite slab raised on granite uprights, the altar. Across its upper surface an image of the Green Lady, in her aspect of the Mother, was incised in the ancient manner: the heavy breasts, the prominent delta, the legs open for impending childbirth. Her face was only a sketch. Between the face and the end of the altar stone was cut a deep, bowl-shaped depression, with an outlet near its bottom. This was where, if Elyssa were to perform a normal offering, she would pour wine and the fragrant oil of the bristlenut.

Against one wall stood a wooden bench, with the ritual objects on it. She went to the bench and inspected them, hoping that something might be missing or obviously defiled so she could escape what lay ahead.

But there was nothing amiss with the objects: the bronze sickle, the stone goblet, the wine in its stoppered wooden jar, the handful of bearded barley in the offering tray. The sickle was recently honed and very sharp.

She turned back to the altar and inspected the floor at its head. The drain was below the outlet of the altar bowl, clear of any blockage and reaching down into the fertile depths of the earth.

"Everything's here?" Larth asked. His voice told her that he liked this no more than she did. The two soldiers hung back by the stair's foot, wide-eyed and frightened. Only Aratu, standing beside the altar stone, seemed self-possessed.

"Can we begin?" he asked in his lilting upland accent.

"Yes." Elyssa composed herself, emptying her mind of the knowledge that he was a murderer and oath-breaker. He was only a young man, going willingly into the arms of his Mother, who in forgiving him would restore his honor and his pride. For his sacrifice she also might look on his people with greater favor, making their upland pastures green and lush and fattening their flocks of argali, the mountain sheep that gave them their meat and cloth.

Elyssa didn't have the formal vestments of a Daughter with her, but those were not strictly necessary. She poured wine into the stone goblet and blessed it. Aratu drank from it, and so did she. After blessing the barley likewise, she placed three kernels of the grain on his tongue, then on hers, and together they ate. That finished, she sprinkled barley into the altar bowl. Then it was time. He looked at her doubtfully, unsure what to do next. She kept her mind almost empty, but a corner of it saw that he trembled a little.

"You must lie on the stone," she said. It was as though her voice belonged to someone else. "And we must tie you."

Aratu nodded; he had to be bound even though he went willingly, so that he would not throw himself from the altar in his death spasms.

He swung himself onto the granite slab, slim and vulnerable in his thin tunic. Elyssa eased him gently to the correct position, facedown with his hips between the Mother's thighs, his forehead resting on the granite a fingerbreadth from the altar's edge, so that his throat was directly above the bowl. Larth gave her the ropes, and she secured him to the stone.

.

That done, she took the bronze sickle from the table, then went to the altar's side. Standing over Aratu, the blade in her hands, she prayed. Larth and the soldiers stood with their heads bowed, eyes averted, the smoky torchlight a sullen orange on the scales of their armor. At last she came to the end of the prayer, and said:

"Aratu of Rumach, do you go willingly?"

There was the smallest hesitation, and he answered, "I do."

She heard the catch in his voice, and she knew he was very frightened; who would not be? She must send him quickly.

Still feeling as though her body belonged to some other being, she twined her fingers in his yellow hair and drew his head up and back, smoothing the throat. The blade's positioning had to be exact and he took a quick little breath as she found the place and he felt the edge touch his skin.

Elyssa whispered, though it was outside the ritual, "I will be quick. Don't be afraid."

She cut his throat with one quick upward slash, and as the first of his lifeblood poured from him into the waiting bowl, her eyes rolled up in her head, and she fainted.

8

FOUR DAYS PASSED, THE FIRST ONE DEVOTED TO REPAIRING
and securing Rumach Hold, the next three on the march as
Elyssa led the First Levy home to Dymie. But it was not until
her capital's towers crept into sight on the horizon, in the middle afternoon of the third day of the march, that Elyssa began
to feel like herself again.

She knew, however, that she would never again be the old
Elyssa. She had killed a man. She didn't regret what she had
done, for she had spared Aratu a worse and more public fate,
and he'd gone willingly. But she hated that she had needed
to kill him at all.

She had felt so ill for the first day after the sacrifice that
Larth had suggested diffidently that she might consider going
to Velchi. This was a healing sanctuary halfway up the side of
Mount Matunas, a high conical peak in the west of her Protectorate. At Velchi, springs bubbled hot from the mountain's
depths to form small steaming lakes whose waters shimmered
with iridescent greens and blues. The cooler ones were supposed to improve your health if you bathed in them but they
reeked of rotted eggs, a stink Elyssa loathed. Velchi was the
last place she wanted to be, and she told Larth as much.

At the hour of the evening meal they reached Dymie.
Elyssa's capital was the second largest city of Haidra after
Kanesh, being home to some thirty thousand citizens and
about six thousand slaves. It stood on a sloping, fertile plain
near the sea, on the shore of a bay that provided a harbor
both for the Protectorate's navy and for the merchant ships
that plied the coasts of Haidra and the mainland.

Dymie was built around Beacon Hill, a platform of tan rock that soared two hundred feet above the surrounding plain. From the seaward end of the hill's summit rose the tower of Dristra's Light, whose signal flame guided mariners approaching the coast in darkness. Rambling over the rest of the hilltop were the buildings of Dymie Palace, two and three stories high, plastered with white gypsum and roofed with red-brown terra-cotta tiles. Below the heights lay the city, its houses and shops and arcades well white-washed and trimmed with rich colors: carmine, turquoise, saffron yellow, moss green. Gathering them and the harbor into a protective embrace were the city walls, built of cut white limestone, each block the height of a man and the length of two.

The eastern gate was called the Sunrise Gate. Elyssa had sent messengers ahead with news of the victory, and excited crowds already thronged the gate's approaches as the city turned out to celebrate the First Levy's return. As the marching drums growled, she led the column of men under the gate's high lintel and through a cheering crowd along Middle Street, the city's main boulevard. The day had been warm, and Elyssa felt hot and grimy, though she had put her armor aside for a quilted tunic and leggings. Many curious gazes followed her; the news that she had given Aratu to the Lady must have preceded her return. It was the sort of news that would titillate many of her subjects, though the truly devout would be awed at what she had done.

She and Larth halted by the Shaft Stone in Old Square, to watch the men tramp toward their barracks over by the Sunset Gate. When the last billowing standards of the rear guard had passed, she turned to the pronoyar, and said, "Come to the palace tomorrow, at the hour before midday. We have to decide who is to replace Aratu."

He saluted. "I'll be there, Protectress."

Elyssa left him and rode with her escort of twelve troopers out of the square. The young men chattered brightly among themselves and flirted with the girls in the crowd. Like most cavalrymen, they were younger sons of the lesser rural nobility, as Larth had been before he climbed to his high office. By contrast, the great city aristocrats and their offspring disdained most forms of work, including service in the Protectorate's government. Descended from clans that were ancient before the Fall of the Great Garden, they were arrogant and imperious, and devoted themselves mostly to the defeat of boredom. They paid for their diversions from the immense revenues of their landholdings, which occupied the most fertile parts of Haidra. Auvas Seitithi, the man who itched most to marry her, was probably the richest of their number. His clan did have one redeeming characteristic, however; a few of its members, including Auvas, showed at least some interest in the army.

But for Elyssa, the best that could be said of the high nobility was that most of them seemed content with her rule, though some spoke a little too well of the Hazannu God for her taste. She had instructed Larth to watch these men, for their real loyalty was to their own interests. Elyssa suspected that they would stand aside while her brother deposed her, if he could, as long as he didn't threaten their wealth.

The horses were nearing the foot of the flagstone ramp that rose along the side of Beacon Hill. Many people remained in the streets; women called the Lady's blessing on Elyssa, and men held their children up to see her as she rode by. Like her, they were golden-haired and green-eyed. But there were others, too, who cheered less if at all, and their eyes were blue and their cropped hair was closer to copper than to gold. These wore the iron wrist rings of slavery.

There was a steady traffic in humans on the mainland, for the Hazannu tribes constantly raided each other for slaves. Some the raiders kept, others they sold across the water to Haidra, and occasional Haidran punitive attacks on offending mainland tribes brought more to the island. Adult Hazannu males were considered too dangerous for domestic work, so most went to heavy labor in Haidra's quarries and mines, and on the vast farms of the nobility. Hazannu females, though, were deemed safe in household service, as were mainland males taken in childhood and brought up in servitude. Crossbreed children, usually sired either by their mothers' Rasennan masters or by male slaves of the household, were also common in the island's slave population. But there were no citizens of Haidra's two Protectorates among the slaves, for while citizens could be executed or otherwise punished for offenses against the laws, they could not be sold into bondage.

Elyssa's little cavalcade reached the foot of the ramp and began the steep ascent. The very first thing she was going to do, after she'd dismissed her young men, was take a hot bath and eat. Then she'd see Nenattu, her Grand Domestic, and make sure no administrative disasters had fallen on her head. After that she could rest as much as she ever did.

Rest? That was not quite the word for it. Tonight she would see the man she loved, and that would not be restful at all.

Two hours later she was clean, well fed, and wearing a long flounced skirt and a high-necked bodice of embroidered linen that had been perfumed with essence of lilies. Nenattu, efficient as always, had kept everything in order during her absence, and she'd had less to deal with than she'd expected. Now she was out on the Harbor Terrace in the soft air of the spring dusk, alone except for the hovering presence of her body slave Tamti. The terrace was an expanse of paving that ran along the palace's east arcade and was embellished with ornamental plantings of spring heliotrope, flowering juniper, and silver yew. On the slow evening breeze drifted the fragrances of Haidra: sage, wild thyme, mint, the scent of stone dust.

Elyssa leaned on the balustrade. Beyond it stretched a ledge of smooth rock, which ended in a sheer drop to the city roofs below. From this height, the buildings looked to Elyssa as small as the pottery dolls' houses she had played with as a child. Far below her spread the docks and shipyards of the naval basin and the warehouses of the shipowners and maritime traders. The harbor district lay in the blue shadow of the hill, and its stone quaysides were already speckled with the dim glow of torches. To the west, sunset blazed along the rim of the sea.

Elyssa gazed into its distant splendor. Beyond that golden

horizon, hundreds of miles away, lay the last two mainland cities of the Rasenna. A score of such towns, survivors of the Garden's Fall, had once clung to life along the mainland coast, like dim beacons flickering in the barbarian ocean that lapped at their gates. Over the centuries, one by one, they burned out. Only the two strongest remained, Ushnana and Kla, and they, too, were slowly failing. When they went, the Rasenna would be wholly an island people.

Unless, Elyssa thought with a bitter grimace, *we manage to restore the Garden. Wouldn't Tirsun love to do that—he'd be worshiped forever. All he needs for the purpose is what he'll never have: ten of us for every Hazannu, instead of the other way around, and all the gold and iron of our ancestors. It's the old, useless, hopeless dream. Everyone has it, even me. Even Larth; he acts so hardheaded in everything else, but still he dreams.*

She turned to look past the squat tower of Dristra's Light, out across the indigo waters of Monument Bay. On the far shore, five miles distant, the marble remains of ancient Charunna stood pale and silent in the gathering dusk: Charunna of the Roses, so named for the white flowers that bloomed among her crumbling sepulchres. As so often when Elyssa watched night falling over the old sacred city, she experienced a stab of melancholy. She only went there once a year, but the time she spent among its brooding monuments left her with a sadness that lingered for days.

For distraction she returned her attention to the harbor. A merchant ship, a new vessel from Kanesh judging by its sleekness, was gliding through the harbor entrance. Elyssa frowned. Her own shipwrights still built the slow, fat, clumsy hulls that had always carried Haidran goods, and she wondered occasionally if the new Kaneshite vessels would make Dymie's merchant fleet so old-fashioned that it couldn't pay its way.

But despite its appearance, the Kaneshite ship's design wasn't a new one at all; Tirsun's wrights had in fact based her hull and rig on records that dated to the last days of the Great Garden. According to Elyssa's ambassador in Kanesh, these records had come to light while Tirsun was rebuilding his palace. His men unearthed a sealed and forgotten store-room at the palace's foundations, and in it had found cen-turies-old vellum documents that bore shipwrights' sketches and measurements.

Like everyone else, Tirsun and Elyssa knew the tall tales that sailors told about alien lands on the far side of Ocean. Indeed, the palace library at Kanesh contained fragmentary records from the Great Garden's end time, which suggested that large, swift Rasennan vessels had, for a few years at least, sailed into the distant north and survived to return. On Ocean's far side, the writings implied, the mariners had found islands and rich cities where the people were friendly and willing to trade. But when the Garden fell the ships rot-ted and the fleeting contact was lost. When maritime com-merce slowly resumed, it was with the traditional clumsy coastal vessels, because people had forgotten how to build anything else.

But Tirsun had apparently added these bits of old infor-mation together, found his curiosity piqued, and ordered his shipwrights to construct a vessel based on the ancient records. After much labor and expense they succeeded. The new design, from what Elyssa had heard, surpassed all ex-pectations. It might even be able to sail to the distant lands of the stories.

Mind you, she thought, *it's been at least three hundred years since anyone went north. Who knows what might have happened there by now? But there might be great opportu-nities for wealth. Perhaps I should consider building such ships in Dymie. The problem is, none of my wrights know how to do it. And Tirsun's not about to help me.*

The sunset was fading. Far across the bay, ruined Charunna had fallen into shadow. Suddenly, unasked and unwelcome, Aratu's account of the Hazannu God's priest-sorcerer returned to trouble her.

She'd thought about it often on the way home. The man-ner of the sorcerer's death suggested that he'd been a secret traveler of the Foul Road; as she had angrily told Aratu, that would account for his sacrifice of the lamb, which would look to the innocent eye like a normal sacrificial offering. In reality, it had been the death that Walkers of the Road needed to make a spell work. Aratu's sorcerer had used this one to produce some exceptionally vivid illusions.

But he'd miscalculated somehow. He raised a specter with an aura so terrifying that it unmanned not only him but every clansman present. It actually frightened some of them into incontinence. That was a considerable achievement; upland clansmen didn't piss themselves easily.

But, she thought suddenly and uneasily, *what if it wasn't deception? The Foul Road doesn't always lie. What if the vision was so frightening because it actually showed how Haidra will end?*

It seemed unlikely, though she didn't quite dare dismiss the possibility. Not for the first time, she wished that magic didn't work. Of course, most of what passed for both benign and malign magic was fraud used by charlatans to fleece the gullible: useless amulets, counterfeit word-spells, powerless rituals, sleight of hand masquerading as sorcery.

But here and there one could find the rare practitioners of the real thing. Most were kindly, those who had the Grace of the Green Lady and who used their powers on the Golden Path, and the greatest number of these became priestesses or priests. But others were not so benevolent. They twisted their gift out of shape for their own pleasure and profit, forsook the Lady, and walked the Foul Road.

Religious sanctions and legal punishments against Walkers existed, but they were ineffective and rarely enforced. Consequently every window and doorway on Haidra had some protective talisman or spell on it, though most were useless. The common people found these guards comforting, but Elyssa, like other educated people, knew that the real protection against malevolent sorcerers was their rarity. And they were rare indeed, for talent for any magic was unusual, hard to nurture, and difficult to use. Few who possessed it chose the Road, and those few feared the Road even as they walked it, for such sorcery could rebound on the Walker with dire consequences. In such people the Poisoner was at work, he who was the Well of Bitterness, the power that envenomed light and life, whom the Lady and the Firebringer hated. The man who deceived

Aratu must have been one of those, and he deserved his death, having most likely brought it on himself by his malformed spell. She was glad he was dead; it spared her the trouble of having him hunted down and killed.

But what had he seen, really, in the phantasms of his sorcery? Was it a real future? She rarely wished she had the sorcerous powers of the Lady's Grace, but just now she did. A ruler's life was never simple, but hers grew daily more complicated: Tirsun's plots, the stealthy inroads of the Hazannu God, the feuds and factions of Dymie's indolent and dissolute nobility. The Grace, if she had it, might help her see her way more clearly, and oh, how she needed clarity of sight.

I don't have the Grace, but I could try the mask.

In sudden dismay she clutched at the balustrade, as if she stood on the deck of a storm-tossed ship. "But that's sacrilege," she told herself aloud, hearing her voice croak.

The earth steadied. She did not understand why she had even imagined putting on the Giftbearer's mask. No one had dared to do that for centuries. Those who had long ago done so had not come happily out of the experience, according to the stories. And it had played a baneful part in the catastrophes that ruined the Great Garden.

"Forgive me, Giftbearer," she murmured. "I'm tired, and I don't know where to turn. I only wanted to know what to do. No more than that." Perhaps, she mused, she was still overwrought at giving Aratu to the Lady. That had been an act of justice and piety, but its memory still made her shudder.

Suddenly she craved music. Now that she thought of it, she had needed its healing touch for the past three days. Turning from the balustrade, she called, "Tamti, come here!"

Her body slave, wearing a belted, knee-length smock of white wool, materialized from the arcade that ran along the palace's east wall. The girl's coppery hair seemed even redder in the setting sun. She reached Elyssa, and said, "Yes, mistress?"

"Tell Halicar and Mereth to come to the aviary, with their instruments. Have the lamps lit there, also."

"Yes, mistress."

Tamti hurried away, smock swirling about her knees. Elyssa watched her go. Sometimes she puzzled over the fact that the old Rasenna, the Rasenna of the Great Garden, hadn't had slavery. She couldn't imagine how they had managed a civilized society without it. Some people should not be made slaves, it was true; the Rasenna certainly were too fine for servitude. But the mainland barbarians were ideally suited to the station. They were strong and adept, but a naturally obedient race, happiest when they had someone to tell them what to do. And they were grateful for the privilege of living in a civilized society; they would eagerly tell you as much if you asked them. They knew themselves to be much better off than their poverty-stricken brethren on the mainland, subsisting in squalid villages and living in constant fear of bloody raids by their neighbors.

They bred no musicians, though. Elyssa felt the familiar bittersweet surge: soon she would be with the man she loved, who healed her with his art. Had he guessed the effect he had on her?

She didn't know, or not yet. She squared her shoulders and set off for the courtyard that held the palace aviary.

By the time she reached it, the slaves had lit the courtyard's hanging lamps. Within the fine bronze mesh of their enclosures, the birds twittered in sleepy protest at the renewal of the light. Their spacious cages held small trees and flowering plants collected from their native haunts, so that they would thrive even as captives. Elyssa loved birds, and added specimens to her collection whenever she could. Her favorites were the sunbirds whose feathers had the metallic gleam of gold, and the drab gray nightlarks, whose song in darkness was the sweetest of all.

The door at the far end of the courtyard opened. Through it, carrying a small water drum and her double flute, came Mereth. Behind her, with his harp, was Mereth's brother Halicar.

Elyssa, standing in the shadow cast by the trees' foliage, watched the pair from her concealment. They were lithe and slender, with long hands and strong, tapering fingers. Neither had her coloring of skin or hair, nor that of the Hazannu; their complexions were a pale, creamy brown, and their hair also was brown, with a deep, lustrous gleam like that of polished hazelwood. Their eyes were large and dark, so very dark that they were almost black.

Elyssa envied their grace as they sat down on a stone bench to tune the drum and harp. Halicar was a little older than she, Mereth somewhat younger. They were of the race the Rasenna called the Antecessors, though the Antecessors themselves did not use that name. Their kind had lived far up in the mountain glens of the mainland since the world was formed, or so they said. It might be true; they spoke a language so ancient and difficult that no one else seemed able to learn it. There had never been many of them, though it was certain that they had been there when the Rasenna came from the cold lands of the far southeast, more than two thousand years before the Fall. But there had been little conflict between the two peoples, for the old Rasenna of the Great Garden had never been fond of mountains, and the Antecessors were content to herd their flocks among their crags and upland pastures.

But the Antecessors were not only herdsmen. Some had an exquisite ability as musicians and poets, even in languages and traditions not their own, and every great Rasennan house of the ancient days had employed Antecessors to provide music and song. Even in these ruined times a few still roamed the world, trading their flawless art for a roof and food. Because their gifts were believed to be divinely bestowed, and even a little eerie in their perfection, all Antecessor musicians were inviolate. Even the barbarous Hazannu did not dare harm someone who wore the signs for music woven into a tunic or engraved on a medallion.

Elyssa at last moved into the lamplight and Halicar saw her. Startled, he rose swiftly to his feet and bowed. He wore a high-necked, sky-blue tunic edged with white, its sash drawn tight at his narrow waist. As he straightened she saw his shoulders moving beneath the fabric, and in her mind's eye she saw the glide of the hard, flat muscles under his smooth skin. Her own skin sensed his strong warmth.

She folded her arms across her bodice, clasped her bare elbows, and felt the dampness of her palms on her flesh. Her mouth was suddenly dry, and she forgot what she had been about to say. They would know about Aratu's sacrifice by now. Would she see disgust and horror in their faces when they looked at her?

Halicar's sister Mereth had also risen to present a formal obeisance. Now she smiled, and said in her dazzling voice, "Good evening, my lady."

Elyssa felt a little relief. Perhaps they understood. "Good evening," she answered, and was pleased that her voice sounded perfectly normal. "I need music, Mereth. I've been too long with soldiers and hobnailed boots." She hesitated, and said, "And you will have heard about the other thing."

Mereth inclined her head. "Yes, Protectress." And then she said, "I'm truly sorry. I wish he had not asked you to do it."

Tears stung Elyssa's eyes. "I had to. There was no choice, once he'd asked me."

"We know," Halicar said. "What will it do you most good to hear?"

She wished he'd say her name, in that resonant voice that made even his flawless harp sound subtly flawed. *Elyssa.* But he wouldn't, of course; he was of a different race and a paid servant. He was grave this evening, perhaps sensing her lingering distress over Aratu, and had put aside the whimsical humor that so often delighted her. But she wished he'd let it show. In the three months since he and Mereth had stepped over her threshold, she had grown to need his wit and lightness. But she had never imagined, when she took them into her service, that she would fall in love with him in so short a time, or at all.

For a fact, though, what had happened troubled her. She was of the Rasenna, and of the purest of the blood. How could she have permitted this to happen? Of course it was not disgraceful and lewd, as if she'd begun lusting after a virile Hazannu male, as some women did. Halicar was not . . . inferior, exactly, except in rank. But he was *different*. She'd never expected to fall in love with someone so different. Perhaps that was what made her fret. It wasn't like her, to step so far outside the customs of the Rasenna.

But though they might become lovers, she would never marry him. Even if she were willing to bind herself to an outlander, which she was not, marriage would be impossible. Custom dictated that she must take a husband with an ancestry as exalted as hers, or no husband at all. And the *not at all* seemed the more likely prospect, although several men of the appropriate station lived in her Protectorate. But Elyssa found all of them repellent. Most were indolent and dissolute, and the remainder were either stupid, or haughty and disdainful, or mindlessly cruel, or all these together. By the time she turned twenty-three, she'd already given up hope of bearing a legitimate son or daughter to provide for the succession.

And now she'd found the man her heart wanted, but he was so far removed from her blood and rank that he might as well have lived in the rumored, distant north. Though she didn't like to risk impiety, Elyssa sometimes felt that the Lady had played a cruel joke on her.

She saw that he was waiting for her to choose the music. "Something light," she said. "A country dance. Then a song. Any song."

A deeply cushioned couch, its cedarwood frame embellished with ivory-and-gold rosettes, stood near the center of the courtyard. Elyssa sat on it and folded her hands in her lap, like an attentive child. The birds sang drowsily. Overhead, dimmed only a little by the yellow lamplight, the first stars were coming out.

Mereth took up her double flute and blew gently into it. Halicar tapped the water drum. Brother's and sister's eyes met, in an intimacy of a kind Elyssa knew she could never share. She was momentarily jealous, then saddened.

They began. There were no words to the dance, only the skirl and lilt of the flute and the rolling, hollow rhythm of the drum. The dance was a cheerful, sprightly Rasennan one called "Sleepy Maida Blow the Fire," but it became deeper, older, subtler, in their hands. Elyssa's right foot tapped out the beat, and she swayed to it; in the flow of flute and drum

DENNIS JONES

it was impossible to keep still. Her gaze rested, unfocused, on the patterned green and blue and white paving of the courtyard. The birds had fallen silent.

After a while the drum softened, and the flute lilted almost alone, its notes treading delicately on the night air. Then the harp awoke. Halicar began to sing, and soon Mereth's voice twined with his in the melody. Elyssa thought she knew the song, then that she did not, then that she had heard it long ago, for the words were almost familiar. Then she forgot to wonder if she had ever known it, and only listened.

A little later she noticed that birdsong had joined the human voices. The nightlarks were weaving their melody into the counterpoints of harp and flute, and the notes were no chance trill, for in their rise and fall and pauses she could hear design. It should have been astonishing, but instead seemed very natural. Was this some Antecessor magic? Did Halicar and Mereth walk a Golden Path of their own people, and had never told her?

She was still gazing at the pavement when a strange soundless quiver in the air made her look up. Not three steps away from her, in the nightlarks' enclosure, there was something that was not a nightlark.

Terror brushed her. She would have screamed, but her breath stopped in her throat. In the crown of a laurel tree was a winged and footed serpent, with an eagle's head. Its talons were silver, and its plumage and beak were gold. It studied her with an eye bright as a star, and she knew that the creature saw straight into her, through her, as though she were clear water. She struggled against that scrutiny, but for an eternal instant it would not release her. Shock and awe struggled within her. What *was* it? A portent? A warning? Some retribution for Aratu's death?

It's a fireshta, whispered a small, wondering voice from her childhood. *The plumed serpent. The hero's companion from the bedtime tales.*

The air shuddered again. Elyssa blinked, and in that blink the creature vanished. She looked around and caught her breath, trembling and dazed. The birds were silent, the music had ended. The nightlarks stirred softly on their perches. But everything around her was revealed in astonishing clarity; she felt as though she could see into the very stones of the walls, and know the eons of their long sleep in the earth.

The clarity faded as she saw Halicar and Mereth staring at her. Alarm and concern stood in Halicar's face, but with these was something more. In the last flicker of her heightened perception, Elyssa's gaze met his, and she knew.

He loves me. Lady, he loves me. What am I to do now?

"Protectress?" Mereth ventured, in a puzzled voice. "Are you well?"

"I—I think so." Her thoughts were a jumble, too much had just happened: the vision of the winged serpent, her sudden awareness of what Halicar felt for her—*what* did the fireshta mean? And why in the Lady's name had she seen one? Was a sorcery at work against her? Or was some unknown magic her ally? And hadn't Halicar and Mereth seen the creature, too?

Gazing at them, she realized they couldn't have, for she saw no awe or astonishment in their faces. Suddenly she was reluctant to speak of the thing. It didn't seem they'd been walking the Golden Path after all. The vision had been for her alone.

But she had to be sure. "How did you make the nightlarks sing with you?" she asked. "You've never done it before, and I didn't know anyone could do that."

Halicar's eyes opened wide. After a moment he said, "But no birds sang. There was only the flute and the harp, and us."

"You didn't hear them?"

"No, my lady," Mereth answered. "But we were . . . puzzled. You stared so long at the nightlarks. You didn't move or speak."

Because I *saw* something, Elyssa wanted to tell them. But there was an aura of the half-divine about the presence in the laurel tree; she realized now that this was what had terrified her so. She was not sure she should reveal it to anyone. But was its appearance somehow linked to Halicar and Mereth, or to their music?

Now she recollected vaguely that the Antecessors also had a belief in the creature she'd just seen. Hesitantly, she said:

"I was thinking about stories my mother told me when I was little, the ones about the fireshta, the hero's companion that helps him talk to animals. You have stories about the creature, too, don't you?"

Mereth seemed a little perplexed by the change of subject, but nodded. "To us the creature is more than that," she said. "We call it the Hidden Singer, who sings Creation into being. I hope you won't think this blasphemy, Protectress, but . . . well, it's said that even the Green Lady and the Fire-bringer are its songs. And the Hazannu God too, I suppose."

Elyssa could make nothing of this; there was no connection she could perceive. She glanced at Halicar, who was watching her closely. Intruding again came the new knowledge: *He loves me.* It made her feel dizzy.

"Are you sure you're well, Protectress?" he asked.

He looked worried about her, not as a servant concerned for his mistress, but as a man worried for a woman, and she knew, helplessly, that it must all happen. They were fated. This wasn't the night for them to speak of it, but she knew that they would be together very soon.

"I must be more tired than I realized," she said. Suddenly she could no longer bear the agitation his presence brought her. "No more music tonight, I think."

"Yes, my lady," he answered. He was easing the harp strings, not looking at her. Though Mereth was.

"You have my leave to go," she added, as if she were indifferent to his departure.

They glided out together. Elyssa sat alone, except for the shadowy presence of her body slave. At length she called, "Tamti, bring me a triple wick."

"Yes, mistress." The girl brought a silver lamp with three yellow flames. Elyssa said, "Go to my sleeping quarters. I won't need you again until I come there."

"Yes, mistress." The girl slipped away. Elyssa rose with the lamp and left the aviary by another door, then descended a flight of steps to a corridor. Lamps burned in niches. She was near the banquet hall. She passed along the corridor, then took another flight of stairs downward past a narrow courtyard. Then another flight, always down. At its bottom she stood in the very foundations of the palace. She crossed another small courtyard whose upper levels vanished in night. In the colonnade on its far side, lamps glowed.

"Who's there?" A man's voice.

"The Protectress." Elyssa entered the colonnade. The guards by the treasury door knelt, then rose. "I need to go in," she said. "Open it."

They obeyed, and she went into the palace treasury. Around her, crates and bales bulked shadowy in the wavering lamplight. She ignored them and passed through the dim room, through another doorway, and into the sanctuary of the Old Shrine beyond. This chamber was lavishly decorated; the floor was a mosaic of red, blue, and white pebbles laid in geometric shapes, and the walls bore paintings done in the stiff, old-fashioned manner. Even in lamplight they were bright and vivid, having been recently retouched at Elyssa's orders.

She made an obeisance to the altar and murmured a quick prayer. Then she put the lamp in a wall niche and went to the wooden chest that stood against the shrine's north wall. Resting her palms on its lid, she stood motionless and stared down at it.

Why was she doing this? It might be sacrilege. But she'd had some sort of divine or semidivine vision. Could she be punished for doing her best to understand it? There could be no impiety in that, could there?

The Green Lady will protect me.

She undid the clasps of the chest's lid, opened it, and brought out a bundle of red wool. Carefully she unrolled it and saw bronze glinting in the lamplight, a convex metal oval with black holes for eyes, the black slit of a half-open mouth. The mask.

Holding the thing by the cloth so as to avoid touching it, Elyssa held it on her flattened palms, at the level of her breasts, like an offering. She had last taken it from its coverings at the winter solstice five months ago, at the Oblation of the Giftbearer. Though she saw it only once a year, the mask's beauty always awed her. It was bronze, or seemed to be, but showed no trace of the green patina of the common metal; never polished, it always gleamed. Its maker had shaped it cunningly, so that the visage shifted from that of a young man to that of a young woman, depending on how the light caught it. Both faces were finely featured and comely, but what held the attention was the impression they made of brooding attentiveness, as if the mask listened carefully to some grave conversation taking place just out of hearing. Elyssa found herself straining to catch the words, and felt a shudder pass through her. Despite its beauty the mask always filled her with disquiet; she felt, in its presence, as if she stood too near the edge of a very high cliff.

Still, she had never feared any inherent evil in the mask; in fact it could not be evil, being from the hand of the Giftbearer. A hundred generations ago he had come from the north to teach the Rasenna the arts of civilization, and with that knowledge and skill they built their first city, Charunna of the Roses, which was the root of the Great Garden. Soon after that a servant of the Poisoner sought the Giftbearer out, and in the sorcerous combat that followed they were both destroyed; the hot springs and sulfurous vents in the mountains at Velchi were the traces of the Giftbearer's weapon forges, or were said to be. So all that remained of him now was his enduring legacy of the knowledge of civilized life, and the mask. Elyssa believed, as had the other custodians before her, that the Lady and the Firebringer had allowed a trace of their natures to pass into its making; this explained why its visage shifted constantly from a man's to a woman's. Thus the mask was not only sorcerous, but sacred.

For most of the history of the Garden it was kept in Maghan, the Rasennan capital city on the mainland. No one knew the Giftbearer's purpose in making the mask, nor how he had intended it to be employed, but it *could* be used, and had been. And while it might not be evil in itself, it appeared indifferent to the acts of its wielder. Three centuries ago the High Protector Thanchvil, during one of the dreadful civil wars of the Garden's last years, had ignored the sanctions against sacrilege and enlisted the mask's help in his struggle. Perhaps he had a touch of the Grace of the Lady, or of the Foul Road for that matter, for the histories said that when he wore it, he seemed to understand something of its nature. He turned that sorcerous understanding against his enemies, and at first the magic seemed to succeed, for crop failure and famine fell on their lands and cities. But then the blight spread to his own, and he could not stop it. Myriads died; Thanchvil cursed the day he took up the mask, and opened his veins in expiation. But the cities and farms of the Garden did not recover, and then the years of the cold summers came, and the plague, and the Hazannu. As the barbarians occupied the old Rasennan heartlands, the mask was brought to Haidra for safekeeping, and had remained there ever since.

Thanchvil used the mask to starve the people he should have fed, Elyssa thought, gazing into its dark sockets. *He used it impiously, to hold on to a power he no longer deserved. I only want to understand a divine vision. How can that be sacrilege?*

Do it, before you lose your courage.

Still holding the mask in its cradle of wool, she turned it over and raised it to the level of her eyes. Her heart pounded, her blood thumped in her ears.

Do it.

Still she hesitated, and in the hesitation she saw, in the hollow of the mask's chin, a bright rippling scratch. If the light hadn't been just so, it would have remained invisible. Had she ever noticed it there before? No, she hadn't. It must be a tool mark. Nothing of importance.

Do it. Stop wavering.

She clasped the mask to her face. For an instant it seemed to flow over her skin, fitting itself to every pore. Then, without warning, she found herself in a place without length or breadth or height, but at the same time labyrinthine, as if infinitely many passages lay in a vast but finite spiral space, with her bodiless self a still point at the spiral's turning center. And she realized she could see deeply and utterly into that self, as if everything she had ever been or known or done lay there for her perception.

Wonder bathed her for three heartbeats. But then, as she looked outward into the labyrinth, she was suddenly seized by unreasoning fear. Within the vast spiral she sensed stupendous chambers, halls, interminable galleries, colossal arches over wells of silence. What lay within them she did not know, but she could tell that they were not empty. And she knew that if she slipped from this still center, where her self knew its being, she might wander in those galleries and halls forever, lost utterly, never finding her way out, forgetting who she was.

The spiral tugged at her, trying to draw her awareness into those interminable corridors. A deeper terror seized her. She could barely remember why she had come. *The fireshta,* she thought, but the vision was a fading dream of gold and green, a wisp, a tendril of mist. The answer was not there.

I have to get out. Lady, please help me, I have to get out.

She knew dimly that outside the monstrous cavern of the mask, her body stood in the shrine. She struggled to reach it, managed to find her arms, then her hands as they held the bronze to her face. Eons passed as she commanded her muscles to pull the mask away from her flesh.

Without warning she broke free of it. The thing fell from her shaking hands, its wrappings fluttering, and struck the floor with a faint metallic thud. Elyssa clung to the chest's edge, her knees almost unhinged. Saliva dribbled from the corners of her mouth, and her heart hammered at her breastbone. Little by little, her terror ebbed.

"I'm sorry," she whispered, a husky croak. "I should never have. Done this. I didn't know. Forgive me."

She wiped her mouth. Then, trembling, she knelt to pick up the mask and folded it reverently into its cloth. It and its power were beyond her grasp. She must never be tempted again.

But she knew the effects of what she'd done would not pass in a hurry. The mask had shaken her in mind and body; at every blink she glimpsed receding spirals, as though the webs of orb spiders drifted in the air, and her head ached violently and her very bones shook. People would notice. But she could tell no one what she'd done.

But she'd make restitution. She would return to the Old Shrine tomorrow, and sacrifice and pray for as long as it took her to recover. She'd allow herself as much as three days. People would think her trouble was because of Aratu, and she'd not say differently. Even more important, her actions would serve as an atonement to cleanse her and the mask of any defilement she might have caused.

And then, after she'd recovered, she would go to Halicar. As for the vision of the fireshta, she must be patient. The Lady would help her recognize its meaning when the time came; and as for Tirsun and the rest of her troubles, she must rely on her own wits to see her way clearly through them. The mask would not help her, but at least she now knew it would not.

She closed the chest, took up the lamp, and left the shrine to darkness.

9

KAYONU'S NATIVE CITY OF KLA STOOD ON A CURVE OF the mainland coast opposite the western tip of Haidra. It had once been a refuge for Rasenna fleeing the ruin of the Great Garden, and even after the Fall the city's fine harbor and massive walls had kept it rich and strong enough to survive. But for two centuries the harbor had been silting up, and Kla's prosperity had waned with its depth. The city's opulence had become shabby and threadbare; needy Protectors had long since stripped the gold leaf from her temple decorations, and weeds grew in her public gardens. But her rulers had kept the walls strong; though the Hazannu tribes in the region were more farmers than warriors, they would pluck even the withered fruit of Kla for slaves and loot, if they could get it cheap.

Some two months had passed since Theatana sailed into Kayonu's dilapidated birthplace, but nothing about Kla or its inhabitants had improved her first dismal impression of either. She knew that Ushnana, the other surviving Rasennan city of the mainland, lay a few days' sail down the coast, but no evidence suggested it was any better. Kayonu had told her that the cities of Haidra were far more rich, luxurious, and comfortable than either Ushnana or Kla, especially the capital of the Protector Tirsun. She'd see for herself when she got there, which she had every intention of doing.

Her apartments in the Protector's palace were not the best rooms in the domestic quarters, but neither were they the worst. The floors were laid with patterned tiles of red, yellow, and white, and on the walls were frescoes of lilies and long-legged herons. She had a bed with wool blankets, two chests of honey-colored aromatic wood for storing her clothes, two chairs, and a small round table for dining. The window had irregular glass panes in it, in a frame that opened and closed, though the glass was too thick and flawed to see through. By Ascendancy standards the appointments and furnishings were sparse, though in Kla they amounted to luxury.

Her bedroom was in an upper level of the palace, and from that height one could see well into the countryside beyond the city. Out there lay the farms and orchards that provided Kla with the necessities of life; beyond these rose hills clad in dense forest. This was the domain of the Hazannu, where the azure-eyed barbarians worked rough fields in their woodland clearings. A long green tongue of the forest, cloaking a ridge too steep and rough for the Klaian farmers to cultivate, ran to within a mile of the city walls.

Theatana was sitting at her bedroom window, gazing out at a landscape of freshly planted fields and orchards in new leaf; this was the month the Klaians called Last Spring. Soon her personal slave Rehua would bring food from the kitchens, light the lamps, and another interminable evening would begin with her solitary meal. The domestic quarters were almost deserted, for Alfni the Protector had been unlucky in his wives and his offspring. Two of the wives had died in childbirth, the third of the spotted fever. Alfni's only surviving son had sailed two years ago on a routine trading expedition westward along the coast. Neither ship nor son had returned, and his father presumed him dead. The third wife was just twelve months in her tomb, and Alfni had no apparent plans to remarry. Instead, he had made Kayonu his heir, keeping the rulership in the family since Kayonu was his blood nephew.

It was not actually necessary for Theatana to eat alone. Rasennan men and women commonly dined together, and, moreover, Theatana was formally ranked among the Protector's retinue, since she had been of the same status in Kayonu's household. Even so, she rarely joined the Protector for the evening meal; Alfni's retainers and guests usually ate with him around the hearthfire in the banquet hall, and Theatana disliked the company. It wasn't that she couldn't understand what people were talking about, for almost four months had passed since Kayonu had plucked her from her exile, and by the pressure of necessity she'd become quite fluent in their tongue. But the banqueters were mostly male, and they chewed with their mouths open, and they often drank too much and became boastful and boisterous. Moreover, a female retainer was an oddity, and Alfni's men tended to ignore her. The few women who visited the palace were of the aristocracy and clearly considered her to be a mere concubine of the Protector, and a barbarian to boot. Theatana had carefully memorized their names and faces.

So this evening she would be served another meal of the alien food and eat it by the window. Later, if the Protector decided not to remain in the banquet hall with his men or his guests, he would call her to his rooms for a session of the tedious Rasennan game called rebec. After the rebec, which she was careful to let him win but not too easily, she'd share a cup of wine with him, and then he would bed her.

She had parted from her virginity two days after she left Kayonu's retinue and went to live in the palace. Her exit from the shipmaster's house had come none too soon, since the situation there had been growing difficult. Kayonu's wife had disliked Theatana on sight, and Kayonu was not sure what role this alien woman should play in his establishment. Because she had saved his life, he hadn't forced himself on her during the voyage south, and Theatana had seen no value in forming a liaison with him until she found out if better candidates might be available. Alfni the Protector was the best Kla had to offer, so she made sure her exotic looks caught his eye even on his first visit to Kayonu's household. Only days afterward, Alfni told his nephew that Theatana would be welcome in his retinue, if she chose to join it. Looking over his shoulder at his wife, Kayonu agreed. So did Theatana. She knew from the way Alfni's gaze lingered on her that sharing his bed was a condition of her joining his household, but this did not trouble her. She had never much treasured her virginity, and disposing of it got her into Alfni's palace. That in turn would open a path to other destinations.

What she hadn't expected was to enjoy coupling with him. But to her surprise, and once the initial discomfort was over, she found the act to be highly pleasurable. Alfni was older than she was, weather-beaten and balding, but an active life had kept him trim and strong. Moreover, he was a fighting man with scars to prove it, and the aura that surrounded men who killed other men had always excited Theatana. So, in the dark where she couldn't see his face, she found Alfni's attentions quite stimulating. As for the risk of pregnancy, she'd been of two minds about it. If she provided him with a son, it would strengthen her hold over him even though a mixed-blood child could not be his heir in the Protectorship—though she might find ways to change that. On the other hand, Theatana loathed children, and the whole idea of bearing one disgusted her. But though she still bled at irregular intervals, she was fairly sure she was too old for impregnation. If it did happen, she'd find some way to deal with it.

Alfni had been astonished to discover that at her age she was still a virgin. In fact, he was sure at first that she was some kind of celibate priestess, and that she'd been concealing it. In response she pointed out that her condition merely confirmed what she had told Kayonu: She had been imprisoned in her youth to keep her from claiming the rulership that was hers by right, and that her jailer was her sister, who had usurped the throne. This bore only a cursory resemblance to the truth, but Alfni would never find out what had really happened. He said he believed her, though he refrained from offers to help her regain her position.

Since he was powerless to do so anyway, Theatana didn't bother to pursue the matter. She had a more immediate design, which was to bring him firmly under her control. She'd succeeded in this more quickly than she'd dared hope, but not as she'd expected, through the manipulation of his fears and ambitions. What had happened was much simpler: His male vigor had been flagging badly before she came to his bed, and she had restored it. He had told her, and clearly meant it, that her abilities surpassed even those of the famous courtesans of Kanesh. He was, in a word, besotted.

Indeed, Theatana had discovered in herself a surprising erotic inventiveness. But she suspected that it arose not from her but from that shadowy entity within her, the wisp of Erkai that she had discovered within herself while she was on Kayonu's ship. The suspicion seemed reasonable. Erkai had been male, and her startling ability to arouse and satisfy Alfni's deepest cravings suggested that she understood men's appetites in a way few women—or perhaps no other woman—could.

The talent, if that were the name for it, had given her fresh ideas. She'd intended at first simply to gain control of Kla through Alfni, a task made simpler by the absence of either wife or son in the palace. But she had soon discovered that Kla and the mainland were a meager domain compared to Haidra's two Protectorates. The island realms were rich and powerful, and Tirsun of Kanesh was a man. If she could reach him under the right conditions, she could enthrall him as she had enthralled Alfni, and govern in fact if not in name in Kanesh. Then she would attack the Protectorate of Dymie and bring it under her control, and rule the entire island.

After that . . . though in some ways the islanders' civilization was archaic by Ascendancy standards, the Haidrans knew how to build ships that far outclassed any vessels of her homeland. She could construct a fleet of such ships, fill them with Hazannu fighting men, and sail north. She would take some island city in the Inner Sea as a base and settle down to gnaw at the very guts of the Ascendancy. She might even persuade the Tathar barbarians to help her with a land invasion from the west.

Theatana sighed at the thought. It was all very attractive, but it failed to satisfy her. She needed something more . . .

Is what I need on Haidra?

Alfni had told her a story some days ago, he drowsy in bed, she wakeful as always. It reverberated in her, like a gong's long droning note.

"There's a city of the dead," he had told her, "across Monument Bay from Dymie. It's called Charunna, a city of tombs. Very old. There's a ceremony the Haidrans do there every year, with a sacred sorcerous thing. Its maker came from the depths of Ocean, or so it's said. Like you."

"What thing? What is it?" She felt an odd sensation beneath her skin, like the gong's voice humming along her nerves.

"It's a mask. I never saw it, but I heard it's bronze."

"Why is it sorcerous?" she asked languidly, as if indifferent. She was not.

"Who knows? The Giftbearer made it. It's not the Lady's, nor the Firebringer's either. A High Protector used it in a war. It brought famine on him and everyone else, and the Garden died. So it's said."

"Who was this Giftbearer? Where did he come from?"

Alfni told her what he knew, which was little enough; it was a very old tale, worn thin by time. But it appeared that *someone* with sorcerous abilities had visited the Rasenna more than two thousand years ago, and had made a magical device that still existed. He had come from the north, though that didn't necessarily mean he'd come from the Old Dominion, the long-vanished realm from which the Ascendancy had sprung, and the home of the equally long-vanished White Diviners. Theatana didn't dare hope that the mask might be from a Diviner's hand, though its legend suggested it might be very powerful. But legends, she reminded herself, had a way of inflating a puff of wind to a tempest.

"And what happened to him?" she prompted when Alfni ran down, sleepily.

"He had an enemy who found him. They destroyed each other in a battle in the mountains of Haidra."

"That's all? Nothing was left but the mask?"

"Yes," Alfni said, and fell asleep.

It was an enigmatic conclusion to the tale. But it could be true. There were plenty of folk tales about struggles between sorcerers. There had even been a war, hundreds of years before the Ascendancy existed, between the White Diviners and their dreadful mirrors, the thanaturgai. At the end of the war the latter had been expunged from the earth.

But before that, Theatana mused, *could a White Diviner and his enemy, a thanaturge perhaps, have found their separate ways to Haidra and destroyed each other there?*

It was impossible to know. But she had sensed, as she lay in the billowing feather bed beside Alfni, that the mask might be crucial to her plans. It was yet another reason to transport herself to Haidra.

Now, in the slanting light of early evening, she leaned on the sill of her bedroom window and looked down. By craning her neck she could see into a corner of the stable yard far below. A man wearing a russet tunic stood in it, examining Alfni's white gelding, which Alfni had said was ill. Remembering this, Theatana recognized the man as the horse doctor. He lived somewhere outside the city walls, but she'd seen him in the citadel twice before; Alfni was always fussing over his horses. He was a slim gaunt man in late middle age, with expressionless eyes and many freckles. He seemed mostly of Rasenna blood but had a coppery Hazannu sheen to his hair.

She had paid him little mind and did not even know his name, but now his distant figure held her attention. There seemed an unidentifiable significance about him. She was not sure why.

He led the horse out of sight into the stables. A trifle bemused at her odd reaction to the man, Theatana left the window and sat down in a chair. Her room was silent. Her mind turned inward.

And the wisp stirred in her, as it had not for almost a month. Theatana closed her eyes and wrapped her slender fingers around the chair's wooden arms.

Don't go. Stay with me. Where have you been?

Since that first encounter on the ship, the presence had melted into her and become part of her, as a grafted branch became part of the tree. Even so, she sometimes felt its *otherness* in her, just as the grafted branch remained different from the tree that nourished it, and when this happened she called it the Other. But it was a benign graft, and she had never known it to interfere with her actions or her thoughts, nor even attempt to do so.

Since escaping Selemban she'd had plenty of time to puzzle about its origins. Her best guess was that Erkai had implanted a seed of his nature within hers, almost certainly at the time of his destruction—his final attempt to perpetuate some trace of his being, in a last spasm of sorcery before the whirlwind sucked him down. Theatana had never been able to recollect clearly the moment of Erkai's death, but there remained a vague memory of a fearsome pressure in her head, as if her brain would burst from her skull, and an instant's sense of an almost-physical invasion. If her guess was right, it was an invasion she would have invited, had she been aware that it was possible. From the first day she knew of Erkai, Theatana had lusted to possess a nature like his, to possess its knowledge and its power, to *become* Erkai. To nurture even this tiny fragment within herself was to nurture hope. And if it was a seed of him, it might carry greater power in it than she could imagine.

She knew he had grasped the Deep Magic before he died. He became a thanaturge, if only for the last beat of his heart. Did she then carry in her the wisp of a thanaturge? The possibility enthralled her, though thinking of it sometimes made her skin crawl with frost. She knew what the thanaturgai had been.

But she still had so far to go. She sat rigid in the chair, her aching jaw locked tight as a barred gate, eyes still closed. *Stay with me*, she begged the shadowy thing within. *Show me what I must do.*

Unfortunately the Other's powers, whatever their nature might be, were not under her control. Assuming the thing was once of Erkai, she had hoped it might have carried into her some of his knowledge of the Black Craft, but days and nights of searching within herself hadn't wakened any such lore. As for the ability to sense another's state of mind, the ability she'd first experienced on Kayonu's ship, she'd tried it a dozen times, though only with slaves. Usually nothing had happened. Only twice had she brought the touch about, and even then she hadn't managed to sense identifiable emotions in the slave's mind, only the lightest brush of her awareness against another's. And making the touch work became no less painful or exhausting with repetition.

She'd tried other approaches to nourishing and wakening the growth within her: secretly killing three mius, small furry creatures with pointed ears that caught vermin in the palace stables, and a mouse she managed to trap. She'd even, to her humiliation, resorted to crushing insects. But nothing had come of this, no revelations. She had expected that after almost four months the Other's powers would be more known and available to her, but it wasn't falling out that way.

She was, in truth, losing heart a little. If only something would happen *soon*. Her shoulders slumped and her hands tightened around the arms of the chair until her wrists and fingers ached. *Soon. Let it be soon. How long does it need, curse it?*

Her nails bit into the wood at her fingertips. *I need a human death. I haven't given us a death since I killed Tabar on the island.*

With the thought came a sudden craving to kill. But did it rise from the Other, or from her own urges?

The craving strengthened. Perhaps it was not only her, then. Her palms dampened against the chair's smooth wood. Could she slip down to the stable and kill the horse doctor? Ridiculous; she'd surely be detected. Furthermore, the thought of killing him roused a faint reluctance. She couldn't tell if it were in her or in the Other.

"My lady?"

Theatana jerked upright, her eyes flying open, and twisted around in her chair. Her body slave Rehua stood in the doorway, holding a tray of dishes. Odors of herbs and fried mackerel wafted through the room.

Rehua stepped back at the expression on her mistress's face. "My lady?" she faltered. She was a plump woman of perhaps twenty-five years, with chubby freckled arms. "I . . . I have only brought your supper as you ordered."

Theatana allowed her lips to cover her teeth, forced composure into her features, and displayed a smile. "Yes," she said in a soothing voice, "I had forgotten." She did not treat the palace slaves as roughly as she would have liked to, nor even as harshly as she once treated her servants in the Fountain Palace. She was no longer a foolish young woman, and she knew that a well-treated slave would be of more use to her than a surly and cringing one. Consequently she had acquired a name among the palace domestics for fair treatment and even a little kindliness. The knowledge sometimes made her smile.

Rehua brought the heavily laden tray into the room and set it on the table. Klaians liked their hot food to remain hot, and served it in thick pottery dishes with ponderous covers. Theatana said, "The evening is warm."

Rehua bobbed her head. "Yes, mistress. For this time of year, very warm."

Most of the palace buildings had flat roofs, used in the searing heat of midsummer for sleeping and eating. "I need to take the air," Theatana said. "I will eat on the roof."

Rehua made a Hazannu gesture of assent and picked up the tray. Theatana followed her out of the room and along the short gallery that ended at stairs leading upward. The younger woman ascended carefully, unbalanced by the tray's burden. Theatana mounted behind her, watching the sway of Rehua's plump behind. She was not thinking about anything in particular. It was as if she were about to do something without actually forming the intention of doing it. She felt suspended in the moment, as one remained suspended for an instant after stepping off a precipice, just before the earthward plunge began.

A low wall bounded the building's wide flat roof. Near the roof's south edge stood a wooden table and benches, and the sleeping platform. A light breeze blew from seaward. Theatana walked to the wall and looked down. The palace-citadel was on Spring Hill, the highest ground in the city, and from this height she could see across the city roofs and down to the foreshore. The tide was half-out and a big cargo ship, apparently too large to enter the harbor at the ebb, was dropping anchor in the sheltered water beyond the sandbars near the harbor entrance. The freighter's master would be cursing, having missed his tide for entering the port before dark. Now he would have to wait for tomorrow's flood.

"Would my lady wish me to uncover the dishes?" Rehua asked from the table behind her.

"In a moment." The parapet rose only to Theatana's upper thighs, making its flat capstone a convenient place to sit if one wanted to. Few would want to, however, for on the capstone's far side was a sheer drop into a courtyard that abutted the palace's outer wall. Most of the courtyard was given over to a garden that contained kitchen and medicinal herbs, and several rows of bottle-gourd vines supported on slender wooden stakes. A masonry stair, part of the system for quick movement of defenders within the palace walls, ran from the rooftop down to the courtyard.

"Come over here, Rehua," Theatana said.

With a look of perplexity on her round face, Rehua left the table and approached the parapet. When she was a foot from Theatana, she stopped.

"You can look right down into the garden," Theatana said. "Look how many gourds there are! They're like copper when they're ripe . . . what's the matter?"

"Mistress," Rehua answered nervously, "my head goes around when I look down from a high place."

"Oh, don't worry. I'll hold your arm. Don't you think it's a wonderful prospect of the city from up here?"

Rehua inched a handbreadth closer and halted again. "Yes, my lady, but may I please stay here? I truly don't want to look down."

Theatana gave a soft laugh. "Does everyone know you're afraid of heights?"

"No, mistress, hardly anyone. I try not to say."

"Come then, my girl, I'll teach you not to be afraid. We'll go down the stair together, so you can conquer your fear. We'll go down to the garden and pick some mint."

"Mistress—" Rehua began, an edge of desperation in her voice.

"Ah, I've found you," came Alfni's voice. Angry frustration swept through Theatana and she felt her mouth drawing taut.

Be patient. I must be patient.

"My lord Protector," she said calmly, and the anger slid away from her like a discarded cloak. "I didn't hope to see you until later." She added a sly smile for his benefit and sensed the quick heat it raised in him. He wore a scarlet tunic that bared his tanned and heavily muscled calves; a cloth-of-gold sash was knotted at his waist. Across his right shin angled an old spear scar, white and puckered. He had recently been shaved and his yellow hair, streaked with the pale ash of middle age, was washed and bound back in a gold fillet.

"We will be going to my nephew's at the eighth hour," he said, halting by the table with its rust red pottery dishes. He looked a trifle chagrined as he realized that if he were in Kayonu's house he would not be in bed with Theatana.

"Is there an occasion?" Theatana asked, not unhappily. This meant she would get out of the palace for an evening, even if it entailed putting up with sidelong looks from Kayonu's wife.

"Last fall's young wine is ready to drink, and we will drink some. The festival of the vintage will be in three days." Alfni lifted the lid of a dish, took a wedge of hot preserved melon, and bit the end off it. "Also, Kayonu is getting a trade cargo together, to send westward along the coast in that ship of his. I am contributing a share, the returns on which are to be discussed this evening. There may be good profit."

Theatana heard a hopeful note in his voice. Alfni needed to make his city prosperous again, for he had powerful enemies among certain merchants and nobles who blamed Kla's decline on his family's rule. These men also disliked his resolute devotion to the Green Lady, and muttered that the old Rasennan faith in her was misplaced. Despite their heritage, many of these men had adopted the Hazannu Storm God as their patron deity, along with the belief that the Green Lady was no more than his submissive consort. Chief among these was the most powerful of Alfni's enemies, an aristocrat named Rimash Idu. A branch of his family had furnished Protectors for Kla until its male line died out, and Rimash was of the opinion that he should be the next Protector, not Kayonu.

Alfni spurned the idea, for he believed that Rimash's reverence for the God in place of the Green Lady bordered on sacrilege. Theatana was indifferent to questions of piety, though not to Rimash's disaffection with the Protector. She knew it would be useful someday, though she had not yet calculated exactly how.

"Your nephew's not sailing north again, then?" she asked, feigning an interest she did not feel. When would the old fool finish so she could get on with her business? Rehua had sidled away from her and was standing near the stairway to the floor below.

"No," Alfni said. "He's still hoping Rook Arnza turns up alive, with his ship, before he tries that again. They'd sail north together, as last time. It's better on a really long voyage if there are two vessels. I mentioned Rook to you, do you remember?"

"You did? Oh, yes." She'd first heard the name from Kayonu—Rook Arnza was the master of that other ship, the companion whom Kayonu had hoped to find during the voyage home, but hadn't. Rook was from that city a few days' sail down the coast, Ushnana.

Alfni replaced the lid on the melon bowl. For a moment she feared he would tell her to come and eat in his chambers, which would lead to bed, usually a pleasant way to pass an hour or two. But at this moment . . .

"I have to speak with the horse doctor," he said. "Be ready when I come for you."

He vanished into the stairwell, followed by a wistful glance from Rehua. Then the slave woman recollected her duty, and said, "May I serve the mistress now?"

Theatana ignored her and walked to the opening in the parapet, from which the outside stairway descended three stories to the garden courtyard. Then she said, "No, Rehua, you may not serve me. We have a small lesson for you first, about being brave. Come, and we'll go down to the garden together."

"My lady—"

"Rehua," said Theatana in a soft voice, and the slave woman began to tremble. Then, submitting, she walked slowly to where Theatana stood by the stair's top.

Theatana looked around, then down. No one else was on the palace rooftops, no one walked in the garden below, no sentry paced the battlements of the wall on the courtyard's far side. She could proceed.

"Now," she said kindly, "just come to the first step. Look, girl, it's quite wide. The stair was made for soldiers to run up and down. You don't think the Protector would want his soldiers falling off it, do you?"

"Mistress, my lady, please. There's no *rail*."

"But if it were a flagstone on solid ground, you'd step on it without even thinking. Rehua, *do as I say*."

Trembling and sweating, the slave edged out onto the top step of the stairway. Her body shook violently. Theatana wondered, with mild interest, whether Rehua sensed her death hovering nearby, or did she shake only out of terror of the height? A pity she couldn't ask.

"Very good," she said encouragingly. "Next one, go on."

Rehua put her left hand on the parapet capstone to steady herself, tentatively placed the tip of her right sandal on the step below, let herself down, and followed with her left foot.

"See how easy it is?" Theatana told her. "Another, Rehua."

Trembling all the harder, Rehua managed the second step. For the third she would have to release her hold on the parapet.

"Have pity, mistress," she whispered hopelessly.

"I'll be right behind you," Theatana said. "Be brave, Rehua. Soon you'll be down in the garden, you'll see."

The slave woman let her hand trail down the stones of the parapet, but very slowly and carefully. She put her right foot on the third step. Gingerly she shifted her weight from her left foot to her right.

Theatana braced herself against the capstone and pushed Rehua off the stair.

The woman plunged with a long high scream, her smock flapping, her arms and legs flailing in a demented midair dance. When she was halfway down the scream rose to an animal shriek, stark with terror. Theatana imagined she had just realized where she was going to strike.

The shriek ended in a thud and crackle. Theatana hurried surefooted down the steps into the shade of the garden. She reached the bottom and ran back along the staircase's masonry wall to the place where the slave woman had struck. The pops had been the sound of ripe bottle-gourds breaking; Rehua had fallen onto two of the slender stakes that supported the vines, and the gourds had somewhat cushioned her fall. She lay on her back, arms and legs clumsily splayed, eyes wide with shock. The first stake had stabbed up through her back to emerge red and dripping from her belly, and the second rose like a blunt and bloody spear from her left breast.

To Theatana's delight the woman was still not only alive but conscious, for her eyes moved to look up at the figure standing over her. Rehua's mouth was agape, and she breathed through it in shallow gasps, though she seemed unable to speak or even moan. Theatana knelt by the slave woman's head and felt the Other's stirring.

I know what to do.

She realized she knew this because the Other knew it. Leaning over, she brought her mouth close to Rehua's. There was recognition in the blue eyes even through their mists of agony and terror.

"You're already dead," Theatana crooned, so softly that only Rehua might hear. "You've just got your dying to finish. And what a terrible dying it is, too. Having stakes pushed through you like that, and all those broken bones. Do the stakes hurt very much? This one must be right next to your heart." She prodded the sticky wet shaft to move it about, and Rehua tried to shriek but could not.

"Oh, it *does* hurt," Theatana murmured. "I thought likely it would. But soon people will come to find out why you were screaming, Rehua, and I'm afraid you'll have to be dead before they arrive. I suppose you'd prefer to wait for a physician, but I don't think one would do any good. You're very lucky you can't see what you look like now—you're truly a disgusting mess. Completely ruined for anything. It will be much better for everyone when you're under the ground and out of sight."

Rehua's eyes were mad. Her gasping quickened, gurgled.

"Good-bye, Rehua," Theatana said. "I'm going to hurt you very badly, but you're only a slave, so it doesn't matter."

She grasped the bloody shaft protruding from the woman's breast and gave it a pull. It resisted, and Theatana had to wiggle it about to loosen its hold on the earth under Rehua's back. Astonishingly, given her smashed bones, the woman somehow manage to arch her back and squirm violently while this was going on. Theatana twisted the stake twice more and felt it come free of the dirt; then she gave it a good tug and it slid all the way out of Rehua's body. Rehua slumped flat and died.

Theatana knew exactly what to do next, the awareness sliding into her from the Other and becoming hers so quickly that she might have always known it. She drew all her concentration down to a single point of ferocious intent and then, still holding the stake, leaned over Rehua as the last breath slid rattling from the torn lungs. The waft came warm and moist on Theatana's lips; she opened her mouth, inhaled it, swallowed it, raised her head, and spat into the air. The spittle became a smoky wisp in the shadows of the courtyard, then swelled into a cloud so transparent it was almost invisible, as if a column of very clear water had formed in the air before her.

Theatana blinked in perplexity and alarm. The form of cloud was that of a naked woman. The face was not quite impossible to see, and it was Rehua's. Theatana perceived in it an unspeakable fury. She had no doubt who was its target.

Still kneeling, she brandished the bloody stake. "Go! You're dead, go and *be* dead."

Now she heard voices calling faintly within the building. Rehua's screams were at last being investigated, though no one had yet looked out a window or over the roof parapet. Meanwhile, the Other gave her no help, no knowledge of how to deal with what she'd created.

The wraith seemed to drift toward her. A cold unease gathered in the pit of Theatana's belly, and she scrambled to her feet. What had she created by her rash action in putting the Other's lore to work? This thing could not *hurt* her, could it?

"Get away from me!" she hissed. *This isn't good enough*, she thought furiously. *If I can create such a thing but not control it, what use is that?*

It hung, disobedient, in the shadows before her. It seemed to Theatana that she saw it more clearly now, the rage in the pellucid features, the mouth agape as if in a soundless scream of fury.

"Get *away* from me," she snarled again. She gathered her will as she had gathered it to suck in Rehua's death rattle, and multiplied it with her fury. She became more than herself; her awareness again contracted to a point, a point that was neither in this world nor out of it, and she found there the soft trace of the Other and the presence of the dead woman. She drew the Other into herself—

And found within it something else. Like a passage into a place that was no place, vast beyond measure yet smaller than a seed of grass, and dead with cold. There, far at the passage's end, she knew a presence. It was aware of her.

Come in, it said silently, in a voice of cold amusement. *The gate he made is open. You will be safe.*

Through the Other she understood what it was: With shock and fear, she realized she brushed the presence of the Adversary. Erkai had touched it long ago, and this passage was a relic of his link to it, now at her disposal or so it seemed. She was very afraid, but her will held her in command of herself. And, eerily, she felt a kind of kinship with that icy awareness.

The Other seemed to whisper: *It is also the Father of Lies.*

She willed herself to draw back from the dark passage mouth, succeeded, and it dwindled to a speck, winked out, took the deadly presence with it. She was in the half world of shadows again, with Rehua gibbering, flailing.

Theatana found a voice that was her voice but more than hers. It was a voice of command, low and hard and certain, of herself and the Other blended.

I instruct you to pass on. Do so and trouble me no more, or I will bind you in this place until the sun goes out, and after.

In that dim half existence the specter heard her. Its essence quailed.

Go, or suffer.

With a voiceless wail the wraith dwindled, faded, and was

gone. Theatana's awareness expanded, returning to the courtyard and the created world. To her chagrin she realized that she was trembling as if afraid, but then she saw that the wraith had indeed vanished. Relief swept through her, and with the relief a vast wonder at what she'd achieved. *I have stood before the Adversary and survived,* she thought, marveling. *And I have commanded the dead. I told the wraith to go, and it went.*

She had done more than that, now that she considered it. She had created an apparition from a woman newly slain, a woman she herself had killed. That must be an act of the darkest Black Craft; no other sorcery needed a human death to achieve its results. Moreover, she had carried it through unscathed, though she knew from her investigations of long ago that sorcery of such power was horribly dangerous to its user. Few practitioners of the Black Craft ever dared go so far.

And I didn't even need a spell-book. She felt a stab of excitement at this realization. Could the Black Craft be practiced without such artificial aids, relying solely on will, talent, and knowledge? Perhaps so. She'd never heard that Erkai used such books, and he was certainly the most fearsome sorcerer the Ascendancy had seen in hundreds of years, if not ever. Perhaps, as she had hoped, some of his skills might still be alive in her, and she wouldn't need aids at all, or not many. She hadn't been able to harness the wraith to her will, true, but she'd had the power to send it away without book, spell, or incantation.

But what of her contact with the Adversary? That was truly a matter for awe: She had found a passage by which she could approach it, and had awakened it to her existence. She would be very unwise to walk carelessly in the presence of the old power of chaos and evil, but its nature and hers were in some measure akin; she'd felt that, unmistakably.

A door banged open behind her. Theatana dropped the stake across Rehua's carcass, assumed a distraught expression, and turned around. Alfni, his scarlet tunic flapping about his legs, was running toward her through the herb beds. He'd drawn his long dagger and was scanning the battlements of the outer wall as he ran. Behind him hurried the horse doctor.

"She fell," Theatana called to him, her voice shaking. "Rehua fell. I tried to help—"

She broke off. "We were coming down to pluck mint," she added as Alfni reached her. The scent of crushed herbs drifted after him.

"I was afraid it might be you," he said, breathing hard. "She fell, you say?"

"Yes. It's my fault. She said she was afraid of heights, but said she'd come with me anyway, I suppose she got dizzy—" Theatana gestured at the stakes. "Those went through her. I pulled that one out, tried to help, but she was already dead. Look at my hands. Oh, the poor girl."

"Vindisi, you're a healer," Alfni said to the horse doctor. "Is there anything to be done? She wasn't cheap."

Vindisi looked at Theatana, then at the body. Sweat stood on his forehead and upper lip. "There's nothing to do, my lord Protector," he said. His voice was rural-accented, with a guttural slur. He looked up again. He seemed unable to drag his gaze from Theatana. A buzzing began in her head, like that of treehoppers in high summer. The Other stirred again, coiled and slithered.

"Ah, well then, so be it. Can you make do with one of the bathhouse girls for a few days, Theatana, until we can replace her?"

"Of course," she managed to say.

"She'll have to be removed before sunset or her ghost will walk." Alfni, bellowing for slaves, turned and strode for the door through which he'd come. His voice receded as he went inside.

Theatana stared into Vindisi's blue-green eyes. He made a low sound in his throat.

Touch him.

She gathered herself and struck toward him with the strength of the awakened Other aiding her. The contact was fleeting, but all she needed she found. The same taste was there, the sweet dark taste that Erkai had carried, though in Vindisi it was far less potent. But Vindisi was a Walker nevertheless, a secret practitioner of the Black Craft. He *knew* things.

The touch recoiled on her as always, leaving her sick and shaking. But Vindisi shook even more. His ruddy skin was greenish white; freckles stood out like moles. He fell to his knees, and said in a choked voice, "Mistress. Forgive me. I thought I sensed it when I came here and the woman was dead. But I didn't know until now."

Theatana stopped her body from swaying. "You're a Walker," she said softly, because that was all she had strength to do.

"Yes, mistress." He added a word she didn't know: "simurgh."

"What did you say?" she demanded, still quietly.

"*Simurgh*. A hand of our lord the Poisoner, the godhead of Walkers. You're one such. I knew it when you brushed my thought, and I felt the Poisoner's touch in you. And there was something else," he added wonderingly. "Something that was a man, once." He shuddered. "What *are* you, my lady?"

What, indeed?

"I don't wish to speak of it," she answered. "You have skills of the Road, don't you?"

He bowed his head. "I do, but I practice only at dire need. I'm afraid of the Road, my lady. Anyone who walks the Road is afraid of it."

"I'm not," Theatana informed him. She gazed down at him, studying his lank reddish hair. He was still shaking a little. She heard Alfni in the building, coming back with slaves.

"You will teach me," she said.

10

IT WAS THE FOURTH HOUR AFTER DAWN. ILARION STOOD IN his chains and waited to be hanged.

The place of execution was a stone platform squatting at the edge of the harbor's east quay. On the platform were ten gibbets. Their uprights and crossarms were the smooth gray of old wood, though the nooses were new, the color of straw. The early light cast the shadows of the dangling ropes over the wind-ruffled water of the harbor, and where the ripples passed under the ropes' shadows, the shadows twitched and jerked.

The crowd around the gibbets hummed excitedly as it watched Ilarion and the other condemned men, manacled to each other with lengths of chain, waiting on the stone platform. He and his eight companions wore nothing but filthy breechclouts; welts, savage bruises, and scabbed wounds mottled their half-naked bodies. A multitude had turned out to watch them die; all up and down the quay, on the roofs of the warehouses overlooking it, spilling out of side alleys, even bobbing in small boats out on the harbor, was a cheerful mob. Women were as plentiful as men, and many of both wore the emblem-brocaded cloaks of the noble houses. The aristocrats, unlike the noisy, eager members of the lower orders, maintained a languid poise. Only the delicate flush and bright eyes of the women, and the slightly quickened gestures of the men, betrayed their pleasure and anticipation. There were slaves in the crowd, too, wearing their iron bracelets; Rook had told Ilarion about the slaves the Rasenna used. Unlike their masters and mistresses, these stood expressionless and silent.

Among the condemned there was no talk; even if the guards on the platform had allowed it, Ilarion and the others were too worn down by deprivation and fear for speech. They had been given only water and a little rough bread for the last three days, two of them spent on the Haidran war galley and the third on shore, imprisoned in a warehouse.

They'd had little enough to eat or drink even before that, during the last days of *Statira*'s thirst-tormented, starving, three-month voyage from the north. They were barely alive by the time they made landfall in a sheltered bay on the mainland coast, but that salvation had proved no salvation at all for Ilarion and half *Statira*'s crew. Rook and Lashgar had staggered ashore with a foraging party to find game and water, and while they were absent, warships bearing the insignia of Kanesh appeared in the bay mouth. In such confined waters and with little wind, there was no escape for *Statira* or the men still aboard her, and they were too few to put up much of a fight. Victorious, the Kaneshites chained them belowdecks in the galleys, and triumphantly brought both their captives and Rook's ship home as trophies. *Statira*'s battered hull now lay moored at the quay, only a hundred paces from the gallows.

At least Lashgar wasn't among the men on the platform. None of the foraging party had been taken, apparently, for none had been brought aboard the galleys either living or dead. So Lashgar could still be free somewhere, and Ilarion found a small comfort in the hope that this might be so.

The Kaneshites had noticed immediately that Ilarion didn't look like the rest of their captives, and seemed mildly puzzled at his presence among them. They spoke the language Ilarion had learned from Rook, though with a different, softer accent, and they seemed to think he was something called an Antecessor. During the voyage Rook had mentioned such a race, but Ilarion could no longer remember what he had said about them. He knew his captors would have been even more puzzled if the dark-complected Lashgar and Mersis, the Mixtun seaman, had been among their captives. But Lashgar was gone, and Mersis had died

during the second month of the voyage, poisoned by the bite
of a small fringed eel with silver eyes.

Now he was to die, too. He was still shocked and disbelieving that he had reached the end of his life, being so far
from finished with it. Even as he stood here, next to his own
gibbet, he could hardly believe that he was going to be
hanged this morning; that he, Ilarion Tessaris, late of Captala Nea in the Ascendancy, was to wriggle and squirm at the
end of a rope, face slowly turning a dark crimson as the
noose throttled him.

His eyes stung a little. He was so far from home, and his
family would never know how he died. They'd never even
know the place of his death. He'd only identified it yesterday, while he and the other prisoners were being shifted
from the galley to the prison warehouse and he'd gotten a
glimpse of their surroundings. Rook had told him of the
Citadel Stone, the colossal rock that reared high above the
city of Kanesh, bearing as its crown the palace of Tirsun
Velianas, ruler of the eastern half of Haidra. And there the
Stone was, a half mile distant across the city rooftops, soaring into the morning light. So this was Kanesh, and he was
to die in it.

Next to him, Shagall stirred in his chains. Ilarion glanced
sideways at him. Shagall was the youngest of Rook's crew,
a cheerfully violent youth of wiry strength and not much in-
telligence. His face was set, his skin ashen, and he was trembling slightly, though he showed no other sign of fear.
Ilarion could hardly bear to look at him and turned his eyes
quickly away.

As he did so, he heard drums thud in the distance and a
brassy hooting from some metal instrument. The music
came from the broad avenue leading from the harbor quays
toward the Citadel Stone, and accompanied a tasseled scarlet canopy that swayed above the crowd. Ilarion watched
dully while the thing progressed toward the harbor, the
crowd parting before whatever vehicle bore it, like waves
before a galley's ram.

At last the canopy reached the harbor, and a lane opened
in the throng between it and the gallows platform. Soldiers

formed a cordon to hold the passage open; they wore armor brightened with a wash of silver and inlaid with bronze. Along this passage, moving at a stately pace toward the gibbets, came a high-wheeled carriage painted red and trimmed with elaborate gilt carvings. It was drawn by two white horses and protected from the sun by the scarlet canopy. A driver, riding on a raised seat at the carriage's front, held the horses' reins; their harnesses were gold and crimson, and crimson plumes waved above their heads. Now Ilarion could make out the shouts: *Protector, Protector.* So the ruler of Kanesh himself had come to see them die. They were to be even more a spectacle than Ilarion had dreaded.

The carriage, accompanied by its trumpeters, drummers, and armed escort, stopped at the steps that led up to the row of gibbets. In it was a man of about Ilarion's age: Tirsun Velianas, Protector of Kanesh. He was pale of skin, and Ilarion realized, even in his daze, that Tirsun was astonishingly handsome. He was clean-shaven, with a rippling mane of golden hair drawn back by a silver fillet, and he wore a richly patterned blue mantle over a belted tunic of white and silver. His pale fingers bore many rings, set with carnelian and bloodstone and grass green chrysoprase, splintering the sunlight.

Tirsun stood up in his carriage and waved to the crowd. It responded with a roar. He gave another wave, then stepped down from the carriage. On his feet were boots of glossy blue leather, embroidered with pearls. The roaring and the cheers diminished. The crowd waited, like a leashed hunting animal, to find out what he would do.

Accompanied by a pair of his soldiers, he climbed the platform steps. When he reached the top, he went to the end of the line farthest from Ilarion. Unable to see what the man was doing, Ilarion waited. The crowd fell quiet. A little time passed.

Then Tirsun was standing a few spans away from him, in front of Shagall. Ilarion turned his head to look. The ruler of Kanesh was studying Shagall up and down, like an aesthete contemplating a rare and intricate, if unlovely, carving. But he said nothing.

Under that relentless gaze, Shagall began to shake, and a single tear escaped from the corner of his eye. Tirsun, his face grave, extended a fingertip and put it to the tear. Shagall winced. Tirsun smiled, withdrew his finger, and studied the dampened tip with grave enjoyment. Then he appeared to lose interest. He flicked away the tear and stepped back to survey the line of doomed men.

More long moments passed. The crowd remained hushed. Above the harbor, seabirds wheeled and keened. Then the Protector's glance flicked sideways to Ilarion, and he spoke softly to one of the soldiers. The soldier stepped forward and yanked at the chain shackled to Ilarion's waist. Ilarion stumbled along the flagstones, iron links jangling at his ankles, until he stood before the ruler of Kanesh.

"Ah," Tirsun said. His voice was light and musical. "You're the curiosity they were talking about. Do you understand me when I speak?"

The accent was strong but intelligible. "Yes," Ilarion answered, looking full into the Protector's face. Tirsun's eyes were a pure dark green and flecked with gold, like the sea after a storm when the sun has come out. They were intelligent eyes, full of merriment, savage with appetites.

"You're going to be hanged," he said. "Are you afraid?"

"Yes."

The ruler of Kanesh frowned. "They said you were an Antecessor, which was odd in itself. I've never heard of an Antecessor turning to seafaring and piracy. Furthermore, your eyes are the wrong color. So is your hair. It has too much bronze in it. *Are* you an Antecessor?"

"No, Protector, I'm not," Ilarion managed. He tried to think of what to say next. Every sentence was a breath or two more of life. As long as he talked, he lived. It was so sweet to live.

"What are you, then?"

A dim hope flickered in him. The man was curious. How much might he want to know? A week's worth of talk? A month's?

"I'm from the far north," Ilarion said, summoning strength from somewhere. "From the other side of Ocean.

The ship your men captured me on was returning from there. And I am no pirate."

Tirsun blinked. Then his head tilted a little to one side, and his eyes narrowed in a skeptical look. "Ah. That's quite an insolent speech, for someone in your position. And a considerable *claim*, indeed, from someone in your position." He paused, then said, "I am no fool. You hope that my curiosity, if you should succeed in arousing it, might save your neck."

The grammar was intricate, but the meaning seemed clear. "I do," Ilarion answered.

"And why would my curiosity result in your redemption from death?"

Ilarion summoned his wits as best he could. "Because what I know might be of interest to you. Possibly of profit."

"I see. You say you are from the far side of Ocean."

"Yes, Protector."

"Convince me of this."

It was utterly unexpected. Off-balance, Ilarion groped for a way to make Tirsun believe him. He asked, "Have you ever seen someone who looked like me?"

The crowd was murmuring again, impatient for the executions to begin. Tirsun ignored it, pursed his lips, and minutely inspected Ilarion's face. At length he said, "No, I haven't. But that's hardly enough. You might be a vagary of nature. And I'm really quite eager to hang you. Convince me further."

Ilarion's head cleared a little and he saw the obvious. "Have men look in the hold of the ship. What they'll find there is not from anyplace you know."

"You are suggesting I spare you while this inspection is carried out?"

"Yes, Protector."

"If there are no such things on the ship," Tirsun said amiably, "I won't hang you. I'll have you castrated, your skin burned off, and then you'll be buried alive."

"They're in the ship," Ilarion said. "Truly, they are."

"You'll regret it if they aren't," Tirsun answered. "Truly, you will." To one of his guards he said, "Get the smith from wherever he is. I want this man unshackled and held aside."

The soldier ran down the steps. Shagall's anguished eyes were fixed on Ilarion, and in the white faces of the other crewmen stood the same question: *Why him, why not me?* Near Shagall stood Kegen the musician, who played a bone flute carved from the whorled tusk of a sea mammal, and who had learned Ascendancy dances from Ilarion's hums and whistles; there was Scisso, who liked eating whelks and had taught Ilarion and Lashgar a guessing game called Three Fingers in Your Eye. And Shagall the youngest, who was supposed to marry a girl named Afaia, when he got home.

Ilarion had sailed with them, eaten with them, learned from them, and at the end had fought with them, and he did not want them to die. They were ruffians and sea-rovers, freebooters for whom *trade* and *raid* came to much the same thing; but they were honorable by their own standards, tough and enduring, fiercely loyal to each other, and brave to the point of rashness.

He said, "Protector, these men were in the north, too. They're mariners, and they'd know how to navigate there again. I beg you, let them live."

To his astonishment, Tirsun suddenly appeared undecided. "Do you really think I should?"

"Yes, Protector."

Hearing this, Shagall fell to his knees and bowed his head in supplication, though he did not beg. After hesitating, the others also knelt, with a clank and jangle of chains. Ilarion and Tirsun were left standing above them. The Protector did not speak, merely surveyed his captives with a thoughtful gaze. The crowd swayed and emitted fretful mutters.

The soldier whom Tirsun had sent for the smith returned, accompanied by a stocky man carrying a mallet and a heavy-jawed instrument of black metal. The smith prostrated himself before the Protector and waited.

"Get up and loose this one," Tirsun said, gesturing at Ilarion.

The smith scrambled to his feet, compressed the thick split pins that closed Ilarion's shackles, and knocked the shackles off with the mallet. The wrist irons had left Ilarion's flesh so raw he could barely touch it. The rest of the crew were still on their knees.

Tirsun looked out at the crowd. Some at the front had heard Ilarion's plea for mercy, and the word had passed around. It did not please anyone. There were shouts from the back and angry murmuring from closer at hand.

The Protector said to Ilarion, "You see how I am constrained."

"Protector, I implore you."

"One mercy is enough for today, I think." Tirsun nodded to the executioner. "Hang them." He turned to the soldier who had brought the smith. "Bring this one down to my carriage."

There was no more to be said. Ilarion followed Tirsun down the steps, trying not to hear the grunts, choking gasps, and scuffling noises that began behind him as nooses were forced over heads and drawn tight. Disgust and loathing at the manner of the men's deaths filled him, mixed with feverish exhilaration at his own reprieve.

The executioner carried out his work while Ilarion waited by Tirsun's carriage. He could not bear to watch the death struggles on the platform, and stared at the pavement beneath the carriage wheels. He saw that the stones were well shaped and fitted, the work of good masons. The wheels, however, were clumsily proportioned by Ascendancy standards, the rim and the spokes too thick for grace, although the joinery of the wood was elegant enough. Part of him marveled that his mind could attend to such detail while Shagall and Scisso and Kegen and the others thrashed at the ends of ropes and the crowd bayed and moaned. Perhaps it was hunger; he felt as though his body were slowly becoming separated from his head.

The mob's clamor subsided, and he forced himself to look up. The men now moved only by the slow swings of their ropes.

"There, that's done," Tirsun said from his seat up in the carriage. "Now I must see to you. What's your name, by the way?"

"Ilarion, Protector," Ilarion said, without looking up at the young man.

"Clan or sept name? Or don't you have such niceties where you come from?"

"I am of the House Tessaris."

"Come along to the ship, then. We'll see if you're telling the truth."

The carriage creaked into motion and lumbered off along the quay, accompanied by the Protector's escort. Ilarion followed them, flanked by a pair of soldiers. A large proportion of the crowd, plainly hoping to see Ilarion finished off in some spectacular and original manner, came on behind at a respectful distance.

The cavalcade reached *Statira*. She was under guard; a dozen Kaneshite sailors prostrated themselves as the Protector accompanied his escort and Ilarion aboard the ship. *Statira* was in the same dismal condition in which Ilarion had left her; her decks gaped at their seams, her rigging was slack and frayed, and her planks were spattered here and there with the dark russet of dried blood.

The hatches to the lower deck and the hold had been sealed with lead seals and straps. Tirsun ordered a sailor to bring tools, which the man did.

"Where should we begin?" the Protector asked. "You choose."

Ilarion indicated the small afterhatch, the sailor cut the seal's straps, and the soldiers levered the hatch cover off its base. A reek like that of a cesspit surged from *Statira*'s innards. The soldiers and even the sailors backed away and screwed up their faces in disgust, and Tirsun held a perfumed cloth under his nose. The stench bothered Ilarion less; he had, after all, lived in it for weeks while they were at sea.

They waited for the morning breeze to allay the stink. Finally, it lessened enough to be bearable, and Tirsun, Ilarion, the tool-bearing sailor, and two soldiers descended the afterladder into the small stern hold. That was where Rook had stored the more valuable items he and his crew had acquired on their expedition to the Blue Havens. From the open hatchway above the men, a shaft of morning sun fell into the ship's interior; visible in its light were a score of wooden boxes and kegs, stacked against the massive frames of the hull and secured in cribs against *Statira*'s roll.

The containers were few enough. Now that the moment was at hand, Ilarion thought of the death he would endure if Tirsun refused to believe his account of his origins, and a sick horror washed through him. Would the Protector be convinced by the scanty collection Rook had amassed during his brief exploration of the Blue Havens' fringes, or would he suddenly lose patience and consign Ilarion to a disgusting death? It was impossible to tell. There was a frightening capriciousness about the Haidran ruler.

"What's here, then?" Tirsun asked. He moved to stand beneath the flood of sunlight. His hair shone like metal. The guards, even in their silvered armor and their helmets of polished iron, seemed dim beside him. "Show me, Ilarion of the House Tessaris, and let's get out of here before the stink throttles me."

Ilarion thought desperately. What did Rook have tucked away down here? He and his men had acquired their cargo, one way and another, before Ilarion and Lashgar and poor dead Mersis had joined *Statira*'s crew. Ilarion had never had a reason to inspect the contents of the well-sealed chests and kegs. He did know that the takings of the voyage had been scant, most of it being ceramics and wooden wares and aromatics and the like. Most of the outer islands of the Blue Havens were poor; the few wealthy places, like Lashgar's home of Ammedara, were in the north of the archipelago, and *Statira* had never found them. He could only hope, now, that some object hidden in this stinking hold would save his life.

He said, "We may have to open them all, Protector. I don't know exactly what the captain stored in them."

Tirsun put his head back and laughed; it was a warm, rich laugh. "You mean you laid a bet without knowing what was in your pouch? Really, you did this, knowing what I'd do to you if you lost?"

"Yes, Protector," Ilarion said, because there was nothing else to say.

"Very staunch of you, indeed." Tirsun gestured at the sailor. "Get on, open the things, all of them. We must not scant our guest's chances of survival, must we?"

The sailor got down to work, ripping the lid from the nearest chest. Inside it—

Nothing.

"Ah," Tirsun said. "Perhaps you are not, in point of fact, from beyond the farthest seas. Perhaps you *are* an Antecessor of some kind, after all. If this is so, perhaps you should consider singing, if not for your life, then at least for an easier death. You might achieve the luxury of hanging, if you warble sweetly enough."

Ilarion had no idea what Tirsun meant by this. The sailors continued their prying and breaking. The next case was empty, and the next, and a keg as well. Belowdecks the air was hot, and sweat ran into Ilarion's eyes and down the sailors' temples.

"This is boring me," Tirsun said. "There's nothing here. I think you've laid your last bet, Ilarion Tessaris."

Ilarion knew he was too weak to fight, and too little a threat to make them kill him if he tried to. Still, he measured the distance to the sword hilt of the nearest guard. Not far, but the other soldier would be on him before he could get the blade out. And even if he managed to arm himself, he knew Tirsun wouldn't let them hack him down. He was reserved for a harder death than that.

"There's still the main hold," he said dully. But he knew there was nothing there except empty provision casks, a few bundles of brown Mixtun cloth that might come from anywhere, and a dozen bales of fretwork palm bark. The bark was likely unknown here, but he did not think it would impress Tirsun very much.

"Protector," a sailor said. "There's something in this one."

He was already prying up the top of a chest. Ilarion's heart seemed to rattle against his ribs. The sailor yanked the lid away, and Tirsun leaned forward to look into it.

"Interesting," he murmured, and lifted something from the interior. It was a stack of ceramic dishes packed in straw. Tirsun separated one from the stack and studied it. The dish was plain creamy white, with a green-wave pattern around the rim, and a stylized blue fish glazed into the center. Mixtun work, and simple out-island stuff at that.

"Probably Hazannu," Tirsun observed. "It's not seen here, but that means nothing. The barbarians do all sorts of things we never hear about. Still, let's open another."

Ilarion could not tell whether the Protector was toying with him or was now genuinely interested. He waited while the sailor cracked open another chest. This one also was not quite empty.

"Ah," Tirsun said. "Something different, is it?"

The sailor handed him a small ornamental box made of fretwork palm bark. The complex intaglio patterns in the wood were picked out in blue and white, highlighted with yellow.

"It's made of a kind of bark," Ilarion told him. "It's not carving, it grows that way. There's more of the bark in the main hold. It's not known here, is it?"

Tirsun shrugged. "No, but what of it? It may be common a month's trek inland. I merely thought the painting of the box curious. Ah, it rattles."

He opened the lid, removed something small, then let the object lie on his palm. In the sunlight from the hatchway, metal gleamed.

"A coin," Tirsun said, with a note of puzzlement in his voice. He examined it minutely, both sides. Finally, he said, "Well, then, I admit something, Ilarion Tessaris—I have never seen a Rasennan coin like this. And the Hazannu don't mint silver at all." He extended his flattened hand. "Since you profess to know such things, tell me what it is."

Ilarion peered at the metal disk. It was old and worn, but he could still make out the tiny graven characters around the man's image, and a sudden, terrible homesickness gripped him.

"It's a coin from my country," he said with an aching throat. "It's a minim, struck in the second year of the Dynast Tatikos's reign, almost two hundred years ago."

Tirsun's eyes narrowed. "Really? You're very quick-witted, to make that up so nimbly. You even thought to put in a foreign word or two. What do *Dynast* and *minim* mean?"

"Protector, the first is the title of our highest ruler. The other is the kind of coin."

Tirsun closed his hand on the minim and regarded Ilarion thoughtfully. "Yes. I see." To the sailor he said, "Open some more."

The next chest contained more of the cream-glazed dishes. And the next. And the next. From the chests after that came several dozen painted fretwork boxes, unfortunately empty. Then there were half a dozen small kegs stuffed with aromatic resins. Tirsun sniffed at them with interest, and admitted that he had not smelled quite their like before. Ilarion's hopes rose a little. The Protector seemed a little closer to believing him.

Now the sailor had found a smaller chest, this one with bronze fittings and a hinged lid. Tirsun's face brightened with curiosity, and Ilarion sent up a prayer to the Two: *Lord Allfather, Lady Mother, let this be the thing that saves me.*

"Open it, man," Tirsun said as the sailor fumbled with the hasp. The lid fell back. Inside—

Inside lay a small book bound in faded green leather. On the leather was inked its title, in the flowing script of the Ascendancy.

Ilarion stared at it in disbelief. How the thing had found its way to the edge of the Blue Havens, he could not imagine. But it would save his life. Tirsun would have to believe him now.

The Protector, wearing a newly quizzical expression, had taken the book out of the chest and was holding it awkwardly. "What is *this*, Ilarion Tessaris?"

"A—" Ilarion began, and then realized what was puzzling the man. Tirsun had never seen a bound book. Rook had said that the Rasenna wrote on sheets of vellum, sewed them together, and rolled the strips onto pairs of dowels to make scrolls. Scrolls had not been used in the Ascendancy for a thousand years, ever since paper-millers discovered how to make a tough, close-grained paper from a common lake reed.

"It's a kind of scroll," Ilarion said. "It opens at the side. There, like that."

Tirsun opened the book and stared at the script. "This is your form of writing?"

"Yes, Protector. For convenience, the name of the book is written on the outside."

Tirsun, with every appearance of fascination, closed the cover and studied the script written there. "What does it say? What's the name of the . . . what did you call it—'book'?"

"Yes, Protector." Ilarion was exulting inwardly. He was going to live. He did his best to keep his voice from trembling as he translated and said, "It's called *The Book Naming All Cities in the Southwest and What Is in Them.*"

"You read that here on the front?"

"Yes, Protector."

"Read it the way it sounds in its own tongue."

Ilarion did so. "That's my language," he said when he ended. "It is called the Logomenon."

Tirsun thrust the book at him. "Read some more. In your Logomenon, then give it in my tongue, so a civilized person can understand it."

Ilarion opened it at random, and read, "The older part of the city lies below White Hill, and indeed its central avenue, called Octagon Street, is said to be the oldest city street in this part of the southwest. However, the citizens of Lambesis, a town farther up the river, dispute this." He stopped and translated what he'd just read; fortunately the section he had fallen across was easily rendered into Rasennan. There was a silence when he finished.

"Does the Protector wish to hear more?" Ilarion said, after an interval.

"No," Tirsun said, "the Protector does not. You have convinced me, Ilarion of House Tessaris. You are indeed from the far side of Ocean, and the old stories of lands there are true. I didn't believe you at first, but you have changed my mind." He turned to the soldiers. "Bring him on deck. This stench would choke a blowfly."

He hastened up the afterladder. Ilarion, giddy with relief, dropped the book back into its chest and dragged himself slowly after the Protector. Emerging into sunlight and the sweet spring air, he saw Kanesh as if for the first time, and only now realized how lovely a city it was. Beyond the gibbet, where he was not going to die after all, a broad avenue climbed in a gentle slope toward the south face of the Citadel Stone. Rambling over the summit of that vast mass of rock, painted in vibrant polychrome, were the walls and terraces and colonnades of an enormous palace. Like the palace, the city below it was gaily colored, its facades and gables painted in sapphire blues and dark crimsons and blazing yellows, the hues all the more brilliant against the white plastering of the walls. At roof peaks and cornices stood likenesses of animals, humans, and birds, their colors bright in the spring sun. Smoke from breakfast fires rose in tendrils into the morning air, and on the breeze lay the scent of burning charcoal, the aroma of fish grilled with thyme and lemon, the sharp salt tang of the sea. Black-headed gulls with forked tails sailed above the harbor and the city, keening in soft shrill voices.

He was going to live. It was almost as hard to believe in as dying.

Tirsun was waiting for him on deck, near the gap in the rail where the gangway had been placed. The Protector's face was grave, all amusement vanished. He was, Ilarion thought fleetingly, probably wondering how to treat such an exotic visitor as stood before him: a traveler from a distant land, walking out of the dimness of legend into the hard-edged light of noon.

"You have been reprieved, then," Tirsun said, "as I promised, for exactly as long as it took to prove your case. Since you did in fact tell the truth, you will keep your genitals and remain unburned and unburied."

"Thank you, Protector," Ilarion said. "Thank you, my lord."

"I accept your thanks. Now I'm taking you back to the gibbet, where you will be hanged."

Ilarion's tongue would not move. Silent, stunned, he stared at the Haidran ruler.

"Yes, hanged," Tirsun said pleasantly. "Did you have some other expectation? If you think back on my words, you'll remember I didn't say you would be *spared*. I gave you a reprieve while you provided me with some amusement, no more."

Ilarion still could not speak. He was to die after all. The moments of life he had won with his tongue had almost all fled. He was to die.

"Bring him along," Tirsun said. The soldiers seized Ilarion by the upper arms, dragged him through the gap in the rail, and down the gangway to the quay.

Tirsun was already in his carriage, looking on as Ilarion stumbled onto the quayside paving. Even in his numbness Ilarion realized that the Protector was enjoying the sight of his despair. It delighted him, as a child might be delighted by the agonies of an insect it had impaled on a bronze pin.

I won't let him have the satisfaction. Never.

He heard Tirsun giggle softly. At the sound a savage heat rose in him, straightening his back and flooding his limbs with strength, and he screamed a curse into the face of the Protector. Though he shouted in the Logomenon his meaning was clear enough, and Tirsun gestured. A heavy blow struck Ilarion to his knees, and his mind reeled toward darkness.

The soldiers prodded him and he managed to get to his feet. He looked up at Tirsun. "Gone mad, have you?" the Protector asked. He made an irritable gesture at the soldiers. "Get him to the gallows. Do you think he's going to bite you?"

Held tightly by his guards, Ilarion stumbled off along the quay. Tirsun's carriage rumbled behind him while the crowd in front, forced along by soldiers wielding spear butts, flowed back toward the gibbets. It hummed excitedly, like a host of flies around carrion.

Ilarion could not bear to look ahead at the approaching gibbets with their dangling hanged men. He turned his gaze on the harbor. Its surface moved in sluggish coiling eddies, and just above the eddies a band of sodden weed lay exposed and dripping on the stone faces of the quays.

The water is falling, he thought dully. *But so fast. Why is the tide going out so fast?*

A dense flock of small azure-and-white birds rose from a warehouse roof and flew far into the sky, twittering. Hundreds of the black-headed gulls now swirled and shrieked above the harbor, and from farther back in the streets of the city came a sudden howling of dogs. The near-side horse danced nervously, though it had walked placidly before, and the driver muttered and snapped the reins.

Suddenly, both horses slowed and halted. They were trembling. The birds shrieked and circled.

"What's the matter with those horses?" Tirsun snapped. "Lay on the whip, can't you?"

The driver fumbled for it. Ilarion discovered that he also had come to a stop. His guards, distracted and now holding him only loosely, paid no attention. Like many in the crowd, they too were looking up at the birds. The dogs still howled and yelped. The water in the harbor was dropping steadily down the faces of the quays.

The driver, whip in hand but unused, said, "Protector, the sea is going out."

"It's only the tide, you fool," Tirsun said. Then his face lost its humor and his eyes widened. "But that's too fast," he said angrily, as if affronted by the sea's behavior.

A few in the crowd had seen, and were calling out in astonishment. Scattered mutters of unease and alarm rose here and there. In a few moments everyone was looking at the ebbing water.

Its descent slowed. After a few more heartbeats Tirsun waved a hand at it. "There, look! It's stopped."

This seemed to be true. The birds abruptly went silent. So did the dogs. In the stillness, Tirsun said, "All right—"

A rumble came from seaward, rose to a bellow, and the paving under Ilarion's feet twitched. He heard human screams, the birds again screaming, both shrieks drowned instantly by an appalling roar from underfoot, from the roots of the earth. Ilarion could hear nothing but its thunder shaking the air, the sound palpable, beating against his face, jarring in his skull. The harbor frothed; dust shot from the pavement, from walls, from rooftops, hazing the sunlight. Near the gibbet a column toppled into the crowd, followed by a torrent of brick and stone. Tirsun's carriage danced on its wheels, the horses white-eyed and screaming with fear. One animal tried to bolt, but the other was too terrified to move and held it fast. The carriage heaved, spilling the driver onto the quaking pavement; the lurch almost threw Tirsun himself over the carriage side. The shaking drove Ilarion to his knees. He saw a warehouse collapse on the harbor's far side, and above its ruin a dirty white cloud roiled into the shaking air.

A moment later a frightful grinding sound shuddered from the depths of the earth, then ceased as if cut off by the slamming of a colossal door. The shaking ended with it. A final tremor ran through the pavement under Ilarion's knees and was gone.

Very slowly he got to his feet. The seabirds no longer screamed but the morning air was alive with human shrieks, and dogs still barked and howled. The sounds of terror and anguish rose from every street of the city, so that Kanesh itself seemed to have found a voice.

Still half-deafened, Ilarion looked around, expecting to see the city in ruins. But astonishingly, most buildings still stood, though the air was misted with dust. The carriage driver lay facedown near the vehicle, clutching at the stones of the quay and apparently paralyzed with fear, for he did not move. Tirsun was still in the carriage, and somehow still on his feet. He was gazing seaward. On his face was a look of vast astonishment.

Ilarion peered through the dusty air to see what Tirsun was staring at. A quarter mile distant lay the harbor entrance, with its twin marker beacons and its massive breakwater of black granite. Beyond it was a shadow, obscured by the haze. Ilarion squinted, uncertain what he saw.

The breeze twitched the dusty veil aside. Not far outside the harbor mouth, its crest tipped with streaming banners of foam, a tall blue wave was marching toward them out of the depths of the sea.

11

THE WAVE SWEPT LIKE A CAVALRY CHARGE TOWARD THE
city. The crowd saw it; the cacophony of shouts and screams
doubled and redoubled. Ilarion's mind became very clear,
each thought like a pebble dropped into a pool of still water.

*High ground. Can't run fast enough. Maybe the horses
can.*

He seized the whip from the carriage's prostrate driver,
pulled himself into the man's seat, and seized the reins. The
horses were shaking with terror. Tirsun seemed as stupefied
as the animals, and unable to wrench his gaze from the onrushing wave. Ilarion yelled, "Hold on" over his shoulder
and lashed the braided leather across the geldings' haunches.
They screamed and kicked, but remained rooted in place.
Ilarion laid the whip on again, savagely. Both horses shied,
then began a shambling trot. He whipped them again, and
they broke into a full gallop, foam streaming from their
jaws, hooves battering stone. They were at the edge of bolt-
ing, and he could barely control them.

A dozen yards away was the edge of the fleeing crowd. A
few people still lay stunned on the paving, but most had now
seen the advancing wave and were racing toward the avenue
that climbed toward the foot of the Citadel Stone. They fled
like the horses, wild-eyed, seeing nothing before them but
the salvation of high ground.

The geldings slammed into the throng. The horses might
have been charging through high grass, for all the humans in
their path slowed them. The unlucky ones fell under the
hooves and the carriage rocked as its wheels pounded over

them. Wild shrieks rose from the maimed in its wake. Ilarion shut his ears to the sounds and lashed the horses on.
Though he tried to keep the racing animals to where the
fugitives were fewest, he hit many, and in a narrow corner of
his mind he was appalled by his callousness. But he was not
appalled enough to rein back, even if the horses would obey
him. These people had come to see him die, and he owed
them nothing.

A glance over his shoulder. The wave had reached the harbor mouth and he saw it swallow the entrance beacons and
the breakwater in a gulp. It was the height of four men,
crested with foam and sea wrack, streaked with white. Curiously, it made little noise, only a distant hiss and mutter. But
it was coming fast. He turned back to the horses and
whipped them on.

By the time the carriage was fifty yards along the avenue
that rose toward the Citadel Stone, the crowd had thinned to
those who ran fastest. But Ilarion heard a deep roar and rumble, growing louder. He looked over his shoulder again. The
wave had crested; a great ridge of white water was seething
through the harbor, heaving ships from their moorings and
surging along the quays. The gibbets vanished, and in another heartbeat the thunder of the breaking wave had
drowned the screams, drowned even the clatter of the heavy
carriage wheels and the drum of the geldings' hooves. There
was nothing in the air but a vast sliding block of sound, solid
as a hammer stroke.

The carriage lurched. Any moment now the wave would
be upon him.

There came a dank, wet smell and a chill wind. Past the
spinning carriage wheels hurtled a knee-deep flood of roiling, dirty foam, laced with wreckage. In an instant it was up
to the carriage steps, then to the horses' bellies, and he saw
people flailing in the wild surge, struggling helplessly as
they swept by him. The carriage heaved; the struts of its
parasol snapped, pitching the crimson-and-gold cloth into
the water. The horses screamed, audible even above the tu-
mult. Then the carriage was no longer a carriage, but a boat
dragged behind the terrified animals. They were swimming

instinctively, carriage and team both flailing in the wave's grip, borne pell-mell up the street amid a wrack of debris and bodies. Water swirled cold about Ilarion's knees. He could no longer guide the horses; he cast the reins aside and clung to the driver's bench. The carriage tipped, spun, pulled the team under, the harnesses broke, the horses swirled away. In the maelstrom he saw a face almost at his feet, a young woman drowning, her mouth a dark O calling soundlessly to him for help. He reached out and seized her arm. She clung to him, and he saw hope in her eyes, but then a broken beam surged from the churning waters and smashed her from his grip. The shock almost pulled him after her, but somehow he held on to the carriage seat. For an instant her hair streamed gold in the foam, then vanished.

He looked back. Tirsun was still in the carriage, clinging to a parasol strut, his face white and his eyes bulging from his head. The carriage was nearly full of water and almost sinking. Down the hill, where the harbor and its quays had been, there was only sea, thick with wreckage, with a few reefs of masonry protruding from the green-and-white welter. Many buildings farther up the slope had lost walls, and their roofs had fallen in. Even there the water was neck-deep. But its headlong rush was slowing at last. It had caught him but not drowned him.

His relief lasted only moments. The torrent was still ferocious; a violent eddy seized the carriage, spun it about its axis, and swept it sideways. It jolted, and a shiver ran through it as the wheels touched ground. Then it slammed into the portico of a small building, scraped between two thick portico columns, and lodged there. A wheel shattered, and the seat tilted. But the flood had begun to reverse itself and rush back downhill. The filthy water poured over the carriage, gaining power with every instant, threatening to tear Ilarion from his perch and sweep him away. The vehicle, still trapped between the columns, jerked in the torrent, and Tirsun howled wordlessly. The carriage offered no safety; if it broke loose, the receding wave would carry it like a leaf down to the harbor and drown them after all.

Ilarion looked up and saw the portico roof four feet above him. He would have only one chance.

He let go of the seat and launched himself upward. Instantly the torrent pulled his legs from under him, but in the same instant his hands clamped on the edge of the roof. It was stone, and there was a rain gutter. Like talons his fingers curled into the trough and he hauled himself from the racing water and got his leg over the gutter's edge. One more heave, and he rolled onto the portico's sloping roof. Under him its tiles vibrated to the current's rush. A *crack* came from below, and the whole portico sagged.

"Help me! In the Lady's name, help me!"

Ilarion rolled onto his belly and put his head over the roof's edge. Tirsun was still in the carriage, still holding to the canopy strut, water swirling about his waist. He stretched out an arm. Another crack, and the carriage jolted farther out into the torrent. Under Ilarion the tiles shuddered and groaned. Above and behind him was the main roof of the building, only a short scramble away.

Leave him. Save yourself.

He may be my only road home.

Ilarion reached down, and shouted, "Stand on the seat and jump!"

Tirsun hesitated, and the carriage shifted suddenly. It was almost free of the columns' grip. "Jump!" Ilarion screamed. Tirsun heaved himself from the water and clamped both hands around Ilarion's manacle-lacerated wrist. Ilarion yelped with the pain. The carriage broke loose from the portico, rolled over in a splintering mass of wood and gold, and fled toward the sea.

The two men's eyes met. Ilarion's wrist was a ring of agony.

"Your life for mine, Ilarion Tessaris!" Tirsun shouted. His feet dangled in the racing water. "I swear it on the Lady!"

Teeth clenched with the agony in his wrist, Ilarion dragged him upward until the Protector could grab the rain gutter. Tirsun struggled onto the portico roof as the tiles sagged again. "It's going," he yelled.

They scrambled for the building's cornice, hauled themselves over it. Under them the portico collapsed into the water in a smear of stone, wooden columns, and broken tiles. Ilarion lay on his back, gasping as the pain faded a little, looking into the sky. It was cloudless, blue, and utterly serene. Birds wheeled far above.

The rumble of the waters faded. Replacing it came a vast stunned silence, broken at length by the voices of humans, suffering.

After a while Tirsun sat up and looked over the edge of the roof. "The water's gone," he said. His voice was flat, his features wooden, and his eyes were distant. It was a look Ilarion had seen on the faces of men who had just survived a savage battle: a kind of shock, a dazed astonishment at being alive.

But the Protector was made of harder stuff than Ilarion had thought, for he shook himself, rose to his feet, and gazed around at the devastation. Then he said, "Have you ever seen anything like this happen? Seen such a wave?"

"No," Ilarion croaked, sitting up. "I haven't."

"Neither have I." Tirsun's voice had lost its flatness and shook a little. He squinted into the morning sunlight. "Gods and goddesses preserve us, what a mess. It will take months to rebuild." Then his tone suddenly brightened and steadied. "But we can rebuild more *magnificently*. A new harbor beacon, new arcades along the quays . . . statues, a park. What do you think?"

Ilarion took this for a babble of relief, from a man who had just escaped death. "As my lord deems best," he mumbled.

"Yes, of course." Tirsun surveyed the street below. Babbling or not, he seemed to be pulling himself together. "Well, it looks safe enough now. How do we get down from here, do you suppose? I suggest you don't run off when we do—you're very easy to identify."

Ilarion had no intention of running off. They reached street level by jumping to an adjoining roof, then descending by an outside staircase. Debris and bodies littered the avenue, and the air was full of wails, shouts, and pleas for help, and supplication to the Lady and the Firebringer.

"Come with me," Tirsun said, and set off uphill toward the Citadel Stone. Ilarion obediently stumbled after the Protector. Now that he was no longer fighting for his life, he was exhausted. But in spite of his daze, he realized that the damage to Kanesh was less than he had imagined it would be. From the shaking he'd received on the quay, he'd thought the city would be laid flat. But it was not so; the wave seemed to have wrought most of the destruction. Above its reach, most buildings had remained intact although a few of the pillared arcades lining the broader avenues had fallen, and a lot of roof tiles had slid into the streets. Still, many must be dead and many more injured. Survivors, recognizing their ruler, cried out to him as he went; Tirsun, who was showing few signs of his earlier shock, spoke comforting words to them, promised help, and even spent a few moments helping a man pull an injured woman from beneath a fall of roof tiles.

They had reached the avenue that ran along the foot of the Citadel Stone when a dozen soldiers, accompanied by several slaves carrying two litters, came hurrying toward them. One litter was empty; the other bore a chubby Rasennan in brightly colored clothes. All except the chubby man prostrated themselves in front of Tirsun, all babbling together in mixed fright and relief. They were palace staff, come down from the Stone to look for the Protector; the chubby man, whose name Ilarion heard as Entash, seemed to be in charge of them.

Ilarion was at the end of his strength. Tirsun apparently noticed his distress, and to Ilarion's dull surprise he ordered Entash to give up his litter. Entash was clearly astonished and infuriated, but just as clearly knew better than to protest. Ilarion clambered into it, the Protector got into the second litter, and the little procession set out along the avenue. As they went, Tirsun questioned Entash about the condition of the palace; the man's replies appeared to reassure him. Entash seemed more distressed than the Protector, though he'd been in no danger from the wave, and worried aloud that either the Lady or the Firebringer was enraged over some inadvertent neglect of them by the worshipers of Kanesh.

Apparently nothing like it or the earth tremor had befallen
Haidra in far longer than the longest living memory, and the
disaster was clearly a sign of divine displeasure. Tirsun
agreed; propitiation was urgently needed, and would begin
as soon as possible.

The ascent to the palace began a hundred yards up the avenue, in a tall gateway cut into a spur of the Citadel Stone itself. Past the gateway was a dim passage, ten feet wide and
equally high, cut through the solid rock. It was intact,
though the quake had brought down a few flakes and lumps
of stone. As they climbed, Ilarion tried to pay attention to his
surroundings in spite of his weariness. Three times the tun-
nel ended in a level courtyard; in each one, the narrow road-
way made a hairpin turn, then plunged into another passage
in a higher spur of the Citadel Stone. Massive and formidable gates guarded the entrance to each new passage.

At last they reached the top and passed into the open. The
transition was abrupt. At one instant they were in gloom and
dankness; in the next, they burst into the sunlight and
warmth of a spacious courtyard paved with blue tiles. Along
two sides ran a colonnade of red-painted pillars, and at the
far end a broad staircase of white marble led to an upper
level. The air was cool and touched with the scent of flowers. No damage had befallen the courtyard except that some
chunks of carved stone had tumbled from a frieze.

"Have this man taken to the Old Quarters," Tirsun told
Entash as he and Ilarion got out of their litters. "Feed him
and make him civilized." He turned abruptly away, and Entash gave sharp orders to one of the slaves. The slave gestured, and Ilarion followed the man into the right-hand
colonnade. Thus he came to Kanesh Palace, the jewel at the
summit of the Citadel Stone.

Dusk was not far off. Female Hazannu slaves flitted about
the long gallery, filling the hanging lamps with oil, as Entash
the Grand Domestic escorted Ilarion to his audience with the
Protector. Ilarion now knew, because Entash had told him on
the way up to the gallery, that the Grand Domestic was the
supreme authority in the palace, after Tirsun. Though the

man was babyish of face, both the heavily armed palace guards and the slaves were plainly terrified of him. The latter were everywhere, and to Ilarion they were an unpleasant novelty, for slavery had been outlawed in the Ascendancy for all its seventeen hundred years. Kanesh had been alien to begin with, and the slaves made it more alien still.

As they walked, he tried to orient himself. Judging from the angle of the sun, this gallery was on the southwest side of the palace. A frescoed wall was to his right, but on his left the gallery was open to the air, with a low wall supporting the russet columns that held up the gallery roof. Between the columns, a distant green headland and the sea were visible. The gallery must be at the very summit of the Citadel Stone.

Ahead was a low couch liberally supplied with red-and-gold-tasseled cushions. A man reclined on it, and as Ilarion drew nearer, he saw that the man was Tirsun. The Protector wore a calf-length, belted tunic and short brocaded jacket. A silver wine cup was in his hand and he was gazing at the sunset-purpled vista of the sea.

At the whisper of the men's sandals on the tiled floor, he turned. "Ah," he said. "Entash, and Ilarion Tessaris."

Entash bowed deeply from the waist. So did Ilarion, and to precisely the same angle. It was not so different from the bow that a noble of the Ascendancy would offer to the Dynast. Entash made an angry noise and seemed about to speak.

Tirsun raised a calming hand. "Tell me of the city, Entash," he said.

Entash swallowed his outrage, consulted a thin wooden tablet with inked characters on it, and embarked on a catalogue of the damage and the dead. The death toll in the harbor area was high, and many ships had sunk at their moorings or been hurled ashore and wrecked. The warehouses had suffered badly, a terrible blow to scores of merchants. However, farther into the city the damage was less, and salvage, burials, and repairs were already under way. Elsewhere in the Protectorate the damage had been minor. Ilarion realized, listening, that the Grand Domestic was responsible for much more than the palace's smooth operation; he must also control the daily operation of the government.

Entash finished by saying, "As you instructed, I have also ordered animals and birds for one hundred days of sacrifices, proclaimed in your name, to the Lady and Firebringer. The priestesses aren't yet sure what we have done to anger the divine couple, but they say this will turn aside any further punishments, such as the one we have just witnessed." Entash frowned. "My lord, one hundred days still seems somewhat excessive, no matter what the provocation on our part."

"But such lavishness will enhance my reputation," Tirsun said lazily. "Entash, how well does humankind memorialize a niggardly Protector? I wish my rule to be known for opulence and generosity. As an age of gold and abundance."

Entash inclined his head. "Just so, my lord."

"This is all as it should be," Tirsun observed. "I have nothing to add. You may go."

Entash bowed, turned silently, and departed. The Protector shifted his attention to Ilarion, who stood quietly while the Haidran ruler inspected him up and down. Tirsun's hair had been braided into complex golden loops that swung over his shoulders, and a fillet of silver held the braiding away from his forehead and temples. In the Ascendancy such a style would be worn only by women, but it did not make Tirsun look in the least effeminate. It made him look like an elegant and carefree youth.

"Your appearance is less appalling than when I saw you last," he observed after a while. "Are you feeling equally improved in spirit and body?"

"Yes, Protector. Thank you." Since arriving at the palace the previous morning Ilarion had been treated extremely well, and he felt better than he had in a month.

"In fact, you're a fairly presentable specimen," Tirsun said. "Especially with clothes to cover the bruises."

"Thank you, Protector." Ilarion's new garments were of good quality, though simple: a buff-colored tunic, woven of a slightly coarse wool, with a brown sash and leather sandals.

The Protector was still observing him as if he were some

exotic creature from an unknown clime. Which he was, of course. Ilarion resisted an urge to speak, unsure whether doing so might give offense. His ignorance of this place was profound; the slaves who had tended to him refused to answer any of the questions he asked.

"It is customary," Tirsun finally said, "to go down on both knees when first brought into my presence, unless you are the Grand Domestic or someone of similar elevation. You, however, merely inclined from the waist, as if you were Entash. Is this, where you come from, the normal mode of demonstrating respect for a ruler?"

He'd made a serious mistake, though Tirsun appeared unperturbed by it. "Yes, Protector. Although a member of the common orders, in my country, would customarily kneel on one knee to the Dynast or to a noble of the higher ranks. Failing to do so would be considered ill breeding or ignorance, rather than culpable disrespect."

"I see. Therefore you consider yourself a person *not* of the common orders. Is this correct?"

"It is, my lord." He ransacked his memory for Rook's sketchy account of the Haidran hierarchy. "I am of the landed orders, in your terms." Until he knew Tirsun better, he was reluctant to reveal his true status. Claims of high rank were easily made, anyway, and Tirsun probably wouldn't believe he was a ruler's son. For that matter, even Rook had never found out how exalted his foreign deckhands were. Ilarion had realized, soon after boarding *Statira*, that it wasn't Rook who had attacked Selemban, but he'd suspected that a comrade of Rook's might have done it—Kayonu of Kla, as later became obvious from Rook's account of their voyage north. If Ilarion and Lashgar someday encountered this Kayonu, it would be better if he didn't connect them with Theatana or with Selemban. With this in mind, they had kept their ranks to themselves. Doing the same with Tirsun had at least the virtue of consistency.

"I see." Tirsun pushed a braided loop of golden hair back over his shoulder and gestured at a stool near the couch. "Come, sit."

Ilarion hesitated; this man was capricious. "If it would

please you to guide me," he said, "is it permitted to sit in your presence?"

Tirsun laughed. "You're very careful, aren't you? Yes, you may sit, if I tell you to." There was amusement in the amiable voice, and the green eyes were friendly and open. "Is this sufficient instruction for the time being?"

"Yes, Protector." Ilarion walked to the stool and sat on it. It was softly upholstered, like Tirsun's couch. The latter was deeply carved with garlands of flowers and fruits, all brightly painted or covered in gold leaf. Next to the stool was a small round table; on it was a tray of baked goods, a golden jug, and a silver cup like the one Tirsun held.

"Take wine and sweetmeats," Tirsun said. "The wine is very good. It comes from the north slope of Mount Atur. But that wouldn't mean anything to you, would it?"

"No, my lord. I am unfamiliar with your geography." Ilarion obediently took up the jug and poured. The wine was a deep rich purple-red, and the cup's polished silver shimmered dimly through it. Around the outside of the cup was embossed a band of sea creatures, each fin and scale and tentacle flawlessly etched. The wine jug depicted graceful horned animals that gamboled among trees and tall ferns.

Tirsun said, "We call the wine Alasdine, because it has the same color as a gem of that name. Taste."

Ilarion did so, and blinked in surprise. It was as good as any served in the Fountain Palace. The connoisseurs of the Ascendancy would go into raptures over this vintage. "It's superb," he said.

"Yes, it is," Tirsun admitted carelessly. "Everything here is superb."

This seemed true enough. What Ilarion had so far seen of the palace was of breathtaking opulence, though its loveliness and luxury were of an alien kind. Its frescoes depicted exotically garbed men and women, painted with curiously elongated eyes, surrounded by bizarre animals and strange flowers. He'd eaten a fine-crumbed brownish bread with an unfamiliar sweetening, a round yellow-skinned fruit called an ambercup, and a fish that tasted not quite like tunny. For his bath, the cleanser was a jellylike substance scooped from stone crocks, rather than the Ascendancy's cakes of hardened soapseed extract. He'd also been shaved by a palace barber; apparently the Rasenna of Haidra considered beards uncouth, though their mainland kin, such as Rook, did not.

Tirsun drank the last of his wine, then contemplated the interior of his cup. "I admit you intrigue me, outlander," he said. "You saved my life, when your temptation must have been to let me die. So you must have concluded that your true interest lay in my survival, rather than in taking revenge on me. Given the circumstances surrounding us, that suggests uncommonly quick wits, and a profound ability to resist temptation." Tirsun stroked the rim of the cup thoughtfully against his chin. "For that reason at least, I'm pleased that I didn't hang you—you do intrigue me, as I said. And since my life is one long flight from boredom, I find this pleasurable."

"I am elated to hear it, Protector."

"You also show signs of being civilized. This piques my interest. How can it be possible? It's well known there *is* no civilization where you come from."

"With respect, Protector, when I lived among my countrymen, I didn't know there was a civilization here on Haidra."

"By which you mean, I might be mistaken, just as you were mistaken?"

"My command of your language is imperfect, my lord. I did not mean to suggest such a thing."

Tirsun snorted. "It seems adequate enough to my ear, though you have a barbarous accent. You learned Rasennan from that bloody-handed Rook Arnza, I suppose."

"I did, Protector."

"Give me some more wine," Tirsun ordered, extending his cup.

Ilarion leaned forward and poured carefully. When he finished, Tirsun took a pastry from the tray and ate half of it with neat, sharp bites. He balanced the remainder on the back of the couch. "You knew I knew of him, did you?"

"Yes, my lord. Rook mentioned you a number of times."

"I can imagine in what words. Never mind. I've wanted to

get my hands on him and *Statira* for two years now. I sincerely wish he hadn't been ashore when we caught the ship and the rest of you. I suppose he heard the fighting and ran off inland. Maybe the Hazannu will get him, though I still hope to have the pleasure of killing him myself. He and those brigands in Ushnana stole that ship from me, did you know that?"

Ilarion hesitated, unsure of how to respond. On the voyage south with Rook, as he picked up the language, he had learned a good deal about the Rasenna. Haidra was the last major remnant of the Great Garden, the powerful civilization that had once occupied the mainland to the south of the island. But the Garden had collapsed in civil wars, recurrent famine, and, at the last, a virulent plague. The sickness killed nine people of ten who fell ill; only the Rasenna on Haidra escaped its full fury, as they had by chance escaped the worst of the other disasters.

But when the calamities had passed, so had the Great Garden, and into the mainland's depopulated ruins moved the Hazannu, barbarian tribes from the deep south. They created no empire but a patchwork of petty realms, which fought each other continually in a shifting tangle of alliances, trivial wars, and slave raids. Rook had said that a few enclaves of Rasennan civilization survived for a while on the shores of the mainland, but of these only his city of Ushnana now remained, and Kayonu's, which was named Kla.

Tirsun was frowning. "Well?" he said. "Did you *know* he stole it?"

It was unwise to argue the point, so Ilarion said, "My lord, Rook *said* he had the ship built in Ushnana."

"He still stole her. He found out I was building exceptional vessels, and he abducted—or bribed—two of my better shipwrights. He took them to Ushnana and they built *Statira* for him. If he didn't steal the ships themselves, he stole the men who knew how to make them. *That's* piracy. And I gather he built another one as well, for a friend of his, one Kayonu of Kla. No doubt you'll have heard of him from Rook."

"Yes, Protector. He was mentioned."

"What do you know of his travels?"

"My lord, very little. Kayonu sailed his ship north in company with Rook. But they were separated by a storm before they reached the islands. The two ships never met up again. *Statira* was alone all the return voyage."

"I choose to believe you. Klaians"—Tirsun made a disgusted face—"they're not much better than the Hazannu. Nor are the Ushnanans, for all they call themselves Rasenna. Too much mixed blood. So Rook sailed north, did he, and you fell into his hands out there somewhere?"

"Yes, Protector. I was shipwrecked with a friend, a nobleman of the islands we call the Blue Havens. Rook picked us up just in time to save us from starving. But he sailed for Ushnana, and we had no choice but to go with him as crew."

"Didn't you ask him to take you home?"

"We tried to, but he was heading home himself and had no real reason to believe us. Eventually I convinced him that my family and my friends would reward him well for our safety, but by that time we were too far south to turn around. But he promised to take us on his next voyage north."

"Where *is* this friend of yours?" Tirsun asked. "The brigands I hanged yesterday were all Ushnanans."

"He was ashore with Rook, Protector, when your galleys came into the bay."

"Ah. You're very lucky, you know—I'm surprised Rook didn't slit your throat for the enjoyment of it, when he found you. What possessed him to take you on as crew? You didn't even speak the language."

Casual throat-slitting seemed more Tirsun's style than Rook's, but Ilarion was not about to say so. "He needed men to work the ship on the voyage back," he said. "He'd had a mutiny shortly after he reached the Blue Havens, when he wanted to go on northward and a lot of his men didn't. He lost half the crew as a result. So then he had to go back south, anyway. He picked us up on his way home."

Tirsun sipped his wine, looking thoughtful. "I've been wondering about sending a ship northward myself. So Rook had a reasonably good voyage to your islands, did he, barring the mutiny?"

"I gather so."

"And the return?"

"That was much worse, my lord. Rook planned to replenish our food and water halfway through the voyage, on some islands that lie between here and our Blue Havens. He'd found them on his way north, with Kayonu, but we missed them returning, because of storms. Without the fresh supplies, especially the water, several of us died before we finally made landfall and your ships caught us."

"Ah," Tirsun said, "the Meridian Islands. So they really *are* out there. Are they inhabited?"

"It appears they aren't, Protector."

Tirsun ate the last of the pastry, reached out, and took another. "You're not eating. Eat."

Ilarion took a pastry and bit into it. There was almond-flavored honey in it, and a sweet nut that was not an almond.

"*Statira* sank at her moorings yesterday," said Tirsun. "The wave did it. Her cargo was ruined, so what little value it had is gone. However, I knew my men could have removed small articles before they brought the ship back to Kanesh, so I made . . . stringent inquiries. Little of consequence came to light, except for one item. Now, where did it go?" He rummaged among the cushions, then held up a shining object. "This is neither Hazannu nor Rasennan, nor, I believe, is it Antecessor. Would it be from your part of the world?"

Ilarion's throat tightened. It was his seal ring. His last link to home. "Yes, my lord. It's a ring made in the Ascendancy. Its stone is green, the one we call an emerald, and it's carved with a winged serpent."

Tirsun's eyebrows rose. "You know it?"

"It belonged to me. We call the serpent a pandragore. Its representation is the symbol of my house and family. One of your men took the ring after the fighting ended." It was still painful to remember their defeat, for he'd never experienced such a thing until that day: the powerlessness, the humiliation, the fear.

Tirsun was frowning down at the jewel. "It's a lovely thing, but I am not sure it would be lucky for me—I don't care for snakes. Here."

To Ilarion's astonishment, Tirsun suddenly held the ring out to him. "My lord?" he said.

"Take it, put it back on."

Ilarion obeyed. He slid the ring onto his finger and closed his fist tight on the carved emerald. "Thank you, Protector," he said, hearing his voice husky.

"I might have thought it was Antecessor work," Tirsun went on conversationally, "because of the winged serpent, except that the Antecessors aren't known for gem-cutting."

Ilarion felt a tiny thrill along his skin. "The creature is known here?"

"Well, they're in a few of our old stories that mothers put their children to sleep with. But I gather that the Antecessors take them more seriously than we do, at least my father's Antecessor bard did. It's called a *fireshta*. It means 'The Hidden Singer.' What was your name for the creature again?"

"Pandragore. It's said to stand for the union of opposites, because it goes on its belly on the earth, and on its wings it's a denizen of the air. It signifies the gaining of hidden knowledge, and of transformation."

Tirsun laughed. "That's far more portentous than the creature in our tales—in ours, the fireshta is a magical pet for the hero, that allows him to understand the speech of beasts. The Antecessors may have given it other attributes, but I don't know what those might be."

"Might I at some time ask your court singer?"

Tirsun stretched his arm out with his empty cup at the end of it. "More wine. No, you can't. He was old, died just before my father did. But this talk of magical creatures, it reminds me what I wanted to ask *you*—what kind of sorcerers do you have in the north?"

The change of subject was abrupt, and Ilarion paused to collect his thoughts. Rook had quizzed him about Ascendancy magic, as well as passing on rudimentary information about sorcery among the Rasenna. It had become clear that the Rasenna had never known the Deep Magic, and once Ilarion realized that, he avoided any mention of it and cautioned Lashgar to do the same. Until they knew more about the south, the existence of such a power was best left unspoken.

Tirsun was awaiting an answer. The Protector's gaze was still warm and open, but Ilarion glimpsed in the green eyes the feral light he had seen when Tirsun stood with him in the shadow of the gibbets: appetites intricately perverse, ripe with depravity. If anyone should *not* know of the ancient sorcery, it was the Protector.

"My lord, it appears that the laws of magic are much the same everywhere—a small number of people have a gift for it. A very small number of *that* small number twist their gift to serve their own purposes, however infamous. Under our laws they're proscribed, and they suffer serious penalties if they're proved to have used what we call the Black Craft."

"Hm. These are similarities, indeed—we say that the benign ones have the Grace of the Green Lady, and walk the Golden Path. The others walk the Foul Road, and they can be dangerous if no one draws attention to them. Our laws against the Walkers, unfortunately, seem rather ineffective. I can't remember the last time I executed one . . . Now, I want to ask you another question. Where you come from, does the God take precedence over the Goddess? If he doesn't, do your priests think he should?"

Ilarion weighed his answer before making it. He found the Rasennan religion perplexing, at least as Rook had described it to him. The Green Lady was far more powerful than her consort, the Firebringer, who seemed to be little more than her chief servant. This was quite unlike the beliefs of the Ascendancy, where the Lord Allfather and the Lady Mother stood as equals in the Sacred Marriage.

"He doesn't exactly take precedence," he answered, and hastened to add, as Tirsun's eyes narrowed, "but she doesn't take precedence over him, either."

"Ah. What *is* the relationship, then?"

"They're equal. Each provides what the other lacks, to make a completeness. Sky and Earth, for example. Or the seed, and the rain for the seed. Our priests and priestesses are agreed on this. Questions of precedence do not arise."

Tirsun snorted. "I find this equality a difficult concept.

Someone *always* takes precedence. Among the Hazannu, the God who brings storms is all-powerful. His concubine is the Earth, who is the female. She's a goddess, but not much of one. Women don't rule among the Hazannu. But here, my sister rules the other half of Haidra. What do you think of that?"

This was dangerous ground; the Protector's nostrils had become pinched, his mouth suddenly drawn tight at the corners. Ilarion said, "My lord, it's not my place to judge the affairs of rulers."

Tirsun hurled the cup at him. The dregs of the wine flew in a red spray as the rim struck the corner of his mouth, and he felt the sting of a cut lip. He jerked back in shock. The cup clattered to the floor and rolled in a circle, making a hollow ringing sound. Drops of wine bit into the cut, and he felt a trickle of blood between his lips. He licked it away and sat very still.

Tirsun's hands were opening and closing. *I am near death,* Ilarion thought. *He's half-mad. Demented.*

At last Tirsun said, "Pick it up. Give me more wine."

Ilarion rose, retrieved the cup, and poured. When he handed it to Tirsun, the Protector had regained his composure, and was reclining just as languidly as before. When Ilarion resumed his seat, Tirsun asked conversationally, "Did you think I was going to kill you just then?"

Ilarion said, with no expression on his face or in his voice, "The thought crossed my mind, Protector."

"I almost did. I almost threw you over the cliff here. It's six hundred feet straight down. Don't think I couldn't have done it. You're still weak, and I'm very strong when I'm angry. Now, answer me properly, without prevarication. What do you think of the fact that my sister rules the western part of this island?"

"I think it is against your best interests, my lord."

Tirsun scrutinized Ilarion thoughtfully. "Did you really learn such shades of meaning at Rook's elbow?"

"I seem to have a gift for tongues, Protector."

"So you do. Now, where were we? Yes, magicians. Do you have any really *powerful* sorcerers in the north? Ones who can fly through the air on a magic cloak, or change iron into gold?"

His changes of tack were dizzying. He had drunk most of the wine in the jug but so far showed no intoxication. Ilarion said, "Not that powerful. A few might be able to produce such illusions, but they're just for entertainment. People with the Kindly Gift, as we call it, use it for healing, or to help crops grow, things of that ilk. Or if a nature sprite's causing trouble, they can often persuade it to go away."

"But none who make magical devices?"

Ilarion thought of Erkai the Chain, and the deadly artifact he had owned, and was instantly alert. "Devices, Protector?"

"A mask, for example. There's one my sister has custody of, made of bronze. It's very ancient. It was brought here from beyond Ocean by a magician we call the Giftbearer." He eyed Ilarion with a sudden hint of alarm. "You're not the Giftbearer returning, are you? Say so if you are, and I'll prostrate myself. But be careful. If you make the claim, and it proves false—"

"No, Protector, I'm not."

"You're honest, aren't you? But I want to know if you have things like the mask where you come from. It helped bring about the Fall, though it's not supposed to be evil. But it's so sorcerous that no one's dared use it since then. Except for one day a year it's kept locked up in Dymie, my sister's capital."

"No, my lord, I don't know of such devices." Ilarion felt a flicker of unease. Erkai's chain had been an artifact of the Deep Magic; could a similar thing have somehow found its way here to Haidra, long ago?

Impossible. Improbable, anyway. If it really is some magical device, and it's not evil, it's likely a talisman of the Kindly Gift. As for its powers, these things grow in the telling.

And if I'm too curious about it, he'll want to know why. Better to let this dog lie sleeping.

"It's the only one like it here in the south," Tirsun observed languidly, "so it truly is a rarity, then." He yawned without covering his mouth. He had perfect teeth, very white. Ilarion sensed from the gesture that the audience, like the day, was nearing its end. The sun had suddenly fallen into the sea, in a wash of crimson and orange and purple, and he still didn't know what Tirsun was going to do with him.

"My lord," he said, "may I speak?"

"I suppose so. What do you want to say?"

"I long to return home. Would the Protector consider working toward this end? The Ascendancy and the Rasenna could both benefit from knowledge of each other."

Tirsun stopped yawning and stared at Ilarion. "You are treading the edge of insolence," he said. He looked around. A slave woman with a burning taper glided along the gallery's inner wall, and paused to light the wicks of a hanging lamp. The flames trembled, rose, and burned in yellow petals. Tirsun called, "You, come here."

The woman did so, eyes cast down. She was perhaps eighteen, and wore a dun-colored smock of rough cloth, short-sleeved, tied at her narrow waist with a sash. She was a Hazannu and very lovely, as were all the younger female slaves Ilarion had seen in the palace. He'd as yet spoken to none of them, though; his attendants in the Old Quarters had been an aged woman who fed him and two Hazannu youths who he suspected were eunuchs.

Tirsun took the taper from the woman, blew it out, and dropped it to the floor. He gestured at the couch beside him. She sat down, folded her hands in her lap, and stared at her knees. Around her left wrist was the iron ring that marked her as one of Tirsun's many belongings.

"I'm sure you *do* want to return home," Tirsun continued. "However, the exotic interests me, and my friends and I might find tales of your distant land diverting." He pursed his mouth, and a trace of unease slid into his face. "Hm. Does your ruler have many soldiers?"

Ilarion dared not answer the question correctly. The Ascendancy's army numbered 150,000 men, and he knew Haidra could never dream of fielding such a force. If he told the truth, Tirsun might kill him, in case he might escape and someday alert the Ascendancy to Haidra's existence. Or the

Protector might think Ilarion was lying, which presented equally unpleasant possibilities.

"Between ten and twenty thousand men," he answered, "depending on need."

Tirsun relaxed visibly. This seemed to be an answer he could believe. "Do you have any military experience?"

"I have led men in battle, Protector."

"Did you win?"

"Yes, Protector."

"Hm. Perhaps one might learn some minor items of military usefulness from you, at that. I'll question you on the matter." He sat up, pulled on a gold chain that ran about his neck, and drew a slender gold cylinder from beneath his tunic. He blew into it twice, and two shrill whistles echoed through the gallery's shadows. Distant footsteps responded, hurrying. "You will be a *karapan* of the palace."

Ilarion did not know the word. "My lord?"

"Exactly." Tirsun rummaged among the cushions. The slave woman watched the Protector sidelong as he searched, plainly hoping that he had forgotten about her. Ilarion tried to imagine what Tirsun was looking for, and failed. Two guards clattered out of the shadows and stopped at the end of Tirsun's couch. The bronze inlays on their breastplates glowed a dull orange in the sunset light, and they carried spears with slender iron heads.

"Ah." The Protector sat up. "Here it is."

It was two semicircles of polished gray iron, hinged together at their ends. Stamped into it were symbols in the script of the Rasenna. A notched tongue of the gray metal projected from the free end of one semicircle; in the free end of the other, there was a slot. Tirsun handed the contraption to the woman. "Put the chattel ring on him," he said.

"A *slave*?" Ilarion burst out, and the guards suddenly were pointing their spears at his belly. But he could not restrain himself. "You make me a *slave*? I saved your life!"

Tirsun raised his eyebrows in mock surprise. "As I saved yours, by not hanging you. That evens the score, I think. But surely you didn't think you were free to come and go as you *pleased*? You've been my property ever since you were captured. You still are."

Ilarion had no words, none he could speak to Tirsun and not die.

"It's not so bad as you might think," Tirsun told him cheerfully. "A karapan has the highest grade of bondage. In your case, only Entash or I can give you orders. You'll attend me at my pleasure, and tell me how my army compares to yours, and other things that might interest me. I enjoy your company, Ilarion Tessaris. You're so *different*."

His arm flashed out suddenly, and a sharp *crack* resounded through the gallery. He had struck the slave woman across her cheek. "Why are you sitting there, girl? I told you to put it *on* him."

She stood up, cheek reddening from the blow, and gazed expressionlessly down at Ilarion. He didn't move; he could not bring himself to extend his arm. The guards shifted their stance, waiting.

Tirsun reached out and gently took a spear from one of them. He brushed the slave woman's hip with its needle point, and she quivered.

"Ilarion," the Protector said in a soft voice, "if you don't cooperate, I'll mate her with a foot of iron. Would you enjoy seeing her like that?"

The woman shuddered, went white, and closed her eyes. When she opened them, they were full of horrified pleading. The threat was real, and she knew it. Her mouth was working and she shook all over in tiny jerks and twitches.

Ilarion put his left wrist out to her. With trembling hands she closed the semicircles around his flesh. The toothed tongue slid into the slot, clicking as it went. The semicircles met, the chattel ring closed. He was a slave.

"The ring can only be cut off," Tirsun said, handing the spear back to the guard. "Tamper with it, and you'll be found out at inspection and killed. Run away, and you'll be caught and killed. Woman, come here."

He took her by her wrist, made her sit on the couch beside him, and began untying her sash. She looked at Ilarion with the same hopeless horror that he'd seen in the eyes of the drowning woman, whom he had not saved. He could not save this one, either.

"Entash will instruct you further," Tirsun said. He was lifting the hem of the woman's smock, and at the same time pressing her back onto the couch. "For now, the guards will take you back to your quarters. When you get there, stay there. All right, remove him."

They took him away down the long gallery. He heard the woman cry out once, and then fall silent. But she was only a slave, and so was he.

12

DUSK HAD LONG PASSED, AND ONLY STARSHINE AND THE flickering beacon of Dristra's Light illuminated Elyssa's surroundings. She was standing, in unaccustomed hesitation, at the top of a stairway that led downward from the Upper Palace's South Arcade. On her right, the dark bulk of the palace's residential annex rambled down the same slope as the stairs, to end on a natural rock platform that jutted from the citadel's summit. Part of the platform had been left as an open-air terrace; paved with gold-tinted marble, it was called Setvil's Promenade, after the Protector who had built it two centuries earlier. At the Promenade's outer edge was a waist-high wall, guarding a sheer drop to the roofs of the Lower Palace. On its inner side, a columned porch ran along the palace's facade and shielded the interior from the direct rays of the summer sun.

Elyssa held her breath and listened, but heard only silence; it was about the tenth hour, and the palace was asleep. There was no moon, but drifts of stars hung in the sky and the horizon was faintly visible by their gossamer light. Beyond the foot of the steps, a faint orange gleam lay along the Promenade's pavement; she thought it must be from a lamp burning within the porch, though the porch's interior was out of her line of sight. The dim illumination revealed some outdoor furniture scattered here and there: tables, a couch, two stools. No one occupied them.

Should she go down? No one would see if she did. She had already sent her body slave Tamti to bed; as for the garden slaves, they weren't about at this hour, and this side of the palace-citadel was so high and sheer that no sentries walked its terraces.

Still, her hesitation did not abate, and indeed took on a tinge of annoyance. It should be Halicar who was seeking her out, not the reverse. She certainly shouldn't be wandering around the gardens like this, and so near his quarters.

Elyssa thought: *And why shouldn't I? It's my palace, and I'll do what I want to in it.* And then she thought: *Mereth will be there, anyway. It will only be awkward.*

Oddly, that broke her hesitation. She took a deep breath and made her way down the dozen shallow steps to the level of the Promenade. Now she could see into the porch. No one was there, though a triple-wicked lamp burned on a bronze tripod. The door to the palace interior, and to the suite of rooms she had assigned to Mereth and Halicar, was closed. Some careless slave must have left the lamp alight. It was a minor infraction, but she would have the light-steward spoken to.

With a faint whisper of sandals on stone, she moved across the paving. The still night air was heavy with the languorous scent of dusk roses, and the spicier perfumes of lamp-flowers and goldenfoam. These were the fragrances of spring's last bloom; soon the fierce summer heat would fall upon the city, and the well-off among its citizens would depart for the cooler airs of their country estates. Elyssa was no exception; every year she moved herself and the core of her household to the sea breezes of her summer villa, some ten miles along the coast from Dymie. In a few days she would be gone.

And who else would be gone from the palace, but not with her?

Elyssa felt the now-familiar wind of fear and grief blow through her, as if she were some ruined house, hollow and roofless. Along with this came bitter mortification that she could have been so wrong about Halicar. Not about what she felt for him, but about his feelings for her. Only she knew of her self-inflicted humiliation, but even so the ignominy of it was enough to make her grind her teeth.

Had it really been almost a month since that night in the

aviary, when she was so certain that he loved her? Yes, and it felt even longer than that. Almost a month, and nothing had happened between them. And nothing *would* happen, naturally enough, because she'd imagined it all. Only that could explain why he'd said nothing, done nothing, made no gesture to show that he cared for her.

But how could she have been so mistaken? She'd looked deep into him that night, and she'd been *sure*. Was it some illusion riding in the wake of her vision of the winged serpent? She still didn't understand that, either.

A few yards away, the lamp flickered gently in the porch. Elyssa stood perfectly still in the darkness, staring at it. There was no point in going on—she might as well return to her apartments, go to bed, and try to sleep. Sleep would not come, of course, until dawn whitened the sky. It never did, these days. Her mirror of silvered bronze told her that faint bluish smudges, like leaf smoke, had appeared under her eyes.

She struggled to summon a little hope. Perhaps, just perhaps, Halicar did care for her, but dared not speak. Probably she was being foolish to think he might. Antecessor bards ranked high even in the noble households of the Rasenna, but she was the Protectress. No sensible man in Halicar's position would declare his love without knowing if it would be returned. If it weren't, he'd be guilty of appalling presumption. He would be instantly dismissed, with considerable damage to his professional reputation.

But how could he *not* know how she felt about him? Hadn't her looks, her tone, her words, been signal enough? She knew her entire demeanor softened when she was with him; hadn't he noticed it? Why couldn't he see past Elyssa the Protectress and perceive Elyssa, the woman?

Resentment welled within her, bitter and hot. She was in an impossible situation. If he didn't love her, his disinterest was an endless excruciation. If he did, then his silence betrayed an utter lack of perception about her feelings. Such blindness seemed almost willful—did he *want* to hurt her? Or did he want her to speak first? But how could she expect her to do that, if he gave her no encouragement? It was horribly cruel of him.

The best thing she could do was send him away. People would talk behind her back if she did, but what of it? She was the Protectress, and they wouldn't dare say anything to her face.

And sending him away now, before anything could happen between them, was the expedient thing to do—expedient and preferable, for both their sakes. An affair between them would cause nothing but trouble; Halicar was an outlander, she was the Protectress, and there would be fury among her nobles that she'd chosen him as a lover rather than one of them. The political consequences of this were incalculable, but certain to be troublesome. It would inevitably end in tears.

But I'll miss his music so—

It wasn't the end yet, but the tears were already at her eyelids. Elyssa bit fiercely down on her nether lip and blinked them away. Why in the Lady's name had she come here tonight? What was she going to achieve, apart from making a fool of herself?

She was about to turn on her heel and go when he stepped from behind the far column of the porch. Her heartbeat tripped over itself, and she blurted, "Halicar?"

He gave a low exclamation of surprise, and Elyssa realized he hadn't known she was nearby. She came farther into the lamplight and somehow kept her voice steady as she said, "I'm sorry. I didn't mean to startle you."

"Protectress." He made his usual graceful obeisance, and she realized suddenly how much it pained her, for the gesture expressed all that separated them.

Halicar straightened, and said, "I was looking at the stars. I've always imagined they're brighter here on Haidra than they are on the mainland."

She stopped some two paces away from him. Her hands were trembling, and she clasped them in front of her. Though the night was windless and mild, and she'd been warm enough on setting out, she now felt cold and shivery.

"Are they really, do you think?" Elyssa answered, and cursed herself for her witless response. "Brighter, I mean?"

"I think perhaps they are." He sounded very composed,

almost indifferent. He had turned toward her, and the lamp-light now lay softly on his face, but she could not read his expression. She knew, however, that he would be wondering why she was there. So was she.

"I haven't been on the Promenade for a while," she said desperately. "Are your quarters and Mereth's proving adequate?"

"Yes, Protectress. They're excellent."

"And the domestics? They're performing their duties as they should?"

"Faultlessly, my lady."

"Is Mereth inside?"

"She's gone to bed, Protectress. We were composing today, and it's tiring. But if you want music—"

"No, no, not at all," she stammered. This was ludicrous. She, who was never at a loss for words, could barely put words together. She was acting like an imbecile. First she wafted out of the dark like an unquiet ghost, then began asking these idiotic questions. Halicar must believe she'd taken leave of her wits; indeed, she thought his voice had become a trifle uneasy, as if he wondered why she was babbling so foolishly.

"I don't usually wander the palace grounds at night," she said in a rush. "I was restless . . . sometimes I can't sleep. Just lately."

"I'm sorry to hear it." He sounded concerned now, but as a friend would be; or, perhaps, as a faithful servant would be. "Is there anything I can do to ease your mind?"

She had no trouble thinking of several things, but she could speak of none of them. Her earlier chill had vanished, and now her skin felt hot, almost feverish. Her temples throbbed.

"Your music does all it can," she said. "As for the rest, I think it comes with . . . with being who I am."

"The weight of rule isn't a light one," he observed quietly. "I wouldn't want to bear it."

Vexation stabbed at her; he had misunderstood her again. "I have no regrets about being Protectress," she said, and was appalled at the sharpness of her voice. Moderating it, she added, "I was trained to rule. I do it well, and it satisfies me. I keep the wolves away from my flock, as the Green Lady wants me to. There are worse ways to spend one's life, Halicar."

He had stiffened at her tone, and even when she softened it she knew she'd put him on his guard. Why, oh why had she reminded him so pointedly who she was?

"I spoke from ignorance," he said. "I ask your pardon if I've offended you."

"It's no matter," she replied, trying to sound light. "It's an old refrain, and most people believe it. It may be true of other rulers, but it's not true of me. Did you really think I was oppressed by my station?"

"I didn't think so, when Mereth and I first entered your service. But—"

His silence continued, so Elyssa said, "Go on." Out to sea, beyond the mouth of Monument Bay, a tiny yellow light showed where a lone ship rode the night waves. She wondered for a moment where it had come from and where it was going, so solitary in the darkness.

"You've seemed troubled this last month," he said. "I wondered if it was—" he hesitated again, but then continued, "if it was what happened at Rumach Hold."

"No," she answered. She'd made her peace now with Aratu's ghost, or hoped she had. At least the Lady had sent no nightmares about his sacrifice, so she must approve of what Elyssa had done. "It isn't that. Not at all. It's a . . . it's a restlessness."

"Ah. I'm afflicted with that, myself. I've never been able to stay in one place for a long time. After a while, I chafe. Eventually, as my people put it, I go to look for the other side of the mountain. Mereth has the same wanderlust, though not as much as I do."

With false lightness, Elyssa said, "And do you have it now? I hope not."

"Ah, I'm going to disappoint you." His voice was flat. "I regret I must admit it's been troubling me lately."

Elyssa noticed suddenly that he'd dropped her honorifics. There was less of *my lady* and *Protectress*. But that small comfort was washed away in a cold breaker of foreboding. She said, with numb lips:

"Do you mean by this that you're planning to leave my service?"

Halicar bowed his head; she couldn't see his face. The fragrance of the dusk roses stole along the night air. She knew that the scent would forever remind her of this moment of desolation and loss.

"I haven't put it to Mereth," he muttered. "But I think it may come to that. With your permission."

"Which you know I can't refuse. Can I?"

He said nothing. Suddenly and uncontrollably, her frustration and grief swelled like a boil, burst into speech. "Why is it," she hissed, "that you must so suddenly leave, even though you've been here for so little time? Is it really wanderlust that sends you away, Halicar?" Her fists clenched till her fingers hurt; she was shaking uncontrollably. For an instant she tried to hold her tongue, but then she failed, and her anger poured molten from her mouth. "Or has my brother made you a better offer? He's had no Antecessor singer since Matunas died, and he only wants the best, and you and Mereth are the best, and you know it. Are you off to Kanesh in the morning, then, Halicar? To sing for my rich and powerful brother? To escape from backward, contemptible Dymie and its petulant, sullen Protectress? Is that what you're going to do?"

Her voice died away. Halicar still didn't look at her, but his stance was rigid. In the night's stillness Elyssa heard her breath flying through her nostrils, ragged and fast. She wondered, despairingly, what she had done. But she could not, would not, disavow a word she'd said. He had hurt her too much. This was the last thing she had expected: that *he* might decide to leave *her*.

You told yourself you were going to send him away. So send him.

"You needn't answer," she said, seeing the brink of the cataract approach, but utterly powerless to keep herself from being swept over it. "You have my permission to leave Dymie. You may go tomorrow. I do not wish to see you again. Or Mereth."

.

He still didn't speak, only stared across the black sea.
Elyssa saw there the far-off ship's lantern, a frail spark in the
ocean of night, and it seemed to her that the world was being
devoured by darkness. She thought: *Oh, tell me you can't go.
Tell me how things might be between us. Tell me you love me.*

Halicar said, "It will be as the Protectress wishes. We will
be gone by midday."

His voice was expressionless. She knew now that she had
slid over the cataract's brink, and that beneath her lay a
lightless whirlpool where she would drown forever. How
had this happened so quickly, happened with so little warning, like a palace shaken down by a shudder in the Earth?
How had it happened at all, when it needn't have?

Her lips seemed frozen, but she spoke with them, somehow.

"Very well. See Nenattu to render your account. He is to
be generous. Tell him I said so."

He inclined his head. "Yes, Protectress."

Turning on her heel was like cutting her heart from her
breast, but Elyssa did not know what she would do or say if
she stayed near him. She set off into the darkness toward the
stairs to the South Arcade, a howl of anguish at her lips but
still unvoiced. If only she could reach her apartments before
it escaped, throw herself on her empty bed, bury her face in
her arms to muffle her grief. There, where she was safe from
him, she could weep and sob and wail.

The bottom of the steps was before her. What was he
doing? Was he watching her go? She dared not turn to see.
Her breath would hardly come; she was suffocating. And
silently, she had begun to cry.

She put her sandal on the first step. Up. The weight of
mountains dragged at her feet. The second step now. Up
again. Tears blinded her.

*I'm leaving him I'll never see him again I've sent him
away.*

You fool.

Her sandal caught on the third step, and Elyssa pitched
forward. She threw her hands up to break her fall and her
palms slammed into stone; pain shot through her wrists,

and the edge of a step banged hard into her ribs. Gasping for breath she lay across the stair, tears running down her cheeks and gathering hot at the corners of her mouth. They tasted salt as blood.

"Protectress!" A rush of hurrying feet and suddenly he was kneeling at her side. He'd watched her leave, after all. And his voice astonished her; it was wild, almost panicked. "My lady, Elyssa, Elyssa, are you hurt?"

She tried to get her breath back, found barely enough. "Don't go," she blurted. Her pride had deserted her, left her groveling, but she didn't care, she would do anything to keep him. "I didn't mean it, Halicar. Don't leave. Please, oh, please, don't leave."

"I won't," he said. "I won't. I can't. It would kill me."

"It would?" she asked stupidly, incredulously. The distant lamplight brushed his face with dim gold, and suddenly she realized he was grasping her arm as he helped her sit up. He had never touched her before, and it took away the breath she'd just regained.

"Yes." He was kneeling on the stone now; he looked down at his hand holding her arm and snatched it away. Then he slid from his kneeling position to sit on the step, and dug his fingers into his dark hair as if he would pull it out by the roots. "It's driving me mad. All the time so near you. Knowing it's hopeless." She heard him take a deep, shuddering breath. "I can't leave, and I can't bear to stay. I'm half-demented. Mereth's afraid I'm sick." He laughed, low and bitter. "She's right, I am. Lovesick."

Stunned, Elyssa could only stare at him. Halicar stared back, then put his head in his hands. "I should have held my tongue," he muttered. "But I've got nothing to lose now, so tell me—I've insolently presumed to love you. Is that why you're sending me away? Because you've realized it, and it offends you?"

"No," she said with a dry mouth. This moment, spanning no more than a few heartbeats, was transforming her life. "No, it isn't. I wanted you to leave for the same reason you wanted to go. Because of being so close, and not knowing. And not daring to ask."

Even in the dim light she saw the astonishment in his face. "Is it true, then?" he almost stammered. She'd never seen him so out of poise. "You really—"

"Yes. I really. Love you. Yes." Elyssa discovered that she was weeping again. Her left palm stung where she had scraped it in falling, and her ribs hurt from hitting the steps. She was beside herself with joy.

She reached out, and Halicar put his arms around her. His strong back was under her hands, his broad shoulders, his narrow waist. Never would she have enough of him. He said nothing, only held her, and after a little while she stopped crying. His tunic felt damp under her cheek.

"I've wept all over you," she murmured, lifting her head from his chest.

"I hope," he answered, "that it wasn't from sadness."

"You know it wasn't. It's from being happy."

He squeezed her shoulders. "I'm dreaming, aren't I, Elyssa? I love you, and I'm dreaming this because of it. You're not really here at all."

Elyssa put her face up to his and kissed him open-mouthed. After some while she took her lips from his, and whispered, "Do you still think I'm a dream?"

"Not now," he said huskily. "I think you're very definitely real. Ah, I'm thoughtless—did you hurt yourself when you fell?"

"Not much. I scraped my hand a little." She laughed. "For some reason I don't seem to feel it much now." Borne on a waft of the night air, the scent of goldenfoam came to her. They kissed again for a long time. Eventually, breathing fast, they drew apart a little, and Elyssa took his hands in hers. "We have so much to talk about," she murmured. "Come and walk with me in the upper gardens. They're beautiful in starlight—the lamp-flowers are like the stars themselves."

He hesitated, and said, "Your domestics may see us."

"Let them. Tongues will wag in Dymie soon, and some people will grumble at our being together, but they can be ignored. Anyway, on Haidra there's nothing unusual about a noblewoman, or any woman, having a lover." She hesitated.

"But there will never be a marriage. You must understand that, Halicar. I would marry you if I could, but I can't."

"I know. This will be enough."

She rose to her feet. "Come with me to the garden."

Arm in arm, they climbed the stairs. Above, among the night blooms of the dusk roses and the lamp-flowers' pale sparks, they talked of their pasts: Halicar of his harsh mountain glens, of blizzards and sunlit snow, of barbarian kings and the music of their courts; Elyssa of growing up in her father's palace in Kanesh, of Haidra's white towns and Velchi's steaming sapphire and emerald lakes, of the Lady's autumn festivals. All this they spoke of until the night grew old and the first light stole into the east and then, as the Dawn Star rose, they at last found their way to Halicar's bed, and became lovers.

13

By the time the Rasennan month of Last Summer came, Theatana was much in Vindisi's debt. She had, of course, no intention of repaying it.

On the sixth day of the new month, on horseback as usual and with a single guard as escort, she went again to his holding. Vindisi's two-room log shanty and his thatched, ramshackle stables were an hour's ride from Kla; he lived up on the thickly wooded ridge she could see from her bedroom window, the green finger that jutted from the inland forests toward the city.

She always went alone except for the guard, whose name was Chatal. Rasennan women were far less sequestered than those of the Hazannu, so Alfni hadn't objected greatly to the time she spent in Vindisi's company, learning his healing skills. What he did object to was her apparent interest in horse doctoring; it was, he said, a craft unworthy of anyone of high rank, man or woman. His other retainers would not demean themselves with such an occupation, so why should she?

But by now Theatana had perfected her control of him. She'd done this so subtly and so skillfully that by the time he'd realized what was happening, it was already too late for him to resist. Now he covertly feared her, but was so firmly in her grip that he could refuse her nothing, though he might—as with the horse doctoring—go through the motions of exerting his authority.

So, for two days, she had alternated sweet persuasion with cold noncooperation in bed and elsewhere. Alfni's po-

194

tency began to leave him; once he raised his fist to strike her, but she gazed silently at him, and his arm fell to his side. The palace slaves walked very carefully in his presence, and gossiped in whispers on the back stairways.

Shortly thereafter, Alfni discovered that he had changed his mind, and Theatana became the horse doctor's apprentice. On learning this, Alfni's other retainers sent her sidelong looks of disapproval, or grinned openly at her female caprices. She noted their behavior for later reference, then ignored them.

They'd laugh from the other side of their mouths, she thought as she and Chatal reached the foot of the track that led to Vindisi's holding, *if they knew what I was really learning.*

"Wait here for me," she told Chatal. He was a very junior member of the palace staff, little more than a stable hand though he wore a short sword and carried a small round shield of boiled leather. Twenty years her junior and awed by her foreignness, he gave her no trouble at all.

"Yes, mistress," he answered. He hadn't dared object, the first time she made him remain here instead of going up to Vindisi's with her, and now it was habit. He'd doze the day away under a tree until she came down again.

She gave him a brilliant smile. "You're a fine strong soldier," she said. "I feel very safe when I'm with you."

Chatal flushed scarlet and stared down at the packed dirt of the road. "Thank you, mistress. I'll be here when you need me. As always," he added with a crude attempt at gallantry.

"Yes," she answered. She reined her horse around and started up the track that led to Vindisi's holding. The track was steep, winding among rough ledges and stony outcrops, but her mare was surefooted and by now had learned the ground. Trees closed around her as she climbed toward the crest of the ridge: barrel-cypress, camphorwood, long-leafed weeping mylax, goldenrain, silver oak. Their shade was welcome after the heat of the morning sun.

At the top of the track was the narrow clearing that contained Vindisi's shanty and his stables. The logs had been roughly peeled of their bark, and had weathered to a silvery gray. Though the buildings had a ramshackle air to them, their thatch was new and in good condition. Discreet talismans hung at the shanty's door and at its single, horn-paned window; unlike most charms Theatana had seen in Kla and its domains, these were not charlatans' shams but real devices of protection against hostile spells.

She dismounted, tethered her mare to a post outside the stable, and called, "Vindisi! Show yourself!"

A few moments passed. Then he appeared at the stable doorway in his shapeless farmer's smock, wiping his hands on a twist of old straw. He was more gaunt than ever and his blue-green eyes seemed haunted. He dropped to his knees, said, "My lady," and waited.

She motioned him to rise. As he obeyed, she said, "Is he here yet?"

"No, honored one. But it's still early."

"Don't call me that. It smacks too much of the Road." She eyed the straw. "What are you doing to Alfni's horse?"

"Only a rubdown, my lady. The horse is much improved."

The animal had been suffering from some intestinal ailment, and Theatana had brought it to Vindisi, promising Alfni she'd cure the beast herself. Though Vindisi was far from a master sorcerer he did know a number of working spells, some of which were benevolent and curative, as befitted his horse-doctor profession. These she had learned, along with many of his mundane ways of healing by potions and salves, as a necessary cover for her real business of learning his darker craft. Being benign and natural, the healing spells didn't require a death, and she found that working them was straightforward. However, doing so gave her strong sensations of nausea, as if she were performing an act that her inner nature found highly repulsive.

Still, the sorcerous talent she had discovered long ago in Captala was developing quickly under Vindisi's tutelage. She was sure that the presence of the Other stimulated it, for the talent seemed deeply in accord with those spells that were malign or perverse; one among them, a coercion spell of the inhuman, was quite powerful. Theatana had already practiced it once, and intended to use it in earnest today.

"Take me inside," she ordered.

He made an obeisance, then led her into the dusty, hay-smelling gloom of the stable and onward to its rear, where an adjoining shed served him as a storage place for his purges, lotions, herbs, and instruments. It was also, now, a place of sorcery. A narrow window admitted a warm breeze and a bar of hot sunlight.

"I need to strengthen the aspect spell," she told him. "But I want the one for coercion ready to hand. Did you find a death suitable for bringing it about?"

"Yes, my lady," Vindisi answered, gesturing. "I found a very strong death. It's over there."

"Ah," Theatana answered. She saw a cage of fine bronze wire in the shadows by the log wall. Moving closer, she peered through the mesh. In the cage was a slim, iridescent russet snake with a speckled head; stretched to full length, it would be no longer than the length of her forearm and out-stretched hand. She had never seen one before.

"I expected something more impressive," she said, a little disappointed. "What is it?"

"A coppercoil. It's also called the three-pace snake. If it bites you, you die before you can walk three paces. Its nature makes it a very potent death for sorcery. Your control will be powerful."

Theatana scrutinized the creature with increased respect. "Ah. How must I do the killing?" In her earlier practice of the coercion spell, the sacrifice was a carrion hawk that Vindisi had snared. The hawk was a vigorous and vicious crea-ture but not lethal.

"Very carefully. Pin it, crush its throat, and make sure the back is broken. The other thing you need is there, also. I've already prepared it."

She'd already seen the peeled branch, a pale mylax wand on the earthen floor by the cage. "Good. And for the aspect spell?"

"I trapped a stable rat."

"Let's get on with that one, then."

Vindisi set the wards about the shed, so that no emanations of the sorcerous activity within would escape. Theatana thought it extremely unlikely that anyone spied on him for evidence that he was a Walker, but she approved of his caution. Given his secret craft, she'd hoped he would own spells to control specters of the dead, such as the wraith Theatana had raised when she killed the slave woman Rehua. But she'd discovered, to her annoyance, that such powers were beyond the boundaries of Vindisi's personal Road.

Just as disappointing was the horse doctor's lack of esoteric knowledge about the reputedly sorcerous mask on Haidra and its maker the Giftbearer; he knew no more about them than Alfni did. When she eventually reached the island, Theatana had concluded, she would have to investigate the ancient artifact for herself.

As Vindisi finished setting the wards, she opened the tiny bag she had brought. It was of finest leather, thin as a moth's wing. "Hair, nail clippings, phlegm," she said. "The last was very difficult to get without him noticing. You're sure it will give me his voice?"

"As sure as I can be, mistress. That is, if it came from his throat and lungs, as breath and voice dơ."

"It did. Show me the method."

Vindisi took the bag, put it into a mortar, and ground it into a pulp with other ingredients, all of which Theatana memorized. In the lost days of her youth she'd used an aspect spell to make her look like her serving maid; this was a different approach, and its results were clumsier, but it worked. She'd already succeeded in wearing Alfni's appearance with it, though she lacked his voice. This next step would perfect the illusion.

"Do you need the spell-scroll?" she said as he neared the end of the grinding. Vindisi kept this ancient and priceless instrument of sorcery hidden in the stable, but he'd willingly revealed its location to her on the first day she came to him as a student. Like Alfni he could refuse her nothing, though for a different reason: She was, in his parlance and belief, a hand of the Poisoner. He had been fearful of her even to begin with, and the ease with which she was unmasking her talent for Walking made him even more frightened. He believed this gift to be wholly her own, knowing of but not understanding the presence of the Other within her.

"No," he answered, "I've fixed the syllables in my mind and tongue. But remember, my lady, you must imitate me exactly. If your phrasing is wrong, it will either fail or go unpleasantly awry."

"You've told me that, time and again," she answered irritably. "Why must you keep repeating it?"

"One can never be too careful, my lady. Acquiring spells by imitation is not the best way of proceeding. But we have no other."

This was true, since Theatana couldn't decipher the spell-scroll for herself. Learning to read or write the Rasennan language was excruciatingly difficult, and few people except scribes, priests, priestesses, and a sprinkling of the high nobility were literate. Vindisi had once been a priest of the Firebringer, but the Road had called him more powerfully than the God.

"I'll be careful," she said, banishing her annoyance. Walking the Road with an unsettled mind was unwise and unsafe. "Are you ready?"

He was. They were about to begin the aspect spell when a voice outside called, "Vindisi!"

"He's here," she said. "Will that mess still serve if it has to wait?"

"Yes, my lady. It will stay potent even when it dries. We can do this next time you come, if necessary."

"Good. Bring the coppercoil and the mylax and come with me."

They went through the stable and out into the bright midmorning of the clearing. Rimash Idu, wearing a belted green tunic and carrying a hunting bow and a quiver of arrows, was standing at the tree line a dozen yards away. The Idu clan-lord was a stocky man of some forty years, bearded like many mainland Rasenna males, with big clumsy hands and a supercilious air; he was, in Theatana's estimation, not overly intelligent. For secrecy's sake he'd climbed up the back of the ridge, on foot, and was red-faced, sweating, and plainly not in a good temper.

"My lord Rimash," Theatana said pleasantly, "how good of you to come."

He scowled at her. "Yes. How good of you to be here."

Theatana smiled at him. Rimash had been an easy mark to hit; he felt he had a better claim on the Protectorship than did Alfni's nephew Kayonu and nursed a bitter grudge that Alfni had disregarded this and made Kayonu his heir. Alfni, for his part, did not want an open breach with the powerful Idu clan, and attempted to heal the breach by frequently inviting Rimash to entertainments at the palace. The clan-lord always accepted, and during these occasions he did his best to undermine Kayonu's position by a combination of fawning and innuendo.

This was fertile soil, and Theatana had sowed it. She began attending the banquet hall for the evening meal, and when Rimash was there she spoke warmly with him. Little by little she intimated that Alfni was not to her taste, and that she believed that Rimash had been denied his birthright, and that she was sympathetic to his cause. For camouflage, she told Alfni she was sounding out the clan-lord for thoughts of betrayal, and reported Rimash to be no serious threat.

Alfni believed her. So did Rimash, and a month ago he'd suggested that if he were Protector, she could stand as Protectress beside him. It was a lie, for no Idu would marry outside the Rasenna blood, and Rimash in addition was devoted to the Hazannu God, who forbade women to rule. Theatana affected to believe him anyway, and displayed enthusiasm. Rimash, puffed up by his success at subverting the Protector's mistress, then proposed that she join him and his two brothers, along with a cousin, in overthrowing Alfni. He and they, Rimash whispered, were already working toward this end. Theatana, having got exactly what she wanted, agreed.

At that time the schemes of the Idu conspirators were amateurish and vague, but with Theatana directing them through Rimash, they began to plot in earnest. The brothers and the nephews didn't know of her involvement; she'd made Rimash agree to this as a condition of her joining them. Since then, she and the clan-lord had been meeting secretly at Vindisi's to carry their planning forward.

Lately, however, Rimash had begun to chafe at her authority. And today, she saw from his tone and stance, he was going to exert his mastery over her. She had been expecting this rebellion and was not surprised.

"Didn't you bring a waterskin?" she asked solicitously, as he wiped sweat from his broad flat forehead. "You look heated."

"There's more than one kind of heat," he said, and ran his gaze up and down her body. How predictable he was; she could see into him like a cup of clear water. He had decided to exert his dominance, and imagined that once he'd done that he could lie with her. He'd been hungry for her since they first met.

Oh, you'll get your belly full of me today, she thought. *But it won't be the meal you expected.*

"Indeed," she said. She turned to Vindisi, and murmured, "Put the coppercoil and the wand down and bring water for the clan-lord. Then leave us."

Vindisi obeyed. As he vanished around the corner of the stable Rimash stared down at the caged snake. "What's the herbalist doing with that? Those things are deadly."

"It's a tool," she said.

"You're thinking of poison, then," he observed. "Well, that's one way to deal with the old man. If the timing's right." He scowled again, and said in an undertone, "That horse doctor still troubles me. What makes you so sure he'll keep silent about us coming here?"

Theatana sighed. "For the hundredth time, you pay him well. And as I've also told you, I have certain sorceries at my disposal. He fears me."

"Hm, yes. Sorcery." Rimash slipped the hunting bow from his shoulder and leaned on it. "Lately there's been talk you've bewitched Alfni. Have you?"

Theatana shrugged. "Talk is wind. Judge for yourself." She'd been very careful to prevent Rimash from finding out that she was learning her sorcery from Vindisi; to dominate the clan-lord, she needed him to believe that she was already an adept. Vindisi feared her far too much to reveal the truth, so Rimash blithely imagined that the horse doctor's only purpose was to provide a safe haven for their meetings.

"One day, Theatana," he said, "you'll have to demonstrate this northern magic for me. You speak of it, but I never witness it."

"All in good time. Ah, refreshment for you."

Vindisi had arrived with water in a jug. He gave it to Rimash and went away. Rimash drank thirstily, guzzling, then dashed the last of the water over his face and tossed the jug to the grass. "So you'll poison him?"

Theatana crossed her arms under her breasts. "You run too swiftly. The problem remains of insufficient armed force on our side. Fortunately, I have a solution to it."

He bared his teeth. "Yes?"

"I know you can read a little. Do you write at all?"

"What for? I have household scribes."

"Very well. This is my plan. I will have Vindisi compose a letter at my dictation. You will put it under your seal, and then you will send one of your brothers secretly to Kanesh with it. He will give the letter to the Protector Tirsun."

Grasshoppers buzzed in the morning heat as Rimash goggled at her. Theatana's fingers twitched.

"Kanesh?" the clan-lord said in a strangled voice. "What's Tirsun got to do with this?"

"A great deal," Theatana told him calmly. "Tirsun has soldiers and ships, and plenty of them. The letter will invite him to lead a force here to help you secure your legitimate Protectorship. In return, you will offer him an alliance between Kla and Kanesh. Your relatives will agree to this arrangement if you propose it—they have no minds of their own, as you very well know." She paused, then went on, "Your brother will then request a written answer from Tirsun, under seal, and return to Kla with it. You yourself will bring it to me, still sealed, and I will let you know what the Protector said."

Rimash was turning scarlet. "Are you crazed with the heat, to suggest bringing Tirsun and his men into Kla? That's no alliance except in name—Tirsun would leave a Kaneshite garrison behind when he sailed home, and I'd rule on his sufferance." He began to sputter. "And who do you think you are, woman, to give me such orders, or any orders at all? The God doesn't like it, and neither do I. I've let you get away with it for too long, and now it has to stop."

"Nevertheless," Theatana told him, "you'll do as I've said. It's the only way we can succeed."

"Never. You're an insolent slut, and I'm tired of your speaking above your station."

"Rimash," she said in a cold voice, "you must obey me, or suffer the consequences."

"Consequences? You make me wonder if I even need you. I wonder if you're really my ally. Or are you perhaps an enemy? I think I'd better find out." Flushed with anger and rising lust, he took a step toward her. "Come into the stable with me, woman, and we'll find a pile of hay. We'll lie down on it together and you can persuade me you're my friend, after all."

Theatana didn't answer. She dropped to one knee and picked up the mylax wand in her left hand. With her right she undid the bronze hook that secured the top of the snake's cage. She flipped the cage open. Within, the coppercoil twined slowly about itself, like living metal.

Rimash had taken another pace toward her but now he stopped short. "What are you doing, you fool? That's a coppercoil. Do you want to die writhing?"

Perhaps she should be frightened of what she had to do, but she wasn't. The snake's head was a blunt bronze triangle with silver eyes. It raised itself a span from the cage floor.

Theatana's hand shot out and seized it just behind the head.

Rimash exclaimed in astonishment and stepped backward. Theatana rose to her feet and the coppercoil wrapped itself in a spiral around her forearm.

"Rimash," she said, "I will give you only this one warning."

He gaped at her, speechless. Theatana raised her arms, holding wand and snake to the sky, and gazed past the clan-lord into the forest's gloom. Then she brought her ferocious will to a needle's point and began the syllables of Vindisi's most powerful spell: the coercion of the inhuman. Rimash listened, eyes stunned and staring, and his face turned slowly from scarlet to white.

She ended the summoning incantation at the death instant, and crushed the coppercoil's delicate throat between finger and thumb. The snake flailed, unwinding from her arm, and she snapped it like a whip; broken in neck and spine, it died. Its death whispered through her, through her fingers, her hands, passed through the wand, became a summons. Rimash looked wildly around the clearing, as if he sensed the unknown creeping toward him. Theatana lowered her arms, the coppercoil dripping molten from her fingers.

Several moments passed. A misty shape began to condense from the air near a silver oak at the wood's edge. Its outlines clarified; shadowy details appeared in the luminosity, though the creature remained translucent. In form it was most like an unclad woman with flowing hair, though no mortal woman's face had ever held such a chilling beauty. The eyes were open but were not human eyes; points of light wandered in them like distant stars. It was a wood sprite, of the kind called in the Ascendancy an alsea, and by the Rasenna an innedota. Rimash, staring at Theatana in gaping disbelief, was as yet unaware of its presence.

"You have a visitor, clan-lord," she told him.

He turned and saw the alsea. He went whiter still and began to back away from the apparition, but slowly, as if a bog mired his feet. His lips writhed, but no sound came from them.

Theatana could sense the alsea's emotive aspect. It was angry at being wakened and at being under compulsion. Drawing more syllables from the spell, she instructed it to approach Rimash. Exuding outrage at this violation of its nature, it did so. Rimash stumbled backward over his own feet and sat down heavily. Sweat poured from him. He had good reason to be afraid; a sprite's presence was deeply disturbing to humans, and if it touched him, he would flop and shriek with mindless terror. Some victims never regained their wits after such an encounter, and the clan-lord might spend the rest of his life in restraints, giggling and weeping, his hands manacled lest they creep to his face and gouge his eyes out.

"Would you like her to embrace you, Rimash?" Theatana asked softly. "She's very beautiful. Perhaps she'll join you on your pile of hay. You could lie with her all today and all night. But I don't know if you'd be much use to anyone in the morning."

He could barely speak but he managed a croak that sounded like "*No!*"

"In that case," Theatana said, "you'll send your brother to Tirsun as I instructed. If you disobey me, you'll wake up some night with one of these ladies in bed beside you." This would be very difficult for her to contrive, since the spell would hold a sprite only for the turn of an hourglass, but Rimash couldn't know that.

"Yes," he squealed. "Yes. I'll do it. I'll do it."

She spoke the word of dismissal. The sprite turned black eye pits on her, and what perhaps was a mouth opened wide in silent, inhuman fury. Then the form drifted into the woods and dissolved into nothingness.

Theatana tossed the coppercoil and the oak wand onto the grass; both were dead husks now, and powerless. She herself felt drained and weary, the aftereffects of working a potent spell. But the sensations would pass.

Rimash emitted a noise like a sob, and she looked down at him. His green tunic showed a dark, spreading stain; the clan-lord had lost control of his bladder.

"You wanted to see my sorcery, Rimash," she said. "Are you happy now?"

14

Evening was drawing on, and the firebringer's disk glowed scarlet on the western horizon. In the blue marble pavilion on the Citadel Stone's highest terrace, Ilarion waited with his silver wine jug by Tirsun's chair and watched the dozen young aristocrats gathered around the banquet tables. The evening breeze was delicate as a child's kiss, for the long Haidran autumn had arrived, its soft warmth at last replacing the dying glare of summer. Four months had passed since Ilarion had stood at the gibbet's foot and waited to die. Now his only physical discomfort was the mild ache of the bruise along his left ribs, and even that was fading.

Tirsun was listening to one of his guests compose a twelve-syllable ode to the rains of autumn, in which these were subtly differentiated from the rains of spring. The man finished to a spatter of applause, in which the Protector joined; then Tirsun drained his cup and set it down on the small round table next to his couch. Ilarion instantly stepped forward to refill the carved goblet. The wine ran dark crimson into the cup's white alabaster, swirled, and found its level. Ilarion stepped back.

He was as invisible as all slaves or servants were, unless he performed his duties incorrectly. He was particularly careful not to err this evening, because Tirsun was drinking more heavily than usual. Fortunately, Ilarion had only to fill the Protector's cup, for half a dozen female slaves attended to the guests. These women were exquisite, their red-gold hair shining in the lamplight like spun copper and their eyes the azure of the afternoon sky. Despite their loveliness, however, they were safe from molestation by the banqueters, for only the Protector had free use of the palace women. Guests who so much as touched one incurred his severe displeasure and were never again invited to the palace. This threat alone made them keep their hands to themselves.

As for the slaves themselves, carnal relations among them were forbidden; Tirsun considered it misuse of his personal property. Discovery in the act meant gelding and hanging for the man and beheading for the woman. This punishment applied also to any guardsman who embroiled himself with one of Tirsun's female possessions. It was no idle threat, either; the Protector had executed a pair of lovers shortly after Ilarion came to the palace. Still, as long as they did not attract Tirsun's annoyance or displease Entash the Grand Domestic, the palace slaves were not treated badly. They had enough to eat, they did not wear rags, and most worked no harder than a free peasant on an upland farm in the Protectorate of Kanesh—which was to say, very hard indeed.

Ilarion did not labor to that pitch, at least not physically. Soon after he arrived in the palace, Entash caught the official Wine Bearer drunk in the cellars; the man was scourged and sent to field labor. After some deliberation, Tirsun moved Ilarion into the post. This made him responsible for the upkeep of the Protector's personal wine cellar and for ensuring that Tirsun's table was always supplied with the appropriate vintages. The work kept him near the Protector almost all the time, for it included tasting food and drink for poison. His status was marked by having his own cubicle near the Protector's apartments, rather than a pallet in one of the palace's service corridors. The latter was the lot of most of the two hundred palace slaves, although a minority worked and lived in the Upper Palace, where most of the tasks were light and revolved around Tirsun's daily routines. The others toiled in the Lower Palace, in the kitchens and laundries and in the workshops that made the furniture, harness, cloth, pottery, tools and utensils needed to keep the palace running.

Ilarion's second duty was to serve Tirsun as a living li-

brary of foreign geography and exotic customs. Lack of curiosity about the world was not one of the Protector's flaws,
and Ilarion's accounts of the distant north fascinated him.
Magic was one interest, but on accepting Ilarion's claim to
know little of it——which was true——Tirsun contented himself with more mundane inquiries. But despite the Protector's inquisitiveness about such things as agriculture, trade,
music, literature, and the erotic practices of Ascendancy
courtesans, it soon became clear that his deepest interest was
in how the Ascendancy's armies and fleets waged war.

Ilarion had already lied to Tirsun by minimizing the military strength of the Ascendancy, and dared not change his
story. This lie had become a trap when Tirsun began questioning him on military matters, for it was all too easy for
Ilarion to let slip a true measure of the Ascendancy's
strength. He had done so twice, and feigned that unfamiliar-
ity with Rasennan methods of reckoning had caused his er-
rors. But he knew that if Tirsun found him out in his lies, the
consequences might be lethal. He was not indeed sure that
Tirsun believed all he was told, but he did his best to keep
his numbers consistent.

He found himself driven to conceal other information as
well. He'd been astonished to discover that the Rasenna
didn't know about stirrups; their cavalry rode loose-footed
and were consequently much less formidable than they
could have been. He hadn't enlightened Tirsun about the devices, but he couldn't avoid describing certain Ascendancy
infantry tactics. Some of these, he knew, were finding their
way into the training of the Kaneshite foot levies.

As well, he'd accidentally mentioned a counterweighted
stone thrower for breaking down field fortifications. Tirsun
instantly demanded an exact description of the thrower, got
it, and within a month his shipwrights had built one. Ten
days ago Ilarion had gone with the Protector down to the
beach, where it was being tried. The shipwrights had understood the machine's principles and executed them well. Its
missiles flew accurately and knocked a stoutly built palisade
to splinters. Ilarion remembered the ensuing conversation
vividly.

"So," Tirsun had said. "A very potent device. You know of others, of course."

He had expected this and was prepared. "No, Protector. This is the only one we use. It has proven sufficient."

The Protector pursed his lips and stared thoughtfully at Ilarion. Then he said, "You wouldn't be suffering from a lapse of memory, would you?"

Ilarion's mouth dried a little. "No, my lord. If there were others, I would tell you." *Like the iron oxen, the kickers, the giants' bows, the firepot throwers, the tortoises.* The Ascendancy's siege train alone was larger than the armed forces of both Protectorates combined.

"When I speak with you," Tirsun observed in a pensive voice, "I sometimes feel that I have gone deaf in one ear. As if you were speaking plainly, but somehow you manage it so that I don't quite hear your words. Do you think that's a strange thing for me to feel?"

"I would not presume to judge the Protector's feelings," Ilarion answered, from an even drier mouth.

Tirsun laughed. "You always say something like that when I ask you a difficult question. One day I shall insist that you actually *do* presume to judge me."

Ilarion swallowed, with difficulty. "Yes, my lord."

"Should I insist today? Ah, I think not, the weather is too fine. Oh, look, they've knocked down the whole palisade now. I shall have my shipwrights build more such devices."

And so the knife-edge moment had passed. But Ilarion's web of lies would necessarily grow larger and more complicated. One day Tirsun would catch him out, and he could not predict what would happen to him then, for he saw two natures packed into the Protector of Kanesh. One was that of an able ruler, intelligent, energetic, perceptive, a lover of beauty and wit. In this manifestation he could be charming, even likable. But the other Tirsun was suspicious, brooding, violent of temper, and ingeniously sadistic, and even when he was affable and even-tempered, a sly malice lay just beneath the glaze of his charm. For some time now Ilarion had wondered uneasily whether the Protector might be playing one of his spiteful, teasing games, enjoying Ilarion's lie-spinning while contriving a suitably elaborate punishment for it.

He let his gaze flicker across the banquet tables and the guests. *Is this perhaps my last evening alive? It would be like him to make an end of me here, as an entertainment.*

He felt his fingers cramping on the handle of the massive silver wine jug, and forced them to relax. He was always in Tirsun's company, and could easily find an opportunity to kill the man; already there had been dozens. But he wouldn't outlive his victim by long, for the palace guardsmen were never far from their Protector.

Even so, Ilarion was puzzled that he hadn't yet died in a fit of Dascarid rage, with a guard's spear through his belly and Tirsun dead on the marble floor beside him. But eventually it was going to happen; every day he felt the fury's slow churn in his gut. Moreover, he'd had a warning sign, of which the bruise on his side was a reminder. A Lower Palace slave, a brawny male from the wine cellars, had taken a slow-burning dislike to him; five days ago, when Ilarion was taking wine from a storage jar, the man struck him hard in the ribs. The fury came, short-lived, but as ungovernable as ever. Ilarion had been trained to fight unarmed, and the slave had not, and he might have killed the man if other slaves hadn't pried them apart. Fortunately no overseer witnessed the incident, for brawls between slaves were punished by flogging. But nothing further came of it; Ilarion was untouched except for the bruise under his tunic, and the other slave, fearing the whip, blamed a fall down the cellar stairs for his injuries.

Tirsun had not yet touched his wine. Ilarion took the opportunity to glance out through the pavilion's graceful colonnade. The sun had drifted below the horizon, trailing long streaks of gold and crimson. Somewhere out there, beyond the Protectorate of Dymie and the far-off western tip of Haidra, was Rook's mainland city of Ushnana, and perhaps Lashgar and Rook as well.

He did not know if Rook and Lashgar were still alive or, if they were, whether they'd reached Ushnana. He did know that he had to get there somehow, for Rook was the only way

he could think of for Lashgar and himself to get home. No
ship would come from the north to seek them; even if his
and Lashgar's parents convinced themselves that their sons
had been carried off rather than drowned, they would never
guess that another civilization lay deep in the unknown
south. And even if they suspected it, no vessels existed in the
Ascendancy or the Blue Havens that could make the voyage
to Haidra.

He dragged his attention back to the banquet tables. The
kitchen slaves had now cleared away the remnants of the
meal, all the pavilion's lamps were alight, and the guests
were settling into the next phase of the banquet, the entertainment and the serious drinking.

Ilarion saw movement between the pavilion columns. Entash appeared from the terrace's dusky gardens and glided to
Tirsun's elbow.

"What?" Tirsun asked irritably, looking up at his Grand
Domestic.

Entash bent and murmured into Tirsun's ear. Tirsun listened, and his face went blank. He said, "Is that so? Well, I
will see the man responsible. Send him here."

Entash made an obeisance and slipped out of the pavilion.
Ilarion watched him go. Except for receiving occasional instructions about his work, he had little contact with the
Grand Domestic. But wise slaves found out as much as possible about those they served, and Ilarion knew that Entash
was the second most powerful man in the Protectorate after
Tirsun, because he managed the humdrum labors of its government. Tirsun preferred to ignore such matters, being
more interested in the works of painters, sculptors, and
poets, as well as the diversions provided by mimes, con-
jurors, and dancing troupes. Everything else he left to Entash's discretion.

Entash's discretion was to extract as much wealth as he
could from Tirsun's domains, then devote it first to Tirsun's
desires and then to his own enrichment. His tax assessors
were omnipresent; no peasant pressed a grape or harvested
a barley grain without a record being set down in the government accounts. Most taxes were collected in kind and

sent to Kanesh; at the foot of the Citadel Stone stood a
walled complex of storehouses stuffed with grain, oil, wine,
metals, hides, spices, scented wax, fine timber, honey, and
pitch. Silver and gold, unlike the taxes paid in goods, were
kept in a strong room in the palace itself. Some of the metal
went for coinage while the rest became ornamentation or
utensils, such as the heavy silver jug Ilarion now held.

Tirsun picked up his cup and drained its contents; Ilarion
refilled it and slipped over to the rack of wine jars to replenish the nearly empty pitcher. As he returned to his post
Tirsun looked up at him. The Protector's eyes were a little
puffy from the wine, though he was notoriously hardheaded
and would not be truly drunk for hours. He waved his hand
for silence, and when he had it he said, "I have decided that
you will contribute to our entertainment tonight, Ilarion.
Perhaps we will ask you to compose an ode to autumn, or a
formal introduction to an epic. Would you do your best to
delight us?"

The pavilion quieted a little. Ilarion said, "The Protector
knows that I have little ability for such pursuits. But I would
be pleased to make the attempt, if the Protector wishes it."

"Yes," Tirsun said, "I so wish. Unless I change my mind."

One of the guests at a far table, a man named Dinclisi, had
drunk a little too much, a little too early. "As well ask a wild
Hazannu to compose," he blurted. "Grunt, grunt, grunt."

Tirsun stared down the length of the pavilion at him. "Is
this whimsy of mine displeasing to you?" he asked in a lazy
voice.

The room fell instantly silent. The man's mouth opened
and closed twice. "Protector," he faltered at last, "of course
it's not. At all. The performance would be extremely amusing. Entertaining."

Tirsun smiled. "Perhaps. Though now the prospect takes
on a tedious aura. Don't you agree, Ilarion?"

Ilarion said lightly, "It is as the Protector says. I would no
doubt only bore him."

"Indeed," Tirsun said, and appeared to lose interest. The
murmur of conversation began again, but Dinclisi did little
to join it. He had ruined his social reputation. Though he

would not have to leave immediately, this was his last evening in the charmed circle of the Protector's friends.

Ilarion found little satisfaction in the man's fall from grace; his hands were shaking with fury. *I'm a slave,* he thought. *If I remember that, I'll live out the night. And I must. After this night I'll be free, or dead, or as good as dead.*

His hands slowly became still as hope calmed him. He must save his rage for a moment when it would serve him, and not his enemies.

My chance is almost here. I only have to control myself for a little longer.

It was the only real chance he'd had since his servitude began. Tomorrow morning, a force of twenty ships and a thousand men was to sail on a punitive expedition against a Hazannu tribe whose leader had robbed and murdered a Kaneshite merchant. Because of the expedition's size, Tirsun was to command it; the Protector was also Kanesh's pronoyar or senior general. The banquet tonight was a celebration, in advance, of the expected victory.

But Ilarion would not be going. Entash had informed him that he was to join a work gang down in the warehouses, clearing storage space for the harvest taxes. He would also sleep there with the gang. This was ominous. Tirsun had twice before left the palace without Ilarion, apparently to inspect the roads that led to the border with Dymie. But at neither time had Ilarion been assigned to the warehouse compound; he'd been put with the gardening staff. This had the odor of a demotion, and the possibility that Tirsun was tiring of him was frightening.

He had always planned to escape while Tirsun was away from Kanesh, but during the other two absences he could find no way to leave the well-guarded Citadel Stone. But getting clear of the warehouses might be possible, and with Tirsun gone the hunt might be delayed or at least less vigorous—although Haidrans pursued escaped slaves with furious resolve, and buried them alive once taken.

He had managed to concoct a plan of sorts. Tirsun had ordered the construction of an enormous, ornate lighthouse on

the harbor breakwater, to replace the beacon destroyed by
the tidal wave. About every ten days he went out in a small
sailing cutter to make sure it made a suitably grand impression when approached by sea. Often he took Ilarion along,
and Ilarion had noted certain facts about the cutter. Two
crewmen normally handled it, but one person could manage
the craft with only a little more difficulty. It was large
enough to deal with ocean swells, and it was fast. Finally,
when Tirsun was not using the boat, it lay moored at a slip
at the edge of the naval dockyards, near a guard post but not
too near. And the guard, Ilarion had noticed, was middle-
aged and lax, little more than a watchman.

He had also picked up as much information as he could
about sailing conditions around Haidra. In this month of First
Autumn the winds were variable, but from overhearing Tirsun
converse he knew that the mainland lay no more than two
days' sail to the south. If he could reach it in the cutter, he
could then work his way westward along the coast and eventually, perhaps, reach Ushnana. He would chance running into
Tirsun's fleet, because he wasn't sure where it was going, but
that was only one more risk added to a host of others.

*At least I'll be my own master again. All the risks are
worth that.*

The servingwomen were gliding among the small three-
legged banquet tables, filling goblets and setting out nuts
and honeyed sweetmeats. Each guest had a table to himself,
and a couch; reclining was a feature of Rasennan banquets,
though on ordinary occasions they sat on stools to eat.

The guests, except Dinclisi, chattered happily. All were
handsome and young, and despite their toadying to the Protector, they were literate, cultivated, and witty. During Tirsun's literary afternoons they would pass hours in poetic
games, vying with each other to construct intricate lyrics
and epigrams. At his evening banquets they ate gloriously,
drank thick Haidran wine sweetened with honey, watched
the elaborate entertainments that Tirsun loved, and later in
the evening enjoyed Kanesh's flawless courtesans. To the
casual eye they were young demigods, cushioned in beauty
and pleasure, delighting in their eternal golden afternoon.

It was illusion. Beneath their grace and accomplishment they were haughty, sensual, and cruel, and their delight in beauty often slid into a taste for the freakish, a taste that sometimes became outright perversion. No one could stop them from satisfying any such craving; with their rank and riches they could do anything they wished unless Tirsun forbade it, and he forbade very little. Ilarion had unwillingly witnessed some of their repellent entertainments—country-house gatherings, where slaves were drugged and forced to fight to the death—and now considered the Haidran nobility to be no more than a pack of golden monsters. Their depravity was constrained by a rind of elegance, like a rotting fish by its silver skin; but slit the skin or arouse their appetites, and the stinking juices trickled out.

But this evening's banquet promised to be a normal one. The poetry and then the musical entertainments would last for some time, but eventually these would end and the guards would bring in the women, pure-blooded Haidran females from the most expensive brothels of the city. It would be late before the revelry ended. The worst thing about a debauch, from a servant's viewpoint, was how tedious it finally became. To cope with such boredom Ilarion had learned the slave's trick of blanking out thought, so that the hours passed more easily. He did this now, while the lamps burned and musicians and dancers came and went. His boredom was slightly relieved when a miu, one of the small gray-and-black animals kept in the palace to catch rats and mice, wandered through the pavilion. The little creatures, with their soft dense fur, neat triangular faces, and long elegant tails, intrigued Ilarion, for they looked exactly like miniatures of the fierce dire-cats of the Ascendancy's far south.

As the miu wandered back into the night a man came out of the garden's darkness and stopped, hesitant, between the pavilion's columns. He was old enough to be Tirsun's father and wore good clothes, but did not have the air of an aristocrat about him; he was too well muscled, and his hands were large and rough-looking. In his accustomed surroundings, Ilarion sensed, he was used to authority. But not here; in the pavilion's lamplight his mouth was cramped with tension.

Silence fell over the company. Tirsun glanced round and saw the intruder. He said, "Ah, at last. Do come in." He waved negligently to his guests, then at the newcomer. "Friends, this is Jerash, who manages the Orosel mines for me. He is a master miner. The silver from which you drink tonight is his harvest. Come closer, Jerash."

Jerash made an obeisance and advanced into the pavilion. He stopped two paces from Tirsun and prostrated himself on the marble floor. Ilarion waited for Tirsun to tell the miner to rise, but he didn't.

"Jerash," Tirsun said quietly, "has experienced difficulties with the said harvest lately. My Grand Domestic has told me some of it. Jerash, please elaborate."

"Lord Protector," the miner said, his voice muffled by speaking at the floor, "there was another cave-in twenty days ago."

"And this is why the metal you promised hasn't arrived." Tirsun's voice had become thin and harsh, like the note of a harp string at the point of snapping. Ilarion's palms began to sweat. Jerash was sweating, too.

"Yes, lord Protector. We've tried to catch up, but we have to shore the tunnels, and the seam—"

"You've sent me half the silver you promised."

"My lord—"

"Half. Or less. Is that right?"

"Yes, Protector."

Tirsun set his wine cup on the table. His hands were shaking, and he sounded short of breath. "I counted on receiving the full shipment today, which you promised. This expedition I sail on tomorrow—you know, it's very expensive. I've built a very costly ship for it. There are many other—outlays. How do you expect me to pay for these things if you don't send me silver? *And* I have a lighthouse to finish before winter sets in."

"My lord, I did my best."

Ilarion knew it was the wrong answer. Tirsun's nostrils became pinched and white.

"Yes," he said, as if he still had trouble breathing. "I'm sure it was your best. Ilarion, give me the pitcher. Jerash deserves a drink for his hard labor in my service."

Ilarion handed over the heavy jug. It was nearly full. The room was perfectly still.

"Drink, Jerash, to your dismal best," Tirsun rasped, and began to pour the wine onto the miner's thinning hair. Jerash jerked convulsively and plastered his face to the floor.

"Drink!" Tirsun screamed, and leaped to his feet. "Turn up your mouth and *drink*!"

The miner whimpered and rolled over. Tirsun shrieked at him to open his mouth and when he did, soused the wine unto his gullet. Jerash choked and gagged. Tirsun kicked him in the side, in the belly, still screaming, incoherent. The flood of purple slowed, the jug almost empty, and the Protector swung its heavy mass over his head and brought it down into Jerash's face. The miner's screams joined Tirsun's as blood and wine mixed with smashed white bone, fragments of teeth, ripped flesh. Tirsun hit Jerash again, and again, and again. The jug's handle bent, its belly collapsed, and still he battered Jerash with its silver ruins. Scarlet and purple spattered Ilarion's tunic and he backed away, dizzy with revulsion and horror. Among the couches and tables the servingwomen stood terrorized and shaking.

At length Jerash bubbled one last time, kicked spasmodically, and lay still. Tirsun stopped shrieking and stood over him, breathing in shrill, racking gasps. Unspeakable fury still twisted his features, and his eyes were demented. They looked up and into Ilarion's without recognition.

Oh Lord Allfather, Lady Mother, is that what I look like?

For a heartbeat he saw himself in the Fountain Palace, years older, the diadem of rulership on his forehead, and his raging face as mad as Tirsun's, as mad as the face of Archates his grandfather. His belly went cold and sick, and he almost vomited.

Tirsun was recovering himself. "What's the matter, slave?" he asked Ilarion in a voice like rusted metal sliding on stone. He tossed the ruined jug onto Jerash's crushed mouth; it landed with a wet thud and toppled clanging to the floor. "You've seen worse than him on a battlefield, haven't you?"

"Yes," Ilarion croaked. "Yes, Protector."

"Of course you have." Already Tirsun's voice was changing, losing its ragged edge, regaining its languid amiable
tone, and the banquet guests stirred a little. The cataclysm
had come and gone, and they'd survived it.

A few more moments passed while Tirsun's breathing
slowed and he regained his color. Then he sat down on his
couch, and said softly, "Ilarion."

"Yes, my lord?" Ilarion's bowels almost loosened. Had
Tirsun really composed himself, or had Jerash's slaughter
merely whetted some playful appetite?

The Protector gestured disgustedly at the corpse. "Go and
get some porters and have this removed. Send a house slave
to clean the floor, too. Jerash can be put in the Lower Court
till morning. If you see the Grand Domestic, tell him I said
to arrange a respectable set of rites, and send some money to
the family. Then come back, and bring a new wine jug—I
seem to have ruined this one. Oh, and change your tunic.
That one's dirty."

"Yes, my lord." Ilarion made an obeisance and walked
carefully out of the pavilion. He still feared Tirsun, as did
everyone on the Citadel Stone, and with reason; but now a
new fear clung to him. For the first time in his life, he was
afraid not just of his anger, but of the madman he might become.

15

THE LEATHER BAG SWAYED CLUMSILY BETWEEN ILARION'S shoulder blades as he hurried through the darkness toward the harbor. A third of the night was gone; the waxing half-moon was perhaps three handspans above the horizon, and Kanesh's streets were unlit and empty.

Escaping from the warehouse compound had been easier than he'd dared hope. The walls of the compound had been built to keep people out, not in, and the sentry posts all looked outward. Furthermore, the Rasenna of Haidra assumed that domestic slaves were unlikely to flee; they could not avoid capture for long on the island, and if they reached the mainland, the local Hazannu would likely enthrall them in worse conditions. Consequently, once the day's labors ended with the evening meal, the overseers went off to their quarters at the compound gate and left the slaves to themselves. The slaves had no separate quarters. They ate in the compound's dusty central court and slept on straw pallets in the warehouses' storage magazines.

The building where Ilarion labored held a vast array of goods. During the day, he had managed to collect a coil of light rope, two strips of fleece, a waterskin, and a block of compressed dried figs. These he concealed in a corner behind a bale of raw wool, along with a leather bag that he had emptied of its slabs of beeswax. It was not much for two days' sail over open water, but it was all he could safely obtain.

Once his fellow slaves had settled down to sleep, he had felt his way to the hiding place, aided only by the thin moon-

light from the warehouse's ventilation slits. There he packed
the figs and waterskin into the bag; the coil of rope went
over his shoulder. Then he stole among the slaves' snoring
bodies to the warehouse's narrow side door, eased it open,
and slipped into the alley that ran between the warehouse
and the adjacent building. Keeping to the moon-cast shadows, he made his way to the compound's outer wall and
climbed the wooden ladder to the wall-walk. He wrapped a
loop of the rope around one of the jutting parapet crenella-
tions, scanned the darkness for sentries, and then down he
went into the narrow street outside. A quick tug and the rope
slithered free after him. Now, half an hour later, he was slipping along one of the alleys that led to the dockyard; he had
already filled the waterskin at a public basin, and his supplies were as complete as he could make them.

His alertness redoubled as he approached the end of the
alley and the harbor quays, for in the harbor he ran the worst
risk of being spotted and taken. If he were, no excuses
would save him. There could be only one reason for him to
be at the docks in darkness, with a bag of provisions, and
Entash would instantly have him in manacles. When Tirsun
returned to Kanesh, he'd be buried alive, or worse.

He halted at the last building before the quays and
scanned the harbor. There were lights here; out on the
breakwater, the temporary beacon glimmered yellow
against the black sea. A few ships' lanterns speckled the
harbor's darkness. Down the quayside to his right, a torch
on a pole flamed smoky orange. The slip containing the
cutter was midway between him and the torch. Its writhing
flame cast a poor light at this distance, but it was still more
than he wanted. He peered into the darkness beyond it,
looking for the watchman. There was no sign of him.

But was the cutter there at all? Ilarion squinted into the
darkness, looking for the vessel's mast rising above the
quay, but it was either invisible in the night or the cutter had
been moved.

That didn't bear thinking about. He paused to judge the set
of the wind. It hissed and rattled among the rigging of the
moored ships, blowing from the east, as he'd prayed it might.

It would be better if his progress did not look too purposeful. He stepped out into the faint illumination of the distant torch and affected a weaving gait, like that of the drunken seamen he'd occasionally seen in the streets. The cutter's slip drew nearer.

A shadow darted across the stones ahead. He almost exclaimed, but bit the sound back as he realized what had startled him. It was a miu. The little animal stopped by the slip and sat down, observing him as if interested in his predicament.

He ignored the creature and kept to his drunken stumbling until he was a pace from the quay's edge. Relief swept through him, for he saw the cutter's mast and then the cutter itself floating almost invisible against the black water. With the tide ebbing, its thwarts were his own height below the level of the quay.

He dropped to his belly on the stones at the quay's edge, let the leather bag down as far as he could, then dropped it softly into the boat. In one more motion he slid after it, holding on to the stones as he felt around with his foot. He found wood and let go, flexing his knees as his weight fell on the boat and it heeled beneath him. Then he was crouched in her bilges, listening and peering into the darkness above. A small head and pointed ears appeared against the torch glow, the miu gazing down at him. After a moment it appeared to lose interest, and vanished.

Ilarion took swift stock of the cutter. The sail was there, still attached to its gaff and boom and protected by its leather wrappings. He felt around his knees and to his further relief found the smooth shafts of the sculls. Judging from the level of the water against the quay, the tide was either half-in or half-out. From his careful observations from the heights of the Citadel Stone over the last two days, he was sure it was half-out, so its continuing ebb would help speed him out of the harbor. This was essential, for he wanted to be well out of sight of land by dawn, and, with luck, a day might pass before someone noticed the cutter's absence. But Entash was no fool, and the absence of both Ilarion and the boat would bring about swift pursuit.

He eased the sculls onto the thwarts, then crawled to the aft mooring rope and loosed it. The cutter's stern began drifting away from the quay. At the bow, he cast off the other line. He couldn't raise the sail until he was out of the harbor, so he seized a scull and began to pole the cutter out of the slip. The water chuckled around its bow, and despite his best efforts the scull thumped softly against the vessel's timbers. But the east wind hushed the noises, the torchlight receded, and soon he was gliding quietly into the harbor's deeper darkness.

Almost under the torch, a man with a spear came round a corner of a ship shed. It could only be the watchman. The dark figure wandered toward the mooring slip.

I nearly did it, Ilarion thought hopelessly, as he hurriedly pulled in the scull and squatted out of sight in the cutter's bilge. *Now he'll think it's come adrift and he'll bring a boat out to get it. Should I swim back and try to get to the warehouse before I'm missed?*

He raised his head carefully above the cutter's side, just in time to see the watchman halt some thirty paces from the slip and stoop over a small dark object at his feet. The object moved, then wandered away from the quayside. It was the miu; the watchman had been stroking it. As Ilarion peered at them, the man took a few paces after the little animal, seemed to shrug, then turned and sauntered back in the direction from which he had come.

Thank you, Lord Allfather and Lady Mother.

He was fifty yards into the harbor now. Quickly he took the strips of fleece from the bag, knotted them about the sculls to muffle them, and began to row toward the beacon at the harbor entrance. Ranks of moored vessels slid by, their masts scratched black against the starlit sky. Until the sun rose, he would navigate by the constellations. On the long voyage with Rook, he'd learned enough about the southern stars to let him find his way to the mainland.

The tidal current speeded up as he neared the harbor entrance. He rowed harder, and the cutter fled through the night like a cloud in a swift breeze. The beacon was suddenly almost overhead, then rushing past, and suddenly the vessel's motion changed as she swayed to the waves of the open sea. Now the beacon was behind him and drawing rapidly away. He was free.

Far to the west, Theatana stood in darkness on the palace roof and watched the wheel of the soft southern stars. Her plans had ripened beautifully, like the figs and apricots turning tawny and gold in the autumn orchards around Kla. Soon she could pluck the first fruits she had so painstakingly nurtured.

Tirsun's expeditionary force must have sailed from Kanesh by now, or was about to. In a few days, wind and weather permitting, the Protector's ships would be a little east of Kla's domains, concealed in a bay in Hazannu territory. Then Tirsun's courier would arrive to arrange the timing of the attack with Rimash, and the clan-lord would let Theatana know when it was to occur. On that night she would drug Alfni's wine with a potion supplied by Vindisi, and Rimash and others of the Idu clan would kill the guards at Kla's harbor gate and admit Tirsun's men. When the invaders approached the palace citadel, Theatana would bespell herself into Alfni's appearance and order the household guards to let the Kaneshites in. The Protector would never wake from his drugged sleep, nor would Kayonu and his family survive the night.

She smiled into the darkness. There had been time for two letters to pass between her and Tirsun, and she'd put more into them than she had told Rimash. Tirsun knew now that his real friend in Kla was a sorceress from the unknown north. Secretly telling him this, and asking him to keep it secret, was a gamble; she would have to see him before she knew how her dice had fallen. But she was confident that she'd done the wise thing. At the least, the nature of his new ally must have piqued his curiosity.

She'd see him soon. Tirsun himself was leading the expedition to Kla, as she'd been sure he would; he was known to thirst for glory, and Alfni had told her that he liked to command his soldiers in person. He also, it was said, had an eye for women. She could hardly have wished for better.

He'll belong to me an hour after we've met, she thought happily, *just as Alfni did.*

And with him Haidra would be hers, and eventually the mask would be hers as well. And if the mask was what its legend suggested, new vistas of greatness would open before her. Dominion upon dominion, power upon power.

How fortunate that she'd been exiled to that little island in the Blue Havens. She'd had to wait there a long time for her luck to come around, but all in all, the year was turning out much better than she'd expected.

16

BY DUSK ON HIS SECOND DAY AT SEA, ILARION KNEW THEY were after him.

He'd spotted the two sails at about noon. He'd seen others since setting out, but they'd always disappeared after a while, so at first these newcomers didn't concern him greatly. He was more worried about his increasing weakness, for he was flagging now, being very short of sleep, food, and water.

And he was still far from his hoped-for goal of the mainland. The winds had shifted just after he sailed from Kanesh, driving him steadily west rather than south, and though he couldn't see Haidra's coastline, he knew it wasn't far away. He also knew that even if the wind changed now in his favor, he no longer had the endurance to reach his destination. In another day he'd have to land on Haidra for water, food, and rest, or risk dying out here.

When he realized this he'd decided to keep his westward course, in the hope that when he did make landfall he would be in the Protectorate of Dymie and out of Tirsun's immediate reach. There would be no hunt for him in Dymie, and perhaps he could hide, get his strength back, and try again for the mainland.

Or that was his plan until he saw the sails at noon. He watched them but they didn't go away as the others had, though at first he did not think they grew larger. But then they did, little by little, and by dusk he knew that they were sailing faster than he was.

No cargo ship could be outpacing him. These had to be

225

military craft, built for speed—dispatch galleys or something like them. They might be only a little swifter than the cutter, but over a day or so that slight edge would be enough. They would catch up with him eventually.

Maybe they're not after me at all. Maybe they're going to join Tirsun, wherever he is.

But even if they were, when they overtook the cutter they'd want to know why such a small craft was so far out at sea. Worse, if they came from Kanesh, Entash would certainly have ordered them to watch for the Protector's boat. And in another day they'd be upon him, so he absolutely had to lose them before then. As soon as night fell, he decided, he'd turn for the coast of Haidra. If they hadn't spotted his sail yet, they might pass him by in the darkness. If they were still after him when dawn came, he'd try to reach shore ahead of them, abandon the cutter, and make a run for it on land.

He forced down his few remaining figs, along with most of his water. Neither did much to strengthen him. The wind still held, but now it had a dank feel to it.

He watched his pursuers' sails fade in the thickening dusk, and when he could no longer see them he changed course to the northwest. Overhead there were now scattered clouds, with more visible around the hazy face of the rising moon.

Good Allfather, keep the stars in view for me. I'll lose my way without them.

He watched his wake. The stars were rising from the sea, all except two. These stayed near the horizon line. They weren't stars but ships' lanterns. He kept an eye on them, hoping to see them pass out of sight to the west. Eventually one did, but the other did not. Instead it grew a little brighter.

He realized that his two pursuers had outthought him; they must have seen Ilarion's sail, known that he might have spotted theirs as well, and had calculated that their quarry might head for land as soon as night fell. So they'd split up, one to search toward the coast, the other to continue westward in case Ilarion held to that course.

There was nothing he could do but keep going; fortunately, despite some gathering clouds, the stars remained visible, and he was able to maintain his course. But he soon knew that this would be his worst night so far, for the wind had become very cold. The chill seeped into him until he was shuddering almost uncontrollably. He stood up sometimes and stamped his feet to try to keep warm, but he was too weakened now for the exercise to do much good. And hour by hour, the pursuing light behind grew slowly but inexorably brighter. As it did, the cold gnawed deeper into him. Every muscle howled, and his hands on the steering oar were so cramped that he could hardly unclench them from the shaft. By the time night was almost done, he was in a half stupor from the chill. What kept him from drifting away altogether was the hope of dawn with its warming sun, and perhaps the sight of land.

The first hint of day was oddly subdued, no more than a watery pink along the horizon. Ilarion forced himself into a kind of fuzzy alertness, and realized that the wind was dropping away. He roused himself enough to look behind. The pursuer's light had vanished.

Hope flooded his blood like a draft of hot wine, and he heard himself laugh in a cracked voice. For some reason they'd dropped the pursuit. Now all he needed to do was reach shore in one piece. Perhaps the Allfather would give him a nice sandy beach, without reefs or rocks or breaking surf. Indeed, the waves had lessened somewhat in height.

He looked up to check his course, and all his hope fell away into despair. The stars were hazing over and a pale smoke was gathering in the air around him. Dawn was bringing not light and warmth, but fog: fog on an unknown coast, with an onshore wind. And the pursuing ship was still back there; its light had only vanished in the murk.

At least, he thought grimly, *they'll be worried about running themselves ashore in this. I, on the other hand, have nothing to lose.*

He did his best to stay alert. He'd been shaking with cold earlier, but now he felt very feverish. His head ached, and his eye sockets felt packed with sand. He seemed to hear two voices in his head, both his. They were debating his future.

I'm sick and getting sicker. If I get ashore at all, will I even have the strength to run?

Don't think about that. All I need is water and food and rest.

And how will I come by those, with Tirsun's men on my heels?

The light had strengthened, and the fog thickened to a pink blanket around him. From ahead, muffled by the vapors, came a low hiss and rumble. Surf, but on what? A sheer cliff, a reef, a shelving beach? The voices in his head fell silent, and under him the cutter lifted as the surge bore it landward. The wind was almost gone, and the sail flapped uncertainly, the boom swinging to the sway of the gathering breakers.

Then, without warning, he was among them: mounds and steep-sided hills of white water, the cutter sluing and yawing, trying to broach sideways to the surf's thrust. They would capsize him and throw him into the sea if he gave them a chance. Ilarion heaved at the steering oar and fought the cutter's bow around. From just ahead came the boom of surf. The fog parted for an instant, and he saw through the gap a line of breakers and a beach beyond them. Then he was shooting forward on a crest, the cutter twisting under him despite all he could do with the steering oar, and suddenly he was in the shallows, the keel grating hard on gravel. The boat lifted, and he held on, riding her up the beach until she grounded again and stuck fast. He rolled over her side, found himself in knee-deep water, and staggered out of the sea onto a sandy beach.

Fog was all around. Fever hammered in his blood and in his ears, a roaring that almost drowned the beat of the surf. He stumbled across the sand, moving in a dank cocoon of smoky white. Then shadows appeared ahead: scrub growth backed by a palisade of trees. It was a wood or forest, offering at least some concealment from his pursuers. But as soon as the fog lifted and revealed the abandoned cutter, they'd know where he went ashore. He had to get farther inland, miles from the beach if he could, and find a place to hide.

He went on into the shadowy, dripping wood. Twice he

stopped to lick water from leaves, but the scant moisture only deepened his thirst. He felt dazed, as if from a blow to the head. He had no idea now how far from the beach he had stumbled. It might be a hundred paces, or ten thousand.

Then, through the humming and roaring in his ears, he heard falling water. He groped onward through the fog and suddenly the water was almost at his feet, a pool fed by a tiny cascade flowing from a cleft in a shelf of rock. Around the pool was a pavement of polished white stone.

He fell to his belly on the paving, put his lips to the water, and drank. The cold hit him in the midriff and weakness swept through him. Fearing he might lose consciousness and drown with his head in the pool, he took one more gulp and rolled onto his back. The paving under him was as cool and smooth as the linen of his bed in the Fountain Palace.

Paving. That meant people. This was no safe place. He had to get up and go on.

But it was early morning. No one would see him here in the fog. He could rest for a few moments. A few moments would be all he needed.

He closed his eyes and fell into darkness.

Belit halted by the bench where Mereth was playing her double flute, and said, "Mistress-Singer, I went just now to the lower spring to gather lamp-flowers, and there is a man of your race lying by the pool."

Surprised, Mereth blinked at the slave woman and lowered the flute. She was sitting in the morning sunshine on the villa's south terrace, where she had gone to practice a new melody. Behind her rose the stucco villa wall, which displayed rough patches where the masons had repaired cracks left by last spring's earth tremor. The minor shaking had caused very little damage in Elyssa's Protectorate and after the temples offered propitiatory sacrifices, people's daily life had gone on as usual.

"You don't mean my brother?" she asked. But it couldn't be Halicar. He'd gone up into the forested hills at dawn, to spend the morning in solitude while he composed. He would not return until noon.

"No, Mistress-Singer."

"But the man is an Antecessor, like me?" Mereth asked. "Is that what you meant, Belit?" She had expected not this announcement, but a summons from Elyssa to play for her; she enjoyed the music of the flute as she took her breakfast. This would be the last of Mereth's morning performances at the villa, however, for early tomorrow everyone would leave the Protectress's summer residence and return to Dymie Palace for the cooler seasons. Elyssa had become melancholy as the day of departure approached and Mereth, bitterly, knew why the Protectress regretted leaving. The past months had been a golden idyll for her and Halicar as they explored their newfound love, and that idyll was shortly to end as they went back to the hard realities of the capital.

Mereth felt the familiar hurt and resentment flare at the thought, like hot coals under her breastbone. She took a deep breath to cool them, but the coals could not really be extinguished, though she'd tried hard to put them out. They'd been smoldering there since spring, when she realized that Halicar and Elyssa were lovers.

The hurt was for no imagined cause. Her brother had almost no time for her anymore; he rarely spent so much as a morning with her, even to practice or compose new music, because he was almost always with Elyssa. When he wasn't, like today, he'd be up in the hills alone, creating songs to the woman he loved. Fortunately for Mereth's peace of mind, he sang them to her in private.

To make matters worse, the generous side of Mereth's nature liked Elyssa very much, and she knew that Elyssa liked her. Even allowing for the barrier of rank, they could have been intimate friends. But Mereth's resentment and jealousy rose like a wall between them, and she could not prevent herself from maintaining a cool reserve toward the Protectress. At first Elyssa did tentatively attempt to confide in her, but in the face of this aloofness (which Mereth could not cast off, though she sometimes tried to) she had drawn back. Halicar said very little about what was going on, no doubt because Mereth presented the same reserved demeanor to him. Neither of the lovers seemed to realize how abandoned

Mereth felt, or how lonely and frightened she was; deep in their luminous world of joy and passion, they saw little but each other. It did no good for Mereth to tell herself she should be happy for Halicar, and for Elyssa, too. Indeed she wanted to feel that way, but she couldn't.

And for this she despised herself. Mereth had never imagined herself a selfish person, nor one prone to jealousy, and was still appalled to discover that she was.

Belit said, "Well, Mistress-Singer, he's got brown hair and his skin's sort of a browny pale gold."

"Ah." Mereth looked over the terrace balustrade. There, a stretch of rather unkempt gardens, now in their dusty yellow autumn foliage and displaying red-and-orange patches of late-blooming poppies, ran down a slope to the wood that hid the spring. The sun was well up now and had burned much of the fog off the land. But mist still hung above the wood's far side, above the beach. The sea beyond the beach was still invisible.

"Did you ask him what he was doing there?" she asked the slave.

"No, Mistress-Singer."

Mereth had noted long ago that most slaves provided exactly the information their owners requested, and that was all. Obtaining more required precise questioning. Most owners imagined that this was because the slaves were stupid, but Mereth knew differently. Slaves rebelled against their owners by displaying a precisely gauged dullness of wit, a dullness that fell just short of earning them a beating. For this covert defiance, Mereth had a carefully concealed sympathy, even when the defiance was applied to her.

"Belit," she asked patiently, "did he speak to you at all?"

"He didn't, Mistress-Singer." And then, surprisingly, she volunteered, "His eyes were closed. He was asleep. But I thought he looked as if he was sick, too."

Sick or not, a stranger on the villa grounds would concern Elyssa's Grand Domestic, who, among other functions, commanded the Protectress's guards. Mereth said, "Find the lord Nenattu and tell him about the man. I'll go down to the spring and see what's to be seen."

A voice from above called, "I'll tell Nenattu myself, Mereth. But perhaps you shouldn't go alone."

It was Elyssa, leaning over the sill of an upstairs window. "May I take Belit, then?" Mereth asked.

"Yes. I'll send Nenattu after you when I find him. Perhaps I'll come myself. I'd like some air now the sun's out. But don't wait for me." She disappeared inside, calling for her Grand Domestic.

"Come with me, Belit," Mereth said. She got up, letting the flute swing from the thong around her neck, and started down the path that led through the gardens to the wood. Belit followed diffidently.

In a few minutes they reached the trees. Though the sun was now pleasantly warm, the night had been chilly and wisps of fog still drifted among the barrel cypresses and camphorwoods. The wraiths of mist gave the place an eerie aspect. Mereth heard the chuckle of the spring ahead, but no mutter of a human voice. Could it have been not a man Belit saw, but some entity that she mistook for one? The possibility made Mereth a little uneasy and she thought, *I wish Halicar were here*.

"You're sure it wasn't a gytash?" she asked the slave woman. Such water sprites inhabited sea caves and lonely stretches of coast, and sometimes appeared in a hermaphrodite aspect that could be mistaken at a distance for a man. Their presence aroused a clammy unease in humans, though they were not particularly dangerous unless approached too closely.

"No, Mistress-Singer. I wasn't much frightened, so it was no haunt."

They reached the glade at the end of the path. Within the small clearing, the spring flowed into a pool surrounded by a ring of marble pavement. A dark-haired man, clad in a dirty, knee-length blue tunic, lay on his back near the pool. Frowning in puzzlement, Mereth knelt beside him. He appeared somewhat older than she was, and well favored and well fed, and for a moment she thought that Belit was right and that he was an Antecessor. But then she saw the golden cast to his skin and realized he wasn't. Yet with that hair he was certainly no Rasenna or Hazannu.

He was sick, though. Belit had been right about that. Fever came off him in hot waves, and he breathed in quick, shallow bursts. Mereth put her palm on his forehead and felt scalded. He was very ill indeed.

"Look at his arm, Mistress-Singer," Belit said in a flat voice. "He's a runaway."

Mereth looked. Preoccupied by his strange appearance, she hadn't noticed the iron bracelet on the man's left wrist. Her disgust at the whole vile business of slavery rose in her, like bile in her throat. If he were truly a runaway and not a shipwreck's survivor, his master would have every lawful right to kill him.

If I knew a place where there were no slaves, she told herself and not for the first time, *I would go there. With Halicar or without him.*

"Go and find Nenattu," she said, "and say that we need a litter to carry him up to the villa. And fleeces to cover him."

Belit turned and scuttled away. Mereth examined the slave iron, searching for an owner's mark. When she found it she rocked back on her heels in surprise. In her profession she had to know all the noble houses of the Rasenna, as well as those of the Hazannu, together with their insignia. This man bore the sea-and-island symbol, which meant that he belonged to the Protector of Kanesh. Mereth had heard unpleasant tales about Elyssa's brother, and she gave a low exclamation of pity for the slave's probable fate.

She was about to stand up when a brightness on the man's left hand caught her eye. She took his wrist and saw that he wore a ring the color of the Protectress's hair. Gold, on a slave? She turned the ring to the light, and blinked in astonishment. A huge green gem gleamed against the metal.

What manner of slave is this?

Cut into the gem was an image. Mereth held it closer, glimpsed what it was, and her breath caught in her throat. Carefully she tilted the jewel to examine the details of the head, plumage, and talons. But she had made no mistake. The image in the stone depicted the winged serpent: the fireshta, the Hidden Singer. But though beautifully cut, it was either a very foreign or a very antique style, one she didn't recognize. It didn't look like Rasenna work and it certainly was not Hazannu. Nor was it that of her people. Perhaps it was Old Rasennan, from the time before the Fall of the Great Garden. That would not quite fit, though, for such a valuable ring wouldn't likely have been carved with a fireshta. Unlike Mereth's race, neither the Rasenna of Haidra nor their ancestors held the winged serpent in any high regard.

She released the runaway's wrist and frowned down at him. Wherever the ring came from, he would not likely be wearing it so openly if he'd stolen it from Tirsun. But would Tirsun let a slave wear a ring that could buy a hundred such as him? Possibly; some owners decked their most valuable slaves out in rich finery, simply to display the extent of their wealth, and the Protector of Kanesh was wealthy enough to do exactly that. Perhaps that was the explanation, though in truth she had not heard that Tirsun did such things. It was something of a puzzle.

The glade was brightening. Mereth looked up and saw that the fog had burned away from its seaward side. Now clearly visible was the broad path that led through the trees down to the beach, which here was only a stone's throw distant. Mist still hung over the water beyond the shoreline, but the surf at the sea's edge was visible, breaking in long low mounds of foam. A boat, its sail drooping listlessly, lay stranded by the falling tide. *He must have come in that*, Mereth thought, and felt a twinge of hope. Perhaps he was not a runaway but a survivor of a lost ship, and they wouldn't execute him.

She took a quick sharp breath. A second boat was nosing swiftly out of the mist. It slid through the surf and grounded beside the first, and she saw that its rowers were armed and armored. A man leaped over the bow and waded to shore. He was close enough for her to see the three blue cetotheres painted on his buff-colored shield, the insignia of the Protectorate of Kanesh. And beneath the cetotheres, there was a stylized green island rising from a blue wavy line representing the sea, the same symbol that was incised into the fugitive's slave iron. The soldiers were from Tirsun's household, and Mereth knew in an instant that they had come for the man by the pool, and she knew in the same instant that they must not have him. She got to her feet and stood at his side.

They'd pulled their craft well onto the sand now. It was small, and she realized they must have rowed in from a ship still hidden in the mist. There were five of them. They inspected the derelict boat carefully but quickly, their movements and voices betraying surprise and glee. Then, leaving one man to guard their own craft, the other four began tramping up the path toward her.

They spotted her immediately, despite the glade's shadows, and as they came up the path she saw curiosity in the faces below the helmet rims. But they were wary, too, with swords out and shields ready, as if they half expected attack from the cover of the trees.

When they reached the entry to the glade Mereth held up her hand, palm outward, and said, "Stop."

To her surprise, they stopped. She stood before them, knowing how frail she looked, and was: a slender young woman wearing a white ankle-length tunic with a blue sash, confronting four men in iron and hardened leather. Each was a head taller than she was and half again her weight. The one in the lead had a sharp hollow-cheeked face, a receding jaw, and a three days' blond stubble that had spread patchily over his cheeks and chin. He was clearly the officer in command. The other three were younger and looked untried.

The leader's gaze went to her hair, to the double flute hanging at her breast, and to the symbol for music that was worked into her tunic. He said, "You're an Antecessor, are you, mistress?"

"Just as you see," Mereth answered. "I am Mistress-Singer to the Protectress Elyssa of Dymie. This is her summer residence, and you are trespassing."

The officer gestured at the man on the ground. "Not for long. We only want to take that article back to our ship, and then we'll be gone without troubling anyone further."

"That article? You mean the man behind me?"

"Yes, mistress. He's the property of the Protector. You must have seen the iron on him."

Mereth took a deep breath, let it out. "You may not take him without the permission of the Protectress. You might be mercenaries, raiding with the Hazannu. How do I know you're from Kanesh?"

The man's eyes widened. "What? Mistress, we're carrying Tirsun Velianas's colors. Our ship's just out there, you'll see her emblems as soon as the fog finishes lifting. We rowed in to search the shore for the runaway's boat, and we fell right over it, thank the Green Lady. So I know that's him there behind you, without even a look at his wrist."

If she were not an Antecessor singer, they would have pushed her aside by now and taken him. She shrugged. "Paint is easy to come by."

"The paint is from Kanesh, mistress." His voice had become sharper. "And how do *we* know this is the Protectress's land? We've only your say on it. Please move aside, and we'll just bind him and be gone."

Mereth backed away, then turned swiftly and went to stand over the stranger, one sandaled foot at each side of his waist. She slid her arms under the double pipe and crossed them. "No. Keep away."

"With respect, mistress, we must." The officer came forward but then stopped when she did not move, and stood a little uncertainly.

"I am an Antecessor Mistress-Singer," she said, her voice harsh. "I am inviolate. If you harm me, your life is forfeit. The Protectress will see to it. Even Tirsun Velianas will not try to protect you."

She hoped that this last was true, or at least that the soldier would believe it. Still, the man might risk moving her carefully aside without inflicting any real damage. If only Elyssa would arrive, they wouldn't dare drag her away from the fugitive. But what would the Protectress do when she discovered her court singer trying to keep an escaped slave from its rightful owner? While Mereth might detest slavery, Elyssa accepted it as part of the natural order.

I may sink in these waters yet. But it's too late to go back. And they must not have him. I can't let him go back to the death the Protector will inflict.

"Return to your ship," she said to the officer. "I tell you, this man is not for you."

In his face, she saw his fear of Tirsun struggle with his fear of her. But she was only a young woman and unarmed, and he might yet decide she was not so inviolate he couldn't inflict a few bruises.

He so decided. He laid his shield down, and said to his men, in a nervous voice, "We'll pick her up easy and put her over there. But we'll do it careful."

The other three also put their shields on the ground, then shuffled forward. Mereth unfolded her arms, took up her flute, and said, "I will blow a tune that will dance you into the sea and under it, and you will stay there forever."

They stopped short, and the leader made a harsh noise in his throat. She could do no such thing as she had threatened, but she saw that they believed her, at least for the moment.

"What is going on here?" Elyssa said sharply from behind her. "What are Kaneshite soldiers doing on my villa grounds? And with drawn swords? I am the Protectress of Dymie! You! Answer!"

The officer gaped at the jewels on her wrists and fingers and at the Lady's golden spiral at her neck. Then, as if hamstrung, he dropped to his knees. His men did the same, and their weapons tumbled clanking from their hands. Elyssa stalked into the glade, followed by Nenattu and two guards. She was clearly furious, her wide mouth drawn taut and her white hands clenched at her side, and looked like a vengeful aspect of the Lady herself. Belit and a pair of male slaves bearing a litter hovered on the path, faces anxious.

The officer's mouth worked, and he half whispered, "Protectress—"

"Speak up. Use your tongue while you still have one."

He lost his voice at this, and took a few moments finding it. "Protectress," he blurted at last, "we didn't know this was your land, forgive us, my lady, we were after this runaway slave; it belongs to the Protector Tirsun, my lady. We were only doing what Entash the Grand Domestic told us."

Elyssa glanced at the prone form. "This is Tirsun's slave?"

"Yes, my lady. A special one, from way north it's said. It's the Protector's Wine Bearer."

"Mereth, have you inspected him? Does he wear a slave iron?"

"Yes, Protectress. But—"

"Mereth, wait. You! Soldier! You say you were following orders from my brother's Grand Domestic?"

"Yes, my lady."

"And he in turn had these orders from my brother?"

"I don't know, my lady. The Protector is away with the fleet, to punish the mainlanders."

Even in her anxiety, Mereth noticed that this did not seem to be fresh news to Elyssa. The Protectress said, "It doesn't matter—in my brother's absence from Kanesh, Entash speaks with his voice. Therefore, Tirsun is responsible for this affront you've inflicted on me. You four are less culpable than my brother or his Grand Domestic, but I am still of a mind to have you whipped for trespass."

Mereth, standing astride the unconscious man, uneasily shifted her stance. There were four of them and only two of Elyssa's guards. But the Protectress seemed indifferent to the threat.

The officer said, "My lady, please don't punish us. We didn't know these were your domains, and you have a name for justice. I beg you, just give us the runaway and let us go. If we don't come back with him, we'll be scourged. The Protector prizes the man highly."

Elyssa seemed to hesitate. Mereth did not know the details of Haidran law about escaped slaves, but she was sure that Elyssa was obliged, by custom at least, to return the man. And the Protectress was known to be treading carefully in her dealings with her brother. Mereth was abruptly certain that Elyssa would give the man up. She would send a sharp protest to Kanesh about the soldiers' trespass, which Tirsun would blandly ignore, and nothing else would come of it. Except that the man at her feet would be dead.

She turned to Elyssa, who now stood only a pace away. "Protectress," she said quietly, "he's very sick, but if he lives long enough to reach Kanesh, they will bury him alive. Or worse."

"It's the law," Elyssa answered. She looked down at the runaway, then up at the Kaneshites. "Go down the path twenty paces, and wait. Leave your shields and weapons here. They will be returned to you."

They scrambled to their feet and retreated. When they were out of earshot she said in an undertone to Nenattu, "Go up to the villa and bring more spearmen. I don't think these are assassins sent by my brother, but I'd rather not find out that I was wrong."

The Grand Domestic hurried away. "I think," Elyssa said to Mereth, "that this is the slave my ambassador heard the stories about—the outlander from somewhere over Ocean, who's been showing my brother how to build war machines. He's dangerous. Better for Dymie if he *is* dead."

Was this an avenue she could use? "But Protectress, if that's what he's been doing, your brother might *not* kill him when he returns. Sending him back to Kanesh would then merely increase the danger." *Unless he dies on the way there,* she thought.

"You're saying I shouldn't send him back."

"I wish you would not. But you are the Protectress."

Elyssa closed her eyes as if weary, then opened them. She said, "I don't think I can refuse. I must send him back, and trust to the Green Lady that he's executed in Kanesh or dies on the way."

Begging for his life would do no good, and Mereth could think of no further arguments to save him. Her shoulders slumped and she thought, *I'm sorry, whoever you are, I did my best for you.*

Suddenly, as if another voice spoke with hers, she heard herself say, "He wears the symbol of the winged serpent."

Elyssa started as if touched with a live ember. "What?" she asked in a low voice.

"My lady, it's carved in the jewel of his ring. It's a fireshta."

"He wears a ring?"

Hope woke in her. "Yes, a very rich one. It looks as though it must be from somewhere far away. Perhaps from his home-land."

"Show me."

Mereth knelt beside the man and held up his hand. Elyssa bent to inspect the jewel. After a moment she straightened, and said, "Yes, it's the winged serpent. And Mereth, I've seen one."

"You *have*?" She almost dropped the man's wrist. Carefully she laid it beside him, then rose to her feet.

"I think so. It was the night I returned from Rumach Hold, and you sang for me in the aviary. The thing was in the laurel tree there. I saw it only for a moment. But I was so tired that night, and so troubled, I half believed it was a phantasm from my mind. But I wasn't sure, and I've been wondering ever since what it might mean, if it meant anything." She gave an odd little laugh. "Though this man's arrival improves my knowledge not at all, even if he wears a likeness of the creature. Do you think it was a foretelling?"

Mereth wished she could say it was and perhaps save him, but she could not bring herself to swear certainty when she had none. "My lady, I have no idea."

"I'm a priestess, but I don't know, either. Do you think I really saw it?"

Despairing at herself for her answer, Mereth said, "Only you know what you saw, Protectress. You must judge."

Elyssa sighed. "I suppose I must, and in doing so settle the fate of this fugitive and perhaps Dymie's, too. Please don't speak of what I saw, though—not until I can discover what it means." She turned and called down the path, "You four! Come here!"

The men of Kanesh tramped forward and stopped, looking hopeful. Mereth watched Elyssa and felt her jaw knot with tension. She had not dared ask what the Protectress was going to do, and she could not tell from her demeanor. Elyssa could be utterly opaque when she chose.

The Protectress settled her gaze on the officer, who stared carefully at the ground. Elyssa said: "This is my judgment in the matter. The fugitive is his master's property, and must be returned wherever he may flee."

Mereth bit her lip to keep from crying out. The officer grinned and opened his mouth to speak.

"Wait," Elyssa said. "There is, however, the matter of redress for the affront you have committed against me in my brother's name. This redress I calculate to be precisely the worth of the slave you have pursued here. He will therefore remain in Dymie as my property. If my brother wishes to object, he may do so through my ambassador in Kanesh.

"You are free to leave, and I wish you to do so now."

The ice under Mereth's heart melted; he was safe from them. But her relief faded abruptly, for the officer's face was like a clenched fist. He opened his mouth, closed it, then opened it again. Elyssa's two guards put their hands on the hilts of their swords.

"Think carefully," Elyssa said in a soft voice to the officer. "If you kill me, my brother will make a profound example of your death, to affirm his heartfelt grief at my demise and his fury at my assassins. That is, if you even get away from this place—I have these guards behind me, with more coming."

As if in response, Nenattu and four soldiers arrived at a run. "Wait there," Elyssa said over her shoulder to the Grand Domestic, then turned back to the Kaneshite officer. "Well?" she asked.

The man's face slowly lost its anger to an expression of defeat. He bowed clumsily, and said, "I would not think of harming you, my lady. I know you're a priestess, and it would be sacrilege. But may we take the slave's boat in tow when we leave? It belongs to the Protector, and he might whip us the less if we bring it back."

"Do so. Tell my brother that the responsibility for his loss is mine, not yours. He may lay on the whip a trifle more lightly. The lord Nenattu and his men will accompany you to your boat, to ensure your safe departure. I assume you have a ship waiting out there?"

"We do, Protectress."

"Go."

They turned and tramped glumly down the path toward the beach, followed by Nenattu and the guards. Mereth held her breath until she was sure they were really leaving and it was not a feint, then slowly let it out. The two male slaves who had brought the litter looked uncertainly at Belit, then at the Protectress.

"Belit," Elyssa said, "go ahead of us and prepare a bed for him in the domestic quarters, and be quick about it. Call Utea to tend him. You two, get him onto your litter, cover him, and follow her. Mereth, you can stop standing over him like a miu over her kitten." She scrutinized the man, and added dryly, "Though I admit he *is* well favored, even with the salt stains and the fever."

"Yes, my lady," Mereth said. She stepped aside and watched the slaves prepare to move the fugitive. He was still unconscious. "He looks strong. Perhaps he'll live."

Elyssa gave her a measured look. "You sound very nonchalant about a man for whom we've taken such risks." She paused thoughtfully. "I wonder what I've done? This is not going to sit well with my brother."

"I'm sorry, Protectress. I should not have intervened."

They started up the hill toward the villa, the slaves hurrying on ahead with the litter. "You mean, by telling me about his ring?" Elyssa asked. "No, I'm glad you did. I cannot think that his arrival here and my vision were coincidence." She gave a wry smile. "Even if they were, my keeping this man will give my brother a boil on his rear, which doesn't displease me at all, though I may someday pay richly for the pleasure."

"I hope not, Protectress."

"So do I." She looked sideways at Mereth. "You protected him at some risk to yourself."

Elyssa seemed to require an answer, so Mereth said, "That's true, my lady."

"But it wasn't only the fireshta that made me do it, Mereth. Or spiting my brother. I wanted to save him partly because you did."

"Oh, Protectress," Mereth said, disconcerted and touched all at the same time. "Thank you."

"This being the case, would you like to own him yourself? You and Halicar might find him useful. Perhaps he knows foreign music you'd find interesting. Though I'd like to borrow him sometimes, for military matters."

Mereth stopped short in astonishment. "Me? Own him?"

"Yes. Don't you want him?"

"Protectress, I've never . . . Antecessors don't own slaves."

"I've heard as much. But does that mean they *never* do?"

"As far as I know, my lady," Mereth answered. Her people's belief was that owning slaves harmed the owner as much as the owned. Mereth's experiences with the Rasenna and the Hazannu had done nothing to make her think differently. To her, slavery was a thing of disgust, like the disease called silverskin that ate away the limbs and the face of the afflicted, but so slowly that the sufferer took years to die. Sometimes she imagined that Haidra itself was dying from such a disease, even though the mutilations lay hidden beneath the sunlit facades of the island's gracious cities.

She was sometimes astonished that Elyssa could not, or would not, see the evil in slavery. But though the Protectress was usually a good mistress to her human property, they were still her property, and she would never perceive them otherwise. A slave of her household who showed signs of questioning this, or who betrayed any trace of insolence or defiance, could expect harsh punishment. In this the Protectress was like all Rasenna. They assumed that showing any sign of weakness to the slave population was to invite revolt, and Mereth knew enough about their slaves to believe that the assumption was probably correct. The Rasenna had ensnared themselves in a trap of their own making.

They walked on toward the villa. "If you gave him to me," she said, "I would only free him. I'd have to."

Elyssa nodded. "Ah. In that case, I'll manumit him myself, as a gift to you, and take him into my household as a free servant. He can build for me the same war contraptions he built for my brother. He'll earn his keep and then some. Would that please you?"

It was utterly unexpected. But as soon as Elyssa had spoken, Mereth knew that this was a peace offering, and that she was unworthy of it. Suddenly she wanted to weep.

"It would, Protectress," she managed to say. "I'd like him to be free. He's so far from home."

Elyssa halted suddenly and turned to her. Mereth stopped, too. "My lady?" she said, blinking back tears. "Is something the matter?"

"Please," Elyssa blurted, "please, Mereth, don't be so angry at me. I love Halicar as I've never loved anyone in my life. It's not dalliance. I won't throw him aside for someone else one day, if that's what troubles you so. You know he's the only lover I've ever taken. And it was no whim. I fought against it. But it's made you so angry . . . do you understand what I'm talking about, or am I even more a fool than I thought?"

Mereth couldn't get her breath for several moments. How much pride had Elyssa swallowed to make this plea? Finally, with a tight and aching throat, she said, "My lady, it's not foolishness, I know what you're saying. But I swear I never believed it was dalliance. I know you better. It wasn't that. I—" Her eyes filled, and she couldn't stop the flood. She stood wretchedly on the path, and hot tears ran down her cheeks.

Elyssa put a hand on her arm. "Mereth, dear Mereth, please don't. What is it, then?"

"I'm all alone," she said brokenly. "I'm frightened. You and Halicar have no time for me. He was the only person I had in the world. And now he's yours. What will happen to me if he leaves the music behind, and me with it?"

"But he won't do that," Elyssa said, astonished. Her eyes, too, were wet. "He *lives* for music. Even when he sings of me, he's still delighting in his art, and I sometimes think the art is the greater delight. But he loves you as well, Mereth. You're his only kin. He loves me deeply, I know, but I can't be to him what you are. Don't you know I've been jealous of you, just as you've been of me?"

"I'm sorry," Mereth answered miserably. "I didn't know. I didn't look." It was a revelation. Elyssa, who never lost her poise or her control, could actually be envious and resentful, just as she was.

"Well, it's true. But . . . even with all that, I would be grateful to have you as my friend, Mereth. The Lady knows I need one. I'm not fool enough to think you and I can

change our ways all at once. But might we try to put an end
to our differences, and see what happens?"

"Yes," Mereth said, and wiped her eyes with the back of
her hand. "Oh, yes. Let's."

"Halicar's been neglectful, and that's at my door. I'll ask
him to spend more time with you, so you and he can practice together and do whatever else is needful to raise your
spirits. And mine, come to that. I've hated seeing you look
so forlorn."

"Thank you, my lady." Mereth tried not to sniffle, and
managed it.

"Then let's begin as we mean to go on." Elyssa put her
arm through Mereth's and together they started up the hill.
"I meant what I said, I need a friend, and especially when we
return to Dymie. This . . . thing between me and your brother
will annoy certain people very much, once they find out
about it. We've been lucky here at the villa this summer—
it's been easy to be discreet. And we tried to be careful while
we were still in the palace in the spring, but I doubt if we
were careful enough, and people will be watching when we
return. I'm not such a fool as to think we can hide this in-
definitely. Or even for very long. And when it's known, if it
isn't already, there will be rumbles."

Mereth nodded. Not for the first time since the spring, she
wished they had never come to Elyssa's household. Every
great noble of Haidra would be furious that the Protectress
had taken a foreign lover, a man without a trickle of the pure
Rasenna blood. They would hate Halicar and no doubt hate
Mereth, too. And perhaps they would turn on Elyssa also, in
the end.

"Look," Elyssa said lightly, gesturing ahead at the slaves
and the litter, "our poor sick scrap of flotsam is nearly at the
house. You know, we can't move him to Dymie in his condition. I'll have Utea and some of the household staff stay to
tend him till he recovers. And some guards, in case Tirsun
tries to take him back by force."

Mereth felt a sharp jab of unease. How careful would the
household slaves be with him? She didn't want to be left behind in the villa while Elyssa and Halicar went to Dymie,

but she'd saved the man's life once and she didn't want his
chances squandered by sloppy nursing.

"With your permission, Protectress, might I remain here
also, until he's well enough to travel? He's very ill, and I'd
feel as if I were abandoning him if I left."

"You're sure? It might be weeks." Elyssa glanced sideways at her, a downcast look in her eyes.

"Yes, I'm sure. But my lady, it's . . . it's not a sulk, truly
it isn't. I'm not trying to avoid you and my brother. I'd just
feel more easy if I stayed."

Elyssa gave a smile of relief. "In that case, of course you
may stay. And I'll look forward to seeing you again when
he's recovered."

"And I you," Mereth said. The coals under her breastbone
still burned, but less fiercely than before. Perhaps one day
they might go out.

Elyssa squeezed her arm. "Everything will come right in
the end," she murmured. "It will, Mereth. You'll see."

17

ON THE DAY HE WAS RESCUED FROM THE ENDS OF EARTH, Lashgar had promised himself that someday he'd hang Rook. But now, as he followed Rook along the narrow, deeply shaded street that wound uphill from Kla's harbor gate, the broken promise gave Lashgar some wry amusement. Far from dangling the Rasennan from a gallows in Ammedara, Lashgar had become one of the man's loyal retainers—a member of his household guard and a permanent crewman with a one-hundredth share in the profits of Rook's future voyages. That was assuming such voyages ever took place; before they did, Rook would have to get his hands on enough wealth to replace his lost *Statira,* which was proving difficult.

The possibility of sailing for home caused Lashgar to wonder, as he often did, whether Ilarion might still be alive. Four months had passed since *Statira*'s shore party watched from a wooded bluff while the Kaneshite galley squadron took their ship, but Lashgar's grief at losing his friend had not diminished. It was like an arrow wound that was healing with the arrowhead still buried in it; a dull throb punctuated by unpredictable jabs of pain.

Lashgar knew there was little reason for hope. Tirsun of Kanesh considered Rook a pirate and his crew likewise, and must inevitably have executed all the prisoners by now. So Ilarion had long gone to the Serene Fields, and no one at home would ever know what had happened to him unless Lashgar returned to tell them. This he had sworn to do, so that Ilarion's family could at least perform the proper rites for him.

There was the other matter, too, of Theatana. If only the information about Kayonu's voyage had been more precise, he'd have a better idea of what to expect here in Kla. It was well-known in Ushnana that Kayonu had returned to his city with a good cargo, and that he'd brought with him a woman from some exotic place in the north. But her identity and race were maddeningly unclear. What made tongues wag in Ushnana was the story that she wasn't a captive, but a retainer—apparently she'd saved Kayonu's life somehow, and he owed that debt to her. Saving lives didn't sound like Theatana, and Lashgar clung to the hope that the woman with Kayonu was just some Mixtun girl lifted from the Blue Havens.

He wondered again if he should have warned Rook about Theatana by now. But doing so seemed pointless until he was sure the northern woman was Ilarion's dangerous aunt. And to make the warning believable, he'd have to admit to Rook that he was more than just a nobleman named Lashgar of Ammedara—that he was the heir to Ammedara's throne, and his father had been Theatana's jailer. He didn't know where such an admission might lead, given Theatana's good standing in Kla. Who knew what plausible lies she might concoct about him, out of revenge? Also, he'd have to admit to Rook that he'd lied about his identity for months, and that wouldn't sit well with Rook.

But even if he'd decided to speak, this particular moment was highly unsuitable for it. Rook's party of four—it included Mastarno and Beritar, two more of Rook's retainers—had disembarked from the Ushnanan trading galley as soon as it docked, and now they were tramping through Kla's Lower Town toward Kayonu's residence. It was midafternoon, but the streets in this part of the city were so narrow and twisting that the sunlight didn't easily penetrate their depths. The city market was down by the harbor, and the district was busy with porters carrying oil and wine jars, sacks of wool, bundles of vegetables, and wooden crates stuffed with the domestic fowl called rancolin. Many Klaians had the telltale ruddiness of hair and complexion that betrayed mixed Hazannu-Rasennan blood, and it seemed to

Lashgar that there were more of these than he had seen in Ushnana.

He had also noticed, back in the harbor, that the quayside had not only a shrine to the Lady and the Firebringer, but another to the Storm God of the Hazannu; this was identifiable by a triple-pronged spear, pointing downward, cut into the plaster above the shrine's doorway. To Lashgar's eye it looked like a trident, though he knew from Rook that it represented a lightning bolt striking the Earth. The shrine's exterior was freshly whitewashed, and trimmed with the God's colors of blue and black, and beside it the shrine of the Lady and her consort appeared rather shabby. Rook had looked extremely annoyed at it; apparently it was a recent addition to the harbor, built after he sailed north with Kayonu, and paid for by a Klaian nobleman called Rimash Idu. Lashgar had heard Rook speak of Rimash before; he was a troublemaker in Kla, a devotee of the Hazannu God, and was thought to have designs on the Protectorship. Because Kayonu was the Protector's heir, Rimash was Kayonu's enemy, and consequently Rook's as well.

Lashgar had begun to wonder how long they would tramp through this maze of streets, when they turned a corner and came out into a small square, vivid with the gold of the autumn sunlight. In the center of the square was a public well, where three women were drawing water in cream-glazed pots with handles like jutting ears.

"Is this Shipmaster Kayonu's house?" Lashgar asked Rook as the Rasennan marched straight for a doorway on the far side of the square. The women at the well—they were, from their coloring, of mixed blood—watched the men approach and drew their head scarves across their mouths as Rook and the others passed. It was more a Hazannu gesture than Rasennan.

"This is Kayonu's place, yes," Rook answered, and Lashgar felt the knot of tension draw tighter inside him. Would Ilarion's aunt be within these walls? He'd never seen Theatana, but he'd know her—no one else in Kla would have the golden skin and black hair of the Ascendancy. As for him, Theatana wouldn't know him by sight, though she could well know that Lashgar was the name of the Ammedaran heir. If she were here, he'd have to make sure she believed him to be another Lashgar; it was, fortunately, a common name.

They reached the door, and Rook banged on it. The timbers reverberated and a spy-hole in the middle plank shot open. An eye appeared in it.

"Shipmaster Rook Arnza and party," he said. "Tell Shipmaster Kayonu I'm here."

A voice answered, the words muffled by the heavy planks. The spy-hole closed, there was the scrape of a bar being drawn, and the door swung inward. A Rasennan stood there, blinking, then grinning. "My lord shipmaster!" he exclaimed. "Welcome!"

Lashgar and the others followed Rook over the threshold into the cool shadow of the interior. Rook said briskly, "It's good to see you, Hirumin. Did Kayonu get my message that I was coming?"

"He did. We thought you'd be showing up, once we heard you'd got back to Ushnana." Hirumin's grin got bigger. "You should have heard us bellow and cheer when we found out you'd reached home. We had a feast, and we all got drunk for a day and a night, to celebrate. Then my master was going to sail down to Ushnana, to find out how you'd fared, but we got your tablet that you were coming here, so we waited. The whole household rejoiced that you were still alive—we'd thought you lost for good."

"I'm happy to be alive," Rook said, "but I'd have rejoiced more myself if I'd brought my ship and my men home. A bad-luck voyage, Hirumin, all the way. I'm glad you and your master were more fortunate."

"We were, my lord—I wish you'd had the same luck. The master's going over the accounts with the scribe, but come with me to the courtyard, and then I'll tell him you're here."

They followed Hirumin through a shadowy reception room into a spacious tiled courtyard. Above them a gallery ran around the courtyard's four sides, giving access to the second floor of the house. In the middle of the courtyard was a pool, where rainwater falling from the roof was collected for household needs. Half a dozen wooden benches awaited them; they sat down, and Hirumin vanished into the house. Moments later, a young woman brought a large pottery jug of wine and a reed basket containing thin-walled pottery cups. Red glints in her hair showed that she was of mixed blood, but unlike the women by the well, she didn't hide her face. Nor did she wear the iron wrist ring of slavery. She seemed pleased to see Rook, and went away smiling.

Lashgar was the junior retainer present—Mastarno and Beritar had been with Rook on the voyage north and were both older than he was—so he poured his wine last. It was the straw-colored vintage called "Daylight." The Rasenna, Lashgar had learned, made two kinds of wine: a strong full-bodied type called "Sunset" that they drank when they didn't need to stay sober, and this one, which was much weaker and was consumed to quench thirst during the day.

He had just set the jug on the pavement when a huge yellow-haired man bounded into the courtyard, bellowed with delight, and threw his arms around Rook. The two men pounded each other on the back, with thuds and slaps. Hirumin stood a little way off, grinning from ear to ear under his flowing yellow mustache. Lashgar quickly scanned the dimness behind him and unobtrusively glanced up at the courtyard gallery. There was still no sign of Theatana. Maybe the rumored northern woman was someone else, after all. He relaxed, and turned his attention to Shipmaster Kayonu Lauchmai.

Rook was a big man, but Kayonu was even bigger. He was, however, not much handsomer than the homely, broken-nosed Ushnanan, for he had a broad, flat face from which a sharp nose jutted like the ram of a galley. He appeared jolly, but his green eyes were sharp, and Lashgar knew from Rook's stories of Kayonu's belligerence that the Klaian shipmaster was not to be taken lightly. This was the man, then, whose raiders had slaughtered a dozen Ammedaran soldiers, looted an Ammedaran fort, and abducted a woman whom Lashgar's father Jaladar had sworn, on his honor, to imprison until she died. For these three reasons at least, Kayonu's life was forfeit if Ammedaran law ever laid hold of him.

On the other hand, the man was brave, tenacious, tough, skilled, and with all that, lucky. Lashgar knew enough about governance to know that it would be a shame to waste such a leader. If he paid blood price, he could be pardoned. All in all, it was better to think of Kayonu as an ally, not an enemy.

The shipmasters sat down together and Hirumin joined Lashgar, Mastarno, and Beritar on the benches. Moments later the wine girl returned with two more jugs, and then an older woman arrived, pink-faced from the heat of the kitchen. She carried a huge wooden platter stacked with thick disks of warm bread, chunks of smoked redfish, a dish of pickled fennel root, a large pot of sailor-bean paste, and another of spiced honey. Like the wine girl, she wore no iron ring on her wrist. Watching her go, Lashgar wondered if Kayonu owned any slaves at all. Rook didn't; he said they were more trouble and expense than they were worth. Only the extremely rich in Ushnana and Kla kept slaves, though apparently they were very common on Haidra. But then, according to Rook, the Haidrans were so wealthy they could afford armies of them.

"So tell me," Kayonu was saying to Rook, "how is it you didn't get home to Ushnana till the end of Middle Summer? I've heard scraps of the story, but not all."

Rook scowled and used a bronze spatula to spread bean paste on a slab of bread. "We had to come overland because I lost *Statira* to Tirsun of Kanesh, may the Firebringer piss on him sideways." He bit off a chunk of the bread and paste, and added, through a full mouth, "That's a long walk, and I've added the price of every blister to Tirsun's account. I'll make him pay it somehow."

Kayonu looked Lashgar thoughtfully up and down. "I'd heard that Rook picked up some foreign crew in the north. You'd be such a one, I think."

Lashgar heard no hostility in the tone, and said easily, "Yes, my lord. I'm Lashgar of Ammedara."

"There were two others, too," Rook said glumly, picking up his cup. "Lost them both."

"I didn't hear that," Kayonu said. "What happened?"

Rook swallowed wine. "One died at sea, and the other

was taken with *Statira* by the Kaneshites. That one, Ilarion, he was a good man. Learned Rasennan in thirty days flat. Never saw anything like it. I was sorry to lose him. He was a good friend of Lashgar's, here."

"I regret your loss," Kayonu said to Lashgar. "You speak our language well, in fact."

"I've had several months to learn it, my lord. Necessity is a good schoolmaster."

Rook swallowed noisily, and said, "You're putting the rudder at the bow post, Kayonu. Let's begin at the beginning, when our ships got separated. How much of the sorry tale do you want?"

"The gist, to begin with. Then we'll eat properly and you can give me the details of what you ran into up north, and then we'll drink ourselves onto the floor."

"As you wish." Rook started by giving an account of the mutiny, for which he blamed himself—he'd taken on a group of Haidran seamen as paid crew, not as retainers, and they'd been the source of the trouble. (Kayonu made angry, sympathetic noises at the treacherousness of Haidrans.) Consequently he had to sail homeward short of men and with almost-empty holds.

"And to put the seal on it all," he said angrily, "that piece of excrement Tirsun took my ship, with the little cargo I did have, and half of what remained of my crew."

"Tirsun rides higher on his horse every month," Kayonu observed. "Will Ushnana threaten war if he keeps chasing you and yours?"

Rook displayed a sour grimace. "I think not. Our Protector knows we're no match for his power. So I must shift for myself while I'm outside our walls or yours. Someday, though . . . Never mind, I'd better get on with the tale."

He did so, recounting the disasters that dogged the voyage from the Havens to the southern mainland. As if those calamities were not enough, then came the loss of *Statira*, which stranded Rook and his shore party in thinly populated and unfriendly Hazannu territory a good eight hundred miles east of Ushnana. Fortunately the area had plenty of game and water, and once they recovered their strength, they headed west. It was slow, hard going; they had to avoid Hazannu settlements, because half the barbarian clans along the coast opposite Haidra were slavers, and all regarded any outlander as an enemy. Traveling by sea would have been far easier, but Rook did not dare to signal the trading ships that plied the coasts. They were quite likely to be from Haidra, and it was well known that Tirsun of Kanesh had put a large price on Rook's head. No Haidran captain would have passed up the opportunity for a quick fortune.

After weeks of exhausting travel they were within a hundred miles of Ushnana. Ushnanan ships often plied this stretch of the coast, so Rook decided to risk signaling one. Before they could they ran into a Hazannu war band, and were captured. Rook made a virtue of necessity by telling the leader that he would be lavishly paid if the Hazannu would escort them all to Ushnana, instead of selling them inland as slaves. Three weeks later they stumbled in through Ushnana's Mound Gate, free and safe, and with Rook much poorer for the ransom.

It was then that Rook asked Lashgar to join his household retinue and his permanent crew. Flattered in spite of himself at the Rasennan's regard, and not knowing how else to support himself or find his way home, Lashgar quickly agreed. So here he sat, in Kayonu's house in Kla, and heard Rook praise him and the other survivors for his loyalty and perseverance.

The story of the voyage took a while to tell. By the time Rook drew it to a close, the light in the courtyard had turned orange and a smell of fresh bread, mixed with grilled mutton and garlic, was drifting in from the kitchen. The rest of Kayonu's retainers had joined them now, and the additional twenty men made a small throng in the courtyard. Still there was no sign of any northern woman.

"And that's the gist of it," Rook ended. "And a dismal gist it is, too. My worst luck was to run into that galley patrol from Kanesh. If I hadn't, I'd at least still have my ship."

"Pah!" Kayonu exclaimed. "Ships can be replaced. You'll be rich again in no time. Look here—and all of you around me witness this—I, Kayonu Lauchmai of Kla, will finance Rook Arnza of Ushnana to build a ship, repayment to be made out of proceeds of trading done with that ship, to the amount of one part in ten of the profits. We'll draw up a tablet later. Agreed, and then we feast?"

"Agreed," Rook said, with obvious gratitude. Lashgar knew that this was what he'd hoped for from Kayonu, but he was too proud to ask outright. Aware of this, the Klaian ship-master had made the offer. It could not have been done more gracefully in Ammedara.

Now servants appeared and, with a great clatter and scrape, four long trestle tables were carried into the court-yard, benches added and rearranged, lamps lit in the dim-ness under the gallery, and the girl brought sealed jars of the strong Sunset wine. Kayonu's wife, a tall and striking woman with no apparent Hazannu blood, came out to su-pervise the arrangements. Like the Rasennan women Lash-gar had seen in Ushnana, she was not at all meek in the presence of men, but joked with Rook as she kept a sharp eye on the servants. Rook obviously enjoyed her teasing, and looked a little abashed when she chided him because he still hadn't married. As if to make her point further, she brought out her three children, a pair of boys of seven and nine, and a wide-eyed daughter of perhaps four. Kayonu grinned with pride.

His wife declined to stay for the feast. After she and the children left the courtyard, Lashgar found himself sitting at a side table between Mastarno and Kayonu's man Hirumin. Lashgar warily took his first sip of the aromatic spiced wine. Once he would have plunged into the feasting and drinking with reckless gusto, but he'd learned from Ilarion the virtues of self-possession and watchfulness.

Next to him, Hirumin was ladling bite-size chunks of grilled mutton from a platter onto a disk of hard bread. Lashgar did the same. The Klaian seemed amiable and will-ing to converse, so he said, "Tell me about your voyage up north with Kayonu. It was better than Shipmaster Rook's, I hear."

Hirumin regarded him thoughtfully. "We did some raiding as well as trading, and I gather you're from those islands. What would you do if it happens we pillaged some of your clan? Would you be sworn to go measure for measure?"

Lashgar thought quickly, made up an emblem, and said, "Did you see any banners or shields marked with a beast's head with three horns?"

"No, nothing like that."

"Then we're not at odds. But tell me . . . it's said that you came back with a northern woman. It was said she saved Shipmaster Kayonu's life."

"She did, though nobody but him saw her do it. So I say he's an honest man, to admit the thing and make her a protected woman, when he could have put her on his sleeping mat. She's no green girl, but good-looking enough for all that." Hirumin grinned. "Long in the leg, good hips and bottom, and a fine balcony. Quite a stiffener, even if you hadn't been at sea as long as we were. But the master would have cut our balls off if we'd looked at her sidelong." The grin faded. "She might have done the same, too. There was something about her . . . golden skin and those eyes of hers, dark, dark blue. When she looked at you in a certain way it'd make you feel, well, uneasy. And she'd killed a man to keep the shipmaster alive, so she was no stranger to bloodshed. We raided this fortified island, you see, where she was a prisoner, and during the fighting her warder was about to spit the shipmaster, but she stabbed the man in the eye before he could do it."

Lashgar's hunger fled. A woman imprisoned on an island: It could be no one but Theatana.

"She's not with us now, though," Hirumin went on, and speared a mutton chunk with his belt knife.

"She's not?" Lashgar asked. "Where is she?"

Hirumin shoved the chunk into his mouth and chewed. "Well, as for that," he said around the mutton, "maybe you knew that the Protector of Kla is also Shipmaster Kayonu's uncle?"

"I did. Shipmaster Rook told me. He said Kayonu is the Protector's heir, too."

"Indeed he is—has been since the Protector's son was lost

at sea. Well, a day or two after we got back from the north, our Protector came to dine here with his retinue. He does that often, he and the shipmaster being good friends as well as Protector and heir. Anyway, he saw the northern woman and took a liking to her."

"What's her name?" Lashgar asked, attempting a note of idle curiosity. The northern woman must inevitably be Theatana, but he had to know for sure.

"Theatana of the Dascaris clan, she said."

"Ah." A wave of gloom swept through him but then he thought: *Well, how much damage can she do in a dilapidated place like this?*

Hirumin was eyeing him. "Now I think of it, you're a northerner, too, but you don't look much like her. Do you know the clan?"

"I'm an islander," Lashgar said, avoiding the question. "The golden-skinned people are from the mainland to the north of us. We don't see much of them except their traders. What happened when your Protector saw her?"

"Well, he was smitten, believe it or not. His third wife's dead, and I suppose he was losing interest in bedding the palace slaves. Pretty soon he came to some arrangement with her and the shipmaster, and off Theatana went to live in the palace."

Lashgar raised his eyebrows. "You said she was no girl. What did he see in her?"

Hirumin shrugged and picked a bit of gristle from between his upper incisors. "The Protector's not a young man now, so I suppose she'd look young to him. And as I said, she's a stiffener, even if she's no fresh-ripened girl." He glanced over his shoulder and lowered his voice. "It might be more than that, too. Rumors have gone around about the way he dotes on her. Talk of sorcery—that she's bespelled him."

"She's a sorceress?" Worse and worse.

"Well, I wouldn't say that. Old men do make fools of themselves over women. But he lets her do anything she wants, which isn't like the Protector."

"What sort of things does he let her do?" Lashgar asked, wild visions tumbling through his head.

"Well, she goes often to the house of Vindisi, and she goes alone except for a single guard. Vindisi heals animals, especially horses. She's learning the skills from him, it's said, to help with the Protector's mounts. But Vindisi isn't from here—he came from way down the coast, near Ushnana or so he said, and he's odd. Some think he uses magic in his healing. But that's benign, so no one questions him about it. And if Theatana learns the odd spell to ease pain, there's no harm in that."

"But animal doctoring is no pastime for a woman of rank. Why does the Protector let her do it?"

Hirumin pulled at his chin. "Well, that's the mystery. That's why some people think he's bespelled. I don't think so, myself. Some women can lead a man around by the short arm, and he'll follow without a squeak. That's likely all there is to it."

"Probably," Lashgar answered, a little reassured by Hirumin's air of conviction.

"Speaking of the Protector," Hirumin went on, "he may be here later this evening. Shipmaster Kayonu invited him to help celebrate your master's survival. He'll likely want to talk to you. He's interested in foreign parts and people. Maybe you'll get to meet Theatana, though she doesn't usually come. The shipmaster's wife doesn't care for her."

Thank the Allfather that Ilarion and I never told Rook who we really were, Lashgar thought. *As long as Theatana thinks I'm a backwater noble who happens to have the same name as Jaladar's son, I've got the advantage of her. But maybe she won't come, and I won't even have to concern myself with that.*

Night fell and the jugs went up and down the table. For all his care with the drink, Lashgar's head began to buzz slightly, and he pushed his cup aside. He wasn't sure how long they'd been eating and drinking; several hours at least, for the autumn sunset seemed to have passed a considerable time ago. Hirumin was telling him a complicated joke when the metallic bray of a horn sounded from outside the house. The Klaian broke off, and said, "Ah, he's here."

"The Protector?"

"Yes."

In a few moments an older man appeared in the courtyard doorway. He wore a belted green-and-white tunic and a cloak worked with running blue horses on an emerald ground. Around him were half a dozen of his retainers. But no woman accompanied them.

"It appears she didn't come," Hirumin muttered in Lashgar's ear. "Well, I'm not surprised. She usually doesn't."

The Protector came into the room with his men; voices were raised in greeting. Lashgar studied the Protector carefully, looking for signs of bewitchment. He saw none, but wasn't sure he'd recognize them even if they were present.

Hirumin had put his cup down. Suddenly he tilted his head, listening, and a frown crossed his face. "Hunh. Did you hear that?"

"No. Hear what?"

"Horns in the distance. No, it's gone." His nose wrinkled as he sniffed the air. "*Hai*, that's not cooking smoke. By the Lady, I think we've got a fire in the city."

Others had smelled it, too. The Protector turned and hurried toward the street door with his men. Kayonu yelled, "Steward, get buckets, there's a house on fire somewhere." Everyone scrambled to their feet and a general surge out of the courtyard began.

Lashgar had lost track of Rook by the time they spilled into the square in front of Kayonu's house. A cloud-hazed moon hung in the sky, casting a dim light over the whitewashed buildings and making a squat ghost of the public wellhead in the square's center.

"The palace!" someone shouted, and Lashgar looked up into the star-dusted sky, toward the hulking darkness that was the citadel hill. At its summit red flames were flailing the night, shot through with sparks and streamers of smoke. A slow breeze blew down from the heights, carrying the reek of burning buildings with it. And on the breeze, faint but unmistakable, came the sound of battle: men's shouts and screams and curses, the clang of iron against iron.

"Treachery!" someone yelled. The voice was enraged,

shrill, and Lashgar thought, *Allfather help us, the Hazannu have gotten into the citadel. The city's taken.*

Oaths and confused commands filled the moonlit square as Alfni's and Kayonu's men tried to organize themselves. Abruptly Rook was beside him. "Lashgar, is that you?"

"Yes."

"I've got Mastarno and Beritar here. Stick close. We'll head for the harbor and try to get away on the galley we came in on. There's no point in us staying—with the citadel gone, whoever's in here is in for good."

"Who is it? The Hazannu?"

"Who knows? But some traitor opened the citadel gates, maybe the city gates, too, by now. My guess is Rimash."

"But shouldn't we stay and help Kayonu?"

"I don't know where he's gone. We can't help him; four swords won't make any difference. His men will do what they can for his wife and the children. But we've got to get away. If Rimash did this, he'll hand us over to Tirsun in a blink. Come *on*, man."

He set off at a run, Lashgar following. "But the Protector—" Lashgar got out between breaths. "Shouldn't we—"

"We're Ushnanans, not his sworn men. He can make a run for it, same as us, if it suits him. Now save your breath for the oars. We've got to sneak out of the harbor before the enemy gets a good grip on it."

18

WITHIN THE WALLS OF KLA'S CITADEL, THE PALACE BAN-
quet hall was burning. Theatana, standing on the ramparts
above the citadel's main gate, boiled with frustration and
rage as she watched the flames leap and writhe through windows and roof. Too much was going wrong. It was no part
of the plan to fire the palace; some fool of a slave must have
dropped a lamp on the rush mats of the hall floor. But losing
the palace hardly mattered; what did matter was that Alfni
wasn't lying drugged in his bed as he was supposed to be.
He was down in the city with Kayonu.

She peered through skeins of smoke down into the
citadel's outer court. Flames lit it a dirty orange; the fire,
which had now taken firm hold of the banquet hall's roof
timbers, was spreading toward the palace's residential quarter. Bedlam filled the night: the smoking air was full of
screams from slaves trapped in the burning hall; other slaves
ran hither and thither in the courtyard like beheaded chick-
ens; Kaneshite soldiers and the survivors of the palace guard
fought across the blood-slicked paving. Steel clanged on
steel, the fires roared. No one was even attempting to put
them out. Tirsun and Rimash had left her to go somewhere
else, she didn't know where.

None of this, except getting Tirsun's men into the city and
the citadel, was supposed to happen. The plan had begun to
go awry just before the time of the evening meal, when Alfni
announced that he was dining later that evening at Kayonu's.
The decision was completely unexpected. Theatana did her
best to dissuade him but this once, to her fury, he was im-

movable. She had no opportunity to get a cup of drugged
wine into him, because he decided to go to the bathhouse before leaving the palace. In near despair she considered knif-
ing him in his bath, but he always kept his guards close by
when he was that vulnerable. So at the tenth hour off he
went, alert, unscathed, and hearty, to dinner at his nephew's.

And then she hadn't been able to get word to Rimash that
Alfni had left the palace. The clan-lord didn't find out about
it until he, Tirsun, and Tirsun's soldiers were inside the
citadel and the fighting with the garrison was under way.
Then, to her appalled disbelief, she discovered that Rimash
had failed in a key part of the plan: Overexcited and wanting to make sure the citadel was held by as many soldiers as
possible, he hadn't reminded Tirsun to divert men to Kayonu's house and dispose of the Protector's nephew.

If Alfni were lying drugged and helpless, a delay in
killing his nephew would not have been so serious. But the
Protector was on the loose, and the conspirators were now in
a dangerous position. The citadel would soon be theirs, but
Alfni had his own allies and supporters in Kla. If he and
Kayonu managed to rally their friends and their friends' re-
tainers, the night could end with the plotters and the
Kaneshite troops sealed up, powerless, in the citadel's ruins.
Theatana could imagine a variety of futures for herself
thereafter, none of them pleasant.

A man wearing the insignia of Kanesh on his surcoat
came up the stair and stepped onto the rampart wall-walk. It
was Tirsun, his armor glinting russet in the light of the burning palace. He pulled off his helmet, releasing a flood of
golden ringlets.

"My lord Protector," Theatana said, as calmly as she
could manage, "what's happening? Where's Rimash?"

Tirsun seemed only mildly interested in the fighting in the
courtyard. It was dying down, with only three of Alfni's
guardsmen on their feet. As Theatana watched, it became
two. The guards' situation had been hopeless once they let
the enemy within the walls; they were so outnumbered that
Tirsun had needed only half his soldiers to crush their resistance.

"Ah, Rimash," Tirsun said lightly. His accent was different from that of Kla, more lisping and sibilant, but Theatana understood him easily. "I lent him fifty men to go and deal with Alfni and Kayonu. If he catches the Protector, the city belongs to him. If he doesn't, it may still be Alfni's. I won't stay to find out. If Rimash misses the mark again, my men and I will promptly return to our ship, and depart."

Theatana wanted to say, *Take me with you*, but held her tongue; she wouldn't ask favors unless she had to. But she felt a small measure of relief. Tirsun, at least, seemed to know what he was doing.

She turned and looked over the parapet, down to the lower city. A three-quarter moon gleamed on the harbor waters, and she could just make out the dark blot of the big Kaneshite freighter by a quay. But the ship hadn't carried trade goods; into its capacious hold had been packed the best troops of Tirsun's First Levy. She'd seen it moving into the harbor at sunset, as planned, not long before Alfni told her he was leaving the palace.

"Let me congratulate you," Tirsun said from beside her. "I had some doubts, reading your letters, that you really were the sorceress you claimed to be. Such skills are easy to profess, especially at a distance. But that was a clever and very convincing spell you used to get us in here. Even to the voice. I was beginning to wonder if you really *were* Alfni, and he was playing some very deep game against me."

Tirsun was referring to the aspect change; that, at least, had worked perfectly. Near the appointed time she'd slipped down into the dark herb garden and bespelled herself into Alfni's semblance. There she waited until she heard the citadel guard challenge Tirsun's approaching men, and then rushed from the garden into the outer courtyard, where she ordered the guards to open the gates. Though puzzled—they had seen Alfni leave the citadel not long past, and the presence of so many armed men on the approach ramp disturbed them—they dared not disobey orders given from their Protector's lips, in their Protector's voice. They opened, Tirsun's soldiers stormed in, and the fighting began.

The Kaneshites had orders to capture the seeming Alfni

but not to harm him, and within moments Theatana stood before Tirsun. As he gazed suspiciously at his elderly prisoner, she spoke the word of dismissal, and Alfni's appearance slid from her like smoke. Tirsun looked alarmed, then astonished, then delighted, and Theatana knew she was nearer her goal.

"All my claims are true," she told him. "Know me long enough, and you'll find out." She wondered if anyone had found Vindisi's body yet or if, after two days, it still dangled from the stable rafters. He hadn't taught her quite all he knew, but even so it was time he went—it wouldn't do for Tirsun to find out that she'd learned her sorcery, no matter how potent it was, from a horse doctor. Rimash also wanted the man dead, for secrecy's sake, so the clan-lord garroted him as soon as he handed over the sleeping drug for Alfni. Vindisi died with everyone's secrets still behind his lips, and they strung him up in the stable as a suicide.

"I certainly *hope* to know you that long," Tirsun said to her. He glanced down into the courtyard. "Ah, we've killed the last of them—I think we've got control of the citadel now. That's a good start. Now I'm going to take some men and find out what Rimash is doing about the opposition. I hope he hasn't bungled again."

"I'll accompany you," said Theatana, and to her satisfaction he did not object.

Dawn had come. Smoke hazed the streets of Kla, rasped the throat, and stung the eyes. In Temple Square, by the stone-capped shaft that symbolized the passage to the Underworld, Theatana stood watching a ragged double line of some sixty or seventy girls and women. Many of the younger ones were weeping hysterically. Behind them a broad flight of red-granite steps rose to a huge stone platform where the slab of the Green Lady's altar hunched in the tarnished light. On the platform behind the altar rose the massive walls of the city's chief temple, its white limestone portico shadowing the copper-green doors that led to the inner sanctuary. It was shabby, like all the Lady's shrines in Kla, and Theatana wondered idly what the building would look like when Rimash got through with it. He'd told her more than once, as they plotted, that when he became Protector he'd replace the Lady's worship with that of the Hazannu Storm God. Now he had his chance. Tirsun, she knew from Alfni's disapproving comments, was not much devoted to the Lady, and might well help him do it.

She turned her gaze to the far side of the square, where another group of captives, these male, huddled under the eyes of the Kaneshite soldiers. They were rich merchants and aristocrats of old Klaian families, many with their sons. Unlike the women, they were bound to each other with ropes. Theatana recognized the majority as Alfni's friends or supporters. She also knew many of the captive women to be wives or formal concubines of the male prisoners; anguished calls passed between the two groups.

Alfni and Kayonu weren't among the bound men; they were dead. Theatana knew this to be true, because she'd seen their bodies. They and their retainers had been cut down in the street before they could organize any serious resistance. So, despite all that had gone wrong, she'd won this particular battle; Tirsun had Kanesh, and she had her path to Haidra.

She looked up through the smoky morning air at the summit of Spring Hill. The fire there had burned out, but it still smoked; the palace was utterly destroyed, and all that remained of the citadel defenses was the outer curtain wall and the gate towers. Rimash wouldn't have much joy of his new possession. It would cost most of the Idu fortune to rebuild it.

Theatana leaned against the stone cap of the shaft. She was tired and hungry, reeked of smoke, and wanted a bath. A few paces away, the two guards Tirsun had assigned for her protection shifted stance uneasily. She'd noticed that they wouldn't look directly at her; the word had obviously gotten around among the Kaneshites that she'd been using sorcery.

Tirsun was still with Rimash on the other side of the square. There the clan-lord and a dozen other men of the Idu clan, assisted by the Kaneshite soldiers, were sorting out the

male captives. They separated the prisoners into two groups,
a small one made up of the richest and most powerful of
Alfni's friends, the second and larger consisting of males of
less consequence. Baskets of slave rings were brought; soldiers clamped them around the wrists of the men in the second group and fastened the irons also to the captive women.
These, never having imagined that such a thing could happen to them, shrieked and wailed as the rings closed around
their white wrists. Then they and the newly enslaved men
were marched out of the square toward the harbor, where the
slave buyers Tirsun had brought with him were already
preparing their bids.

Of the twenty or so males that remained behind, two-
thirds were adults and the rest were boys or youths. These
were the Idu clan's strongest enemies in Kla. Rimash gave
an order, and the Kaneshite soldiers forced the bound prisoners to their knees. Rimash spoke again, and four Idu
clansmen began working their way along the line of kneeling captives, pulling heads back and slitting throats. The air
filled with choked, bubbling screams interspersed with
moans and gurgles. Theatana looked on with interest at first,
but found that crude butchery soon palled.

When all the captives were dead, Tirsun turned his back
on them and sauntered across the square to join her. Rimash
followed, trying not to look like a servant beside the Protector of Kanesh. Behind them, the clan-lord's relatives were
searching the bodies for concealed valuables.

"That's out of the way, then," Tirsun said as he came up
to her. "I think it's almost time for breakfast. Don't you?"

"Yes," she answered. "Incidentally, I didn't see Kayonu's
wife and his brats here today. Where are they?"

"Rimash?" Tirsun asked, smiling. "Where are they?"

"Dead," Rimash muttered.

"He killed them himself last night," Tirsun told her
blandly. "Wife, sons, and daughter. The new Protector of
Kla likes to be tidy. Don't you, my brother Rimash?"

The clan-lord shrugged. Theatana felt a jab of disappointment. She'd hoped to have the pleasure of doing away
with Kayonu's wife. The woman had hardly bothered to

conceal her loathing for Theatana, and deserved a notable death.

"Brother Tirsun," Rimash said, "about the Lady's temples—"

"Ah, yes, the Lady. You had plans for her, I believe."

Rimash lowered his voice to a guttural, angry whisper. "I want her images thrown in the muck. The God has to rule in Kla, not her, or everyone in the city will be punished. I want her temples emptied of every trace of her, and the priestesses thrown into the street."

"This is quite a serious business, Rimash," Tirsun observed, raising his eyebrows sardonically. "Won't the priestesses object?"

The clan-lord spat on the pavement. "This isn't Haidra. Here the Lady's priestesses are poor, and their power has deserted them. The God has ground their Goddess's face into the dust, and they know it. That's why they haven't put their noses outside the temple this morning." Rimash waved an arm at the slaughter on the square's far side. "They don't want to end like *that*. And if I'm wrong, and the Lady still rules, let her destroy me now and break the God's shrine that I built in the harbor. Unless that happens, the rule of the God is here in Kla. And his house is going to be *that* one." He pointed at the temple.

"Yes, yes," Tirsun said. "I don't want to engage in theological dispute." His voice became ironic. "But Theatana, aren't you a devotee of the Lady? Does Rimash's proposal not shock you?"

To Theatana this was a sheer waste of time, though Tirsun seemed to find it amusing. She said:

"He can toss her statues into the nearest dungheap, for all I care. And then, if he's inclined, he can send the Storm God's images after hers and piss on them all together."

Rimash, already breathless with emotion and suppressed anger, seemed to lose the power of speech. Mouth twitching, he could only stare at Theatana.

His fury seemed merely to amuse Tirsun further. "A clearly held position," the Protector said amiably. "All this aside, Theatana, I assume our bargain still holds?"

She gave him her most intimate smile. "Why shouldn't it, my lord? I gave you Kla, now you take me to Kanesh as a free member of your household. It's more than fair."

Rimash made strangled noises. Then he said, in a low, choking voice:

"*You gave* him Kla? You lying slut." His eyes glittered. "I've held my tongue long enough. Brother, this one walks the Foul Road. I'm warning you now, as a fellow ruler."

"Are you sure of this?" Tirsun asked. He seemed un-alarmed. "I find it hard to believe that so lovely a woman could be a Walker. How do you know this?"

"She draws sprites from the woods and commands them. I've seen her do it. If you take her to Kanesh, you let your doom in by the main gate."

Tirsun studied Theatana. "*Do* you walk the Road?" he asked softly. "I don't really care. I'd just like to know."

She said, "I walk where my path leads me."

He laughed. "As we all wish to." But he sounded very, very slightly uncertain, and their gazes locked.

She saw his eyes, really saw them, for the first time. They were the green of emeralds, flecked with gold as if inlaid by a master jeweler. And in their depths coiled appetites like soft fanged mouths, sweet and violent.

It has to be now, she thought. *He's capricious, and Rimash has worried him a little. I have to snare him quickly. I must promise what he most desires.*

She summoned all her waning strength, honed her will to a blade of intent, and thrust her awareness toward the Protector.

The moment became suspended in time. Tirsun, unblinking, still looked at her. The people in the square were motionless effigies; two small birds flitting over the roofs seemed barely to move. From Theatana's belly rose a searing whirlwind; it seethed across her vision and in it she saw specters with beautiful violent faces and long, streaming hair, their bodies writhing in passion and torment, twined in grotesque couplings and perverse ecstasies.

They blazed before her for the space of two heartbeats, then winked into nonexistence. She felt herself sway and forced herself to stand upright, though she felt on the point of collapse. Tirsun was leaning forward, his lips a handbreadth from hers, his gaze unfocused. Then he blinked, shook his head a little, and she knew he saw her again.

Theatana opened her mouth a little and took a soft slow breath. Tirsun gazed at her parted lips, then looked up and said in a thick, wondering voice, "Your eyes are almost black. It is like looking into a mirror."

"Yes," she murmured. She moved her aching body a little, as she had moved it to inflame Alfni, and swayed an inch closer to him. "I am a woman of singular abilities, Protector. And of singular desires."

His nostrils flared, and she saw him swallow. "Are you, now?" he asked.

Theatana said, "Yes. I would soon come to understand your tastes, I think." She had him on the hook's barb now. She was tired, but not too tired to play him in.

"Ah," he breathed. "Yes, I think indeed you *would* understand."

"Believe me," she whispered.

Rimash snarled, "God above, woman! Have you bespelled him now, too, the way you bespelled Alfni?"

Theatana kept silent. "Rimash," Tirsun murmured, without looking at him, "my men are near, and you walk the brink of a cliff."

"But brother," the clan-lord protested desperately. "Brother, Protector—"

Theatana turned on him, and he closed his mouth. After a moment she said, "I'd leave a strong garrison here if I were you, my lord."

"I intend to do so," Tirsun agreed dryly. "But Rimash, don't worry about the Green Lady. I'll help you deal with her. It's partly in my own interest to do so. Some of my nobles will be quite pleased at the news of her diminishment."

"Yes," Rimash said woodenly. "As you wish."

"Thank you. Now, you'd better get on with ruling your city. Begin by feeding my men—they're short-tempered when they're hungry, and I'm sure you don't want Kla pillaged. My officers will help you see to them. As for me, I'm going back to the ship for my own breakfast. Will you join me, Theatana? We have so much to talk about that I hardly know where to begin."

19

IN THE AFTERNOON OF THE SECOND DAY OF MIDDLE AU-
tumn, Ilarion came to Dymie Palace.

That morning the wet season had begun in earnest. Rags of
soft cool rain fell about him and Mereth as they rode with
their small cavalry escort up the paved ramp that climbed the
flank of Beacon Hill. Above, shadowy in the mist cloaking the
hill's summit, loomed the fortification walls of the citadel. On
Ilarion's left, spreading away below the ramp, were the streets
and roofs of Dymie itself, but he could gain no real impression
of the Protectorate's capital. Indistinct in the fog and drizzle, it
seemed more a phantasm than a reality, like the spectral Underworld cities he had seen in the fever-drenched dreams of his
sickness. But he knew the sea was out there somewhere, though
invisible, for he could smell its salt tang. He shivered.

Mereth glanced sideways at him. She'd suggested traveling to the city in a cart, but he'd refused, tired of being an in-
valid. After they set out he'd begun to suspect that the cart
might have been as much for her benefit as his, for she was
an inexpert horsewoman. The Rasennan ignorance of stirrups, of course, made riding even more difficult for her.
He'd learned to manage without them in Tirsun's service but
still felt slightly precarious in the saddle.

"Are you warm enough?" she asked. She worried about
him, though he had regained almost his full strength and no
longer shook like an aspen when the air was cool. He supposed her worry was natural; she'd told him he'd almost
died of his fever before it finally broke. He didn't remember
that, but she'd been tending him and should know.

271

"I'm fine," he told her reassuringly, and gave her a smile. Like him, she wore felt-lined riding boots and a hooded rain cloak of black leather. Beneath the cloak was a thick woolen tunic with a belt under it, to which felt leggings were laced. Neither the Rasenna, the Hazannu, nor the Antecessors had apparently ever thought of breeches, and Ilarion had decided to try making a pair before the colder weather set in. Mereth, intrigued by the idea, had promised to help.

"But Ilarion, you just shivered," she said, peering more closely at him from beneath her hood. "I've seen you shivering enough to worry when you do it."

"It's nothing to worry about," he told her. "It was the thought of being at sea again, in a fog. Anyway, the most I'll admit to is a single shiver. No, not even that. More of a slight tremor."

"Only that?" she asked, her face grave but with a touch of a smile at the corners of her mouth. "I would not like to see you really shivering again, Ilarion Tessaris."

"Only that," he assured her, and smiled in return, a little awkwardly. He still felt abashed that this young woman had tended to his most basic physical needs when he was ill: fed him, washed him, changed his soiled bedding, ladled willow-bark infusion into his mouth to cool his fever. There was little about his body that Mereth didn't know, and he recognized, with some embarrassment, that she had gained that knowledge in rather unpalatable ways.

As for Mereth herself, he did not think she was precisely beautiful, though she was well favored enough to turn a man's head in the street. She was always immaculately groomed but otherwise made little of her physical appearance. She applied none of the eye shadow or lip and cheek colorings that upper-class Rasennan women habitually used, and she employed only a pair of unadorned silver clips to keep her glossy brown hair drawn back from her face and forehead. Her coloring was closer to his than to that of the Rasenna, but she could never have been mistaken for a woman of his race; her face was too delicately boned, her mouth too wide, her long dark eyes too tipped up at the outer corners, her skin too much the color of pale tawny sand.

But if her appearance was simply that of a well-favored young woman, her voice was a different matter. After Ilarion came to need less constant care, her singing had frequently drifted to him from her quarters in the villa, and it was flawless, exquisite. Learning from Belit that she was an Antecessor Mistress-Singer, he had not dared impose by asking her to sing for him, but her far-off melodies often touched him with a bittersweet melancholy. Others made the back of his neck tingle, as if he had unknowingly stepped into the presence of a divinity. He understood now why Antecessor singers were so highly prized, and so rare.

He also suspected, from a memory almost washed away by his illness, that Mereth had sung to him while he lay in his fever. If she had, he thought that perhaps her voice had called him back from death. He would have liked to tell her so, but was afraid he might sound foolish, especially if the memory were a false one.

As for memories, he recollected nothing of his landfall below the villa, though Mereth had told him how the Protectress had refused to give him up to his pursuers, though in doing so she risked violent hostility from her brother. She'd saved his life by her action, for he'd certainly have died before he reached Kanesh —no doubt to Tirsun's profound disappointment.

And Elyssa had given him his freedom, into the bargain. He wore no slave iron now; Mereth had summoned a smith to cut it from his arm once he'd regained some strength. He was so weakened by the illness that he almost broke down when she told him he was to be freed, and when the iron at last fell away he did weep a little. Mereth had pretended not to see.

He hadn't yet been able to thank the Protectress in person, since she had left the summer villa for the palace before his sickness ebbed. Today, however, he would do so. He would also, he had decided, tell her who he really was. He would tell Mereth at the same time. He owed the two women his life and health, and continuing to conceal his identity from them would be dishonorable.

He was aware that telling them would also entail letting

Mereth's brother Halicar know. Ilarion hadn't met the Master-Singer yet, because Halicar had returned to Dymie when the Protectress did, but it was obvious from the way Mereth spoke of her brother that she cared deeply for him. Expecting Mereth to lie to him was out of the question.

As for the Protectress, Ilarion had gleaned a certain amount of information about her from Mereth. Elyssa Velianas was twenty-six, a just ruler by all accounts, and a full priestess of the Green Lady. She also was intelligent and literate, and took none of her brother Tirsun's delight in cruelty. This last, to Ilarion, came as a profound relief.

He'd been startled to learn from Mereth that Halicar and Elyssa were lovers; Rasennan aristocrats, both men and women, were very particular about the blood and rank of those with whom they formed liaisons. But the two were deeply in love, Mereth said, and determined to stay together. She did not sound entirely happy about the affair; no doubt, Ilarion supposed, she was worried about her brother's safety even though he was an Antecessor bard. And with some reason. Most Rasennan nobles would be livid with fury that a foreigner was the Protectress's consort, and while Halicar might be immune from physical injury, they could make his life—and Mereth's—very unpleasant in spite of Elyssa's protection.

Their horses reached the top of the ramp. It ended abruptly in a small triangle of level ground, an outcrop of Beacon Hill's main summit. Looming above this tiny plaza was the palace's fortification wall and a pair of towers flanking the main gate. The gate's wood and iron leaves stood open. Its two sentries saw Mereth among the cavalry escort, grinned at her, and waved them through.

As Ilarion rode under the lintel, he passed a professional eye over the gate and its setting. Its timbers were gray with age and would burn well; their iron fittings were old, and though they were bitumen-sealed against the sea's salt air, he saw the telltale pitting of rust. The towers were too low and the ground-level masonry suggested that the foundations had settled. As a stronghold, the place did not inspire much confidence. Mereth had said the Protectress might be pleased to employ him in some military capacity, and by the time they left the gate's shadows for the misty courtyard beyond, he concluded that it would be a good idea.

Mereth reined in as grooms appeared from the direction of what must be stables. "Here we are," she said. "I'll arrange for you to eat and rest, and later the Protectress will want to speak with you. Once you're cared for I must go and see my brother." She slid gingerly from her horse. "Halicar will want to talk to you, too, by the way. He'll ransack your head for melodies and lyrics. I hope your memory's good and you can carry a tune."

This was the first he'd heard of Halicar's professional interest in him, but he said gamely, "My singing voice is notoriously bad. Even my mother could hardly bear to listen to me—my sister's is much sweeter. However, I'll try to oblige."

"Don't worry," said Mereth. "He'll be fascinated."

The summons for his audience came late in the afternoon. It was borne by no less a personage than Elyssa's Grand Domestic, Nenattu, a man of middle age with somber eyes and a pointed chin. Nenattu was smaller and slighter than the average among the Rasenna, being a fingerbreadth shorter than Ilarion. Despite his lack of stature he carried himself with authority. He instructed Ilarion in the etiquette of being with the Protectress—a brief instruction, for she apparently took little notice of formal decorum—and they left the guest chambers.

Ilarion realized, soon after they set out, that Dymie Palace was something of a labyrinth compared to the airy vistas of plazas, colonnades, and pavilions that Tirsun had built on the Citadel Stone. He and Nenattu walked down endless dim corridors, up narrow white-gypsum stairways and across octagonal chambers, along galleries faced with dark green mottled stone. From time to time they passed light wells that fell away into shadowy gardens of ferns; here and there were narrow courtyards with marble benches and flower beds now faded to their autumn colors of muted orange, sage green, and dusky yellow. It seemed far older than the palace in Kanesh, closed in and brooding, its fading resplendence a dreamlike glimpse into the ancient world of the Rasenna.

"How old is this place?" he asked at length.

"Parts of it are very old," the Grand Domestic answered. "A palace has been here for a thousand years, rebuilt and restored many times." He reached out as they walked and gently brushed a fingertip over a painting of a woman's face. "Haidra was once a province of the Great Garden, and Dymie was the capital of that province, and Dymie Palace was then the residence of the Provincial Protector. After the Fall, the Protectors of Haidra moved their capital to Kanesh; the Citadel Stone is more defensible than Beacon Hill. But the Protectors kept up the palace here, for their visits to the west of the island. When the old Protector divided Haidra between the lady Elyssa and her brother, this was the suitable place for her to live."

Nenattu was more talkative than his dour appearance would suggest. They were now walking through a pillared room that was empty except for a trio of vast bronze cauldrons near the exit door. Nothing suggested what purpose the cauldrons might serve, if any. "It's an impressive residence," Ilarion observed politely.

"The lower levels are damp, and in Middle Winter it's chilly," Nenattu said. "Half is closed up and not much used now." He gave Ilarion a surprising sidelong grin. "If you can persuade my lady that your homeland's rulers have a taste for rebuilding their residences from time to time, and that she might do the same, I will be much in your debt. The Protectress prefers to attend only to dire necessities, like leaking roofs and blocked drains."

"In this she is very unlike her brother," Ilarion said, warming suddenly to the man. He was clearly no natural kin to Entash, his counterpart in Kanesh.

"And for that we thank the Green Lady," Nenattu answered with feeling. "Ah, we've arrived. This is the Blue Swallow Room, where my lady receives favored guests."

He stopped at a double door whose wooden panels had been polished to a high sheen. He knocked three times, waited, then called, "Nenattu the Grand Domestic and the esteemed Ilarion Tessaris."

From within a woman's voice answered, "Enter."

Nenattu said, "Come through here, if you please, my lord Ilarion," and allowed Ilarion to precede him into the Blue Swallow Room. A billow of warmth surged around him, bearing a spicy fragrance of lampnut oil, honey, and heated wine. Accompanying the warmth was a sudden pink-and-gold light. Many lamps had been lit in the reception room, and these were the gold. The redder illumination was the late-afternoon sun, which had appeared from behind a cloud bank and was shining through three windows set high in the wall. The windows had many small panes of thick pinkish glass, and these dyed the sunlight the hue of faded roses. The walls were covered with frescoes: Myriad flocks of blue swallows darted through orchards of golden fruit, huge striped cats hunted deerlike creatures with spiral horns, processions of silver butterflies and golden bees floated across ranks of lilies. The scent of warmed wine came from a large pottery wine server on a burnished bronze stand; a brazier glowing with charcoal sat in a rack beneath it. The room was lavishly furnished by Rasennan standards, with couches, chairs, and the small low tables common to every household.

Mereth and a man, who must from his coloring be her brother Halicar, were sitting on a long bench under the windows. Halicar held a curiously shaped harp that appeared to be made of ivory, and Mereth's double flute lay on her lap as if she had just finished playing. He saw Mereth smile, but then his attention flew to the golden-haired woman who sat in the gilt chair at the room's center: Elyssa Velianas, Protectress of Dymie.

She wore a high-waisted skirt of blue with scarlet flounces and a tightly fitted red jacket with a flaring collar. At her throat was a spiral worked in gold, and on her long white fingers were a dozen rings of gold, silver, onyx, and crystal, and a green stone that might have been jade. Her skirt reached the floor, but one slender sandaled foot peeped from beneath its hem. Its nails were painted scarlet, like her fingernails. She was regarding Ilarion with an expression of careful appraisal mixed with curiosity.

Ilarion was momentarily at a loss for words. He had judged from Mereth's description that Elyssa Velianas was well favored, but he had not expected her to be so lovely. Her green eyes were enormous, and her mouth was generous and perfectly shaped. Some very adept attendant had arranged her hair in flowing waves that created a soft frame for her face. A fillet of silver set with onyx bezels kept it in position.

He recollected himself and bowed. "Lady Protectress Elyssa Velianas of Dymie," he said, "I beg leave to present myself as the nobleman Ilarion Tessaris of Captala Nea of the Ascendancy. I am your lady's ally and servant in the name of the Green Lady and the Firebringer, and may they bestow her blessing and favor on this roof and all under it."

Elyssa nodded, and her face relaxed slightly. "I am pleased at your presence under my roof," she answered, "and welcome you in their name. You have the protection of my walls and hearth. I hope you've recovered fully from your illness."

"I'm in all respects recovered, Protectress."

"I'm very glad, and also glad to have you here with us now. I usually take my evening meal at sundown, with Mereth and Halicar, and I would be pleased if you would join us. Until recently I knew nothing of the existence of northern countries and peoples, except for some very old stories, and I'm looking forward to hearing about the place you call home."

"I'd be extremely happy to tell you all I can," Ilarion answered.

"Then we'll all sit together and talk," Elyssa said. "You haven't met my Master-Singer Halicar, though I'm sure Mereth has told you about him."

The Antecessor bard rose, came to stand by Elyssa, and stretched out his hand. It was so unlike a Rasennan gesture that Ilarion was nonplussed. Then he reached out also and the two men clasped forearms in the Ascendancy manner. Ilarion remembered describing the custom to Mereth; she must have told her brother about it.

"I gather that's how men greet in the north," Halicar said,

grinning hugely. His voice was a resonant baritone, rich and melodious. "Did I perform it correctly?"

"An optimate of Captala couldn't improve on it," Ilarion said, smiling in return, for Halicar's grin was infectious. He'd been prepared to like Mereth's brother, and in these first moments of their first meeting he sensed that he had discovered a friend. Mereth had said that Halicar had a whimsical sense of humor beneath his Master-Singer's air of gravity, and indeed there were laugh lines at the corners of his deep brown eyes. He looked very much like his sister, though he was twenty-eight to Mereth's twenty-two: the same long dark eyes, the same wide mouth and thick shining hair. But there was nothing effete about the man. His grip on Ilarion's forearm had been strong and confident, and under his blue-and-gold tunic glided hard flat muscles. But where Mereth's face was delicate, his was hewn from rougher stock. If not for the laugh lines, it would be a stern face, even harsh.

"Thank you," Halicar said. "I try to perfect such customs, since who knows when one may need them? Though I don't know if Mereth or I will ever sing in your homeland. We didn't even know it was there."

"I assure you it is. My people didn't know Haidra was here, nor the mainland either, for that matter."

"There's a great deal to talk about," Elyssa said, and waved at the two low-backed couches near her chair. "Join me, all of you, in taking a cup of spiced wine. It drives the season's dankness away. My lord Tessaris, sit here by me. I had heard that ships of Ushnana and Kla sailed for the far north last year, and that only the Klaian vessel returned. But now I find that you were aboard the ship from Ushnana. Mereth has told me something about how you came to Haidra and fell into my brother's hands and lost your friend Lashgar. But I'm sure there's much more to know."

Ilarion took a place at the end of the couch nearest her. Elyssa clapped her hands softly, and two female slaves appeared from a shadowy doorway to serve the wine. The spices were well blended, but the vintage had a faint acrid aftertaste. Tirsun's cellars were much better than Elyssa's,

Ilarion decided, but the company that came with it was far worse.

"Honored Protectress," he began formally, "before we talk further, may I speak on the matter of my gratitude to you?"

Elyssa nodded, as if expecting this. "You may."

"My lady, I wish to thank you for the two gifts of my life and my freedom. First, Mereth has told me that the Protector's men would have dragged me to their ship and to my death except for your intervention. Second, you gave me my liberty, which to me is a gift beyond price. My words are small enough thanks, but they are heartfelt. I promise that when I return to the Ascendancy, its friendship and regard will be extended to the Protectorate of Dymie without stint."

"This is very gracious of you," Elyssa said with a smile, "and much appreciated. But in fact you are thanking the wrong person. It was Mereth who stood over you at first and kept my brother's men at bay until I came. And it was Mereth who showed me the winged serpent on your ring, and persuaded me it was a sign that you should be protected. Finally, it was Mereth who moved me to give you your freedom. I would like to take credit for these actions, but in truth I can't. Your thanks must go to Mereth, not to me."

Ilarion opened his mouth, then closed it. Mereth was studying him, amusement in her dark eyes. She said nothing to rescue him from his discomfiture.

"Mereth," he demanded at last, "why didn't you tell me what you did? All that, and you brought me back to health as well? As we say in the Ascendancy, I thank you from my blood and bone. As I should have done earlier."

"Well," she said, "it was really both of us who saved you. The soldiers were going to take you in spite of me—it took my lady's power to stop them. As for freeing you, well, she actually *did* it. It was only my suggestion."

"We're happy we kept you from my brother's clutches," Elyssa told him, "and that you're alive and free. Now we'll celebrate the occasion, though I admit the season is somewhat damp for festivities, especially here by the water. Perhaps the winters are warmer and dryer where you come from. The Ascendancy, I believe you name it?" Her tongue stumbled on the unfamiliar word.

"Yes, my lady, that is what it's called. As for our winters, in the far south they're quite warm, warm enough for a second harvest. In the north it's colder. Snow is common."

Elyssa blinked. "Snow? There's that much difference between your north and your south? We get it on the peaks in winter here, but . . ."

She was quick; he waited for the next question.

"Exactly how large *is* your Ascendancy?" Elyssa asked.

"My lady, from what I know of the ancient Great Garden and its size, the Ascendancy would be somewhat larger."

She blinked. "Ah. How much larger? In terms of Haidra, say."

"With respect to Haidra, I gather that a man can walk from its western tip to its eastern in about seventeen days."

"That's correct. In the dry months, at least, when the roads are good."

Ilarion said, "At home it is commonly reckoned that a traveler can go from the western border of the Ascendancy to its eastern in one hundred days. From the northern border to the southern coast requires a little less."

Elyssa stared at him. So did Mereth, and from the corner of his eye he glimpsed Halicar's expression of astonishment.

"The Lady save us," Elyssa said after a moment. "*That* long a journey?"

"Yes, Protectress. I wouldn't blame you for suspecting exaggeration, but it's the truth. The Ascendancy is the largest and oldest state known in the north. It has existed within its present borders for over seventeen hundred years."

"But . . . did my brother know what you've just told me? I have ways of hearing things said in Kanesh, and nothing of it came to my ears. I only knew that Tirsun had obtained a, well, a slave from the north, a man who knew weapons and soldiering. Strange weapons and a different way of fighting, but nothing of such *vastness*."

"He didn't know it," Ilarion said. "I took care not to tell him. I was afraid of what he might do to me if he found out."

"Yes, indeed," Elyssa said reflectively, and Ilarion knew

she was reckoning numbers in her head. "Your Ascendancy has enemies, I suppose. With what numbers of men and ships do you defend yourselves?"

"Again, I ask for your trust that I don't exaggerate. How many men can the Protectorate of Dymie put into the field?"

"I have a thousand foot soldiers and two hundred cavalry in the standing force here in the city. These are always under arms and available at any season. These men are called the First Levy. When I require our full strength, I call on my landholding nobles for aid, which is the Second Levy. If this is complete, which it never is, I have another four thousand foot soldiers and some five hundred more cavalry."

"In all, that's about the size of the force we call a tercia," Ilarion said. "The Ascendancy maintains an army of thirty-six tercias. As for warships, there are about three hundred of them."

The silence was longer this time. At last Elyssa said, "I see. And you didn't tell Tirsun this, because you thought he might take fright and dispose of you?"

"The thought crossed my mind, Protectress. His moods are unpredictable."

"You probably were wise. But hasn't it occurred to you that I might take a similar fright and do the same thing?"

"My lady," Ilarion said, "from all I have heard of you, I do not think you would."

"No, I wouldn't," said Elyssa, and drank. Lowering her cup, she went on, "My lord Tessaris, Mereth has told me you say you're of middling noble rank at home. But is this all there is to be said of your background? Or are there other matters you were wise enough to keep from my brother?"

The moment had come. "I deceived the Protector about my rank," Ilarion said, "for reasons you'll understand in a moment. I'm sorry that I deceived Mereth in the same way, and that through her I have deceived you. I hope you will forgive me. And," he added, "I hope that you'll believe what I'm about to tell you. If you wish, I will swear to it by any oath you please."

"That won't be needed," said Elyssa. "Go on."

Mereth was watching him in perplexity. Hoping she'd forgive him for misleading her, he plunged on. "In my home-land, the title of the ruler is Dynast. His sons bear the title of Luminessos. My father is the Dynast, and I am the Luminessos Ilarion Tessaris." He took a deep breath and said:

"That being so, I am the heir to the throne of the Ascendancy."

A silence. He looked around at the others. Elyssa was studying him with consternation mixed with something like hope, but Mereth and Halicar appeared astonished. Mereth's mouth dropped open a little, and she quickly closed it.

But they believed. A bolt of relief shot through him, piercing and unexpected. He'd returned to his true self, Ilarion Tessaris of the House of the Tessarids, a free man who now sat in the company of free men and women. Months had passed since he last felt this way. It was like being home.

A slave stirred in the shadows beyond the doorway, and he knew he was not.

"This *is* an unexpected occasion," Elyssa said at last. "I've never had the heir to a foreign throne as a guest, much less the heir to a throne so powerful and exalted as yours. But I understand why you kept it secret. Tirsun would have redoubled your humiliations at the least."

Ilarion laughed without humor. "At the very least, I think."

Elyssa nodded and went on, "And if he finds out who you are, he'll worry that you may someday bring an avalanche of Ascendancy soldiers down on his head. To avert that, he may try assassination. We had best keep knowledge of your true rank to ourselves. Do you have any objections to this?"

"No, Protectress. In fact I would be happier if you continued to treat me as a nobleman of, as Mereth put it, middling rank."

"We'll do so, then. But Mereth—you saved not only the lord Tessaris, but also the hopes of his homeland. The heir is alive because of you."

"And the heir will have to return to the Ascendancy," Mereth said quietly.

Elyssa's face clouded. "Yes, of course. You'll want to go home. I'm afraid, though, that I have no ship that could take you there."

"Even if you did, Protectress, I couldn't leave yet. I came to the south with my friend Lashgar, as Mereth has told you, and I must find out if he's alive or dead before I even think of leaving for home. That means finding Rook Arnza, but Rook also may be dead, for all I know. I hope he isn't—he knows the way north, and it would improve my chances of getting home if he were my navigator. If I can't find him, though, there was that Klaian friend of his, Kayonu Lauchmai. He might help me, if I made it worth his while."

Elyssa's expression turned grim. "Ah, of course you didn't know, being off there in the villa—the news from Kla has been trickling in by dribs and drabs over the past ten days. Kla's Protector has been overthrown, with the help of Tirsun and his soldiers. Kayonu, who was the old Protector's heir, is dead, and a creature named Rimash is now Tirsun's tame Protector in Kla. So Kla and Kanesh are allied, if you can call it alliance when Kaneshite soldiers garrison the city and Rimash cannot spit without their commander's permission."

"Kla's fallen?" Ilarion said in dismay. He had lost another avenue of return. "But Tirsun had just set sail when I escaped from Kanesh. He was leading an attack on some Hazannu clan."

"That was also what my ambassador in Kanesh told me. I should have known it for Tirsun's deviousness." Elyssa half shrugged. "Perhaps there *was* such an attack as a feint. But Tirsun himself sailed to Kanesh, with many men hidden in one of his big new ships, and helped Rimash take the city by treachery."

"There's worse," said Halicar. "As if the treachery weren't enough, Tirsun and Rimash have also committed the most serious sacrilege."

"So they have," agreed Elyssa. Her voice was tight with distress. "While my brother's men kept order, Rimash took the Green Lady's images out of Kla's temple and raised statues of the Hazannu God in her place. Then he put her images in a swine-byre outside the landward gates. When the Lady did not strike down the desecraters, it's said that Tirsun laughed. He said that everyone now could tell it was the

Storm God who ruled in the divine household, not the Green Lady. The woman, he said, had clearly learned that her proper place was beneath the man, in every respect imaginable." She shuddered and made a sign of protection. "Tirsun apparently wishes to bring some terrible fate on himself and everyone near him."

"There was no outcry from the people or from Tirsun's own soldiers?" Ilarion asked. Had Tirsun gone utterly mad, to offend so deeply against the Lady? Perhaps she hadn't punished the defilers on the spot, but divinities sometimes preferred to let such transgressors compound their offenses and in doing so destroy themselves. The mills of retribution ground slowly, but they ground exceedingly small.

"Apparently there was very little complaint. Tirsun's men fear him too much to think of protesting, and some are God-worshipers to boot. As for Kla, the old Rasenna blood doesn't run pure there, and many in the city already followed the Hazannu God. Now, however, Rimash and his ilk have made the God supreme. The women of Kla, and in time the men, will suffer for it." She drank, then stared into her cup as she swirled her wine. "And you, my lord Ilarion—in your homeland, is the God supreme over the Lady? How does the action of Rimash strike you?"

"As sacrilege," Ilarion answered flatly. "In the Ascendancy the Lord and the Lady are known as the One in Two. Neither is complete without the other. Each orders his or her own dominion, but they are coequal, and between them they see to the nurturing of the world. What Rimash and Tirsun have done is as vile to me as it is to you."

"Equal?" Elyssa said, in some surprise. "To us the Lady rules, and the Firebringer is her consort."

"Beliefs differ," Ilarion said carefully. "But throwing the image of the sacred into a swine-byre is sacrilege, no matter where it happens. And I would not like to see the Hazannu Storm God destroy the worship of the Lady. From what I've heard, if this God of theirs were human, he would be cruel, vengeful, and capricious. I for one could not venerate him."

Elyssa looked relieved. "I'm happy to hear it. I didn't think Mereth had misjudged you."

Ilarion said, "For what it's worth to you, Protectress, I heard men talk of the power of the God around Tirsun's banquet tables. Some muttered that the Lady could no longer protect the Rasenna from misfortune and evil, and it was time for change. Tirsun didn't outwardly agree, but he didn't stop the talk, either."

"I know." Elyssa's voice had become harsh. "He hopes that if he can overthrow the Lady's temples on Haidra as he did in Kla, and not suffer for it, he will find it easier to overthrow me. That's what he's after—he doesn't care a whit for God or Goddess, but he uses people's belief in them for his own ends. Which is, of course, to rule all Haidra. He strengthens his army, but he also tries to rot my rule from within. His agents whisper that the rule of a woman is a blasphemy against the God, and some in my Protectorate have believed the murmurs. In the spring I had to kill a man who did."

Her fingers tightened on the wine cup, and Ilarion saw pain and grief in her lovely face. "He wasn't an evil man," she continued, "but I had no choice, so at his asking I gave him to the Lady. But others think as he did, and some among them are my own nobles. They swear they're loyal only to me, but I know they wonder if they might prosper better under Tirsun and the Hazannu God. As indeed they might, if they helped in my overthrow." She produced a grim smile. "What happened to Alfni of Kla has not been far from my thoughts these last ten days."

"But," Mereth said in a puzzled voice, "I don't understand what the Protector wants with Kla. Compared to Kanesh it's a poor city. What prize can he find in it?"

"It's a knife at Dymie's back," Elyssa told her. "I'll explain. The iron mines of Haidra were worked out years ago, so we in Dymie must now get the metal by trading westward along the mainland coast. Other things come from there, too—long timbers for ship keels, spices, furs, as well as copper and tin for bronze, but iron is the thing we need most. Kanesh trades in a similar way, but toward the east. We don't use those eastern sources, since they're that much farther away from us, and Kanesh has a tight grip on them.

"But now my brother holds Kla, to our west, and Kla commands our sailing route to the western mines and trading depots. With a dozen galleys based in that city, Tirsun can cut off our iron supply and throttle our general trade. So this conquest of Kla is an act of war against me, though my brother will swear that it is not. And as you are likely aware, Kanesh is richer and more populous than my poor Dymie. Tirsun can put more soldiers into the field and more warships to sea than we can. If he strangles our commerce and then attacks us, I am not sure I can hold him." Her gaze turned to Ilarion. "I will accept help from any quarter that offers it."

Ilarion thought: *This hasn't been idle conversation. She wants me to help her resist her brother. And I can help. But while I'm doing that, I won't be on my way to the Ascendancy.*

But she and Mereth saved my life, and, anyway, I have no ship to take me home. Even if I did, how could I sail away and leave them to Tirsun, whose army I helped to strengthen? I have to get home someday, but I can't leave honor and obligation behind me to do it, even if I didn't help him any more than I had to. And I have a score to settle with Tirsun, myself.

Stirrups. That's what I'll start with.

He set his cup on the table before him, and said, "It was against my will, but I taught Tirsun something of Ascendancy warfare. To make up for that I'll teach you the same and much more, until Dymie is strong enough to beat him. Only then, if you'll help me find a ship, will I go back to the Ascendancy."

Halicar murmured softly, "Ah," and Mereth's somber expression vanished in a smile of delight. Elyssa's face also lightened, and she said, "Thank you, my lord Luminessos. I understand how much you must want to go home, and when the time comes, I'll do everything in my power to get you there."

Ilarion inclined his head. "I'll be in your debt. First, though, we'll deal with Tirsun."

"Good," Elyssa said happily, and for an instant she looked

like a young girl who had just been given an unexpected but longed-for gift. "For the first time in a year, my hopes for Dymie have been lifted."

Ah, and there's one more thing, Ilarion thought. *She hears a lot about what happens in other places.*

"You knew of Kayonu's voyage north," he said. "Did he, by any chance, bring someone back from the north with him? A woman, not young, with black hair?"

Elyssa's brow furrowed. "There was something . . . yes, I believe they said he had a woman with him, of a strange coloring. But she wasn't slave booty. She ended up in Kla's palace as Alfni's free concubine, though she wasn't as young as such women usually are. I suppose when Rimash overthrew Alfni she was taken to be sold. The recent news from Kla didn't mention her. She might be anywhere by now." Her face softened. "I'm sorry, I should have remembered to tell you. She may have been a countrywoman of yours."

At the windows the rosy sunlight had dimmed and reddened with onset of evening. Now the panes and their leadwork were a mosaic of black and crimson, and the air seemed to chill as the light failed.

"I'm afraid," Ilarion said wearily, "that she is. She may just possibly be my aunt. I'm here because of her."

20

EIGHT DAYS AFTER HE REACHED DYMIE, ILARION WAS hard at work in the training field outside the city's Sunset Gate. He was putting a troop of twenty cavalrymen through exercises that would accustom them to the still-unfamiliar device of stirrups, and to the heavy infantry spear that he'd ordered to replace their accustomed light javelins.

The major strength of the First Levy, Dymie's standing army, was its thousand heavy infantrymen. But because the cavalry would benefit most from Ascendancy military techniques, Ilarion had decided to work with the two hundred horsemen first. Both they and the foot soldiers lived in a compound just inside the Sunset Gate, where the horses were also stabled. The mounts' pasturage and the cavalry training ground lay outside the walls on a stretch of level land that ran along the city walls down to the shore of Monument Bay.

The principal function of Dymie's cavalry, like that of Kanesh, was to provide reconnaissance and to keep enemy horsemen away from the army while it was on the march. This task suited their armament and tactics, but they were also supposed to join in battle by attacking the flanks of an enemy infantry line and pursue its fleeing soldiers if it broke. By Ascendancy standards they would be quite ineffective in these latter roles, for they were really no more than light auxiliaries.

Ilarion intended to correct this by arming the men more heavily and giving them stirrups. To his relief the Pronoyar of Dymie, whose name was Larth Tetnias, hadn't balked at

the new ideas, though he was at an age when most soldiers
had turned conservative. He and Ilarion had spent considerable time together over the past few days, and their first mutual wariness had now shifted toward respect for each
other's abilities. Normally the pronoyar commanded both
the infantry and mounted troops, but there was a provision
for a deputy cavalry commander, with the formal rank of
First-Captain of the First Levy Horse. This was the post Ilarion now held.

He and Larth were on horseback, watching the cavalrymen
charge one by one at straw targets suspended from poles. A
wind blew in from seaward, tossing Larth's ash-streaked,
thinning blond hair about his shoulders. Training had been
impossible the previous day because of rain, but a watery sun
was out this afternoon and the ground had dried enough for
practice; the horses' hooves tossed clumps of damp grass and
mud into the air as they pelted across the turf.

Beyond the poles that held up the targets, the training
field ran down to the beach and the gray-blue swells of
Monument Bay. On the bay's far shore, some five miles
across the glinting water, rose the pale ruined towers of
Charunna of the Roses. Ilarion was curious about the place,
for the ancient Rasenna had built it, and he would have liked
to wander for a day in its silent avenues and squares. But
Mereth had told him that people preferred to avoid the old
city; it was both too sacred and too haunted to be visited
comfortably. Not even salvagers would take its cut stone for
new buildings. In any case, Ilarion had little time for leisure.

"Are they behaving themselves?" Larth asked. A trooper
had just missed the target and was suffering good-natured
jeers and heckling from his comrades. "If they're balking at
all, I'll make them dance a different step."

"They've been no trouble," Ilarion assured him. When
he'd proposed the changes in tactics and weapons, the
pronoyar had muttered that the young cavalrymen might resist them, especially as the changes were at the hands of an
outlander. Also, Ilarion didn't have the advantage of age and
obvious battle experience, since he was not much older than
they were.

"In fact, it's been the other way around," he added as the trooper began another charge at the target. "I can barely rein them in."

This was true enough. The cavalrymen were younger sons of the lesser rural nobility, just as Larth had been before he climbed to his high office. They were much less wealthy and much less corrupt than the sons of the great city nobles Ilarion had encountered in Kanesh, and better yet, they were eager to learn anything that would make them more lethal in combat.

When the saddler and the smith first came to provide them with stirrup leathers and irons, they were puzzled. Then Ilarion, using a well-blunted infantry spear and the first of the newly converted saddles, knocked three of them off their unconverted ones in as many minutes. The hardened leather of their small round shields could stop a spearhead well enough, but the men could not withstand the shock of an opponent who was using stirrups. They had been waiting for this foreigner to make a fool of himself, but from the moment the third rider tumbled onto the sod, they were his. Now all two hundred were frantic to be reequipped and start training. Each of these first twenty, once they knew what they were doing, would train two more, and so on until all of them grasped the new way of cavalry warfare. Then Ilarion would start them on full-unit field maneuvers. Räsennan cavalry, he had learned from Larth and the young troopers, ran at the enemy in a loose gaggle. This was good enough for the light lancers they had been, but he wanted more: a hammer of men, spears, and horses that could turn the flank of an infantry line or scatter the horsemen of Kanesh like blown chaff. For that, his troopers would need to charge and fight in close order.

"There, good," said Larth, as the trooper's spearhead impaled the straw target squarely in the center and snapped the light cord holding it. The young man, the target fixed on his spearhead, waved it triumphantly in the air. The others cheered derisively while a slave ran to hang a new target.

"How do our men and horses compare to those you led in the north?" the pronoyar asked.

"The men are as good. Some breeds of our horses are larger than yours. That lets our medium cavalry wear heavier armor and use larger shields."

"That's what you'd call *medium* cavalry?" Larth asked, and snorted in disbelief. "What in the Firebringer's name do you use for heavy troops, then?"

"Not horses," Ilarion said. "Our heavy cavalry—we call them cataphracts—ride a mount called a hippaxa. A hippaxa is like . . . well, imagine a cross of a black bull and a black miu that's my height at its shoulder, and you'll have an idea of it. They're half again the weight of a big horse, with two fighting horns. The only trouble is, hippaxas are hard to train and very hard to breed, and we never have enough of them."

Larth eyed him askance. "How many is 'not enough'?"

"We have about three thousand trained beasts, but it's taken twenty-five years to build the cataphract force even that far. A long time ago the Ascendancy had five full tercias of cataphracts—that's about twenty thousand hippaxas—but there was a century of troubles, and the animals were almost wiped out."

The Rasennan laughed, without much humor. "I'm glad you're our ally and not our enemy."

"We're not conquerors by inclination," Ilarion said. "We're well armed because we've had a lot of trouble over the past two hundred years."

"Yes, trouble. The world's the same everywhere in these latter days, isn't it?" Larth looked wistful, an expression at odds with his hard face. "In the time of the Garden the Rasenna had peace, at least until near the end. Someday, the Lady willing, we'll restore what we had. Ah, what it must have been." Larth turned in his saddle and looked across the bay. A bank of misty cloud was sidling toward the land: rain coming. It was already falling on Charunna of the Roses, and the towers of the dead city had turned indistinct, as if fading into a dream as they watched. "See there?" he said. "We're surrounded by our past, by the memories of our greatness. Here on Haidra the reminders are everywhere. Kanesh is ancient, Dymie even older, Charunna the oldest of all. It's true our hopes have dimmed and the memories with them, but we've never given them up. Whoever gives them life and color again . . . the Rasenna would follow such a leader anywhere."

Ilarion remained silent. He hadn't realized that Elyssa's brusque general was a dreamer as well.

"The Protectress is not the one, though," Larth muttered, speaking as if to himself. He glanced at Ilarion.

"Ah," Ilarion said.

"She knows she isn't," Larth said. "She yearns, like the rest of us, but she doesn't believe it can happen. So she will never make the attempt."

"What about her brother?" Ilarion said.

"He might try someday, if the whim struck him. But would he persevere once he began? I have my doubts. Ah, look. Here comes an audience for your men's work."

Riding toward them from the Sunset Gate were two helmeted house retainers wearing overmantles with a clan badge depicting a stylized yellow lily. Leading them was a burly, long-jawed man on a dappled gray horse.

"It's the clan-lord Auvas Seitithi," Larth said. "You met him the other night."

Ilarion answered, "Yes," and watched the man approach. Auvas had a pointed chin at the end of his long jaw, but his nose was short and snubbed. Ilarion, who had first encountered him at dinner in the palace, thought he looked like a feroe hound, the savage dogs that were used to hunt hagbear in the northern Ascendancy.

According to Mereth, Auvas had long believed himself to be the most suitable match for Elyssa, and he had exerted subtle pressures on her to achieve a marriage and the alliance of their houses. But Elyssa disliked the man, and had evaded his advances just as she had evaded those of every other suitor. Still, she'd taken care to do so without offending Auvas too badly, for the Seitithi family was the senior noble clan of Dymie as well as the richest, and Auvas was the clan's highest-ranking member after his blind and bedridden father. When the full army was called out and both the First and Second Levies of Dymie were on the battlefield, it was the privilege of the senior Seitithi male to command the army's left wing, while the pronoyar led the center and the right. Since Auvas's father had taken to his bed, Auvas served in his place; he would be confirmed in the position when the old man died.

Ilarion had tried not to dislike the man simply because Elyssa did, but by the time his dinner with Auvas was half-advanced, he shared her feelings. Mereth and Halicar had also been present, along with several other Rasenna of the aristocracy. Elyssa's presence had forced Auvas to exhibit a frigid courtesy to the three outlanders, but his repugnance at their presence and his contempt for their foreign blood were clear enough from his manner and face. After the meal, when Mereth and Halicar sang a ballad bittersweet enough to bring tears, he listened expressionlessly, thin-lipped and cold of eye. If Auvas so disliked Elyssa's Antecessor bards and their music, Ilarion could only guess at the man's loathing for him, the northerner who was bringing his foreign ways to the army of Dymie.

And now here was the man himself, out on the training ground. Ilarion's fingers tightened around his gelding's reins. Auvas was powerful; he might, if he put his mind to it, cause all sorts of trouble with Ilarion's troopers and their training.

Larth murmured, "His curiosity's got the better of him. He's come out to see what's really going on." The prono-yar's voice was expressionless; Ilarion listened for either coolness or warmth in it and heard neither. He was still uncertain of the nature of the two men's personal relationship. They did not seem very fond of each other, but so far he'd detected no overt hostility. At Elyssa's table Auvas treated Larth as an equal, although his family was far wealthier than the pronoyar's. But both were of very ancient clans, and within the Rasennan aristocracy that counted for as much as riches.

Auvas put out a hand to halt his retainers, then rode on a few paces and reined in his gray. He said, "I hope I find the prono-yar and the . . . cavalry teacher in good health and spirits?"

"We're very well," Larth answered. "I wish the same on your behalf, from both myself and First-Captain Tessaris."

Ilarion made the suitable gesture of respect but said nothing, Larth having answered for him.

Auvas glanced down at Ilarion's stirrup irons. His upper lip curled, and he said, "I suppose, from what I see, that people in your homeland can't stay on a horse's back without using such aids?"

The affront was calculated. To display anger would only serve Auvas, but neither could Ilarion allow the words to pass.

"On the contrary, my lord," he said in a reasonable voice, "most riders begin learning without the aid. They are allowed the advantage of the foot irons only when they have passed the stage of novice."

It was not an insult, especially delivered in Ilarion's tones. Nevertheless, Auvas flushed a little. "And what advantage is that?" he asked, his tone brittle.

"The irons allow the rider to use his full weight and his mount's impetus against an enemy. He is not so likely to be knocked off his animal by the collision of a charge."

"Bah." Auvas looked Ilarion up and down. "I outweigh you by one part in four. Do you think you can knock *me* from my saddle, even with your foot crutches?"

It was true that Auvas was the heavier man, but this would not help him stay on his horse as stirrups would. Nevertheless, Ilarion said judiciously, "It might be difficult for me to do that, Clan-lord."

"But not impossible?"

"No."

He knew instantly that he had made a mistake. Auvas gave him a sunless smile, and said, "I differ in my opinion. Let us take two of those infantry spears the others are using, and a pair of cavalry shields, and see if you can unhorse me."

He thinks he'll win, Ilarion thought, *and that's faintly possible, and if he knocks me out of my saddle, my men's confidence will suffer. But what's worse, I'll likely put him down on the first pass, and he'll never forgive that. Worse still, those spears aren't blunted. If he moves the wrong way, I might kill him. Allfather knows where that might lead. He's duped me, curse him. I lose no matter what I do.*

He hesitated, and Auvas opened his mouth to speak. Ilarion knew what the clan-lord would say. It would be something like: *I would not have thought to see such caution in such a renowned warrior.*

Larth said, "Clan-lord, with all respect to your rank, I forbid this."

Auvas's green eyes widened, and his jaw clamped tight. After a moment he opened it to say, "What?"

"I forbid this exercise. First-Captain Tessaris, if you accept his suggestion, I will hang you for mutiny."

Ilarion blinked at Larth. He appeared to mean what he'd said.

"For what reason," Auvas said in a hard voice, "do you interfere between us, Larth? It's a friendly test of skills, no more."

Larth's tone was equally hard. "The Protectress has ordered the first-captain to train her First Levy cavalry. She requires me to see that he does this. If the first-captain lies in bed with broken bones or a cracked skull, or worse, I have failed in my duty. I'm sure that you, Clan-lord, would never suggest that I dishonor myself in such a way. Consequently, you must wait for another time for your friendly test, and you must not carry it out unless the first-captain has my exact and witnessed permission to do so. Otherwise, I will indeed hang him."

Auvas pursed his thin lips, and said, "I would not cause you dishonor. First-Captain, I withdraw my suggestion."

"Perhaps another time," Ilarion said, "with the pronoyar's permission."

"Yes."

A trooper impaled a target and received cheers. Then, speaking across Ilarion as if he did not exist, Auvas said to Larth:

"Another matter, Pronoyar. What do you think of these Antecessor twitterers the Protectress dotes on so? They've been less than a year in the palace, and she treats them as if they were born to her rank."

Larth shrugged. "The Lady Elyssa is fond of music."

"Indeed, but she's with them always—the other night they

were at table with you and me and several of the old blood.
That verges on insult."

"Some might think it so. I agree the Protectress treats
them well, but neither of the singers takes advantage of it as
far as I can see."

"Perhaps people see less than they should."

Larth gave Auvas a calculating stare. "Oh?"

"The man, Halicar. He's all too familiar with her. And she
with him. I'm not alone in my opinion. There's been talk."

"Most talk is noise and wind, Auvas, as you very well
know. What of it?"

"It's in my mind, and not just in mine, that he has wrig-
gled himself not only into her household and her affections
but also into her bed."

A brief silence followed. Then Larth said, "I've heard the
whispers. But there's not much harm in it, if she doesn't
marry him or set him over us."

"What? She's already set him over us by taking him as her
lover. It's dishonorable and infamous."

"I'd choose my words carefully if I were you," Larth observed in a flat voice. "And you know as well as I that plenty
of highborn women, married and not, take lovers. Why
shouldn't the Protectress scratch an itch we all have, just as
the Green Lady scratches hers with the Firebringer? We're
not Hazannu, to stone a woman if she finds pleasure with a
man who isn't her husband."

Auvas spat over his horse's withers. "Yes, it's true our
women have always taken lovers whenever it pleased them.
But maybe they shouldn't. Maybe the Hazannu are right,
and we're wrong. The priestesses say the Lady has precedence and protects her faithful. But where was the Goddess
when the plague came and the Great Garden withered and
died? And who lives now on our ancient lands? The Hazannu and their God. Maybe their God's the more powerful,
as they say he is, and he's been angry at us because we follow the Lady and let women do as they please."

Larth made a warding sign. "Auvas, perhaps you speak
without thinking."

"If I do, I see no pit opening in the Lady's breast to swallow me. But as for the Protectress taking a lover, that's not what sours my wine. It's this, Larth Tetnias—*her lover's no Rasenna*. If he were of the old blood, I could stomach any taste she had, even if the man were a pock-faced dolt without the wits to pour piss out of his boot. But to bring this vagabond Antecessor chirper into her bed? The thing reeks. If that itch you mentioned needs scratching, why didn't she choose one of us to scratch it for her?"

Larth grinned a little. "You had yourself in mind, no doubt? Perhaps even for marriage?"

"And why not? I'm divorced, and my house is equal in most regards to that of the Protectress."

"Be patient," Larth advised. "If he is indeed her lover, she'll get tired of him eventually. Or she'll wake up and see she can't go on offending against custom, and send him away. And that will be the end of it."

"So what may be going on now doesn't rub you across the grain?"

"Not much, assuming it *is* going on. I have enough matters of my own to attend to."

"Indeed. There's no more to be said, then. Though to my mind the favor she gives those two Antecessors is an insult to our rank, even if the male isn't in her bed. Pronoyar, I leave you well, I hope."

The farewell pointedly excluded Ilarion. Larth grunted a response; Auvas pulled his horse round, rode off a little way, and stopped with his men to watch the cavalry maneuvers. Ilarion held his tongue but thought hard. Halicar's inviolate status would likely protect him from physical harm, but there might be other ways Auvas could damage him. He must warn Halicar that this talk was in the air. Mereth had said it would be inevitable, and she was right.

"So what do you think, First-Captain Tessaris?" the pronoyar asked after a time. "You live in the palace, so you're there more than I am. Are they lovers?"

"I've seen no evidence such as an open embrace," Ilarion replied carefully. "But they seem very happy when they're with each other."

"That would be enough to start the rumors." Larth shifted

in his saddle and studied the galloping cavalrymen. "Speaking of rumors, sooner or later Tirsun will hear about what we're doing here. He may decide to transform his own cavalry in the same way."

Relieved at the change of subject, Ilarion answered, "It's not as easy as it looks. To take advantage of the stirrups and lances you need the right battle tactics, and that's where the training really begins. Tirsun's people will need a long time to figure them out . . . in that regard, with your permission I'd like to suggest a few changes to Dymie's infantry maneuvers. I showed Tirsun one or two things I wish I hadn't. With me gone he may have given up on them, but I'd like our men to know about them anyway."

A large drop of cold rain slapped the back of Ilarion's hand. Larth said, "Here's the rain. Yes, that can be done. We'll speak of it later. Are you keeping your boys at it in this?"

It was about the second hour after midday, and with the rain clouds moving in, the field would soon be soaked, making the churned and muddy turf slippery and treacherous. Eventually he'd make his men go on even in the foulest weather, especially when training in tactical maneuvers. But they weren't ready for that yet. He said:

"I think not—I don't want any broken necks or lamed horses. I'll get them back to the barracks and tell them everything they've done wrong."

"A long list, no doubt . . . until later, then."

"Until later," Ilarion answered, and watched Larth rein his horse around and trot away. Auvas, apparently having seen all he wanted, joined the pronoyar, and together the two nobles rode toward the Sunset Gate.

Ilarion assembled his troopers in the now-pelting rain and led them back into Dymie. After they'd rubbed down and fed their horses, he assembled them in the arcade of the stable yard and instructed them in the faults and virtues of their afternoon's performance. By the time he left the barracks, the rain had tapered off and the clouds were moving off to admit the honey-tinted sunlight of a waning afternoon.

He rode through Dymie's streets toward the citadel, with the smell of rain and wet stone in his nostrils, tinged with the sharp odor of the public urinals. Mixed with these were the scents of the evening meal being prepared: onions, fish frying in oil, stewed ambercups, the scent of Rasennan flat bread, kitchen herbs. Odors drifted from the harbor, too, of pitch, sawn timber, the weed wrack of low tide, salt water. It was like the smell of the harbors of home, of the vast Commercial Basin at Captala Nea, and the people of Captala too loved fried fish. But here in Dymie even the smell of the bread was not quite the same, and the spiced odor of cooking ambercups had never wafted through Captala's streets.

The absence of public inscriptions was another of the things that was alien about the cities of the Rasenna. In the Ascendancy, three adult citizens in four could read and write, and in any Ascendancy city the Logomenon's flowing script was everywhere: carved on statue bases, cut into memorials, engraved on lintels and pediments. But written Rasennan was so hard to master that only scribes, senior officials, and educated aristocrats received training in it, and it was little seen in public places. Professional scribes wrote business and government records on wax or clay tablets, while committing especially important documents to long-lasting vellum. But even if it had been easy to read and write the language, there was no cheap paper to write it on, because the paper-reed didn't grow here in the south.

Perhaps he missed the inscriptions because it was yet another sign of how far he was from home. This foreign city, with its sharp primary colors, its houses with their images of animals and birds dotting the roof peaks, was becoming familiar now, but it would never be his. Even if he could somehow feel that it was, to its people he would always be an outlander; whenever he was out in the streets, men and women looked sideways at his alien appearance, and children stared.

He reached the foot of Beacon Hill and the ramp to the palace. Near the bottom of the ramp, just as in Kanesh, was a fortified compound enclosing the government warehouses. He rode past them and started his ascent of the ramp's switchback climb. Judging from the angle of the sun, he had enough time to bathe and change before he attended Elyssa in the Blue Swallow Room, where she preferred to dine unless she were entertaining magnates.

At the summit of the ramp the guards, who knew him now, waved him through the palace gate. In the Lower Court he turned his mount over to a groom; like most of the palace servants the man was a slave, and born one. By now word had gotten around among the domestics that Ilarion had once been a slave himself, and had been owned by the Protector at that. Consequently, they were even more watchful and on guard with him than with freeborn Rasenna. He knew why, though he would not have understood it before his own servitude; they feared him because he'd learned all their tricks of handling a master. Moreover, he was sure that some hated him because he had won a freedom they would never know. The oppressed, Ilarion had learned on the Citadel Stone, were not necessarily made virtuous by the fact of their oppression.

The groom silently took the reins and led the horse away. As he passed through the courtyard's inner gate and started up the Grand Staircase, Ilarion pondered the blindness of the Rasenna over their human chattels. There were so many slaves; if their fear of their masters and mistresses vanished overnight, and if they could arm themselves and act together, their fury would engulf the lovely island in a cataclysm of butchery, pillage, and burning. That this was very unlikely to happen did not make the knowledge less perturbing.

At the top of the Grand Staircase was the Middle Court, from which another broad stair led to the Upper Court. At its top, a visitor would find the formal reception rooms of the High Palace, the Protectress's living quarters, the colonnades and gardens of the Harbor Terrace, and the squat shaft of Dristra's Light. Halicar and Mereth, being personal companions to the Protectress and enjoying the traditional high status of Antecessor singers, lived on the upper level in rooms near Elyssa's apartments. Because of Ilarion's rank, the Protectress had given him the finest of the palace's guest apartments, which stood at the level of the Middle Court. For his personal use he had a lavishly appointed reception room, a comfortable sleeping cubicle, and a smaller cubicle for Bres, his body slave. There was also a dining chamber, a private terrace overlooking Monument Bay, and a bathing room with sanitary arrangements almost as good as those of the Ascendancy.

He went into the building on the court's east side. Everywhere the domestics were lighting the clusters of bronze and pottery lamps, and the scent of oil and burned wick-weed drifted through the corridors. Ilarion walked along the passage that led to his quarters; at the end of it, inside a doorway that could be closed with a sliding wooden door, was his reception room. In its far wall was a row of small windows, whose translucent glass panes could be closed to keep out drafts or opened for ventilation and better light; at the moment they were shut against the wind, and admitted an amber illumination. The hearth slaves had kindled a pottery firebox on the tiled hearth in the room's center, and its glowing charcoal radiated a welcome warmth. Also on the hearth, sitting over a brazier, was a gently steaming hot-water basin enameled with sea creatures. No slaves were visible, including Bres, but that would change instantly at a call or a handclap.

Mereth was sitting on a low stool beside the hearth. She looked up as he entered, and said, "Hello."

He was mildly surprised to find her here. Usually at this hour she was practicing her music.

"Hello," he answered, unfastening his cloak clasp, and without warning Bres was at his elbow to help with the wet garment. The body slave had as usual been inside his cubicle, alert for Ilarion's appearance. Bres was a eunuch in early middle age, born into servitude, perfectly trained, taciturn, and extremely able. He was somewhat portly yet seemed to disappear into the walls until needed.

Ilarion freed himself from the cloak's folds, then removed his riding boots and replaced them with felt slippers. "Would my lord and the lady want hot spiced wine for the damp?" Bres asked in his soft, flat voice.

"Yes, bring us some," Ilarion said. "Watered, two parts in three." He'd stopped phrasing his orders like requests, since doing so clearly made Bres uncomfortable.

The eunuch vanished through the doorway to the dining chamber. Ilarion pulled a second stool to the hearth, sat on it, and held his hands to the firebox's radiance.

"You didn't get a chill, did you?" Mereth asked.

"A chill? Mereth, I thought you'd stopped worrying. You've hardly asked me such questions since we came here."

"I know, but it's been a wet day and a cold one for this time of year."

"This isn't cold. I've been on the march when there's snow to the men's knees."

"Then you're either very brave or very foolish, which may come to the same thing. What do you do in the palace when it's so bitter?"

"Oh, Captala never gets that cold. No worse than this, usually. And people in our north have much bigger fireboxes than these, built into the houses, like thick-walled baking ovens. They're covered with tiles, and people sleep on them. In the Fountain Palace there are pottery pipes under the floor and in the walls, and hot air runs through them from furnaces down in the cellars."

"That sounds like a very good idea," Mereth said, with feeling. "The Ascendancy seems to have a lot of such ideas."

"We like to be comfortable," Ilarion answered. He sat on a stool and warmed his hands at the firebox.

"Do you know," she said suddenly, "I once told myself that if I ever found a place where slavery was unlawful, I'd go there. And if Halicar wouldn't join me, I also told myself, I'd go without him."

Ilarion was at a loss for words and could only look at her. Her head was slightly bowed, her long dark eyes pensive, her brown hair thick and gleaming in the rich illumination from the windows. The fading sunlight through their translucent panes touched her skin with the glow of amber.

"Does that shock you so much you can't speak?" she asked, turning to him. "That I'd really think of leaving my brother behind?"

"No," he said, "no, it wasn't that. I didn't realize you'd consider leaving Elyssa's service at all. Or going so far away into the north, with or without Halicar."

"I haven't really thought about it seriously," she answered. "But it's crossed my mind."

"But if you want a place without slavery, your own people don't have it. You could return there, couldn't you?" He realized, as he spoke, how little he really knew of her race and country. He did know that she and Halicar were orphaned when she was a child, but otherwise she was reticent about her early years. She'd always seemed to prefer the subject of his background to her own, and he was dismayed now to realize how much he'd talked of himself and how little about her.

"I could," she said. "But there's little for me or Halicar there. We're a dying race, Ilarion. We always lived high in the mountains with our herds and flocks, and even in the days of the Rasenna's Great Garden there weren't many of us. We were never part of the Garden, but the old Rasenna loved our music and musicians, and even our least brilliant were welcome down in the cities of the foothills and the plains. But being in the mountains didn't save us when the years of the cold summers came, and the plague with them. We suffered as the Rasenna did, all through the famine times and afterward. When things got a little better the Rasenna were mostly gone and the Hazannu had taken the lowlands, so there was no chance of us moving there even if we'd been inclined to it. And we've dwindled even since then. In a century or two we'll be gone, I think, and our music with us."

"I see," Ilarion said. He was profoundly saddened. If their voices and melodies fell silent, the world would be a meaner place.

"So if Halicar and I go home we'll be welcome," she went on, "but who would we sing to? To the garron flocks on the crags, and each other? My people are poor, Ilarion; there are no rich families in the mountains. Halicar and I grew up hungry and cold, and we made our music to forget it, and if we go back, we will be hungry and cold again." She held the wine cup in both hands, tightly as if it might slip away from her, and took a swift drink.

"But your relatives," he asked. "Surely they'd help you?"

"They couldn't. Our mother and father died in an avalanche in my ninth winter, as I think I told you, and we were raised by my father's brother. He was a good man, but he had little enough for his own children even before we fell through his doorway. If we went back to the village we'd have no land of our own, no flock, no trade but singing, and among my people that would hardly keep us alive." She paused, then said, "That's not altogether true, about the flock. Elyssa is generous, and someday we could return home and buy livestock and a farmstead. But that's not what I *am*, Ilarion, a herder. I was made to do what I do here, not to follow beasts up the glens in summer and back down in winter."

Tentatively, because she had never spoken of it, he asked: "There was no lover, no offer of marriage to keep you there?"

She laughed, but not gaily. "Well, there were young men who wanted me, but I told them I was leaving, so there was no point. I knew I'd go, from the time I was fourteen, when I found my true voice, as our saying is. Halicar had already found his, but he was waiting to see what would happen with me—the best Antecessor singers work in couples, the man for the depths of the music, the woman for the heights. Most often they're husband and wife—Halicar and I are an exception. But good pairs are very rare, and we are among the best."

"But you still don't contemplate marriage, even now that Halicar and Elyssa—" He broke off in confusion, afraid he'd blundered. "Forgive me, I'm too forward."

She made a negative gesture. "Not at all, there's nothing mysterious about it. Simply put, I've never met a man I wanted to marry. I'd never be comfortable with anyone but another musician, or some kind of artist at least. Those few who have crossed my path—" She shrugged. "I've always been too busy. I'm married to the music, you see, and that's the most jealous of all spouses."

"Then I must thank you even more for deserting your spouse for me while I was ill. You're a generous and warm-hearted woman, Mereth."

"You're very noble to say so, but I'm far from an exemplar of virtue." A look of weariness passed over her face. "It wasn't until recently that I could be even a little happy for my brother and Elyssa. For the first few months of the affair I was a miserable shrew, jealous and resentful. That's passing, thank the Lady, and the Protectress and I are becoming friends. Though I still catch myself being angry at her, once in a while." She turned a serious face to his. "I hope you don't think too much the less of me for it."

He realized suddenly how she must have felt: If she lost Halicar, what would become of her art? Without her brother in the partnership, where would she go, what would she do? She might have wondered if she could even survive.

"I don't think so at all," he said. "I'm flawed, too, certainly worse than you are."

"I hardly think so. Surely, being the heir to such a powerful throne, you've had all your faults carefully trained out of you."

A moment passed before he realized she was teasing him a little. He thought of confessing his killing rages to her, as a kind of exchange of confidences. But the vision of his own furies in the Protector's demented face, on that last night in the palace of Kanesh, was too appalling to speak of. The mere recollection of it put him into a cold sweat, and he did his best never to awaken the memory.

"I have a few left," he said. The memory stirred again, and to quell it he said, "Incidentally, I've been meaning to ask about Halicar's harp. I've never seen one quite like it, either at home or here."

"Ah." She smiled. "Do you know what it's made of? Guess."

He pondered this. The instrument was a little larger than Ascendancy harps, and the soundboard and sound box more complicated. But he had heard no finer tones in the Fountain Palace; the thing had a resonance that at times was almost eerie. "Carved ivory or bone, I'd say. Very unusual."

"You're close. Actually, it's made from the breastbone

and ribs of a Master-Singer of the last days of the Great Garden. The tuning pegs are carved from his finger bones."

Ilarion sat up straight. "That's *human* bone?"

"Yes, it is. Don't look so shocked, it's not from a sacrifice. There was a tradition that when a truly great singer died, he or she would ask that such a harp be made. So even after death, you see, the singer's music wouldn't end. Only three have survived to our day. They carry the names of their begetters, and Halicar's is the one called Eridan."

"I had no idea it was so important," Ilarion said. "How are they passed down?"

"Each harp is bequeathed by its singer to one who will be worthy of it. Halicar was chosen, and Eridan came to him when he was twenty-two."

"Your flute—"

Mereth laughed. "Oh, it's just wooden, a very good flute indeed, but it didn't come from someone's arm bone, if that's what you mean."

The wine was cooling in Ilarion's cup, so he drank a little. He'd intended to be washed and changed by now, but he didn't want to break the flow of their talk. Something had changed subtly between them. What?

He realized suddenly that this shift had been going on since they came to the palace. A warmth flowed between them now; when they rode through the main gate eight days ago, he could not have called her his friend, because thus far she'd been his nurse and caretaker. Now she *was* his friend, unquestionably. He felt an unaccustomed surge of happiness. He said, "So you left the mountains, you with your flute, and Halicar with Eridan the harp."

She nodded. "We went on the road when I was sixteen. We sang in Hazannu chiefdoms for longer than I'd have liked, but two years ago we decided we were good enough for even the Rasenna of Haidra. We worked in two households here in the Protectorate of Dymie. Then the Protectress found out about us, asked us to sing for her, and took us into her household." She smiled. "I think our former employer was very annoyed, but the Protectress is a determined woman."

The light from the window was sliding from amber to rose and gold. Ilarion reluctantly stood up. "I smell like a damp horse—I must get out of these working clothes before I attend Elyssa at dinner. You're going as well?"

"Yes, I—oh, I'm so foolish, you must be wondering why I'm here."

He grinned down at her. "It had occurred to me."

"I was with her earlier this afternoon, when a message came from the harbor. Ushnana has sent an embassy, and the ambassadors are coming to the palace for an audience. She wants you to be present when they arrive, which will be for dinner. The banquet hall's being made ready, and they're to stay here in the guest quarters, beginning tonight. She wanted me to tell you you'd have company. And I knew you'd want to know they were coming. They might have news of Lashgar and Rook."

"Allfather above, let's hope so," Ilarion said. He was calculating sailing times and coming up short. Elyssa had sent emissaries to Ushnana a few days previously, with a proposal for a defensive alliance against Kanesh. But they would only just be getting to Ushnana, even with fair winds.

"These visitors can't be the answer to our own embassy," he said. "Did you hear their names?"

"Only the chief one was announced, someone called Arkallu. I believe he's Ushnana's pronoyar."

"Ah, well. But he'll know about Rook if anyone will. Wait for me, I'll change and we'll go up together. Bres—"

Bres was already beside him, carrying a washbasin for the hot water.

21

ILARION STOOD BESIDE MERETH AS SHE RAPPED AT THE doors of the Blue Swallow Room. Elyssa's voice called, "Come," and they entered. Within, autumn sunlight falling through the windows glowed on the fields of painted lilies and the birds darting above them. Both lilies and swallows seemed alive, as if merely arrested for an eternal instant by the artist's hand. The Rasenna might be backward in some things, but no artist Ilarion knew could excel them in painting the natural world.

Halicar and the Protectress were sitting together on a divan. He wore his usual simple tunic and she the flounced skirt and fitted, low-cut bodice of a Rasennan noblewoman. The skirt was green and yellow, the bodice a matching yellow with red trim. It appeared that Halicar had been playing the harp, for the instrument lay across his knees. Happiness seemed to flow between the two, like the light of two lamps mingling. But then Elyssa looked up at Ilarion, and her expression became somber.

"Come and sit," she said, and when they had, she went on, "I have news from Kanesh. It came by ship today, from my ambassador there. Let me bring the text."

Next to the divan was a table piled with wax tablets and the sheets of vellum the Rasenna used for paper. Elyssa took up one of the sheets, and said, "I'll give you the meat of it. It appears that while Tirsun was in Kla earlier this month, helping Rimash seize the city, he acquired a woman. My brother has since brought this woman back to Kanesh, and she now lives with him as a wife, in his private quarters in the palace. She was formerly the mistress of Alfni of Kla, and there have been rumors that she not only helped over-throw the old man, she used sorcery to do it. Her hair is black, her skin has a golden cast, and she bears the name" —Elyssa had to work at the pronunciation—"Theatana of House Dascaris. I think this is your aunt, whom you warned me about."

Ilarion let out an exclamation of anger and surprise. The-atana, on the loose again! The woman was indestructible. He'd hoped she had died in Kla or been sold deep into the mainland. Now she was in Kanesh, and worse yet, in Tir-sun's bed.

"This doesn't please you," Elyssa said wryly, "does it?"

Ilarion scowled. "It's bad news indeed. She's allied her-self with Tirsun, and that makes both of them doubly dan-gerous. But Theatana's the worse threat, believe me."

"How so?" Elyssa was watching him keenly.

"You know what your brother's like, Protectress. He craves excess and the . . . the exotic in pleasures. He also likes playthings. I think he wants to rule Haidra so he can have more of them. With the Protector, it's really his appetite for amusement and praise that prompts his cruelty and am-bition."

"An estimate of him I share," the Protectress said in a dry voice. "Go on."

"But that doesn't describe Theatana at all—she's not in-terested in playthings or even in pleasure, not as we'd un-derstand it. I told you what she did at home, when she was only a girl, and I doubt if she's changed. She craves power, and she wants revenge on . . . probably on the world itself. Under her influence, Tirsun will become even worse than he is. And through him she'll have an army at her disposal. This is very bad indeed. It might get worse."

He wondered again if he should have told Elyssa about the Deep Magic when he first told her about Theatana. Not doing so had been an instinctive reluctance to speak of that power to people who knew nothing of it. It had been easy enough to avoid; he'd simply said that Erkai was an extraor-dinarily adept sorcerer who, with Theatana's help and an army of Tathars, nearly won the War of the Chain. But the Deep Magic's existence was of little consequence here. Even Erkai had needed a lifetime's labor to find his way into it, and Theatana was no Erkai.

"How could it be worse?" asked Halicar. "It already seems as bad as possible."

"It probably is. I especially don't like the rumors of sorcery. Theatana walked the Foul Road when she was young, and I know she'll walk it again if she can. It seems she had some ability—she'd learned to use one or two simple spells before my mother and father brought her down. I'd hate for her to find some way of magnifying whatever gift she has. And there's something disturbing about the way she so quickly captured Alfni. She's almost my mother's age, but now she's apparently captured Tirsun, too."

"Ah, but if that's the extent of her talent," Elyssa said, "I'm not much concerned about it. Some women have that magic with men no matter what their age, and no one calls it sorcery. And my brother, as you've said, has unusual tastes."

Ilarion frowned. He felt instinctively that Theatana was more dangerous than Elyssa believed, but the Protectress was probably right. Tirsun's tastes were indeed peculiar. Besides, it would be very difficult for Theatana to indulge her hankering after the Black Craft. He'd thought about her situation again and again, and his conclusions were always the same. She had no tools of the Craft, no deep knowledge of it such as Erkai had possessed, and even if she did manage to learn some minor sorcery—and after all, she'd never shown herself capable of more—it would still be just that, minor. She was much more dangerous as an influence on Tirsun than she was as a sorceress.

He said, "Likely that's true. She makes me uneasy, but I don't see how she can be much of a threat through magic."

"Ah, yes, magic. Which brings me to the other matter that's been on my mind. Ilarion, you wear a ring bearing the symbol of the fireshta."

The abrupt change of subject took him a little aback. She'd asked him about the nature of the pandragore soon after he came to the palace, and he'd told her the Ascendancy beliefs concerning the winged serpent. She'd listened carefully, but when he finished his account, she left the subject and had not returned to it.

"I know you told me about what it means in the north," she said. "But there was something I didn't tell *you*. It's this—well before you were washed onto my doorstep, I saw one here in the palace."

"You *saw* one?" Ilarion exclaimed. Halicar sat up straight.

"Yes, I did. It was while you were singing in the aviary, Halicar, the night I came back from Rumach Hold. It was in the nightlark cage. I was very frightened. Then it went away."

Astonishment stood in Halicar's face as he stared at her. "You never told me."

"I only told Mereth, because I wanted to discover what it meant before I spoke to anyone else. I've been watching for signs of clarification ever since, but it wasn't until the sea brought you to my door, Ilarion, that I realized that the fireshta must have wanted me to recognize you when you came. The carving on your ring was partly why I decided not to send you back to Kanesh." She sighed. "But I don't know why you were prophesied, unless the Lady has sent you to help me against my brother's machinations."

"Or against my aunt Theatana's," Ilarion said, struggling with awe. This woman before him had seen a pandragore.

"Perhaps that as well, or instead. The creature is of no profound significance in Rasennan belief, but perhaps we're wrong—when I saw it, it felt significant indeed." She shivered. "I know something of the numinous, and what I saw was a sacred thing. It's sacred to Antecessors also, isn't it, Halicar?"

"It is," Halicar answered, and touched the frame of his harp. "To us it's a manifestation of the Hidden Singer who is the source of Creation, and even the gods and goddesses of Creation are its songs. It's also said that the rests between its notes are the Silence." He made a small protective sign. "A thing dwells there that wishes all to be silent. What the Rasenna call the Poisoner we call the Unspeakable, and from it comes what humankind calls evil."

"We have a similar belief," Ilarion told him. "We name the power the Adversary. It inhabits what we call the Outside."

"Please stop," said Mereth. "This talking about such things . . . too much of it can draw their attention."

Elyssa said, "I agree, though I don't know what I did to draw the attention of the fireshta. Ilarion told me that seeing one portends a great change in the person who sees it—and it certainly portended a change in me. I knew that night I encountered it that Halicar and I . . ." She smiled and touched his arm. "Well, I knew."

She looked so happy, and so did Halicar, that Ilarion had no heart to warn them against Auvas, not at that moment. Still, a ripple of foreboding swept through him, and he thought, *But it doesn't have to end badly,* and the feeling passed.

"A change indeed," he said.

"Indeed," she replied. Then, in another of her swift alterations of mood, her look of happiness faded. "I'm going to show you something. I want you to tell me anything you can about it. Probably you won't be able to, but I'd like to find out. You'll see why."

"Of course," he said, mystified. "I'd be glad to."

She stood up. "Come with me, everyone," she said, and led them out of the Blue Swallow Room into the formal banquet hall. All through the big pillared space, slaves were lighting lamps, kindling fireboxes, and arranging couches with the small Rasennan banquet tables. Braziers glowed under wine bowls on stands. In a far corner, Nenattu was inspecting a row of drinking cups for chips or cracks.

"Is everything in order?" Elyssa called to the Grand Domestic, as they crossed the room.

"All will be ready, Protectress. The joints are roasting, and the bread will be fresh."

"Good." She darted into a corridor and along it, then opened a door and went through. Ilarion had never entered this section of the Upper Palace, and from their demeanor he didn't think that Mereth or Halicar had done so, either. The door led onto a stair that descended the side of a tiny two-story courtyard; the steps ended at another door, which was painted deep vermilion.

"Leave it open," Elyssa said, as they passed through into dimness. "We'll need the light."

They proceeded along a narrow corridor, the light fading as they went. The corridor walls bore paintings on carved plaster, but the colors were much faded, the plaster chipped. It seemed an old place; the artists had rendered their landscapes and creatures in a stark, angular manner, unlike the flowing designs that appeared in the upper levels.

They descended another flight of stairs, the light so dim now that Mereth, walking ahead of Ilarion, was only a shadow in the gloom. He wondered why Elyssa had not thought to bring a lamp, and wished for the clear light of a glass-paned Ascendancy lantern. If he failed to get home, he reflected, he could likely become rich on Haidra as a lantern maker, or perhaps as a supplier of fitted breeches.

They turned a corner and a dim orange illumination seeped into the corridor ahead. A few yards farther along was a doorway, this one without a door, that opened into a colonnade that ran around the four sides of a small square courtyard. He followed Elyssa and the others into the court; looking up as he went, he saw two more colonnaded levels above, and beyond the topmost one the coral-tinted clouds of evening.

There was a light on the court's far side. Entering the colonnade, Ilarion saw an oil lamp burning in a bracket above a bronze-plated door. Two sentries, each with the crossed-ax insignia of Dymie's First Levy on his leather cuirass, guarded it. They knelt briefly to Elyssa and rose.

"How goes your watch, Orinnu?" Elyssa asked the man on the left.

"Quietly, Protectress, as always."

"Good. Open the door. And we'll need your lamp for a little while."

Orinnu took it from its bracket and gave it to her, while the second guard drew the door's securing bar and pushed it open. The space within lay in near darkness, though a very faint light came from somewhere above. Elyssa stepped through the doorway, and said, "Ilarion, Halicar, Mereth, come inside. This is the palace treasury. Through it is the Old Shrine."

Thus the guards, Ilarion thought, following. Once inside, he saw that the dim light was entering through a pair of shafts, too small to admit the passage of even a child, that opened in the ceiling. Added to the light of Elyssa's lamp, the shafts' illumination allowed him to see that they stood in a large room whose roof was supported by two thick pillars.

He looked around. The walls were rough plaster, unpainted. If this were the royal treasury of Dymie, it seemed a sparse place, though it was big enough to hold great riches. It was far from full, however. Ingots of copper were stacked in piles here and there, with others of a gray metal that might be tin for bronze-making. As for bronze, there was a large pile of the loaf-shaped ingots the Rasenna favored for storage. A much smaller stack of cast-silver bars was near it. A dozen or so roughly built wooden boxes stood against the walls. They were cubes about as high as Elyssa's waist.

"There's gold and ivory here, too," Elyssa said, perhaps a little defensively. "And some gems, but they're packed in the crates. I don't keep the quality cloth or other perishables down here—it's too damp. Anyway, Dymie's real wealth is in its land and what its land produces, and what we get in trade. But I didn't bring you here to see my riches, or the lack of them. Come. The Old Shrine is on the other side."

She went on through the treasury, the lamp lighting the way before her. In the room's far wall was a rectangular opening bridged by a stone lintel almost a yard thick. They went under it into the shrine.

The chamber was only a third the size of the previous room, and unlike the treasury it was full of color. There was a pebble mosaic of red, white, and blue on the floor, and the walls were decorated with the kind of stiff, old-fashioned art Ilarion had seen in the corridors earlier. But here the pigments were fresh and bright.

"I had everything repainted last year," Elyssa said. "This is the oldest shrine in Dymie, and it must be kept in good repair."

There was a light shaft in here as well, which added a pink glimmer of sunset to the gold of Elyssa's lamp. The shaft opened above a slab of rock that must be the altar. Behind the altar rose a wooden pillar, painted red, the height of Ilarion's breastbone. He expected to see an image of the Green Lady on it, but instead there was only a chunk of black granite roughly shaped into a cone. He looked around for the divine image, but other than the pillar and altar, the room was empty except for a wooden chest against the wall to his right.

"The *baetyl*," Elyssa said, using a Rasennan word Ilarion didn't know. She bent a knee to the stone object on the pillar and touched her lips and chest with her fingertips. He imitated her, as did Mereth and Halicar. Then, curiosity getting the better of him he asked, "This isn't a shrine to the Lady?"

"Oh, it is," she said. "But it's to an aspect of her that is too sacred to be spoken of, depicted, or named, so the baetyl there stands in the aspect's place. There are only three such baetyl-shrines on Haidra. Another is at Velchi, which is said to be the oldest. The third is in Kanesh. Don't you have such objects at home?"

"I've never heard of them," he answered. He wanted to ask about the nature of this aspect of the Lady, but doing so would be pointless; she'd told him it was not to be described. The enigmatic stone and what it might represent made him a little uneasy. Just when he began to think that the beliefs of the Rasenna were close kin to those of the Ascendancy, something like this would remind him that they were not. The baetyl was one example, and Elyssa herself was another; last spring this warm, generous, and scrupulously just ruler had opened a young man's throat on the altar of her Lady. The man had requested his own sacrifice, but it was a mark of the alien ways of the Rasenna that Elyssa had felt she must comply. No priest or priestess of the Ascendancy would have done it, no matter how willing the victim, for a human offering was to them a device of the Black Craft. But clearly it wasn't always used as such on Haidra. Here the death could be an offering of atonement, as it had been for the man Elyssa killed.

"We've always had baetyl stones," Elyssa said. "But it's not what I brought you here to see." She set her lamp on the altar, then went to the chest against the wall and opened it. From it she brought a bundle of crimson fabric, which she began to unroll. Metal gleamed, then Elyssa held the thing in her palms, cradled in the red cloth. A face of bronze gazed blindly at the ceiling of the shrine.

"This is the mask of the Giftbearer," Elyssa said in a flat voice.

Silence lay thick in the stone room. Mereth stared apprehensively at the unseeing bronze face. Halicar shifted his weight from one foot to the other.

"Your brother spoke of it to me," Ilarion said into the stillness. "He said it was made by a man from the north, and had some sorcerous or sacred potency, and that it helped bring about the Fall."

"He told you the truth. It was sorcerous then, and it still is. Though no one has tried to use it for more than three centuries."

Mereth was studying the mask. "It's both woman and man," she said. "It changes with the light." Her voice became uneasy. "And it looks as if . . . as if it's listening to us. Or listening to *something*. I don't like it very much."

"It disturbs me, too," Elyssa admitted. "Just as it disturbed my mother, who was the mask's custodian before me. She died when I was sixteen, and the custodianship passed to my hands. I didn't want it, but I had no choice. It always goes to the eldest female in the ruling line, who must also be an initiated priestess of the Lady. If there isn't one, a girl is adopted in."

"It's not an evil thing, though," Halicar murmured. "Is it?"

"No," Elyssa answered. She went to the altar and reverently laid the mask and its wool wrappings on the stone. "It came from the hand of the Giftbearer, so it can't be evil in itself. Though its uses can be, since it contributed to the Fall. I suspect it's indifferent to the intentions of its employer. So it's a dangerous thing."

"It was made to be worn," Halicar observed. "There are holes for a strap. What happens if you put it on?"

"There's a prohibition against that. It's sacrilege, though not as much a sacrilege as trying to use it."

"But surely a few of the custodians tried," said Halicar. "In so many years, there must have been some who did."

Elyssa hesitated and looked down at the mask. Then she said, "Yes, there were. For most it was so frightening they never tried again. Those who persevered usually went mad. Three people who tried did not. Two were custodians and carried out their sacrilege secretly, and found knowledge and power in the mask. But with each wearing of it they risked their lives and minds, and eventually they were detected. Both were taken by surprise, away from the mask, and were convicted of sacrilege and executed.

"The third was Thanchvil the High Protector. He seized it from its then custodian and used it, because he was on the edge of defeat in a civil war and had nothing to lose, or so he thought. But he did. The mask brought crop failure and famine to his lands as well as to those of his enemies. In the end his impiety destroyed him and helped ruin the Garden itself."

"But Protectress," said Mereth, "no one has used it for three hundred years. Are you sure it's still potent?"

She looked at them all. "I'm sure."

"Ah," Ilarion said.

Elyssa took a deep breath and let it out. "I did a terrible thing some months ago. I put it on. It was only for a few heartbeats, no more. It was because I wanted to understand the vision of the fireshta. But it didn't work, and it frightened me out of my wits. I didn't want to *use* the mask, not use its powers. I don't even know what they are. I only hoped it would help me *understand*." Again she looked down at the mask lying on the altar. "I didn't believe it was sacrilege, because I'd had a divine vision. I still don't think it was. But I've made sacrifices of atonement, and repented, and I'm sure I've been cleansed of the defilement."

Halicar looked aghast. "But how could you have taken such a risk? I might have lost you, Elyssa."

"Believe me," she told him, "I'll never do it again. Whatever gift it takes to use the thing, I don't have it. Nor do I want to."

"May I ask," Ilarion said, "what it was that frightened you so?"

"I was at the center of a labyrinth," she said quietly. "It was pulling me outward. I might have gotten lost and never returned. It was full of . . . places like rooms. There were things in them. I don't know what they were. I don't like remembering it."

The lamp flickered in a draft from the doorway. "I'm sorry," Ilarion said. "Let it go."

She was studying him. "Does any of this sound familiar? The Giftbearer, the mask?"

"I regret, Protectress, it doesn't."

"You have no such legends in the north? Since the Giftbearer came out of the depths of Ocean, I thought perhaps—well, perhaps that you'd know something about him that might help us understand his mask. In case the mask might give us a way of restoring the Garden. . . ."

Her voice trailed off. Ilarion said, "I'm sorry. I know of none."

"Ah, well. It was a thin reed to lean on. At any rate, we don't forget the Giftbearer, even after so many centuries. Every year, in a thanksgiving ceremony at the winter solstice, we honor him for the benedictions he gave us. By tradition, we hold that ceremony in Charunna. It's called the Oblation of the Giftbearer. I take the mask there for the rite, for which I'm responsible. It's not all that long till it comes—there's only a month and a half till the solstice." She shivered slightly. "It's an uneasy thing for me. I don't like the mask, may the Giftbearer forgive me if I offend by saying so, and Charunna has been a melancholy place since the Fall. Also—"

They waited for her to go on. After a few moments she said, "Also, my brother will be present at the thanksgiving ritual. He's of the ruling family and must by tradition attend. I'd refuse him if I could, but I can't. It would be a deadly insult."

There was another silence, which Halicar broke. "But is it wise for you to be anywhere near him, even if it's in a shrine in sacred Charunna? You know you can't trust him, Elyssa."

"I know, and I don't. But he's always attended the Oblation, and he's always behaved himself. In any case, I can't forbid him to attend. For one thing, it would be wrong of me to affront the Giftbearer's memory. For another, if Tirsun's looking for an excuse for war, that would give it to him."

Halicar sighed. "Very well, if you must, you must. But if you're in the same room with him, I will be, too."

"So will I," Mereth said. "We'll both come, if you want us to."

"I'd be very grateful if you would," she answered. She turned to Ilarion. "I'd be happy if you'd come, Ilarion, as well. But you might not wish to, since Tirsun will be there."

Ilarion grinned. "It will be a pleasure to stand as a free man before the Protector. My small revenge, if you like. But my presence will remind him that you helped me. If this will be to your disadvantage—"

She made a negative gesture. "He seems indifferent to your escape and to my abetting of it. He sent me a complaint soon after he returned home from taking Kla, but it seemed merely a formality. I neglected to answer, and he hasn't pursued the matter."

"He was becoming bored with me when I left," Ilarion said. "Perhaps acquiring my aunt more than makes up for the loss of my company."

"He'll still kill you if you fall into his hands," Elyssa warned him. "But you'll come, nevertheless? He wouldn't dare touch you in Charunna, not at the Oblation. It would be serious blasphemy. Even he will avoid that."

"Sacrilege didn't worry him at Kla," Halicar pointed out.

"Yes, but that was Kla. My brother, to put it crudely, is wise enough not to pass water on his own doorstep."

Ilarion chuckled. "In any case, I doubt if Tirsun would risk angering divinity over the likes of me. Of course I'll come."

"But I've strayed from why I brought you here, Ilarion," Elyssa said. "*Why* can I not keep to a subject? There's something about the mask I want you to look at. Come and see."

He joined her at the altar. "As I said," she went on, "the mask told me nothing about the fireshta. But then you came

along, and you're from across Ocean, and so is the mask.
That made me remember something I saw on the back of the
thing, the night I put it on. It was like a wavy scratch inside
the chin, and it made me curious. So I came here again yesterday and looked more closely. I'd thought it was a tool
mark, but it wasn't."

"It wasn't?" Ilarion said.

"No. I couldn't make out anything more with my eyes
alone, but our engravers know how to make small things appear larger, using crystals that they grind and polish to the
shape of a water drop. We also use them as gems, and there
were some in the treasury. I found one and looked more
closely. As you can do for yourself."

She went to the chest from which she had taken the mask,
removed a tiny clear object, and brought it to Ilarion. Then
she used the red cloth to turn the mask over. "One is permitted to touch it," she said, "but I prefer not to."

"I won't, either," he assured her. The mask might be nothing more than wonderfully fashioned metal, but Ilarion was
oddly unwilling to lay a finger on it. He bent over it and held
the crystal to his eye. There was the tool mark, a wavering,
slightly jagged scratch the length of his thumbnail.

"Raise the lamp a little," he muttered. The shadows
moved. The scratch slid from a blur into clarity, picked out
by the lamplight. But it was no scratch. It was an engraving,
minuscule but perfect. His skin tingled.

"Do you see it?" Elyssa asked, with suppressed eager-
ness.

"Yes, it's . . . great Allfather above, it's the script of the
Logomenon!" His breath came short and he felt light-
headed.

"But that's your way of writing, isn't it?" Mereth asked in
a startled voice.

The infinitesimal characters were oddly shaped, but they
were unmistakable. "Yes. Whoever engraved this knew my
people's script." He squinted through the crystal. "It's the
Logomenon, all right. But I can hardly read it, the way it's
written is so archaic. That word, I can't . . . oh, *that's* what
it is. We haven't used it in our common speech for cen-

turies—Protectress, you said the mask was here more than two thousand years ago?"

"According to our legends and what records have survived, yes. They say the Giftbearer came to us a few years before our ancestors laid the foundations of Charunna."

"Then he didn't come from the Ascendancy. But I know where he *did* come from—given the mask's age and the fact that he used our script, he must have come from the Old Dominion. That was the heartland of my race, but it was drowned under the New Sea seventeen centuries ago. The Ascendancy is the Old Dominion's successor."

"But then," Elyssa said, with astonishment in her voice, "the Giftbearer, since he made this, must have come from your Old Dominion. He was a countryman of yours!"

"A long time ago," Ilarion replied, "and it was another country, really. But in essence, you're right."

"So," she said, with a laugh that sounded wry and rueful at once, "your forebear taught my forebears how to be civilized."

Discomfited, Ilarion shook his head. "No one man could do all of that, Protectress. Perhaps what he gave was the knowledge that certain things were possible, and the old Rasenna did the rest themselves."

"Perhaps." Her brow furrowed. "But how could he have reached Haidra? Did the mariners of your Old Dominion have ships like my brother's?"

"I'm not sure. They might have, but if they made such voyages, the records and the ships were all lost in the Deluge."

"I see I've much to learn of your history," Elyssa said. "But for now, the writing. Can you read what it says?"

"I think so. I had to learn the antique forms in my lessons." His eye began to water, and he switched the crystal to the other. "I think . . . let me be sure, yes, that's it." He raised his head. "It's not very useful. It says, as well as I can translate, 'The Visage of Retrospection.' "

" 'The Visage . . .' I see. No, I don't see. Do you know what it means?"

Ilarion straightened. "I have no idea."

"Perhaps we'll learn more when we go to Charunna for the Oblation. There's a very old inscription in the crypt under the Giftbearer's shrine. I'm not sure, but I think its symbols resemble the ones inside the mask. I suppose they might tell us more about the Giftbearer, if you can read them."

"I'd be glad to try."

"But are you *sure* the Ascendancy has no tradition of the Giftbearer? Did your Old Dominion have one?"

"The Ascendancy doesn't. As for the Old Dominion, I don't know. I can tell you only that if the Giftbearer engraved those words inside the mask, that's where he came from. I still can't imagine how he found his way here."

"But he never found his way home again," Elyssa said gravely. "An enemy, a servant of the Poisoner, sought him out, and they fought. The struggle destroyed them both. The hot springs at Velchi still bubble from the use the Giftbearer made of the fires there."

Ilarion hadn't heard this before, and it sounded ominous. "Where did the enemy come from? The north?"

"Beyond Ocean. They'd been enemies before, it's said."

He thought: *Could the man who made the mask have been a White Diviner? And his enemy a thanaturge? Is the mask a Deep Magic artifact? Or was the struggle merely between a man with the Kindly Gift and one who used the Black Craft, and the mask no more than an amulet or talisman? Though Elyssa said it brought crop failure and famine when Thanchvil used it. But those disasters can happen without sorcery, and do. After so long, who can be sure of any of it?*

He returned to himself and saw Elyssa's downcast expression. "Protectress, what were you hoping for?"

Her shoulders sagged a little. "I'm not certain," she said dully. "I suppose I wanted the signs of the fireshta to mean that the Giftbearer was coming back. That he would help us restore the Great Garden so we could be as we once were." She laughed, a desolate sound. "I suppose I hoped, when you came, that you might be the Giftbearer himself. But it's clear you're not, and the Garden will never be restored. We're a decayed people, even if the beauty of our island and our cities perfumes the stink. Dusk is falling over us, though for a while I was hoping for a dawn instead. But I should have remembered how hope clouds the vision."

Saddened for her, Ilarion could only mutter, "I wish I *were* him, Protectress, so I could give you that help. But I'm not."

Elyssa drew herself up and straightened her back. "I shouldn't be so dire. We live on a beautiful island, and not all the Rasenna are corrupt, and I've found love." She reached out, took Halicar by his hand, and squeezed it. "Perhaps that's worth more than all the glories of the old times—ah, Lady be merciful, what am I thinking of! The ambassadors from Ushnana will be at the gates by now! Upstairs, quickly, or all of poor Nenattu's protocol will go awry."

She put away the mask and the crystal, and they hurried out of the shrine, through the treasury, and into the dim corridors. As they reached the upper levels of the palace Mereth dropped back a little, allowing Halicar and Elyssa to go on ahead. She gestured to Ilarion to walk with her, and said in a low voice, "The murmur of their affair is spreading. You've been with the soldiers. How will it sit with them?"

"Larth seems loyal to the Protectress. My cavalry does, too. I think the whole First Levy is hers, unless there's some monumental disaster. But I was with Auvas Seitithi this afternoon, and he's not happy. I'm afraid he speaks for others of his rank. I was going to warn Halicar as soon as I could get him alone."

"Thank you," Mereth said. "We'd better both warn him, maybe that will make him listen better—he's so stubborn."

"Should we warn the Protectress as well? This could certainly help Tirsun's political scheming."

"I think we should let Halicar do it. This won't surprise her, though. She knows Auvas detests me and my brother."

"We're in this together, Mereth—he detests me as well."

"I know," she said. She gave him a wry smile. "We are all three of us detestable outlanders."

"We're each in good company, then," he answered lightly, as they arrived at the doors to the banquet hall.

They passed into the big columned room behind Elyssa and Halicar, into a blaze of lamplight and warmth. The banquet tables gleamed with silver and bright ceramics, and slaves stood like living furniture in the shadows of the columns. Nenattu was pacing distractedly near the double doorway that led out to the ceremonial portico.

Seeing them enter, he hurried down the long room to meet Elyssa. "Protectress," he said, with relief on his face, "I was becoming worried. They're coming up the Grand Staircase even now."

"I'm here, Nenattu. Where have you decided my friends are to sit?"

"This is a state occasion," said Nenattu. "I've put them at the right center tables. That is, unless the lord Ilarion is to be considered an ambassador from his Ascendancy, in which case he will be with you, Larth, and the emissary from Ushnana."

"What's your preference, Ilarion?" Elyssa asked.

The Ushnanans might have news of Rook and Lashgar. He said, "I'll be pleased to sit with you and the emissaries."

"Good," Elyssa told him. "Nenattu, go see if they're up the staircase yet."

The Grand Domestic hurried to the portico doors and gestured; two slaves swung the heavy leaves apart. The last radiance of day, red as ember light, poured into the hall. The Ushnanans were already striding between the portico columns.

Nenattu called out, in a herald's voice larger and deeper than his frame suggested, "His Eminence the Pronoyar of Ushnana, Arkallu of House Samash of the Protectorate of Ushnana. And his retinue."

The strangers crowded into the hall behind Arkallu, more than a dozen strong. The sunset was behind the men, and Ilarion had to squint to see their faces clearly.

One of them was Rook Arnza. Ilarion took a sharp breath as the huge Ushnanan saw him. Rook's face split in a grin of surprised delight. And then a slender, dark-skinned man stepped from behind his bulk, and Ilarion, with incredulity and astonished joy, saw that it was Lashgar.

III

THE MASK

22

THE TIRITHANA, THE SEVEN-DAY RASENNAN FESTIVAL OF
the winter solstice, had arrived. The festivities began with a
day of fasting and of sacrifices, in which the head of each
household offered oil, grain, and a domestic fowl on the
Lady's altars. As for the Firebringer, his traditional offering
was an incense made of the resin of smoke trees, and soon
after the festival's first daybreak its heady scent was drifting
in aromatic clouds through the streets of Dymie.

The fasting and the sacrifices ended at dawn on the second day, and as soon as the sun crept above the horizon the
festival began in earnest. Haidra was vastly rich in meat,
fish, bread, oil, wine, and fruit, and the recent harvest had
been even better than most. No one needed to stint; even the
poor were fed at the expense of the city magistrates. A buoy-
ant spirit was abroad in Dymie this year, and her citizens, as
well as every other free person on the great island, would
spend the six remaining days of the Tirithana in feverish revelry. It was the major festival of the year and the Rasenna
drank, ate, sang, caroused, and coupled as if the world's survival depended on the ardor of their debauch.

Ilarion had never witnessed the Tirithana, but he knew
from the domestics in Tirsun's palace that slaves hated the
festival. Drunken masters committed assaults, erotic and
otherwise; intoxicated mistresses flew into rages and
reached for the slender whips called wake-ups; children
were permitted to abuse and did so. The seven days never
passed without a crop of bruised and beaten slaves, and a
number of dead ones. Elyssa's were among a fortunate few.

329

According to Nenattu, the Protectress didn't allow such excesses under her roof. The palace slaves wouldn't love her for this, Ilarion knew, but they would at least not hate her.

The Tirithana's licentiousness and uproar much overshadowed the Oblation of the Giftbearer, the thanksgiving ceremony that involved the mask. In the days of the Great Garden, according to Nenattu, the Oblation was an important part of the solstice festival that the Rasenna held in their glittering mainland capital of Maghan. But after the Garden fell, and the mask was taken to Dymie, the Oblation's importance declined until it had become little more than a family rite of the Protectors of Haidra. The great magnates had ceased attending long ago, and only a few pious commoners bothered to accompany the Oblation procession that set out for Charunna in the late afternoon of the Tirithana's second day. The Protector or Protectress traditionally entered the dead city at sunset and carried out the thanksgiving ritual in a shrine within the ancient necropolis; anyone could accompany them as far as the shrine, but even the pious rarely did. Rather than enter Charunna's silent avenues during the hours of darkness, such celebrants waited at the city gate until the ceremonial party returned with the first light of the solstice day. Then they would accompany their ruler back to the city and rejoin the festivities of the Tirithana.

This year was no different; only some dozen of the devout joined Elyssa's small procession as it left Dymie in the pale gold of afternoon. These were on foot and wouldn't reach the old city until after sunset; Elyssa's party, which was mounted, would already be deep in its empty streets by then. The Protectress rode at the head of the procession, with Halicar on her left.

Mereth, Lashgar, and Ilarion rode a dozen yards behind the lovers. For Ilarion, having Lashgar with him again made his loneliness much easier to bear. Better yet, the prince also was now one of Elyssa's retinue; Rook had left Dymie over a month ago with the Ushnanan embassy, but before he did, Elyssa had asked him to release Lashgar from his household into hers. Rook grumbled at losing a good man, but agreed. Then, just before he departed, Ilarion and Lashgar finally explained who they really were and why they'd lied to him. To Lashgar's relief in particular, Rook took the deception well; as an occasional freebooter himself, he understood the need for discretion and anonymity.

Lashgar now lived with Ilarion in the palace guest quarters. He had done his best to help with training the cavalry, but he was no cavalryman, and after several days of frustration Ilarion sent him (with Elyssa's permission) to the harbor to see how Rasennan shipwrights carried on their craft. Lashgar's knowledge of Mixtun ships and sailing methods turned out to be valuable to the Rasenna, and the prince was enjoying himself immensely in his new career.

Rook's appearance in Dymie had had another fortunate result. Elyssa had been pondering for some time over how to construct the long-range ships that Tirsun had so fortuitously rediscovered. One of her shipwrights was willing to try building one, but to be sure of success, the man needed help from someone who was familiar with the design. She'd considered bribing one of Tirsun's wrights to enter her service, but none was likely to risk the Protector's wrath by working for her. Then Rook's arrival gave her a better idea. She offered to back the cost of a new ship for him, in return for a quarter share of the trade profits and the loan of the wright who built *Statira*. Rook muttered that he'd had a much better arrangement with Kayonu, but Kayonu was dead, and in the end he agreed. So, in a few years, Elyssa could hope to have a fleet to match her brother's.

Ilarion glanced back at the rest of their small procession. Just behind him trotted a horse drawing a light cart, which was lavishly painted and gilded. Nenattu drove the vehicle, a thing normally far beneath his dignity though not, apparently, when the cart bore the work of the Giftbearer; the mask rode behind him in an inlaid chest secured with silver-gilt chains. Other boxes in the cart carried the needs of the thanksgiving celebration: food and wine, torches, lamps, and offerings to the Giftbearer's memory.

Rounding out the procession's rear came a troop of Ilarion's newly trained, stirrup-fitted cavalry. The twenty young soldiers had tied green-and-white pennons to their spears, and these fluttered bravely in the breeze above their helmeted heads. There were no slaves; the Oblation was too sacred to allow them to be present.

"A fine day for an excursion," Ilarion said, gazing across
Monument Bay. Three miles off, on the peninsula that
formed the curve of the bay's far side, Charunna slept in the
waning afternoon. The sun poured its soft clear light across
the water, making the wave crests glow white as if from an
incandescence within. Running inland from the coast road
were fields planted with winter grain, the dark soil already
showing a haze of green where the tiny sprouts were poking
into the light. Groves of shaggy bristlenut trees and hillside
vineyards punctuated the landscape, and occasional lanes
led away from the road toward the farming hamlets and
country estates where the rural population lived and worked.
The sun-warmed air was almost balmy, for by Ilarion's standards the weather never became truly cold in Haidra's lowlands—here, the last remembered frost was three
generations back. Even at its harshest, the depths of a
Haidran winter brought cool rain rather than snow, and there
were plenty of sunlit days to help the crops along. And during the month of Last Winter, Mereth had said, there was
usually a warm spell—people went about in summer clothes
for some twelve to fourteen days until the seasonal rains resumed.

"It's fine indeed," Lashgar answered. He had begun growing his beard longer, but it still formed a neat point below his
tapering chin. "Haidra would be a good likeness of the Fortunate Isles if it didn't have people like Tirsun on it."

"And slaves," Mereth put in from his left, though quietly.
Ilarion was riding between her and Lashgar, so he could
keep an eye on her horse. She was as awkward a rider as
ever, and tended to let her mount do too much as it pleased.

"And slaves," Lashgar agreed. Mereth had awed him with
her singing the night he arrived at the palace, and he was still
diffident in her presence, which was unlike Lashgar. But he
had told Ilarion, in deepest confidence, that he thought she
was even more beautiful than Elyssa. Ilarion suspected that
Lashgar was perhaps a little in love with the Mistress-

THE MASK AND THE SORCERESS

Singer, or at least thought he was, and was trying to curb his hotheaded tendencies as a result.

"We don't have slaves in the Blue Havens, you know," the prince went on, his dark face very earnest. "Some of the jungly dukes in the out islands have them, but they're more like bondsmen, not the way slaves are here—in the Havens they can buy themselves out eventually. And we're quite civilized in Ammedara. If you and Halicar ever want to find a new audience to captivate, please come to my father's court there." He grinned at Ilarion. "Don't bother with the Ascendancy—I hear that Captala Nea is much overrated as a haven for artists. They all starve."

"But not as quickly as in Ammedara," Ilarion retorted.

"I'm delighted at your invitation," Mereth told the prince, "but I don't think we'll be going as long as they're together." She nodded at the lovers ahead.

"I suppose not," Lashgar said wistfully. "But perhaps someday."

"Perhaps. Now I think of it, Lashgar, we've hardly seen you lately. Have you been rebuilding the Protectress's shipyards with your own hands?"

"No, not at all. I've been learning how they do things here. And passing on what I myself know, also." He went on to describe both activities to Mereth, in exact and enthusiastic detail. She listened patiently, looking only very slightly bored.

Shortly the little procession turned off the main east–west road and started down the old avenue that led to Charunna. This had once been paved, but apart from a few exposed slabs it had reverted to a green track running along the eastern shore of Monument Bay. The commoners who had been following the procession on foot were now far out of sight.

Lashgar was chattering on. Ilarion listened with half an ear, until the prince said, "We should hear from Rook this month, shouldn't we? About the new *Statira* and when she'll be finished, so he can send us a shipwright."

Ilarion realized the question was meant for him. "I hope so. If *Statira*'s building goes as it should, we should see both her and the wright late this winter." He smiled; Rook had

showed an unexpected streak of sentimentality in naming
his new ship for his old.

Lashgar glanced ahead at Elyssa and lowered his voice.
"Do you think we'll have war inside the next few months?
Tirsun won't be satisfied with Kla, will he?"

Mereth looked at him sharply. Ilarion said, "No, he won't.
The news from Kanesh is that he's arming steadily, and
Larth thinks he'll attack us next spring, when the planting's
finished. I don't think our treaty with Ushnana will frighten
him very much."

The defensive alliance between Dymie and Ushnana had
been in force now for almost a month. It specified that Ushnana's Protector would send troops and ships to Elyssa's aid
if she were attacked, and that Elyssa would do the same for
Ushnana's ruler if anyone attacked him. It did not name the
enemy, but everyone knew who it was.

"Tirsun ought to be disposed of." Lashgar glanced over
his shoulder, at Nenattu and the cart negotiating a rough
patch of the road a dozen yards behind. The cart creaked,
wheel rims thumped on some exposed paving slabs. He lowered his voice still more, and said, "Do you see what I
mean? There'll never be a better chance than tonight."

"In the Lady's name," Mereth whispered, "don't say that
in her hearing. I can't tell you how angry she'd be. She
might *dismiss* you, Lashgar."

"Mereth's right," Ilarion agreed in an undertone, feeling a
rare irritation at Lashgar. "Keep such ideas to yourself, for
the Allfather's sake. Look, I'd like to kill him, too, but not at
the expense of sacrilege, and certainly not in Charunna.
While Tirsun's a religious celebrant he's under the Rasennan
law of protection. If Elyssa let him be killed there, she'd
give people like Auvas an excellent reason to charge her
with sacrilege and maybe even overthrow her. Tirsun would
be gone, true, but that wouldn't help her if she lost her
power."

"Tirsun might do it to her," Lashgar muttered.

"She says he won't. Even if she were wrong, she can't do
it to him. Please, don't take matters into your own hands.
She has too much to lose."

"All right. I spoke out of turn."

"It's tempting," Ilarion admitted, "but it can't be. Wait for the war."

"*Must* you talk like this?" Mereth demanded, her voice low but full of exasperation. "We're going to a thanksgiving celebration, and the day's lovely, and all you two can think of is fighting and death."

They fell silent. "I'm sorry," Ilarion said at last.

"Likewise," mumbled Lashgar. "I'm truly sorry."

"I'm sorry, too," Mereth said with a weary sigh. "My tongue's sharp because I'm worried for them both. You're not alone with her as I sometimes am, to hear her speak of how happy my brother's made her. And every time I see her so, I think of all the enemies here and in Kanesh, and how they wait for her and Halicar to put a foot wrong."

Ilarion nodded. His troopers didn't gossip in his presence, but he'd overheard scraps of their conversation as well as other chatter in the city streets. The rumors voiced by Auvas had inevitably spread, and the city had assumed for the past month that the Protectress and her Master-Singer were lovers. Many people seemed indifferent, and a few appeared pleased for her, but there were enough dark looks and mutters to be worrying. And if the city whispered such things, Auvas must be bellowing them, though in private and only to those who shared his opinions. Ilarion told Halicar what he heard as he heard it, though there was little the lovers could do about the warnings except try to be discreet.

As for Larth, even rumor did not report that he had any opinion at all of the affair, and he'd certainly never ventured one to Ilarion. This seemed a trifle peculiar, for the pronoyar was a Rasennan noble and must share at least some of Auvas's displeasure. This very reserve sometimes made Ilarion wonder if Larth's loyalty to Elyssa was as perfect as it appeared to be; utter silence could be covering up anything. But such thoughts—they were not even suspicions, really—smacked uncomfortably of his grandfather's violently distrustful nature, and Ilarion dared not seriously entertain them.

To reassure himself he said to Mereth, "Well, Larth's certainly on her side, and he's well respected. That will help."

"Yes," Mereth agreed. "I hope so."

They were now riding through the salt meadows toward the neck of land that joined Charunna's peninsula to the mainland. The dead city was not yet in sight, being hidden beyond a low ridge in the distance. From a field on the left, a flock of the big-boned argali sheep watched them pass. The shepherd waved, and Elyssa waved in answer. Ilarion found himself thinking of the crypt beneath the shrine of the Giftbearer, and of the inscription Elyssa had said was there. She had promised that he could examine it after the ritual was finished; like him, she was curious about what it might tell them.

"I'm still wondering what Theatana's up to," Lashgar said. "It's odd—not a whisper about her since Elyssa got that report from her ambassador. It's been well over a month now. It's as though she reached Kanesh and turned herself invisible."

"It is," Ilarion answered. He was very uneasy about Theatana, and the lack of news about her didn't make him less so. She must know of the mask; Tirsun would have spoken to her about it, just as he'd spoken to Ilarion, and it was exactly the sort of artifact she'd want to get her hands on. Ilarion had told Elyssa as much, though he'd avoided any mention of the Deep Magic. He was very reluctant to see the mask allowed to travel outside Dymie's citadel, and had urged the Protectress to hold the Oblation ritual there. Given his dire account of Theatana's past and her nature, he'd expected her to agree.

But he hadn't clearly realized, then, that except where Halicar was concerned the Protectress felt herself closely bound by Rasennan custom. The Oblation was always carried out in Charunna, she told him, and she would not change that. When he suggested Tirsun might seize the mask at Theatana's direction, she stared at him in disbelief. Even her brother, she'd said, would not violate the sanctity of the Oblation in such a way. And she gently derided the idea that Theatana might overcome his scruples; Tirsun, she said, had too much contempt for women to allow one to influence his actions.

Ilarion couldn't move her, and Elyssa showed signs of annoyance when he broached the subject again. She was the Protectress, and hers would always be the last word; so, very unwillingly, he had to let the matter rest.

"It's true there's not been a chick's peep out of her," he said to Lashgar. "I don't know if that's reason for comfort, though."

"Well, maybe she's given up her old ways," Lashgar said hopefully. "Maybe she's decided to settle down and enjoy the rest of her life. What would she gain by trying to get back to the north? If your people or mine caught her, she'd end in prison again. And from what you've told me, Kanesh is comfortable enough."

"That's true. Maybe you're right."

By unspoken mutual agreement, they dropped the subject of Theatana and rode on. The late afternoon dissolved imperceptibly into early evening. Eventually they reached the neck of land that led to the peninsula; it was called, rather somberly, the Throat of the Tombs. Here the meadows petered out into a landscape of rough limestone overgrown with scrubby, thick-leafed, aromatic vegetation: straggling sage bushes, dwarf laurel trees, oleander bushes, carpets of mint. The scent of the herbs mixed with the salt breeze from the shore. A few late grasshoppers, awakened by the day's warmth, still buzzed in the grasses. The road climbed a gentle slope as it crossed the Throat, and as they rode the sea became visible on both sides: Monument Bay to the right, the deep waters of the Sleeve to the left.

"Tirsun's just over that ridge in front of us," Lashgar said. "Him and his thirty men, if that's all he brought."

"Elyssa said it was," Ilarion answered. "He's under immunity, remember. He doesn't need to bring an army."

"Well, I hope he's uncomfortable, sleeping rough."

"I know him," Ilarion answered. "He'll be comfortable." Earlier in the month, Elyssa had politely sent word to Kanesh that her brother would be welcome in Dymie Palace for the Oblation, but Tirsun had declined, stating that he preferred to camp at Charunna's gates. He probably feared assassination, though given Elyssa's sense of honor he would be as safe in her palace as in his own.

Whatever the reason, the Protector was deep within his sister's domains. Some five days ago he and his party had crossed the border into the Protectorate of Dymie, traveling by land although the sea route from Kanesh would have been somewhat quicker. Elyssa had tracked his progress with couriers; when he reached the Charunna turnoff she and Nenattu were awaiting him with supplies, gifts, and a renewed invitation to stay in the palace. Again Tirsun refused, and amid much stiff courtesy and protocol, he and his companions went on to the old city. Today was his second day encamped at its gates.

Elyssa's procession crossed the Throat of the Tombs and moved onto Charunna's peninsula. The aromatic scrub still flanked the ancient road, though it had not penetrated much into the road's trace. Ahead, the top of the ridge was near. Elyssa and Halicar stopped at its crest to wait for the others, and a few moments later they reached it.

Ilarion reined in his horse. At last, he looked down on Charunna of the Roses. Half a mile away the ancient city lay like a dream of the past, its stones luminescent in the rose and gold of the fading light. Even from that distance he could see the vast necropolis in the city's center: tomb upon tomb, monument upon monument, sepulchre upon sepulchre, pillar upon memorial pillar.

"That's the place we're going," Elyssa said softly. "The Garden of the Blind."

They gazed in silence, the sea wind rustling the sage and laurel around them. Even the young troopers didn't speak.

At length Nenattu's cart squeaked as the horse shifted its hooves. Elyssa said, in a tone a little too bright, "Those will be my brother's tents by the gate. Come, we'd better go down. The mask is supposed to enter Charunna at sunset."

They all rode together, the cart trundling close behind. As they came nearer the city Lashgar asked, looking puzzled, "Why doesn't it have walls? It has gates, but they're standing all by themselves. It looks odd."

"In the old days," Elyssa told him, "we had no foreign enemies, and in the civil wars at the end of the Great Garden, Charunna was still too sacred for any Rasennan army to attack. So she never needed walls. She has gates, though, as you can see ahead—that's the Gate of the Living, where people and goods went in and out, as in any other city. But the gates were there only to show the proper places to enter."

"How many are there?" Ilarion asked. The Gate of the Living was a massive structure, two sixty-foot pylons of creamy stone topped by a huge lintel of red granite. Into the lintel was carved an inscription, one of the few Ilarion had seen on Haidra.

"Seven. Each has its name cut into it, as you can see. The most sacred is the Gate of Tears. It's on the seaward side, because that's where the dead and the mourners always entered, close to the entry to the necropolis. The dead always came to Charunna across water. We don't do that anymore, but the old Rasenna were very particular about it. At least, the ones who could afford to be buried in Charunna were. Only the very great or the very holy or the very rich had tombs in the necropolis. Some of the earliest High Protectors of the Garden were buried in Charunna."

"And the rest?" Halicar asked.

"In Maghan, deep on the mainland. The Hazannu destroyed their tombs a long time ago, looking for grave goods. These are the only ones left."

"And they haven't been robbed?" Lashgar asked in surprise.

Elyssa's laugh had a bitter edge. "No, they haven't, because we don't put riches with the dead, only a flask of wine and a loaf of bread as a token of nourishment for the soul. The Hazannu could have saved their labor—they judged others' customs by their own. What we Rasenna need after death, if anything, the Lady will provide. Don't you do the same in the north, Ilarion?"

"Well, Lashgar's people like to furnish their tombs decently, and they do have trouble with tomb robbers. We in the Ascendancy normally embalm our dead and seal them in wooden or stone caskets. But we only put flowers into the tomb with the casket, and a small portrait of the dead person. Consequently the remains lie undisturbed."

"Well, *I'm* not going to the Serene Fields or the Fortunate

Isles with a bouquet of windflowers and marsh violets," Lashgar said with determination. "I want everything I've enjoyed in life."

Everyone laughed, and Elyssa said, "I'm sure whatever it is you desire, Lashgar, you can charm the Lady into providing it."

They were by then a hundred yards from the Protector's tents. "I don't see Tirsun," said Ilarion. His stomach was tightening slowly into a knot. He hadn't expected this. It wasn't fear affecting him, though he had certainly feared the Protector's whims while he lived on the Citadel Stone. It was anger that clenched the muscles of his gut.

"Perhaps he's gone ahead," Halicar suggested.

"Perhaps." *I told Lashgar to wait for the war,* Ilarion reminded himself. *I have to do the same. I mustn't lose myself and stick my sword into Tirsun's throat. Elyssa would have to execute me.*

The sun was a fingerbreadth above the horizon when they reached the dozen tents of the camp. One was obviously the Protector's; it was large, made of finely dressed white hides, and Ilarion saw furniture through the open flap.

An officer wearing the insignia of Tirsun's palace guard was awaiting them. He blinked as he recognized Ilarion, but otherwise kept his face sternly composed. He made an obeisance to Elyssa, then straightened and waited for her to speak to him.

She said, "Where is my brother?"

"Protectress, my lord Tirsun has gone on into the city. He will be waiting for you at the shrine. He wishes you to know he has brought the best wine that Kanesh has to offer."

"Which is better than mine, of course. Who's with him?"

"Honored Lady, there are four. The noble brothers Gurtun and Meteli of the House Vafio, and two servants."

"Servants or guards? Never mind, you don't have to answer . . . Ilarion, did the Vafio brothers frequent the Citadel Stone while you were there?"

"Yes, Protectress."

"Tell me something of them. Their family holds lands north of Kanesh but I haven't seen the brothers since we were children. They were unpleasant even then."

He hesitated. "As I knew them, they were much in tune with the Protector's moods and pastimes."

"Enough said. What a pair to bring to a sacred place! Though maybe a necropolis is the best place for them." She looked westward. "The sun is at the edge of the Earth. It's time to go in."

Ilarion turned to his cavalrymen. "The Protectress will be here at the Gate of the Living at sunrise. You may stay and keep your own vigil with the other citizens when they arrive, or you may go back to the city now, provided you return by dawn." He glared at them. "However, it's the second day of the Tirithana. If you go back and you get drunk or find a woman and you don't show up here at first light, I will speak to the pronoyar and you'll be dismissed from the First Levy. For good. Is that clear?"

They nodded, and one said, "There are still five days of the Tirithana, First-Captain. Plenty of time left to enjoy ourselves. For tonight, we'll stay here."

"Good. We'll see you in the morning."

Elyssa said, "Until tomorrow, gentlemen," and rode into the shadows beneath the gate.

23

Beginning at the gate's other side was a broad avenue that was called, Elyssa said, the North Promenade. Now that Ilarion was actually within the city he saw that Charunna was more ruinous than she had appeared from a distance. Viewed from Dymie, across the breadth of Monument Bay, she could have been a living place, her streets thronged with carts, animals, and people, her markets bustling, her breezes sharp with charcoal smoke or perfumed with flowers and the scent of the sea.

But in Charunna of the Roses all that had ended three hundred years ago. Salt grass grew thick in the streets, moss and lichen pried at the cracks between the building stones, saplings grew from soil blown into fountain basins. Tiles cracked, rain crept into rafters, beams rotted, roofs fell in. The creepers of winter sunflowers drooped from the tops of broken walls and speckled the dusk with their long-petaled yellow blooms.

"Where are the tomb roses?" Lashgar asked, looking up at a frond of yellow blossoms.

"Some are here," Elyssa answered, "but they're a little out of season. Most grow in the necropolis. Oh, there's one by the fountain. The white flower, do you see it?"

Ilarion squinted into the gathering dusk. Growing up a wall next to a dry stone basin was an emerald-leafed bush. On it were many small brown husks and a single rose, pearl white and as broad as his palm.

"They grow only here?" he asked. He'd never seen the flower in Dymie or Kanesh.

342

"Not altogether. You might come across them elsewhere on the island, but they're uncommon except in Charunna. It's true they grow best in the necropolis. The bushes there are quite large, and they climb. In summer, when they're in full bloom, the scent is like no other."

"Pleasant?" Ilarion asked.

"Exquisite. Though a little sweet and cloying for my taste."

Conversation faded as they went on. The horses' hooves thudded on the grass covering the streets, with the occasional clatter as the animals traversed exposed paving, and the cart's wheels thumped and creaked. The wind had dropped, and with the sun below the horizon the air was becoming chill. Elyssa had said the old city made her melancholy, but Ilarion did not find it so; Charunna to him seemed a place of serenity and quiet.

Nenattu called softly, "Protectress, do you want your winter cloak?"

"I think I do," she answered. They halted while Nenattu took the garment from a bag in the cart and handed it up to her. As she pulled it around her shoulders, Halicar asked, "How much farther?"

"Not far."

They set off again. The avenue ended in a broad plaza. In its center was a low circular platform as broad as a man was tall, capped by thick stones. Lying a yard from the platform was a broken column of pink granite. When erect and in one piece, it must have been eighty feet high. On the square's left, facing west, stood an almost-intact building that was clearly, from its size, shape, and detail, a major temple of the Green Lady.

"This is Charunna's Temple Square," Elyssa said. She gestured at the platform. "Under that is the shaft called the Gate of the Earth. This one is said to be very deep. That's the Shaft Stone lying next to it."

"You have those in Dymie, too," Lashgar said.

"Yes. Every Rasennan city has a shaft and a Shaft Stone, though few stones are as big as that one was. The shaft is the emblem of the passageway from the Overworld to the Underworld. It's always kept closed to tell the dead not to return and trouble the living."

"Is it ever opened at all?" Lashgar wanted to know.

"Never. Doing so would invite misfortune."

They left Temple Square and continued down a narrower street. The sunset turned the ruins on their right to black silhouettes and drenched the facades on their left with glowing crimson. The cart's wheels and the horses' hooves made the only sound.

"Here it is," Elyssa said quietly. They had reached the street's end. Ahead was a stone wall twice a man's height, and in the wall a gateway wide enough for two horses to pass abreast. There might once have been a gate in the opening, but no sign of it remained. Through the gateway, dim in the last of the twilight, the Garden of the Blind lay beneath its mantle of trees: mourning cedar, yew, laurel, purpleheart.

And under the trees, everywhere, were the stone memorials of the dead. Among them, the last autumn bloom of the tomb roses hung white and luminous in the dusk. A fragrance drifted through the gateway, like that of the roses Ilarion knew but rich as incense. He tried to imagine their scent in the time of full blossom, and failed.

"The shrine's not far inside," Elyssa said.

They entered the necropolis, following a narrow avenue between the monuments and sepulchres. It was so dim under the trees, and the ancient structures so overgrown, that Ilarion could make out little more than their shapes and some indistinct carvings. The most prominent were slender stone pillars, but even in the poor light he saw that almost all had broken off some distance above the ground. Time had shattered them.

He saw a glimmer of yellow light in the dusk ahead. "Protectress," he said, wishing for his cavalrymen.

"I see it. My brother's here."

"You still don't think he's a danger?"

"He's always a danger, but much less of one in this place. He'd like me dead, but he isn't going to kill me so that everyone knows he did it. Moreover, he wouldn't do it while we're under immunity. I've already told you that, Ilarion."

"Yes, Protectress. I'm sorry for harping on it."

She leaned over and patted his arm. "I know it's only because you worry about me."

Her confidence was infectious. But even if it were misplaced, he and Lashgar and Nenattu could give a good account of themselves, for they were well armed. Halicar, though, was not, for an Antecessor bard was inviolate only if he went unarmored and carried no shield or fighting blade. Hunting spears and a dagger were permitted; Halicar today had a knife at his belt but was otherwise defenseless. But an attack was very unlikely, as Elyssa had said; they were as much under celebrants' immunity as Tirsun and his companions were.

Ahead, a grassy clearing appeared in the forest of monuments. Along its west edge lay a pool of still water that reflected the sky's last crimson, and on its far side stood a white stone building with a portico supported by scarlet-painted columns. The tile roof was intact. A pair of torches burned in brackets fixed to two of the columns. No humans were in sight, but five unsaddled bay horses stood at ground ties within reach of the pool. They stamped nervously at the strangers' approach, and one neighed. Lashgar's mount whinnied an answer. This seemed to reassure the other animals, for after a few snorts and whuffles they returned to cropping the thick grass.

"That's the shrine," Elyssa said. "We'll leave the horses here. There's grazing and water. They'll be all right till morning."

No one came out of the building as they unsaddled the mounts and put them on ground ties. Nothing now remained of the day but an indigo streak just visible through the trees. Stars hung overhead in vast silent rivers. There was no moon.

Nenattu said, "If the men will help me to unload the cart—" And suddenly the door under the portico opened. A bar of warm lamplight fell through the darkness, framing the silhouette of a man.

"Ah, my dear sister, you're here at last."

Ilarion took a deep breath, let it out. He would have

known the Protector's voice even without the words: affable, melodious, urbane.

"Indeed I am, brother. Have you brought your own supplies, or was it just the wine?"

"We have all that's necessary," Tirsun answered, moving toward them along the bar of light. He sounded as if he were enjoying himself.

"So have we. We'll bring it in."

"And the mask?"

"Of course. Do you think I'd forget *that*, Tirsun? What a peculiar question."

"I suppose. Will you come in for wine before you unpack?"

Ilarion thought that Elyssa glanced at him, but in the darkness he wasn't sure. "Very well. Thank you."

"It's my pleasure." The Protector turned and went back into the shrine. Ilarion peered after him and glimpsed furnishings and lamps, and three men in colorful overmantles and tunics, one of whom was Tirsun. The other two would be the Vafio brothers, Gurtun and Meteli. The remaining pair were more plainly dressed: guards, masquerading as servants.

"Come," said Elyssa.

They walked across the grass to the portico and passed under it. Elyssa went first into the shrine, then Nenattu, then Halicar and Mereth, and finally Ilarion and Lashgar. Ilarion paused on the threshold, blinking in the light. The building was one large windowless room, lined with slabs of fine-grained alabaster and well lit by pottery lamps set on terra-cotta sconces. Unlike every other Rasennan shrine he had seen, this one had no wall paintings; the alabaster surfaces were blank white. Running halfway down the room's center was a stone platform not quite the height of Ilarion's waist. It seemed to be a dining table, a vast one by Rasennan standards; wine jugs and cups stood on it, and alongside it were a dozen two-person stone benches.

He looked for an altar beyond the table, but there was none. Instead, a rectangular opening, two yards long and one in breadth, gaped in the floor. Its wooden trapdoor stood open, leaning against the shrine's rear wall. In the mouth of the opening the top step of a descending stairway was visible. Between it and the table's end stood a square pillar of white marble with an oval gold bracket set into its face.

"Ah, it *is* you, Ilarion," Tirsun said. "I'm perfectly astonished." His languid voice suggested nothing of the sort. "Sister, did you bring him as a calculated insult, or is this sheer oversight on your part?"

"Neither," Elyssa said calmly. "Ilarion is of our rank, and he's become my friend. He's under my protection, as well as possessing the immunity of a celebrant. As do all of us here, might I remind you."

"Of our rank. A friend. I see." With a lazy smile, Tirsun examined Ilarion from head to foot. But his eyes were green stones. Ilarion stared into them, remembering his terrors, his humiliations, his slavery. He had already seen that Tirsun wore a slashing-sword; the customs of the Rasenna did not, unlike those of the Ascendancy, prohibit weapons at religious rituals.

Draw, Ilarion thought. *Draw, Tirsun, commit the sacrilege first, and I can kill you.*

Gurtun and Meteli were watching him and Lashgar. They looked doubtful. Ilarion had heard the brothers boast of their military prowess, but he knew they were no professionals. The two supposed servants were another matter: palace guards, the pick of Tirsun's infantry. He knew them by appearance if not by name, for they'd come to the Citadel Stone a few days before he left it. And they knew their trade; they watched his sword hand, not his face.

"In this sacred precinct," Tirsun said, "I won't argue either point. But Ilarion, how pleasant it is to see you again! I thought I'd never have a chance to renew our connection."

Ilarion bowed to the exact degree he would have used for Elyssa. In a voice so steady it surprised him he answered, "I also anticipate the pleasure of the renewal, my lord Protector."

Tirsun smiled, and his even white teeth showed slightly as he did so. "I'm sure you do. Well, tonight you needn't pour my wine unless you wish to. In fact, I'll pour a cup for you myself, to celebrate your change in station. How fortune turns us about, hey?"

"Indeed," Ilarion said. "I'm much honored, Protector."

"Of course," Tirsun said, and picked up a jug. They all drank, even the guardsmen, and when they were finished, Elyssa said, "It's time to bring the mask."

They all went outside and kindled six torches from the two already burning at the portico. The guardsmen and the Vafio brothers, with Lashgar and Ilarion, arranged themselves in two lines in front of the shrine's entrance. Then Elyssa and Tirsun each took a handle of the mask's box and proceeded at a slow, ceremonial pace toward the portico, led by Nenattu. The Grand Domestic carried a small pottery jar of burning incense and murmured softly over it as the mask approached the shrine. Mereth and Halicar stood in the shadows at the edge of the torchlight, watching.

Nenattu, the Protectress, and her brother reached the doorway and entered. Ilarion could see them through the opening as they paced slowly to the pillar with the golden bracket. When they reached it Nenattu moved aside. Elyssa and Tirsun set the box on the floor, opened it, and together removed the mask in its red cloth. After unwrapping it carefully—Tirsun, like his sister, appeared to avoid touching the thing—they placed it in the gold support attached to the pillar. Then they stepped back. The mask gazed down the room's length, eyeholes enigmatic and empty.

"The emblem is in its house," Elyssa called into the silence. "Those who would celebrate the Oblation of the Gift-bearer, come near."

Ilarion, along with the others, thrust the sharpened butt of his torch into the soft earth. When he straightened Mereth was beside him.

"Are you all right?" she murmured. "Tirsun—"

"I'm fine. Don't worry." He walked toward the shrine, with Mereth gliding beside him. "It's just for one night. Then we'll be rid of him."

"Yes."

Elyssa came out to direct the unloading of the provisions and offerings from the cart. Ilarion worked outside as long as he could, but eventually they had moved everything into the shrine. He was the last in. The others had already set more dishes, cups, and food on the stone table to join those already on it, and draped cloth spreads over the seats. Ilarion took a place at the table's foot, with Lashgar, Halicar, and Mereth near him, and as far from Tirsun as he could manage to be. Elyssa and Tirsun sat at the end closest to the mask, facing each other across the table, with Nenattu next to the Protectress. The Vafio men and Tirsun's palace guards were in the middle.

Elyssa had told Ilarion what to expect at the ritual, whose modest nature reflected its antiquity. They would eat a meal together in the mask's presence, then descend into the crypt under the shrine to sacrifice to the Giftbearer. Ilarion had asked Elyssa if the crypt were the ancient teacher's tomb, but she wasn't sure. The tradition was ambiguous about what remained of the Giftbearer after he and his enemy destroyed each other; it mentioned ashes, and that those had been brought to Charunna, but their exact burial place wasn't recorded.

Ilarion wondered again about the inscription in the crypt. He'd be seeing it within the hour. Perhaps, if it were indeed in the Logomenon and he could read it, the words would tell him a little more about who the Giftbearer had been.

They began their meal. The food was by necessity cold, though Tirsun warmed his wine over a small portable brazier. They ate bread, cheese, spiced sausages, pickled mushrooms garnished with parsley, the white breast of hens, ambercups, plums, and cherries preserved in honey. The many lamps warmed the room comfortably, although the shrine's door remained open to admit fresh air and dispel the fumes of burning oil. Tirsun spoke only to the Vafio men and to Elyssa, disregarding the presence of everyone else. That suited Ilarion, and he began to hope that Tirsun would ignore him until dawn came and with it their departure. The superb food and a cup of the flawless wine of Kanesh made the prospect easier to contemplate.

Even so, the meal was hardly one of cordiality and warmth. Tirsun chattered brightly, speaking three words for

Elyssa's one, but he was clearly being cheerful and talkative merely to irritate her. Most of his conversation circled around the rebuilding and embellishment of an enormous country villa he had recently acquired—or confiscated, it was not clear which—from a noble who had slipped into too much debt. Elyssa's responses were brief and tinted with irony. Nenattu spoke only when Tirsun's or Elyssa's words made it necessary for him to do so. As for Ilarion's end of the table, there it was mostly silence. The Vafios pretended he wasn't at the table at all, though they did a poor job of concealing their resentment at dining with a former slave. They attempted conversation with Halicar and Mereth, since Antecessor singers ranked high enough for recognition, but it was stilted, and Mereth in particular did not encourage them. Their interest in Lashgar vanished at the instant he identified himself as Ilarion's friend.

The meal went on for a long time, and by its end the conversation had dwindled to a monologue carried on by Tirsun. Then, mercifully, the final dish—cherries in crystallized honey—made the rounds. Mereth loved this confection above all others, and Elyssa spoiled her by frequently having them at table, but tonight she took only one and merely nibbled at it. Then she put it on a dish and looked up at Ilarion. Their eyes met, and she made a tiny grimace that said, *Isn't this a truly dreadful evening?*

He answered her with a minuscule nod, and then Elyssa stood. She glanced down the table at Halicar and her expression softened. Tirsun saw it.

"Sister," he said, "I had meant to ask . . . there are rumors about you coming out of Dymie. Of course, I'm sure there's no truth to them."

In the corner of his eye Ilarion saw Mereth twitch. Halicar's face was wooden.

"What rumors?" Elyssa asked indifferently as she straightened her overmantle.

"Oh, I wouldn't dignify them with repetition." The Protector's glance flicked to Halicar, then away. "They were of a . . . personal nature."

"Ah." Elyssa laughed. "In that case, you're perfectly correct. You should not add to their substance by repeating them, even to me. But you must know how rumors are, brother dear—those of your peculiar behavior travel even as far as Dymie. However, I never pass them on, though many delight in doing just that."

"Ah," Tirsun said with a sharp little smile, "but you and I differ in one respect. I *hang* people who assault my dignity by repeating such tales in the wine shops. Perhaps you should do the same. The silence afterward is profound and restful."

"No doubt it is to some ears. Enough of this, Tirsun. The offerings should be made."

"And after that," he said wearily, "we sit up here in thanksgiving vigil until the sun rises. With all respect to the Giftbearer, it's very boring."

"Why did you bother to come, then?" Elyssa snapped. "There's no requirement for you to attend, only for me. Why didn't you stay in Kanesh and celebrate the Tirithana? I know how you hate to miss a celebration."

"Ah, but for me every day is a Tirithana, so I'm not missing much. And you and I so rarely see each other, Elyssa. This is one of the few opportunities we have to bask in the familial warmth that flows so naturally between us. I wouldn't miss it for any price."

"Indeed," Elyssa said coldly. "Then let's not miss the offerings. You can carry them down to the crypt."

"Me? Why can't one of your near-speechless companions do it?"

"You know the bearer should be of the ruling blood, Tirsun. Stop being obstructive."

He shrugged. "I forgot. As you wish, however." He took the offering box from the foot of the pillar and waited while Elyssa, using the red cloth, removed the mask from its bracket. She carried it to the opening in the shrine's floor, where the crypt stair led down into darkness. There she halted, and said, "Ilarion and Lashgar, would you be so good as to take those triple-wicked lamps and go ahead of us? It's not far down."

They obeyed. Ilarion went first; by the time he reached

the third step he could already see a flagstone floor below him. He went down the rest of the way, Lashgar following close behind. At the bottom he stopped and looked around. As far as he could tell in the dim light, the crypt was as large as the building above it. Many thick masonry pillars supported the shrine floor above, and the crypt's recesses were lost in darkness.

Elyssa was descending the stair, holding the mask upraised before her. Tirsun came next, and the rest followed, Halicar at the tail of the impromptu procession with Mereth. The Vafios had brought more lamps, as had one of Tirsun's guards.

"This way," Elyssa said. She led them past a pillar, and Ilarion saw a wall of carefully dressed granite ahead. Just in front of it was a waist-high circle of mortared stones, like a wellhead, and next to this stood a shallow brazier of green bronze. He looked around for the mysterious inscription, but the lamplight did not carry far enough into the dark. Perhaps, when the ritual was over, they could look for it.

"There are wall niches for the lamps," Elyssa said. "All of you except Ilarion, put them there. But don't use the niche behind the shaft—that's for the mask. Ilarion, I want your lamp here by the brazier."

He obeyed, setting the light on the flat coping of the wellhead, and glanced into the shaft within. Blackness filled it, and he shivered. It might resemble a well, but he suspected it was not meant for drawing water. He imagined that it was very, very deep: a true passage to the Underworld.

Elyssa, still using the red cloth to hold the mask, placed the bronze face upright in its niche. Tirsun had already set the offering box on the floor by the brazier and opened its hinged lid. Within were two ceramic flasks, a small round offering-loaf, a comb of honey in a dish, and a sheaf of pale green splints. The splints gave off the fragrance of greenheart, the rare aromatic wood the Rasenna burned for their most important sacrifices.

Elyssa came back to the brazier, piled half the greenheart into it, then opened one of the flasks and poured oil over the splints. From the second flask she poured a few drops of wine. Then she added honey and half the loaf of bread. She broke the other half in two, poured wine and honey over the halves, and gave one to her brother. Her portion she set on the coping beside Ilarion's lamp. Then she raised her arms, palms upward, in the Rasennan attitude of prayer.

"See us, Giftbearer," she said softly. "We have come this year, as every year, to honor you. We ask that you accept our bread, our wine, the sweetness of our honey, and the fragrance of greenheart, in thanks for the gift of knowledge and of the building of cities and for the founding of holy Charunna."

She stopped, lowered her arms, and picked up a splint. Touched to the lamp flame, it instantly ignited.

Ilarion tipped his head and listened, but not for Elyssa's next words. Had there been a sound from the stairway? Or had a wind creaked at the shrine door above? He couldn't go to investigate; it would disturb the ritual. He moved a little so he could make out the stair from the corner of his eye.

"Hear us and accept our offering," Elyssa said, and plunged the splint into the oiled kindling. Flames spat and soared, light poured through the crypt. Across its breadth, no longer hidden in the darkness, the far wall leaped into being. Ilarion stared. Carved into the stone were characters in the same archaic Logomenon he'd seen inside the mask. It was the inscription, and he could read it, and what it said hit him like a mailed fist under the breastbone.

ONCE AT THIS PLACE LIVED DAOKOS
THE WHITE DIVINER

He heard himself exclaim with shock, and in that instant a voice came from the top of the stair. It was accented, and a woman's.

"Tirsun the Protector," it said, "are you there?"

"Oh, yes," Tirsun called in answer. He dropped the bread and honey on the floor and drew his sword in a rush. His four companions instantly did likewise and Ilarion saw now, too late, how they had arranged themselves into a sword-wall. He yanked his own blade from its scabbard and saw

Lashgar and Nenattu do the same. Halicar stepped in front
of Elyssa but left his knife in its sheath.

Now their three swords bristled at Tirsun's five. Mereth
was backing away from Gurtun. Ilarion grabbed her arm and
pushed her behind him.

Elyssa seemed struck dumb. Tirsun grinned and called up
the stair, "Everything's nicely arranged. Why don't you
come down and join us?"

"You don't outnumber us by that much," Lashgar said
hotly. "What do you think you're going to do?"

"You're in absolutely no danger at all," Tirsun told him,
still grinning. "Well, you might be, Ilarion, but it won't be at
my bidding—even I won't kill somebody under the immunity of a celebrant. However, I'll do my best to protect you
from *her*. She really doesn't like you—something to do with
your mother. These family quarrels can be *so* bitter. Ah,
there you are, my sweet."

A woman came down the stairs. It was Theatana. She
wore red-leather leggings and boots, a long red tunic, and a
hooded overmantle of thick, dark blue wool the color of her
eyes. In one slender hand she carried a long, leaf-bladed
knife. Behind her, their laced hobnailed sandals clattering on
the stone steps, came eight huge Hazannu clansmen, all
armed and armored for battle, swords drawn.

"Nephew," Theatana said in a happy voice as she saw Ilarion. She sheathed the knife and came forward into the brazier's light. "It's been a long time since I've seen you, hasn't
it? *Imagine* my surprise when Tirsun told me he owned a
slave named Ilarion Tessaris. I was so looking forward to
meeting you in Kanesh—and how disappointing to arrive
and find you'd run off. But anyway, after the Protector and I
had a long talk, I decided it really was you and not some im-
postor. And so it is. You look just like your father."

Ilarion knew he was gaping at her but could not stop. The
woman before him was no young girl, but she had an allure
far beyond that of youth. The hair framing her lovely face
was shining and black, her skin sunlit gold, her wine red
mouth wide and soft and a little open. Theatana gazed back
at him and smiled. It was an intimate, knowing smile, and

instantly he understood how she had captivated Alfni and Tirsun. If he had been innocent of her nature, she might have captivated him as well.

It's as though she's found her way back to the Black Craft and learned some spell of seduction. But how?

"No one saw your galley, I hope?" Tirsun asked her.

"No one. We came in under oars last night. The ship's by an overgrown pier in the eastern harbor, with her mast lowered. She's invisible unless a boat actually enters the basin. The crew whimpered about being in Charunna at night, but I put a quick stop to their whining." She gestured at the Hazannu. "As for your hired mainlanders, they don't seem much afraid of your tomb city."

"They don't fear other peoples' ghosts, only their own. Well done, my sweet Theatana. No officer of mine could have managed this stratagem any better."

"No officer of yours would have thought of it," she said sharply, and Ilarion, surprised at her tone, covertly studied the Protector. What he saw on Tirsun's face startled him. The amiable, slightly mocking expression was as he'd expected, but for an instant it slipped to reveal a look of tormented hunger tinged with dread. Then the moment passed, and the Protector's expression assumed its urbane glaze again. But there was a brittleness to it, a brittleness Ilarion hadn't seen when he was Tirsun's slave.

He's afraid of her, he thought in astonishment. *Allfather above, she's well on her way to ruling him. And he knows it's happening and can't stop it. He can't bring himself to kill her.*

"What do you and your woman want here, Tirsun?" Elyssa demanded at last. "Have you finally lost your wits and decided to assassinate me?"

"Not at all," her brother assured her. "Although the Hazannu I've hired wouldn't hesitate if I ordered it. They don't know anything about the Oblation of the Giftbearer, and even if they did know, it isn't sacred to them. No, we've come for something else. That bronze thing on the wall there."

A breaker of fear curled over Ilarion, and he heard Elyssa say, "What? You'd take the *mask?*"

"Of course," Tirsun answered reasonably. "There's no law that says it has to reside in Dymie. It can just as well stay with me in Kanesh."

"No," Elyssa said. "What right have you to it? It stays with me."

"Enough of this," said Theatana in a cold voice. "Stand aside and let us have the thing."

"And if I don't?" Elyssa answered.

Tirsun said, "You're outnumbered. I think we can move you out of the way and disarm your friends without doing too much damage, except perhaps to your dignity. If you resist, though, I *may* not be able to stop my Hazannu allies from killing one or two of you. And we'll have the mask in the end. If your friends die uselessly, it will be at your choosing."

Elyssa's hands had bunched into fists. "What good will the mask do you in Kanesh that it doesn't do you here? Has your . . . *woman* convinced you it's some magical plaything you can amuse yourself with? You know how dangerous it is."

"Ah, but with the danger comes power. Theatana has told me a very interesting story about some ancient sorcerers in the north and something called the Deep Magic. She thinks the mask belonged to one of those sorcerers, and that it was a tool to control such a power. Be that as it may, we're taking the thing to Kanesh. When we know all its secrets we'll have the power to rebuild the Great Garden, which Theatana and I will then rule as High Protector and High Protectress . . . she also has plans for your Ascendancy, Ilarion. But I don't imagine you'll like them."

"What makes you think the mask is a tool to control the Deep Magic, Theatana?" Ilarion asked desperately, though he knew words were useless. "Tirsun, she's putting you at more risk than you can imagine."

"I am doing no such thing," Theatana snapped. "As for what the mask is, nephew, you could have already found out—if you'd ever bothered to stroll into Charunna and glance at the inscription. Tirsun told me it was here, so I came and looked last night." She gestured at the inscription, which was still illuminated by the brazier's light. "The Giftbearer was a White Diviner named Daokos, and he made the mask. What else does one need to know, to want it? And don't try to frighten me with talk of the Ban. Erkai broke it. I know, because I was there."

"You'll never be able to use it anyway. You don't have any such gift, Theatana."

"I beg to differ," she said in a soft, cool voice. "If we had time, I'd show you how wrong you are. But there'll be another day. For now, we'll be satisfied with the mask."

A silence. The flames fluttered in the brazier and the perfume of greenheart hung in the stone room.

"We'll have it, Elyssa," Tirsun said, "one way or another."

"Take it, then," she answered, her voice harsh. "I want none of my friends hurt. But you'll find it came at a high price. Ilarion, Lashgar, Nenattu, put down your swords."

Dropping his blade to the floor and sick with dismay, Ilarion thought, *She mustn't have it. But I can't stop her. I could die fighting, and she'd still get it. Why didn't I come and read the inscription before now? If I had, maybe I could have convinced Elyssa to drop the cursed thing into the sea.*

Theatana said, "Bring me the mask, nephew, and make sure you touch it. If it does something nasty, I'd rather it was to you than me."

Nothing remained but to obey. He turned and walked slowly past the wellhead and the brazier to the wall. The mask stared at him, blind metal. In the flickering brazier light it was female, then male, then female again.

"Get on with it," Theatana ordered.

He picked the mask up and turned to face the others. Mereth watched him, her eyes enormous with apprehension. The metal between his fingertips made his skin tingle as if to a faint, deep vibration.

Theatana must not have it. He had to stop her.

I could try to use it myself.

It was a mad idea. He knew nothing of the Deep Magic; no one living did. He didn't even have the Kindly Gift, the lesser magic.

But I must try.

It may kill you, or worse.

Theatana is worse.

The mask had no straps. He raised the shell to his face and pressed the bronze onto his flesh. The metal was cool, with an odd softness that was almost like living skin. Within an instant it fit him perfectly, as if it had flowed into every nook and cranny of his face.

"What do you think you're doing?" Theatana asked, and he heard amusement rather than anger in her voice. "You're trying to turn it on me? You pitiful creature. You couldn't begin to know how to use it." Her tone sharpened. "Bring it *here.*"

He barely heard her. With an abruptly different sight he perceived that the mask was not really metal at all, but a whirlpool of force, a spinning labyrinth. At its center was a still point, the totality of his nature: his thoughts, his emotions, the recollection of every experience—

Elyssa said it pulled her outward, into the maze.

Fear woke in him. He felt the tug of the labyrinth, sensed the enigmatic presences within its myriad interconnected chambers. But he could not flee; he had to try the mask's power against Theatana.

He ventured a hesitant step outward. His fear increased; he could lose himself so easily. Now a chamber seemed to open near him, spectral door ajar. On the door was the ghost of an inscription and it said, in the archaic Logomenon: *The Room of the Words of Minor Encouragement.*

"Take off the mask," came Theatana's voice as if from a far distance. "Take it *off.*"

He had no idea what to do. What help was there here in this slowly wheeling maze?

Go the other way. Go inward. Perhaps there.

He fled from the terror of the labyrinth into the knifepoint center, into himself. Suddenly, all about him was silent and filled with warmth and dim light; he hung suspended at the center of a timeless instant, and he understood that he had plunged deep into his own past. He knew he was in his mother's womb but that neither she nor he was in any place of this world.

And in the silence, a woman who was not his mother said: *This is the water of life. Take, and drink.*

He had no idea who she was, nor where he was, nor what she meant. Only that this had happened, and that through the mask he knew of it.

"Give me the mask, or I'll kill you!"

Theatana's voice again, distant. Dimly, he saw her stride toward him, dagger ready. He heard death in her voice and knew he must obey; with a struggle he gave up the peace of the unborn, let the mask fall from his face, and was again in the crypt under Charunna. Theatana snatched the bronze from his shaking fingers, and as they both touched its substance, it was a moment's bridge between them.

And in that moment a wind howled through Ilarion, a wind so bitter that he felt his nerves flayed bare and scalded with ice. Struck dumb, paralyzed, he endured the agony. It lasted only a heartbeat, but that was enough. As he had seen into himself, he saw into her.

She was no longer Theatana, or not only Theatana. She was riddled with the tendrils of a thing unspeakable, nameless, so intimately entwined with her flesh and thought that she and it were already almost one. It was transforming her, and the transformation was monstrous.

And within her, too, was a shaft into an abyss, and within the abyss coiled annihilation and despair, and silent limitless hunger.

Theatana felt the contact. Her eyes widened, and he understood her thought.

He sees me. Kill him.

Then his heart thudded again as she pulled the mask from his helpless fingers. Her dagger was raised to strike. He threw himself backward but the wellhead's stones brought him up short and painfully and he heard Elyssa's enraged shout and Tirsun's furious yell.

Theatana stopped only a pace away from him, the mask in one hand, the knife in the other. Her mouth worked and her eyes were blue-black pools. But he saw that the Protector's command had held her back. She did not quite dare murder him.

She still needs Tirsun, he thought. *But for how long?* He was shaking and queasy and his sight seemed clouded with slowly rotating, ghostly webs.

"You don't know what you've done, Protector," he said weakly. "In the name of all that's sacred, destroy her if you can. She's become something terrible, not human. And there's worse in her than that. She knows the Poisoner, and it knows her."

Tirsun burst out laughing. When he stopped he said in an amused voice, "Is that the best you can do? We all have something terrible in us, Ilarion. Even you do, I'm sure. Still, Theatana my love, it's better if you don't kill him right now. Another time would be preferable."

"But I *want* to," Theatana said in a thick voice. "Can't we take him back to Kanesh and play with him? I know you'd like to, my love. And he's your property, after all."

"I can't, my sweet. He has immunity, even if he used to be my slave. I can't abduct him—Elyssa would get me declared a desecrator and accursed, and that's not a good thing for a ruler. I'd kill him in spite of that, if it were truly important to do so, but the pleasure of it just isn't worth the inconvenience."

Theatana scowled and sheathed her knife. Then she pulled a leather bag on a strap from beneath her overmantle and slipped the mask into it. "I can wait," she said as she pushed the satchel back into place. "I'll peel your skin off you one day, Ilarion Tessaris, and dust you with salt."

Ilarion held his tongue. Tirsun might change his mind as easily as not, and he had to stay alive to get the mask back from Theatana. Nothing mattered but that. He did not know what she might become through its powers, or how she might then serve the Adversary, but he knew that catastrophe and ruin stalked at her side.

Tirsun chuckled again. "Ah, my dear Theatana, you *do* have a bad temper sometimes, but it gives you a savor all your own." He turned to his sister. "Well, Elyssa, I think the bloom is off the evening, don't you? Theatana and I must be away to our ship and put to sea. I'm afraid that you and your friends will have to spend the rest of the night down here under the trapdoor, but I'm sure somebody will come by in the morning and let you out. As for my escort at the city gate, I'd be obliged if you sent them home. But if it would make you feel better, you can hang a few of them."

"You judge others by yourself," Elyssa said, her tone flat and cold.

"How else should one do it? Good night, sister." He turned to Theatana. "Come along, my love, it's time to go."

The Hazannu waited as a rear guard until Tirsun, Theatana, and the others were up the stairs. Then the mainlanders trooped after them. The trapdoor closed with a boom, and scrapes came from above as the Hazannu weighed it down with the stone benches. Then there was silence.

"Now what?" Lashgar asked, in a tight, furious voice.

"Now we wait," Elyssa answered. "He was right. Someone will come looking for us by noon at the latest. But he'll be well away by then, and anyway, he'll have an escort waiting over the horizon. We'll not catch him at sea, I'm afraid."

Lashgar subsided with a mutter. The flames of the brazier burned low.

"Ilarion," said Elyssa at last, "what did you find in the mask?"

"Myself," he answered. He thought: *And a place called The Room of the Words of Minor Encouragement.* And suddenly he understood where he had been, and what the Giftbearer had contrived. "There was a labyrinth round me. I think I know what it is."

"What?"

"It's like a vast building. Full of rooms. The Giftbearer kept his knowledge there, or copies of it, as if he wrote it in a book. That's what the inscription inside the mask pointed to—I thought it said 'The Visage of Retrospection,' but I mistranslated. The words actually mean 'The Visage of Recollection.' A place to store memories of how to do things."

There was another silence. Then Elyssa asked, "What will she do now?"

Fear turned in his belly. "Learn," he said.

24

THE CITIZENS OF KANESH PACKED SARNATH SQUARE, THE broad plaza near the harbor that served as the city's place of public assembly. At the east side of the square, the black pillar of the Shaft Stone of Kanesh reared into the sky, and at its foot was the huge white-granite disk that sealed the city's Gate of Earth.

Theatana stood with Tirsun on a marble dais next to the Gate. To her right rose the sheer face of the Citadel Stone, with the gleaming walls of the palace at its crown. Over Kanesh lay the pale light of the winter sun, washing the city's polychrome buildings and russet-pillared colonnades with a fragile radiance. It was late in the morning, the sky calm and clear, with no hint of rain.

Tirsun stepped forward, raised a hand, and stilled the excited hum of the crowd. When he had their silence, he called out, "People of Kanesh! You have heard the rumors among you. I have felt the hope emanate from the city, from all of Haidra, as the word has spread. But what is the source and wellspring of this hope?"

The crowd murmured, knowing the answer was at hand, and that he would tell them. Theatana, listening to him as he went on, had to acknowledge that the Protector knew the ways of moving his people. His words and images worked on their passions like yeast in dough; he told them of their ancient glory, of how much they had lost, of their hope of restoration, of the despair that the restoration was beyond their strength. By the time the sun approached zenith, they were murmuring and crying out; some wept.

At last he raised his arms in the attitude of adoration and shouted, "But now, though our hope lay dying, it lives again! In the far north our weeping was heard, and from the far north our ancient prayer has been answered. And our answer has come to us in a new guise, for it prophesies a new age of the Rasenna. To us has come the Heiress of the Giftbearer. The Heiress has come!"

He turned to Theatana and made an obeisance. An instant of shocked silence fell, that the Protector would abase himself to her, then the crowd caught its breath and roared.

Theatana stepped forward to the altar at the dais's edge. In her high, pure voice she cried, "Rasenna! I have come to restore the Garden! Our way will be long and hard, but I will be with you! Your enemies will cry out in despair; you will crush their throats under your heel! Your eyes will smoke with fire, your hands will be the scarlet of blood, you will flay all who resist you and drag them in the dust of the earth!"

The multitude bellowed. Women were screaming and weeping. Theatana raised her arms and quieted them. Her power flowed in her blood like hot wine, and she thought: *This is what I was born for.*

"I am the Heiress! Witness me now!"

She opened the wooden casket that stood on the altar. Bronze glittered within it. She raised the shining oval above her head.

"The mask of the Giftbearer! I have come to reclaim my inheritance."

In the mob's roar, she slipped the mask over her face and felt the bronze mold its cool surfaces to her skin. She'd possessed the ancient artifact for ten days, and it was all she had hoped it might be. Even now, as its labyrinth took form with her consciousness at its core, she marveled at the genius of its artificer. The mask was a vast storehouse, the library of a White Diviner, its chambers replete with the images, the sounds, and the writings of his sorceries. Most of the former she could comprehend, but the written records were in a form of the Logomenon so archaic that she understood only half of what they said. She had much work to do.

Her very first experience with the mask came during the
return voyage from Charunna to Kanesh. Tirsun was with
her when she put it on, that morning in the galley's cabin.
She'd had no idea of what to expect, but the instant it
clasped her face she perceived that the mask was not metal
at all, but the manifestation of a whirlpool of forces; and that
in the throat of the whirlpool was her own nature. She was
seeing *into* herself, in her totality. Laid bare to her inner vision were her first heartbeat in the womb, each breath she
had inhaled since her birth, every footstep she had ever
taken. And with that, every memory she possessed: her first
kiss, the face of the first man she hanged for treason, her first
instant of madness.

But that was not all. She probed deeper and perceived
those parts of her nature that were closed to her waking mind,
as they were closed to all men and women except in the language of dreams. They were the wellsprings of her being: secret, wordless, the primeval muck of appetite and urge. She
understood that from those came conquest, mastery, dominion, the need and the power to crush and enslave and rule;
and the lust of slaughter, to expunge whole peoples from existence. She knew the craving to devour all that was not herself, and in so doing destroy all that might ever threaten her.

And deeper, in her abyssal depths, she sensed the mouths
of paths leading beyond herself, glimpses through them of
vast crags of frigid light, gulfs of searing darkness. One led
farther than all others, and at its end was the pit, and in the
pit was the Adversary.

I greet you, sister, it had whispered. *Come into my arms,
as did the others.*

I need nothing from you, she told the thing.

But you do, it murmured in its sweet, poisoned, cajoling
voice. *You have a library in a language you cannot read. In
me are wisps of those who can read it. Only ask, invite me
in, and I will send them to help you.*

No, she answered, and fled its presence. She swept
through the byways of her vast inward country, returning
toward an awareness of the outer world, dimly sensing again
the galley's pitch and roll. The mask still surrounded her, al-

though she also seemed to see it from a distance, like a spiral of fierce radiance. She tried to grasp its structure, to understand its power and how to control it, but doing so was like trying to see every leaf of a tree in a single glance. But she perceived enough to know its likeness to a vast catacomb that was also a library and artificer's forge, a place where sorceries could be made and stored.

Then she became aware that she was still looking through the mask's eyeholes, into the galley's cabin. The mundane world seemed meager beside the immensity of the interior landscape, but the turning spiral dragged at her; she must leave or be drawn into it. With a ferocious effort she found her hands and pulled the mask from her face.

Tirsun had been staring at her, eyes wide and alarmed, for she was shaking violently. The galley rolled to a larger wave and he'd braced himself against it and asked, "What happened? What did you see?"

"All I need," she'd answered.

In the days that followed, she'd tried to accustom herself simply to wearing the mask. Its mental effects made common reality seem very small and far away, or like a landscape in a dream, and at first it was all she could do to navigate a room while it was on her face. But eventually she trained herself to maintain a double vision while she wore it, so that she could function in the world of things and people even while her central self hung within the labyrinth. So far she hadn't dared wander into its mazes or attempt to fathom its sorceries, but she no longer felt as if she were being dragged into its depths. She was gaining control.

Now, as she wore the mask, Sarnath Square appeared dim and remote, the roar of the crowd muted as surf tumbling on a distant shore. Theatana focused her concentration on the altar, where the smoking brazier, the dove, and the necessities of her spells were laid out. She used tongs to draw an ember from the brazier, and thrust it into the powder she'd ground for the aspect spell.

"I am both the Heiress and the Giftbearer returning," she cried. She seized the dove from its cage and held it aloft. "This sacrifice I make to the Green Lady!"

She snapped the trembling bird's neck. Its death flowed into her; she leaned above the smoking powder, breathed it in, and uttered the syllables of the spell. The aspect change swept over her, a variant that Vindisi taught her not long before he died. For this change she'd ground the powder from her own substance, and as the transformation shivered over her she became a male version of herself, a black-haired northerner, golden of skin: sorcerer, Giftbearer.

The crowd shrieked, then hushed in awe. Theatana gazed down into it and pointed at the young man she'd already marked out, a youth with an oozing sore on his cheekbone. "Come here," she called, "and be cured of your wound."

He stumbled to the dais. Tirsun himself helped him climb the steps to her. Theatana applied a salve she'd made according to Vindisi's recipe. Then, her fingers on the youth's cheek, she invoked the healing spell the horse doctor had called The Sealing of the Open Portal. The nausea she'd always felt when she used benign magic swept through her, and as the spell's power flowed through her fingertips into the wound, she had to fight to keep from retching. The physical and mental strains troubled her control of the mask, and she felt her consciousness slipping outward into the labyrinth.

With a fierce effort, she maintained her centering and completed the spell. The young man, white of face, stood trembling before her. Then he fell to the dais, weeping, and tried to kiss her sandaled feet.

Theatana suppressed an urge to kick him in the mouth, and let him press his lips to her skin. "By sunset he will be healed," she called, knowing it was true. She pulled him to his feet and handed him over to Tirsun, who got him quickly off the dais.

"Can you do more?" he asked beneath the crowd's ecstatic roar. "They want more. It would be better."

She knew he was right. "Two," she answered, her voice faint and far away. "Only two. Those with sores, like his."

So she healed two more, and when that was done she restored her natural appearance. And then she took off the mask, and they fell to their knees before her, and acclaimed her as the Giftbearer returning.

Not quite two months later, on the eleventh day of Last Winter, Theatana and Tirsun sat together in Theatana's workroom. The small space was austere and sparsely furnished: white plastered walls bare of decoration, plain reed matting on the floor, a wooden table with the remains of a noon meal pushed aside, a chair with a red-leather seat, a faintly smoking ceramic firebox on the hearth in the room's center. Theatana sat in the chair; Tirsun was lounging among the pillows of a couch that stood against the opposite wall. The window was open and admitted a watery late-afternoon light.

"Did you know they've begun worshiping you?" Tirsun asked. He took a sweetmeat from a tray and nibbled it. "Images of the Lady are appearing in the shrines, and they've got black hair and gold skin. Entash told me this morning."

"What of it?" Theatana had the mask on the table before her and was gazing thoughtfully at the bright metal.

"It's because you heal people. They think you're not just the Heiress but an incarnation of the Lady. Even the priestesses seem to believe it. Even *Entash* believes it."

"Let them," Theatana answered. She had cured another dozen wounds since that day in the square. Doing so disgusted her, but it would disarm any suspicions that she might walk the Foul Road. She was so revered now, though, that even if some priestess made such an accusation, no one would believe it.

As for Tirsun, he was now as much in her control as Alfni had ever been. When he first brought her to the Citadel Stone she'd behaved in the submissive way he expected, but not much time passed before her wishes weighed heavier in the balance than his. She gripped his will all the more easily because of his complete erotic obsession with her, an obsession so consuming that he even stopped coupling with the palace's female slaves. In respect of satisfying his other, deeper appetites, those that inflicted pain and degradation, this was more difficult. If such licentious behavior became known, it could undermine the Heiress's reputation for dignity and kindliness, even if it only involved slaves. Consequently, she and Tirsun had sampled such pleasures only once and in secret, at a secluded country villa he owned. But she promised him more when she had full control of the mask, and that in itself was enough to bind him closer to her.

"What are you thinking about?" he asked.

"Nothing," she answered. "Stop distracting me."

In fact she was pondering Ilarion again, and that instant of connection when they both touched the mask. He had certainly perceived the change in her that the Other had brought about, and she'd had a glimpse into him in turn—an instant's perception of his weariness and fear and rage, and of his hatred for her.

Is there more to him than I thought, she wondered, *or did he perceive me merely because my power was flowing through the mask?*

When she got her hands on him again, she'd find out. He was still in Dymie, and she would be there also, in the not very distant future. Tomorrow morning the army marched on Elyssa's domains, and Haidra would be at war.

"Isn't it about time you did something spectacular with that thing?" Tirsun asked. "It's been almost two months, and you're still investigating it, and tomorrow morning we march west—and that was your idea, my dear, wasn't it? You won't have much time to work with the mask while we're on the march."

She raised her eyes and stared at him. Tirsun said quickly, "I only inquired."

"I will tell you again," she said, "since you can't seem to grasp my difficulties. The mask is a library of spells, among other things. But the spells are in an archaic form of my language, and there are words I don't know, which I must understand before I dare use them. Imagine trying to learn a foreign tongue, but if you made an error in its speech, a flame might consume you. These powers are *dangerous,* Tirsun."

"Very well, I understand."

"So you keep telling me. Now be quiet. I need to concentrate." She was trying a new tack. It had occurred to her as she woke that morning that Erkai might have known the older forms of the Logomenon, and fragments of his knowledge might persist in the Other. She intended to search for the Other's presence within her, and see what she could find.

She picked up the mask, held it a moment, then slipped the strap over her black hair.

Instantly she possessed the double awareness again, of seeing the mask from afar as a slowly spinning whirlpool of white radiance, and simultaneously of being within herself as she hung at the vortex center. She searched along her nerves, along the threads and filaments of her awareness. Everywhere she sensed strands of the Other but they had melded long ago with her own, now almost impossible to distinguish.

Inspiration struck her. She found a tendril that seemed most clearly the Other's, and discovered that she could tease it from its matrix, like a thread being drawn from the weave of a tapestry. She examined it.

It was not only a thread of identity. It was a path into the Other itself.

Instantly Theatana cursed herself for an imbecile; she had missed the obvious. As the mask allowed her to see into her nature, it would also let her see into whatever shared her nature with her. The Other was there for her to know completely. She had only needed to separate its substance from her own, and look.

Now she did look, and she quickly discovered that her conviction about the Other's origin was correct. It *had* begun as a fragment of Erkai the Chain, implanted in her on the Hill of Remembrance in Captala. Over the years it slept in her like a seed dormant in dry earth, until she killed Tabar her jailer and his death watered it awake.

This was no more than she'd suspected. But what else was there?

She searched more deeply into the Other's nature and found that it was a rudimentary being, for it had entered her only as a fragment. Its awareness and purposes were little higher than a reptile's: to survive, to feed, to procreate itself.

But its essence, the essence that had transformed the old Theatana into her new self, was no reptile's.

Thanaturge.

In that instant, through the Other's dim awareness, she understood what she was and how she had become so. She was a seedling of the Deathmakers, the thanaturgai, the terror of the ancient world before the White Diviners destroyed them. She understood that they could implant a part of their natures into men or women whom the Black Craft had tainted, so long as the person was willing. And Theatana *had* been willing; she had wanted to be Erkai's lover, to learn and share his powers. She would have willingly agreed to be sown with such a seed.

She had sometimes wondered how he'd managed to implant it in her. Now, through the Other, she knew. Erkai's chain, which he had used to help him break the Ban, was an instrument forged in the ancient world to control the Deep Magic. Seeding her was his last sorcery with it before he died.

But then she perceived what would have happened to her if he'd lived, and felt a cold shudder. A thanaturge who created such scions used them as lieutenants, giving them powers they could use at will, provided this did not conflict with his ends. But in return they became his creatures. Once the seed had grown into what she called the Other, Erkai could have controlled her every breath.

But Erkai was dead, and she was under no one's control. Wild excitement suddenly coursed through her. She knew her true self, but what other knowledge might have passed into her? Did the Other hold spells of Erkai's craft, or even more ancient stores of learning, perhaps Erkai's insight into the Deep Magic?

She rummaged through murky recesses that still seemed to be more of the Other's nature than they were of hers. Here and there she discovered the sources of her erotic knowledge, and skills of torture as yet unused. Then, in its lowest stratum, she found what she was looking for.

But her first glee turned quickly to bitter frustration. She found the spell that had created and dismissed the wraith of

Rehua back in Kla, but that was all. Much other knowledge was there, but it was in fragments. This wreck was all that remained of Erkai's knowledge; in his death throes he had managed to thrust it into her with the seed of the Other, but the forces destroying him had ruined it as well.

Wait. Perhaps something useful remains. I dismissed Rehua's wraith, after all.

The Other's rudimentary awareness stirred sluggishly against hers. She became conscious of crude excitement.

Help me to know what controlled Rehua.

The Other did. The knowledge trickled into her consciousness, and as it entered her she felt a door open in the labyrinth. Within that chamber lurked a spell of ferocious power, a spell that the Other perceived and understood, as Erkai had perceived and understood it before he died. And now, as the door opened and the shape of the spell hung before her, she also possessed that knowledge: the spell was named Begetter of Myriads, and it was terrible, and she knew how to use it.

And now she *would* use it. Exaltation coursed through her. She drew back from the turgid crannies of the Other's sentience and plunged into the buried parts of her nature, down into the brutal energies that drove her. They did not want to be drawn toward the light, but she dragged a strand out nevertheless, coiled it, molded it like clay on a wheel as it squealed and fought, then rose with it into the sunlit shallows of her inner sea.

Abruptly she inhabited the outward world again. Through the mask's eye sockets she saw her workroom, and from the angle of the sun she knew that considerable time had passed. Savage excitement filled her, but she was shaking as if overcome by palsy, shaking so badly the chair creaked. The fragment she had drawn from her deep being quivered bitter and oily behind her teeth.

Without thinking, she spat it through the mouth hole of the mask and yanked the mask from her face.

Tirsun yelped in alarm, staring. Something hung in the lamplight between Theatana and the far wall. It had no clear shape; it distorted the air, like the heat rising from the firebox. It was like the wraith of Rehua, but Theatana knew it was *she*. She had created an entity separate from herself.

Trembling with exhaustion she thought, *This isn't the Black Craft. I've needed no death to do this. If this is not the Deep Magic, I don't know what is.*

It had her face though the features were so transparent they were hard to see; they shifted like shallow clear water. The eyelids seemed closed. Tirsun cringed on his couch, shivering.

"Sister," Theatana breathed.

The eyelids seemed to flicker open. There were no eyes behind them.

Motion on the windowsill, an animal. A miu had jumped onto the sill from outside and now balanced in the open window, peering in. It was a young animal though not a kit, its silvery fur barred with gray and black. It regarded Theatana curiously.

She was almost too exhausted to move, but she took up a fragment of baked fish from the remnants of her meal and tossed it onto the floor under the window. The miu's ears twitched. It peered at the fish, then jumped nimbly down into the room. It seemed quite unaware of the translucent thing hanging in the air a few paces away. It sniffed the fish, then settled down on the matting to eat. She could hear Tirsun's harsh breathing.

"Sweet sister," she whispered. "Go there."

She directed the command at the sister-shape. The entity contracted into a faintly luminous ball and drifted down to hover just above the miu's delicate pointed ears. The little animal at last looked up, saw the ball, and hissed in sharp alarm.

The ball sank into the miu's head and vanished. The creature froze in mid-hiss, mouth gaping wide as if paralyzed.

Theatana formed an intention, sent it to her substance within the miu. The miu stood up stiffly, marched across the floor. Theatana told it to stop, and the miu stopped. Then she walked the animal across the floor to the hearth and made the creature hop up onto it. It crouched a pace from the firebox.

Jump up, she commanded.

The miu didn't move. The little creature was resisting her. She hadn't expected this. Theatana redoubled the force of her command.

The miu held back for another moment, then obeyed. It hopped onto the thick rim of the firebox and teetered. From its open jaws seeped a screeching noise. The sound grated on Theatana's eardrums. She was getting terribly tired, as though someone had opened a vein in her leg and her blood was leaving her.

Jump in.

The screech became a thin shriek of terror. The miu tottered, pranced stiffly on the firebox rim, then leaped into the coals.

The coals hissed and the miu squalled and danced as Theatana began roasting it. Its fur charred and smoked.

Abruptly her grip slipped away as the miu's agony and mad panic gave it the strength to break her hold. With that went her sense of the sister-thing, evaporating into nothing. The miu screeched, bounded instantly to the floor and then to the windowsill and out. Theatana heard its wails fading as it fled along the roofs of the palace.

The room stank of burned fur and flesh. Tirsun cowered on the couch, his lips twitching, his face stark and white with dread. He made a small high noise in his throat, like a terrified child, but seemed able to utter no other sound.

Theatana ignored him and slumped in her chair, almost fainting, her vision gray with exhaustion. She was fiercely disappointed. The sister-thing hadn't been strong enough to make the miu cremate itself, though it had been close. But if even partial control of such a weak creature nearly killed her with weariness, how would she ever deal with a human?

Through her daze came a whisper, perhaps some faint trace of Erkai awakened in the Other. When the whisper stopped, she knew what to do.

Harness the dead, it had murmured. *Harness the dead, and make the living walk.*

She turned her gaze to Tirsun. He had sat up on the couch and was no longer cringing against the wall. He managed a weak, ingratiating smile.

"Theatana, dearest," he got out in a dry whisper. "My love, that was . . . magnificent."

Contempt rose thick in her throat, choking her. He was a corpse-beetle; she wanted to crush him crackling under her heel.

"Leave me," Theatana said. "Leave me, *now*."

Tirsun opened his mouth, closed it, and obeyed.

25

HAIDRA'S ANNUAL LATE-WINTER MILD SPELL HAD ARRIVED, carried on sultry winds from the northwest. The Rasenna called it the Little Summer and every year basked happily in its warmth and sunlight, until the cooler weather returned with the last of the rainy season. Several minor festivals fell during it and everyone, except for the slaves, put their work aside and enjoyed themselves. Elyssa and Halicar decided to spend the mild weather at the Protectress's summer villa, a few miles along the coast from Dymie, and invited Ilarion, Lashgar, and Mereth to accompany them.

On the afternoon of their second day there, they took food and wine and went down to the beach below the villa. The sky was the crystalline blue of the south, and the light fell with a pureness and clarity Ilarion had never seen anywhere but on Haidra. Waves rolled in from the waters of the Sleeve and broke gently on the sand in white scrolls of foam; above the surf, silver-gray birds with long beaks and forked tails soared and wheeled. The tide was ebbing and left behind it scattered pools and basins, braided with mossy weed. The wood behind the beach, where Mereth had found Ilarion, was still in its emerald winter leaf, and above the wood the white walls and russet tiles of the villa showed among the narrow spires of mist trees. They were the only five people in sight; Elyssa, craving some privacy, had sent the slaves back to the house.

Ilarion and Mereth were sitting on a flat rock just at the high-tide mark. Twigs, tiny broken shells, strands of sea grass, and scraps of bleached driftwood traced a wavering borderline between land and water. Lashgar had found a small fishing net at the villa and was waist-deep in the waves, trying his luck. A hundred feet away, Elyssa was paddling in a tide pool. She had hiked her tunic up to her knees, and Halicar, grasping her hand, was steadying her. He said something, and Ilarion heard her laugh.

"She forgets herself and becomes a child again," he said, smiling. "My sister Katheri used to do exactly that."

"You must miss your sister," Mereth said. "And everyone else at home."

He glanced sideways at her. When they came to the beach she had unbound her hair from its silver fillet and now it rippled, breeze-tossed, about her cheeks.

"I do," he answered. He'd seen little of her during the past two months. Training his cavalry formation in battlefield maneuvers devoured much of his time, and he'd been overseeing the construction of stone throwers for the city's ramparts. Furthermore, he'd been helping Larth work out new infantry tactics for the coming spring training. Consequently, he had spent little time in the palace, and when Larth suggested that both he and his troopers deserved a rest, he'd leaped at the opportunity to spend a few days at the villa. Larth had, in fact, been quite insistent that he go.

"It must be very tempting for you to leave us when Rook brings his new ship," she said. "That will be soon, won't it? Less than a month."

"Yes, but you know I can't leave," he answered. "Not while Theatana's lurking over the horizon. I feel responsible for the threat she's become." He kicked at the white sand. "I should have pushed Elyssa harder to keep the mask safe. I was stupid as an ox not to have told her everything long before I did. I left it too late."

Elyssa and the others knew about the Deep Magic now. In the crypt's flickering lamplight, after the Hazannu sealed them in, Ilarion had told them what the mask might be and why he had to get it out of his aunt's grasp. He asked them for secrecy and then told them the story of the Ban against the Deep Magic, and how even the Ban's creator did not realize the spell's single, fatal flaw: that someone who had already died was proof against its lethality. He told them how Erkai, who fell mortally wounded in battle and then was restored to life by the Black Craft, was such a person: a man who was twice-born. And then he recounted the events of the War of the Chain, revealing how Erkai, being of this twice-born nature, was able to break the Ban and live, and in doing so freed the Deep Magic again. The mere existence of such a power troubled them all, especially Elyssa, and she was only slightly encouraged when he told her that no one had used it successfully for seventeen centuries.

Mereth said, "I don't know if Elyssa would have changed the Oblation even if you'd told her earlier. You know how bound she is to Rasennan traditions. Not to mention how stubborn she is. But she blames herself, not you, for what happened. She knows now she shouldn't have trusted Tirsun even as little as she did."

"He was bad before," Ilarion muttered glumly. "Theatana's made him worse. But I doubt if he's the real ruler in Kanesh by now, though he may think he is. Look how he's proclaimed both himself and my aunt as restorers of the Garden—the Tirsun I knew never would have shared the glory. And he's let Theatana call herself the Giftbearer's heir returning. The old Tirsun wouldn't have allowed anyone to put him in the shade by making such a claim."

"I know," Mereth agreed unhappily. During the time between Theatana's first arrival in Kanesh and her seizure of the mask, even rumor had been silent about her doings. But only days after the mask was in her hands, the silence ended in a thunderclap, with her proclamation that she was the Giftbearer's successor, and her prophecy that she and Tirsun would restore the ancient splendor of the Rasenna. More than a month had passed since then, but the event still reverberated across Haidra like a constant tremor in the earth.

"Do you think people in Kanesh *really* believe she's the Giftbearer's successor, as she pretends?" Mereth went on. "Do many believe it here? Does Tirsun believe it, even?"

"I don't know about Tirsun. But my aunt's from the north, she's definitely practicing sorcery, and she appears to be using the mask to do it. It all supports her claim. And the

Rasenna *want* to believe it, remember. They want their Great Garden back. Larth once told me they'd follow anyone they believed could restore their old power." Ilarion kicked at a stone. "And if Theatana walks the Foul Road to make that happen, even the priestesses of the Lady may look the other way. That may already be going on. At least, none of them has spoken against her magic."

Elyssa had found something in the pool, perhaps a shell, and was showing it to Halicar. Lashgar drew in his net, empty again. Mereth said, "Ah, yes. The restoration, the great dream of the Rasenna. It was clever of her and Tirsun, wasn't it? Stealing the mask outright and then saying that Elyssa was the villain because she tried to keep the thing from the Giftbearer's heir. It makes Elyssa look as if she doesn't want the Garden restored."

"My aunt's very cunning—it was likely her idea. I don't think Tirsun's a match for her, for all his cleverness." He rubbed his chin. "The more I think about the mask, the more certain I am that it's got all sorts of sorcerous information in those chambers I saw—information about the Golden Path as well as the Foul Road. How long Theatana will need to make it work for her, I don't know. But the kind of sorcery that really worries me is the Deep Magic. The White Diviners knew its ways, and the Giftbearer was one of them. So those spells will likely be there in the mask, too, along with who knows what else."

"Do you think your aunt can learn to use the Deep Magic?"

"I don't know," he answered. "Everything I ever heard about the Deep Magic suggests that it's very difficult, even for an adept. I'd think she'd need a long time."

He wished he was as sure of this as he sounded. He had glimpsed the monstrosity Theatana was breeding within herself, but he didn't know what it was, nor how it had impregnated her, nor how much help it could give her. He did know that she was open to the Adversary. He had no idea how that primeval malice might use his aunt, or be used by her, but either prospect was enough to put him into a cold sweat.

If she gets full control of the mask, he thought, *and with the Adversary helping her, she'll be worse than Erkai the Chain ever was. She's picking up where he left off. What in the Allfather's name am I going to do? My parents destroyed Erkai with the Signata, but I've got no such weapon.*

He tried to console himself with the knowledge that even Erkai had needed a lifetime to begin to grasp the Deep Magic. That was true despite his mastery of the Black Craft and his seventy years of study. Theatana had no such stature or experience. She'd need time, and a good deal of it, to become anything like an adept. Or so he hoped.

But given *enough* time, she would likely succeed. Above all, he feared that. So, somehow, she had to be killed, or at the least the mask must be taken from her. How that was to be done, he didn't know. Perhaps he should go home as soon as possible, after all, and return with an army. But before he could do that, many new long-range ships would have to be built in the Ascendancy, the sailors trained, the expedition prepared, the dangerous voyage made. Years would pass before his soldiers set foot on Haidra, and anything might have happened by then.

The only answer was assassination. He'd talked about it with Elyssa; she not only agreed, but made her brother a second target. She was still enraged at Tirsun for the theft of the mask, and she was convinced that he intended war; by killing him, she would achieve both justice and peace, not to mention the rule of all Haidra. But both Tirsun and Theatana were very difficult to get at, and the task would be slow and difficult. Elyssa herself had doubled and redoubled her own precautions against assassins.

"I hope you're right, that your aunt can't learn it quickly," Mereth said. "That will give us some time . . . but look, the day's so lovely! Perhaps we should try to forget the bad things, just for a while."

"Yes. That's a good idea." His gaze went to Elyssa. She was standing in a tide pool, hand in hand with Halicar, to watch Lashgar cast his net. The Protectress's affair with her court musician was now common knowledge in Dymie; indeed, everyone on Haidra, and no doubt in Kla and Ush-

nana, knew that she had taken an outlander to her bed.
Auvas Seitithi, his hopes of marrying her dashed for the
foreseeable future, had used his aged father's death as an
excuse for a sullen withdrawal to his country estates. Hoping to soften him a little, the Protectress had confirmed
Auvas as his father's official successor commanding the
army's left wing, but that had not sweetened him much.

"Look," Elyssa called suddenly as she turned to face
them. "Lashgar's caught a fish."

It was true. The prince was dragging his net toward shore,
grinning. Ilarion applauded with handclaps and a yell of encouragement. Elyssa and Halicar left their pool and sauntered up the beach.

"That's a good-size fish he's got," Ilarion said. "We could
find some driftwood and cook it here."

"Perhaps we could," Mereth answered. "I used to be able
to grill fish very well. I've hardly touched a skewer in years,
though."

Halicar and Elyssa reached them. Elyssa knelt on the
sand, then sat down cross-legged. Halicar dropped onto his
haunches next to her. The Protectress shaded her eyes with
her palm and gazed out across the aquamarine waters of the
Sleeve. Then she let her hand fall and sighed. "Still no Rook,
no ship, and no shipwright. I'd hoped for both during Little
Summer. How much longer does he *need*?"

"Not long, Elyssa," Halicar said. "Ten or fifteen days. Be
patient."

"I can't be. I want my own ships laid down before my
brother decides to attack us. If he chooses war this year, he'll
be over the border in a month, as soon as the spring planting's finished."

"It might not be this year," Halicar observed. "He's been
very quiet, militarily speaking. So far all he's done is make
noises about restoring the Garden, and how Elyssa's pre-
venting him from doing it."

Halicar may be right, Ilarion thought hopefully. Tirsun
had attempted no hostile operations against Dymie during
the two and a half months since he and Theatana seized the
mask, and relations between the two Protectorates had settled

into a state that was on the edge of war but not quite over it. Elyssa sent frequently to Kanesh to demand the return of the mask, with compensation, but stopped short of threatening to attack her brother. She needed time to strengthen her forces, and to gain it she avoided any hint of overt hostilities. As for protective measures, she had called up men from the Second Levy to reinforce the border forts that secured the invasion routes from Kanesh. But there was no fighting yet; the merchants of both Protectorates still sailed in and out of each other's harbors, and Elyssa and Tirsun maintained their ambassadors in each other's capitals. Months of armed truce might still pass before the armies marched.

"But it has to come sooner or later," Elyssa observed irritably, "unless Tirsun dies, or that woman does, or better, both." Her face darkened with anger. "My brother keeps sending those filthy God-priests over the border, to skulk around and tell my backcountry lordlets and my peasants that I'm keeping him and his northern sorceress from restoring the Garden. That the two of them can't even start because I'm hostile to that *woman* and my hostility is some kind of sacrilege. *That's* the pot calling the kettle black— some of those priests walk the Foul Road, for all they pretend to be servants of the God."

Halicar said, "Elyssa, really, it's too pleasant a day to darken it with such talk. Let's be cheerful."

She was silent for several moments. Then she took a deep breath and let it out. "I'm sorry. You're right. I'm spoiling things . . . Lashgar, what *are* you going to do with that creature?"

Lashgar had come up with his net. He had caught a good-size, slender silver fish with an elegant blue stripe on each side. "I thought we could eat it. Do you know what it is? I've never seen one."

"A thorny. They're full of bones, I'm afraid. The fishermen always throw them back."

"Oh." Lashgar looked disappointed. "I'll do the same, then." He turned around and trotted toward the surf, the fish wriggling. He released it, then sauntered back to join them, the net over his shoulder.

382   DENNIS JONES

"You know," Mereth said as the prince sat down on a nearby rock, "on such a day I have to hope that everything will turn out for the best. It still could, you know. Imagine how it might be . . . Tirsun will be gotten rid of somehow, and Theatana, too. Haidra will be one Protectorate again."

Elyssa's expression brightened. "Yes. And my people will be better off, once my brother isn't spending the wealth of half the island on his palace." She smiled at Ilarion and Lashgar. "And now we know we're not the only civilized people in the world. Would your Ascendancy and the Blue Havens send traders and merchants to us?"

"Indeed we would," Ilarion said, suddenly caught up in the dream. "We could share our craftsmen's skills. We need ships like yours, and we can send you knowledge of our own to pay for it. And goods, too—spices, herbs, aromatics, tin and copper for your bronze. All sorts of things. Ways of building in stone."

"And writing," Mereth said excitedly. "The Ascendancy way of writing. Ilarion says it's much easier than the Rasennan or my own people's. I could learn to *truly* read and write, and I wouldn't have to memorize so much."

"And songs," said Halicar. "New music."

"Poetry," Lashgar added. "The jade carvings of Ammedara."

"Jewelry. Jokes."

"Musical instruments," Mereth said. "The best harps in the world."

"Cloaks of silvertip otter."

"Cloth of gold."

"Lanterns," said Ilarion. "Leather breeches." He looked sideways at Mereth and she grimaced at him. She had tried to make a pair. They had not been a success.

"Stop, stop," Elyssa exclaimed, laughing. "Such riches. It's too much to imagine."

"But it can happen," Mereth said. "It *can*."

"And it will," Elyssa murmured. "Won't it, Halicar?"

"Of course," he told her, touching her hand. "Of course, my love."

"All we have to do is remove Tirsun and his sorceress,"

she said. "That should be possible." She smiled dreamily. "And then all will be one long sweet afternoon, like this one. Friends, lovers. Happiness."

Mereth look up toward the villa. "Someone's coming," she said.

"Who?" Elyssa had leaned back against Halicar and closed her eyes. Her face was calm and relaxed, almost peaceful.

"I'm not sure, he was in the trees. Oh." Her voice faltered. "It's Larth."

Ilarion's gaze followed hers to the sandy slope that led from the wood. Down the path, striding at double pace, almost running, came the pronoyar.

Elyssa opened her eyes. "Help me up, my love," she said.

Halicar did so, and she rose to her feet. The rest of them did the same.

"What is it, Larth?" she asked as he reached them.

He was breathing in harsh gasps. "Protectress—it's your brother. He's come over the border."

Elyssa's face became very still. "Go on."

"He's got an army, Protectress. The news just came in by courier, from the fort at Adnana, on the coast road. The border pickets spotted him and his bodyguard a day's march from the fort, and coming this way. He's leading an army."

"At *this* time of year? You're sure it's not a raid? A feint with his First Levy?"

"No, Protectress. The report said he's got Kaneshite troops but even more are Hazannu tribesmen. Thousands all told. It's war."

Over the bay the gray birds soared and keened. The waves tumbled in from the sea and fell back, one by one.

"So soon," Elyssa said.

26

THE ADNANA BORDER FORT FELL IN THE LATE AFTERNOON, after a determined attack by a battalion of the Hazannu mercenaries Tirsun had hired, supported by the infantry of Kanesh's First Levy. They had tried twice the previous day to take the stronghold, but the defenders had repelled both assaults. The third, against the weakened garrison, finally succeeded.

Tirsun was not much perturbed by the delay the fort had imposed. Theatana, on the other hand, chafed to get the war over with, for she looked forward to the final victory and especially to spending a few zestful days with Ilarion.

Despite such prospects, however, the war had been so far quite frustrating, because it kept her from a thorough exploration of the spell called Begetter of Myriads. Since they left Kanesh with the army eleven days ago, the demands of the steady march westward had left no time or opportunity to investigate it further.

Today, though, as she watched Tirsun's Hazannu mercenaries assembling the captured defenders under the fort's gray-brick walls, she was excited and happy. The next step in her investigations was at hand. The taking of the fort figured in this, although she had not yet informed Tirsun of what she was going to do. He would be delighted when she told him, although his pleasure or lack of it was of no consequence to her whatsoever.

I'm so much more powerful than I used to be, she thought. *Who knows what I may someday become? I already have an army, even if Tirsun thinks the army's his. Most of all I have the mask.*

384

Unwillingly, she heard the Adversary's whisper in her memory: *You have a library in a language you cannot read. In me are wisps of those who can read it.*

No, she told herself fiercely. That was far too dangerous. She would work out the spells eventually; Erkai had begun with less than she already possessed.

But the possibility was there. If all else failed—

She dismissed the thought of failure. Even with her present, limited knowledge, she controlled enormous power. *Erkai gave my sister and her husband bad dreams,* she thought, *but in a few years I'll show them waking nightmares. I'll trot them around the Fountain Palace and make them hurt each other.*

She realized that her thoughts had wandered down pleasant but distracting paths, and returned her attention to her surroundings. She had just come up the track that led to the fort and hadn't really looked around. Now she did.

The fort stood on a flat-topped spur of the rugged hills that ran down to the narrow coastal plain. Below the spur, Theatana could see the dusty white band of the coast road, running along the constricted strip of level ground between the hills and the waters of the Middle Gulf. The army's camp lay along both margins of the road, tents sprouting like brown mushrooms, smoke drifting from cooking fires, horses tethered in dark clumps. The road was the easiest route into the Protectorate of Dymie, and the fort's capture meant that no real barriers stood between the army and Elyssa's capital. After about ten more days of marching, they'd be under Dymie's walls. The men needed a rest before going on, though. They'd force-marched along muddy roads during the first few days out of Kanesh, and even the barbarians were tired.

Tirsun's voice came from over her shoulder. "Ah, my dear, here you are. I'm sorry to have kept you waiting."

She didn't bother to turn as he halted beside her. He wore battle armor, not the bright flimsy parade-ground stuff he used on ceremonial occasions. He'd removed his helmet, which was painted in red-and-black stripes. Its gold-and-scarlet sunbird plume fluttered in the sea wind as he held it in the crook of his arm.

Theatana turned to smile at him and touch his arm. She'd taken care to behave warmly to him while on the march; he'd be a better general if she kept him content and happy. "It's no trouble—I was just standing here being delighted. This is our first victory together."

"A small one. Still, a victory is a victory. And it's been a fine day for one."

She nodded. The Little Summer had smiled on the army for six days thus far, and had helped the advance by drying out the roads. Attacking at this time of year had been her idea, inspired not long after she reached Kanesh by Tirsun's idle mention of the seasonal warm spell. After a little thought and investigation of geography, she had suggested to him that this was the time to move against his sister. Elyssa would not expect an invasion at this season, and would not be prepared for one if it came.

Tirsun had admitted this but explained that traditionally, the Rasenna never made war until First Summer, because of the needs of the spring planting. Only the standing army, the First Levy of Kanesh, was available all year round. To attack Elyssa successfully he'd need to gather the strength of Kanesh's Second Levy as well. But he couldn't call those men to arms until the end of Last Spring, because they were needed on the land till the planting was finished. That was the reason for the tradition.

"Well," Theatana had said—they were in bed, Tirsun sated and compliant—"what about those Hazannu mercenaries you hired to help us at Charunna? There must be plenty more where they came from."

He had argued cost, and the infamy of using Hazannu against pure-blooded Rasenna, but she could tell that the audacity of the scheme attracted him. In the end, he dispatched negotiators to the mainland clans. So, by the time Kanesh's First Levy set out from the capital, three and a half thousand well-armed Hazannu warriors and their warleaders had quietly arrived on Haidra and bivouacked in small encampments along the army's expected line of march. Land travel was difficult and slow in the rainy season, and there had been little danger that Elyssa would hear about the mercenaries before the invasion was under way.

Tirsun also quietly called up a hundred of the First Levy's retired veterans to swell the army's strength. So, by the time he and Theatana had reached the border and added all the Hazannu contingents to the army, they had a force of six thousand men including cavalry. Elyssa could reasonably expect to field no more than two-thirds of that. Even allowing for stragglers and garrisons in captured towns, they would still outnumber her when they reached Dymie.

Tirsun's gaze followed Theatana's to the encampment on the narrow plain below. "We need two days before we go on," he said. "They're weary, even the mainland savages."

"I wish we could keep going. We must get into Dymie in the good weather. It would be better yet if we can force a decision before the rains come back."

"The wet weather won't start again for six to eight more days," Tirsun said. "It never does. We'll be well into my sister's lands by then."

Theatana turned to look at the prisoners. The Hazannu had collected about thirty of them on the stretch of bare dusty stone near the fort's gateway. She touched the satchel that hung at her waist on its leather strap. She carried it always, slung over her shoulder with the mask inside in its cloth wrapping.

She said, "And if Elyssa doesn't come out and fight? If she sits behind her walls and tries to wait out a siege?"

"Theatana, we've been over this. If most of Kanesh's aristocrats believe you're the Giftbearer come back to restore the Rasenna, you can be sure that plenty of Elyssa's do, too. And she's no favorite of her great nobles these days, anyway. To begin with, taking that outlander lover annoyed them. Furthermore, a good many of them have come to prefer the Storm God to the Green Lady, and they've taken careful note of what I allowed to happen in Kla—the God rules there now, and they hope it might happen in Dymie. If my sister tries to wait us out, they'll start coming over to us. Once she's lost her military support, somebody inside

Dymie will open the gates. And that will be the end of
Elyssa and the divided rule."

Theatana shrugged. "This may be as you say, but armies
evaporate if they sit too long in front of a city in the rain."

"That won't happen. She knows her situation as well as
we do, and she won't accept a siege. There'll be a battle, and
we'll win it."

She studied him. "You're very confident."

"If I weren't, I wouldn't have embarked on this venture."

This was true enough. He was cunning, though not so
cunning as he thought himself, and in particular not as cunning as she was. Still, it was better that he should be confident, rather than reluctant and uneasy.

"I want two of those," she said, gesturing at the captives.

"Two prisoners? Of course. What do you want to do with
them?"

She smiled softly. "Come and see."

He looked puzzled, then eager. "You're going to do something with the mask?"

"I am," she said.

"You only want two? You could have more."

"Two will be enough for now. And after we have Dymie
there'll be as many as I need."

"Very well," he answered, and together they walked over
to the line of dejected captives. War wasn't chronic on
Haidra, but during the centuries since the Fall there had been
enough fighting to produce some conventions. These men
would be expecting imprisonment at hard labor until hostilities ended or they were ransomed, and then they would be
freed to go home. Sometimes, depending on how alliances
shifted, they would be recruited into the victor's forces until
hostilities finished.

Two of these captives wouldn't be going anywhere, however. The barbarian guards looked on curiously as Theatana
walked along the line, inspecting the prisoners. Their wrists
were tied behind their backs and most were naked or nearly
so, the Hazannu having pillaged them not only of their
armor and weapons but also of their clothing.

"This one," she said, looking up into the man's green

eyes. In spite of the sweat and dust and bruises, the soldier was handsome, as indeed were most Rasenna males. She touched the young man's chest with a fingertip and he twitched and shuddered slightly. Theatana smiled at him and passed on.

She found the second one a few paces down the line. He was tall, slim in the hips, and beautifully formed, skin unblemished in spite of the fighting. He did not appear much afraid of her.

"You have the look of an officer," she murmured. "Are you?"

He remained silent. Tirsun smiled, and said, "I'd advise you to answer her. Sometimes she isn't very patient."

"I'm a third-captain, Protector."

"He'll do," said Theatana. "Now, we need somewhere more private than this. Best inside the fort, I think. And I'll want some rope."

The place had to be cleared first of looters. Tirsun sent one of his Rasennan officers with a dozen Hazannu to see to it, while he and Theatana moved the two prisoners into the gateway. Someone brought Theatana a coil of rope, which she slung over her shoulder. Tirsun had drawn his sword but held it negligently. Prisoners, expecting eventual freedom, were little threat.

When the fort was empty, Theatana led the captives and Tirsun into the interior. The stronghold was a small but well-built place, with brick quarters for the men, wooden stables, and a separate building for the fort commander and the armory. A windowless brick storehouse stood next to the armory. Its stout wooden door stood wide, opening into shadows.

"What are you up to?" Tirsun asked.

Theatana didn't answer. The whisper hissed in her mind, the whisper she'd heard after the miu escaped, telling her what to do.

Harness the dead. Harness the dead, and make the living walk.

"Go in there," Theatana said. The captives obeyed, though the soldier was beginning to look alarmed, and even the young officer was showing signs of fear. But they were bound, Tirsun had his sword, and Theatana wore her long dagger belted over the sash of her tunic.

Within the storehouse, thick wooden posts supported the roof timbers. "Make that one sit down," she said, indicating the officer. Tirsun gestured with his sword, and the man sank to the earthen floor.

Theatana drew her dagger, set its tip to the belly of the man she'd selected first, and said, "That post. Put your back against it."

Wordlessly, the soldier obeyed. Tirsun and the officer watched while Theatana bound the soldier to the thick upright. She made the bindings very tight: chest, hips, knees, ankles.

"What are you doing, my lady?" the soldier croaked, at last frightened enough to speak. "Please. My family will pay ransom."

"Oh," Theatana said, "that's good." She sheathed the dagger, moved around in front of him, and opened the satchel. His eyes widened as she took the mask out and put it on. "No," he said, voice quavering. "No. I don't want to go to the Green Lady."

"This isn't for the Green Lady," Theatana told him through the mouth of the mask. "Be quiet."

Perhaps reassured a little, he fell silent. Theatana was already deep within herself, seeking the energies she needed. She found them, and did as she'd done the night she tried to kill the miu. She drew forth a strand of herself and shaped it. It resisted as before, but she bludgeoned it into obedience and dragged it up into the light, into the world where she could use it. The wraith seemed to coil in her mouth. She paused, summoning all her strength and all her will.

Now. She spat the bitter thing into the air and pulled off the mask.

All three men were staring at the shape hanging in the gloom, Tirsun nervous but fascinated, the officer with quivering alarm, and the soldier with stark, speechless terror.

Theatana dropped the mask into the satchel and made her spectral sister drift toward the tightly bound soldier. When she was sure she fully controlled it, she halted the thing. In the dimness it seemed a fluttering shadow, as if it sucked light into itself. The soldier's mouth opened and closed but only thin squeals came out.

Theatana stepped forward, drew her dagger, and stabbed him just left of his breastbone. Blood spurted around the knife's guard, driven by his heart's last convulsive beats. Holding the knife's hilt to steady herself, Theatana went up on tiptoe and put her open mouth almost to his. Then, as she'd done with Rehua, she drew her concentration to a single point of savage intention. As the soldier's final breath rattled out she sucked it into herself, swallowed it, and spat.

The spray thinned, became a mist, a shape, a wraith of the dead man. Theatana heard Tirsun's muffled exclamation. As Rehua's shade had done, this one seemed to want to turn on her.

But this time she knew how to deal with it. She swept her sister-thing over it like a cloak, melted the two together. A soundless struggle took place; her vision blurred, puffs of dust rose from the floor, the roof beams creaked.

Tirsun edged slightly toward the door. "Stay," she ordered harshly, and he stopped.

Her spectral self subdued the soldier's wraith and became one with it. It hovered in the gloom, a roiling shadow. Fierce exultation swept through her. It was working. She turned to the officer sitting on the earthen floor.

"*No!*" he whispered, and she coiled the specter into a shivering ball and thrust it into his gaping mouth as he tried to scream.

Silence fell instantly. The officer sat motionless in the dirt, his eyes wide and staring, mouth locked open in a voiceless shriek.

Theatana made him close his mouth, then scrutinized him carefully. His skin was twitching a little. She wondered if she could force him to speak with her words, but before trying such tests she should find out how deep her control of him was.

"Watch him carefully," she told Tirsun. "He's mine just now, but he might break free." She sensed the man strug-

gling and had to exert much of her will to keep him confined. The effort was tiring, but not as tiring as with the miu.
The whisper had been right. The correct technique was to
raise an entity from someone she'd just killed, then harness
it to a sister she'd drawn from her own being. Why waste
your own strength when you could use another's?

"What are you going to do?" Tirsun asked. He seemed to
have some difficulty speaking.

"You'll see," she murmured. She slipped behind the officer, bent over his wrists, and with one quick slash cut his
bonds. Then she moved around in front of him. Tirsun
backed off a little, to give himself sword room if the man
lunged.

Test him. Theatana made the officer get onto his knees.
That wasn't very difficult. His arms hung slack by his sides.
She tossed the dagger into the dust just in front of him.

"What do you think you're doing?" Tirsun said. "Just kill
him, if that's what you want."

"No," Theatana said. She formed the purpose in her mind,
imagined it as vividly as if she saw it before her, then hurled
the command to her other self, the self embedded in the officer's brain and nerves and muscles.

He reached out, picked up the dagger, and with one furious sweep of the blade he slit his throat.

She heard Tirsun grunt with surprise, but ignored him and
watched her handiwork. Arterial blood spurted in jets from
the officer's throat, quick and urgent, then slowing. He made
a choking liquid noise and she released her hold on him; he
fell forward into the dirt, twitching. Theatana swayed as a
vast fatigue swept through her, followed by vast relief and a
fierce satisfaction. She'd *done* it. If she could make a man
kill himself when he wanted to live, she could make anyone
do anything.

Her sister-thing was still in him. She tried to withdraw it
and discovered that she could not, for it had sealed itself to
his nerves and brain, a brain that was already darkening.
Letting it be, she sank to her knees and watched him die.
With him went the wisp of herself, into blankness. It occurred to her that creating too many of them might be un-

wise. Her inner resources might not be limitless. There was still so much to learn, so many tests to carry out.

Tirsun said, in a shaken voice, "You made him do that, didn't you?"

Theatana lifted her gaze to his. He had been frightened of her before, despite his outward nonchalance. Now he was terrified, and his face showed it.

"Yes," she answered. "I did." As she rose unsteadily to her feet, he diffidently reached out to help her. She was about to shake him off, then remembered that she'd need him for a while yet.

Giving him a warm smile she said, "Thank you, my love. Isn't it wonderful? And this is just the beginning for us."

27

IT WAS THE DAY OF BATTLE. THE MORNING WAS SUNNY AND warm, though the weather signs foretold that Little Summer was about to end; a steady humid wind blew from the southwest, and toward the mainland a long band of white cloud clung to the horizon.

The army of the Protectorate of Dymie tramped along the coast road in the morning light. It had left the city the previous afternoon, moving slowly as armies always did on the first day of a march, and was still only twelve miles east of the capital. Elyssa rode with the vanguard; Ilarion had learned that she always accompanied her army into the field, though Larth was in tactical command during the approach to battle and during the actual fighting. The pronoyar was far more experienced at war than the Protectress was, and she did not, apparently, interfere with his battlefield decisions.

Ilarion's cavalry unit was riding some distance ahead of the column of foot soldiers. Larth had assigned him to screening duties, and after breaking camp that dawn he had sent a score of his troopers out to locate Tirsun's army. The Protector's strength remained uncertain, though earlier reports suggested that he had about five thousand men in all.

A little before midmorning, two of the scouts came back and reported the approach of the enemy. A few miles to the east, they told Ilarion, they'd run into a small unit of Tirsun's light horse, also on reconnaissance. Armed with their heavy lances and with the advantage of stirrups, Ilarion's scouts had scattered these; then they went looking for his main force. They'd glimpsed it, but a mass of Tirsun's cavalry was

394

nearby and had kept them from getting close enough to count numbers. They estimated that the Protector's army was by this time about two hours' march away.

Ilarion dispatched one man to locate Larth and Elyssa and give them the news, then sent the other to rejoin his fellows on reconnaissance. As he rode on, he found himself wishing that Lashgar were with him, with his spiky black beard and eager grin. But Lashgar had been gone for eleven days; as soon as Larth brought the word of the invasion, Elyssa had sent the prince to Ushnana to invoke the defense treaty. Even with good sailing weather, he couldn't be back in Dymie for a day or two yet. And then another half month would pass, at least, before any soldiers could arrive from Ushnana. For the moment at least, Elyssa was on her own.

It wasn't long before she trotted up on her gray mare, Larth beside her on a black stallion. The Protectress had donned the expensive lamellar armor of an aristocrat, a knee-length surcoat made of narrow rectangles of linked iron plates, worn with tough leather leggings. Her helmet was painted green and white, and a green-and-white crest bobbed above it. Larth wore similar protection, except that his helmet was red and yellow with a black-and-white plume. Ilarion's gear was considerably less elaborate: a cavalryman's cuirass of glued layers of linen reinforced by bronze disks, a black, bell-shaped iron helmet, and bronze greaves. He was used to the Rasennan cuirass, but it was stiffer than he liked. He often wished for a good, flexible shirt of Ascendancy chain mail, but the Rasenna didn't have the craft of making it. For weaponry, he carried a heavy lance, an oval shield, and a horseman's slashing-sword.

Larth and Elyssa fell in beside him. The cavalry column was traveling at a brisk walk; the road was dry and white with the warmth of Little Summer, and the wind blew wisps of dust from the plowed fields to its south. The sea was about three miles away, though out of sight. To Ilarion's left lay more rolling farmland, set with scattered groves of fruit trees and small vineyards.

"No word on Tirsun's strength yet?" Elyssa asked him.

Golden hair fluttered at her helmet rim. Her face was grave, but she seemed neither tense nor apprehensive.

"No, Protectress. He's being careful to keep our scouts away."

She nodded. "Well, at least we know where he is. Larth, what now?"

Larth squinted into the morning light. "If he keeps coming, we'll shift into battle line on the flat ground at Demacda and wait for him. We've got good flank protection there, and if he outnumbers us, as he likely does, it won't matter so much. *Curse* this wind."

A gust had blown a cloud of fine dust around them. Ilarion's gelding snorted and tossed its head. "Is this how Little Summer usually ends?" he asked. "Windy?"

"It's changeable," Elyssa told him. "But there'll be rain by tomorrow or the day after at the latest. If it comes today we'll have to wait it out, then deal with my brother."

Ilarion still wondered if coming out to do battle was the best strategy Elyssa could have chosen. If she declined to fight, Tirsun's men would have to sit in the rain for fifteen or twenty days, until the weather cleared. Unfortunately, though they would be uncomfortable, they wouldn't be short of supplies. Last autumn's harvest had been so abundant that the granaries and the wine cellars in the farms and villages around Dymie were still half-full.

In the councils of war that had preceded Elyssa's decision to call up the Second Levy and accept battle, Larth had stressed the supply situation. With plenty of food on hand, he said, Tirsun could continue a siege of Dymie for months, giving him time to frighten the magistrates of the Protectorate's lesser towns and cities into joining him, and to cement his claim of being the leader who would restore the Garden. Elyssa might, he pointed out, wake up one morning and find that the capital was all she had left of her Protectorate.

"So you're sure we should fight him when he gets here," she'd said to the pronoyar, on the night she made the decision.

"I am, Protectress," Larth answered.

"Well," Elyssa had said pensively, her face weary in the lamplight, "it's true his army's coming to the end of a very long march. His men will be tired. Leaving garrisons to secure his rear has cost him strength, and there's always the loss to straggling. Very well, we fight. Make the preparations."

Auvas Seitithi, on the march in command of the army's left wing, had agreed with her decision. In his outrage over Tirsun's attack, he seemed to have forgotten his anger at the Protectress. Ilarion still didn't trust him, but the outrage appeared genuine—Auvas was particularly incensed because Tirsun was using Hazannu troops on Haidran soil. And the clan-lord had done good work in getting much of the Second Levy called in and organized at a very difficult season of the year.

Not all the Second Levy was present, however. There hadn't been enough time for the far western contingents to reach Dymie, although Larth had waited until yesterday to march out of the capital to meet Tirsun's approach. Consequently the army had only eight men in ten of its strength, to the number of some four thousand. As far as it was possible to tell from long-range reconnaissance, the Protector's forces were larger than Elyssa's, though more than half the Protector's men were the Hazannu mercenaries whose presence on the island had so infuriated Auvas.

"Those mercenaries," Ilarion said to the pronoyar. "You know the Hazannu better than I do. How brittle are they likely to be, after this long a march?"

Larth frowned. "I fought them on the mainland, years ago. They're undisciplined, and unless their leaders have a tight grip, they come at you in a mob. On the other hand, it's a dangerous mob. If they crack your line, you'd better have reserves nearby, or you're in trouble. They go foaming mad when they smell blood and decide they're winning. It's hard to stop them then." He wiped dust from his mouth with the back of his hand. "But they can be brittle if they're hard-pressed. They're barbarians, and they like to fight, but once you've broken them and they're on the run, they keep going. They don't try to form up again—it's all over but the pursuit."

"Yes, Pronoyar. My men will make sure they keep running."

Larth gave a curt nod. "See that they do. All right, here are your orders. Demacda's two miles down the road from here—it's a fishing village, just a few houses on the shoreline. When you get a little way past it, you'll see a hill off to the right of the road. Just south of the hill are the beach and the sea. Put your men up on the hill—I'm making you the anchor for our right flank. The beach is too narrow there for Tirsun to get around our line, as long as you hold the high ground. There's a deep marsh half a mile inland, and I'll have Auvas pin the extreme end of the left wing there. We've got good flank protection that way."

"Yes, Pronoyar. I'll keep my scouts out and send word to you when we see the Protector's main force."

"All right. Do so."

Elyssa said, "But watch him carefully, Ilarion. My brother's a slippery fish."

"We'll keep him in the net," Ilarion told her. "Pronoyar, do you want us to try harassing him while he deploys into line?"

"No. Sit tight. You can make threatening motions to keep him worried, but don't leave the hill. I'll work on weakening his right and center. He'll shift his left wing's reserves in that direction, I hope. Once he does, I'll order you to try rolling him up from his left. If he puts the Hazannu in front of you, so much the better. They don't like cavalry much, and your lads will be a surprise to everybody." Larth looked down at Ilarion's stirrups and grimaced. "I'd never have thought those footrests of yours would make such a difference. Auvas still doesn't think they will."

"We'll show him differently, Pronoyar."

"Good." Larth turned to Elyssa. "As for Auvas, my lady, we must go and set his orders now."

"Yes. Wait one moment, though. Ilarion, Halicar needs a vantage point to see the fighting. The hill at Demacda would be the best place. Have you any objection if he joins you there?"

"None, Protectress." Halicar had a professional responsibility, for the lords of the Rasenna liked to hear ballads about their martial heroism, and court singers traditionally attended battles to gather raw material for the songs. "I'd be glad of his company till it gets started."

"I'll send him up to you when we get there," she said. In her eyes he saw a silent appeal: *Please don't let anything happen to him.* She would never say it, though. She was too proud to ask for such protection, and Halicar was too proud to accept it.

"I'll bring him back to you at the end," Ilarion told her, offering what comfort he could. He was glad Mereth was absent; Antecessor inviolability or not, a battlefield was a very bad place for a young woman. Even so, she might well have been there if she were not so awkward with horses. She had been riding up the palace ramp on a misty morning four days ago when her mount slipped on the wet stones, and she came off. The agitated animal then kicked out, giving Mereth a set of badly bruised ribs. She was in no danger, but the injury slowed her down, another very good reason for her not to be anywhere near a battle. Ilarion was covertly glad that she'd taken the tumble.

"Thank you," Elyssa said. She reined her horse around and trotted back down the cavalry column, Larth following. Ilarion returned his attention to the road ahead. The wind from the southwest was damp, and in spite of the sun he shivered.

Three hours later the armies faced each other on the plain at Demacda. It was a little before midday.

Ilarion and Halicar sat on the salt grass at the crown of the hill and studied the opposing lines. The cavalrymen waited by their mounts, the nonchalant among them munching soldier-bean bread and drinking watered wine. Nearby, Ilarion's two signalmen, their long bronze horns ready at their saddlebows, talked with each other in low voices. The white road ran from west to east at the hill's inland foot, and below the hill's steep seaward flank a heavy surf crashed and boomed on the beach's gray shingle. The sun shone brightly, and the wind had dropped to a gentle breeze. Gray-white tendrils of cloud, far up in the sky, were reaching slowly from the southwest horizon. The sea glittered.

From this height Ilarion could see the whole length of Larth's battle line, beginning in the distance at the long green smudge of the marsh. From there it stretched toward him across dusty plowed fields to the infantry battalion at the hill's foot. Farthest away was the left wing of the army, fifteen hundred men and three hundred light cavalry under Auvas's command. Forming the center and right wing were the two battalions of the First Levy and two more of the Second, all led by Larth. Because of the lie of the land and the position of the marsh, Auvas and his left wing were a little advanced. That wing would contact Tirsun's line first and, Larth likely hoped, would tempt the Protector to shift some of his strength toward it, thus weakening him elsewhere.

"We're outnumbered," Halicar observed. It seemed a professional comment rather than a worry, part of the background for his ballad cycle.

"Somewhat." Ilarion turned his attention to the enemy line that ran across the plain parallel to their own and about a quarter mile from it. It was a longer line, its left wing squarely on the seashore and its right also anchored on the marsh. A mile farther east was Tirsun's baggage train, extremely vulnerable if the Protector's army broke and ran.

They've got about four to three against us in infantry, Ilarion thought. *About equal in cavalry. His men must have lamed a lot of horses on the march.*

"It doesn't help him much, though," he observed, "as long as we hold this position. He can't use his longer line to get round our flanks."

Tirsun had put most of his mercenaries on his right wing, and at the right of his center. They were still getting into position and appeared to be setting up a reserve behind the main fighting line. Ilarion could identify the Hazannu formations by their raggedness. They didn't seem much concerned with good battle order. Larth's advanced left wing would work even better because of that. Near the foot of the hill he saw Elyssa's green-and-white helmet plume bobbing about as she rode along the front rank of infantry. Their cheers reached him. The common soldiers' loyalty seemed intact, despite the campaign of defamation and rumor Tirsun and Theatana had been carrying out.

"I hate to admit it," Halicar said, gazing down at Elyssa's distant plume, "but I've never seen a big battle. When Mereth and I were on the mainland I was at a few skirmishes, but nothing like this."

"You won't actually see much when it starts," Ilarion told him. "Dust gets kicked up if the ground's dry, and hides a lot. When you're actually in the middle of a fight you have no idea what's going on, even if you're an officer. And the dust will be worse now the wind's dropped—it'll hang in the air."

"That will make it hard to get the details for the ballads."

"Make the details up," Ilarion told him with a grin. "I suspect that's how it's done anyway." Elyssa had reached the bottom of the hill, and her mare was gingerly starting up its steep slope. "Ah. It looks as if the Protectress is going to join us."

"I wish I could fight for her," Halicar said, a little morosely, "but I can't."

This was true, for a bard's inviolate status came at a price. He could defend himself at need, but he could never be a soldier, not if he wanted to keep that status. To show what he was, he wore a surcoat bearing the Hazannu and Rasennan symbols for music. By tradition it would keep the enemy from slaughtering him. Or it was supposed to; his only weapon was a long dagger, not much defense against someone in a battle fury. He had a helmet on and wore armor like Ilarion's beneath his surcoat, but those were to protect him against unaimed spears and javelins. He'd left his harp in the palace with Mereth; it was far too valuable to risk on a battlefield.

"Don't worry about the fighting," Ilarion told him. "Soldiers can be had by the day for a copper coin. Your gift is beyond price."

"So I tell myself," Halicar said. "Elyssa tells me the same."

The Protectress had reached the hilltop. She rode to Ilarion and Halicar's vantage point and dismounted. "I'll join you, if I may," she said, as a trooper took her horse's reins for her. "I can't do much when the fighting starts—it's all up to Larth." Tension was at last showing in her face, though her voice was perfectly calm.

Halicar grinned at her as she sat down on the grass beside him, clearly relieved that she was farther from the lines. "You can see better from here, too," he said.

She sent him a quick answering smile, and said, "Ilarion, you've been in battles. How does this one look to you?"

"Not bad at all, my lady. The Protector's a long way from home, and his men are tired. Ours aren't. It was a mistake for him to fight, I think."

Her face relaxed a trifle. "I think so, too. Remember all the wonderful things we talked about on the beach? Once we've won this battle, we can start making them come true. We only need to get through today."

"We will, Protectress."

"Look," Halicar said. "I think it's starting."

The two men and Elyssa got to their feet. Tirsun's line had begun to move forward. Drums growled, signaling the march tempo. A ripple ran down Larth's battalions as the men advanced their spears. Polished metal winked in the sun. Kicked up by the feet of Tirsun's men, clouds of pale dust rose from the dry earth and hung in the air, hardly moving.

"He's not very subtle," Ilarion muttered. His mouth had gone dry as it always did before combat. "It's a frontal attack. I'd have expected something more devious."

"Our position doesn't leave him much choice," Elyssa pointed out.

"No, it doesn't. Still—"

The distance between the lines was shrinking steadily. It appeared that Larth and Auvas had agreed to receive the onslaught rather than countercharge. They wouldn't want to lose their flank protection by advancing. Ilarion could see Larth's helmet plume and his standard in the line's center, and Auvas's huge personal banner not far beyond it.

"Mount yourselves," Ilarion called to his men. He swung

into his saddle. "Halicar, Protectress, you also should get into the saddle. There's always a chance some loose ends of his cavalry will get up here."

They did so. Then all three watched as the battle opened below the hill.

Tirsun's line was now two hundred paces from Larth's. Ilarion could see the Protector's battle flag and a knot of horsemen around it, a quarter of a mile away. Tirsun would be there. Farther north, and advancing behind the Kaneshites' main battle line, was a solid block of Hazannu. Near it was a cavalry unit. These were the Protector's reserves, and they were so strong, Ilarion now saw, because he'd weakened his left to make them that way.

But Larth also had kept men back, though they were much fewer. They were opposite Tirsun's thinned-out left wing, and well away from his formidable reserve.

We've got him, Ilarion thought. Tirsun had made himself vulnerable because he didn't know that here on this hill was the first true heavy cavalry the Rasenna had ever seen. Given the Protector's flawed dispositions, Ilarion knew that even his small number of horsemen could break through the enemy left and shatter it, leaving it an easy target for Larth's First Levy infantry. He had to attack at exactly the right time, but he'd seen enough fighting to know that time when it came. Even if Larth missed the moment, he would not.

Another growl of drums. Ilarion blinked in perplexity as the Protector's advance ground to a halt. Tirsun had stopped his men well short of contact. The Hazannu of his right wing were perhaps a hundred paces from Auvas's battalions.

"What's going on down there?" Halicar muttered. Elyssa was silent, but in her stance was the tension of a harp string.

Without warning a horn blared from Auvas's end of the line. A rumble rose to a bellow, the shouting of men about to join battle. An instant later the army's entire left wing charged headlong at the waiting Hazannu.

"What is he *doing*?" Ilarion burst out, appalled. The action was mad, unless Larth had changed his plans and wanted a general attack. But though the center and the right swayed uncertainly, they didn't move forward to join the left wing in its rush. Dust billowed from Auvas's formations, but Ilarion saw enough to know that their sudden advance had disordered them. Far worse, the whole left wing was pulling away from the center, leaving a huge and expanding gap in the line.

Elyssa cried out in appalled disbelief. Ilarion realized with horror what would happen next, and it did.

The Hazannu opposite the gap charged. A wedge of howling warriors smashed into the breach, then turned to strike at the flank of Auvas's detached wing. Dust shot up in billows, screams and shouts and the clang of iron and bronze filled the air. Through the thickening haze Ilarion saw the Hazannu reserve race forward, then swing left, intent on attacking Larth's now desperately vulnerable center. He glimpsed some of Tirsun's cavalry trotting forward, also making for the breach. In moments they vanished in the growing dust cloud. Larth's small reserve below the hill began to hurry toward the fighting, but they were moving far too slowly to intervene in time. Now the men in the right wing, unable to see what was going on but sensing disaster, began to look over their shoulders. Many were shouting, but their voices were lost in the growing pandemonium of the battle.

Elyssa and Halicar sat transfixed, watching ruin and catastrophe unfold below.

If the Hazannu got behind Larth's line, all was lost. Ilarion shouted, "First Levy Cavalry! We have to seal the breach! Form wedge, follow me, charge the Hazannu!" He kicked his heels into his mount's ribs. The horse neighed, sprang forward, and pelted down the hill. His troopers thundered after him, his signalers galloping on his right and left. He glimpsed a flash of green and white over his shoulder, looked again. Elyssa had joined them. Her short sword was out. Halicar was coming too, farther back and empty-handed.

"Protectress," he screamed at her, "ride to Dymie! Close the gates! Go, now!"

White-faced, she screamed something back. In the uproar he could hear no word except *"Larth!"* and he knew she would never run. All he could do was try to close the broken line.

On the plain the dust was already thick and getting thicker. He raced past Larth's hurrying reserve and positioned his lance and shield. On his right, the rear ranks of the infantry line seemed to be wavering. He drummed heels on his gelding's sides, urging it to greater speed, and spared a glance over his shoulder. His men were with him in a flying wedge of horses and lance heads and armor. The ground shuddered as they rode. Elyssa had vanished and Halicar, too. She would be trying to find Larth, hoping to salvage something from this disaster.

Cavalry plunged from the dust ahead. Tirsun's light horsemen had broken through, scores of them. In a moment they'd be cutting the infantry down from the rear. Ilarion took a firmer grip on his lance and went for them. All thinking stopped. Lance head crashed through armor, jarring in his bones, screams, a stab at the nearest. Blinding dust everywhere, sunlight dim yellow, sight fading at a dozen feet. Horses, men, spears looming out of the murk. A heavy blow as lance met enemy shield, the shaft shattering, drop it, sword work now, he took a blade on his own shield, slashed, a howl suddenly cut off, blood—not his—spattering his lips. Three of his men nearby, one going down, javelin in the gut.

Abruptly the light brightened, and his horse raced from the dust cloud. A score of his troopers were still near him, but no enemy were close. He slowed to a trot and looked wildly around.

Catastrophe. They were too late. Auvas's left wing was falling apart, the foot soldiers panicking and turning to flee. The enemy light cavalry was well through the breach and swarms of Hazannu were breaking out of the dust clouds to turn and attack the rear of the already-disintegrating center. Farther distant, toward the hill, torrents of men fled from the enemy. Sickened and shaking with despair, Ilarion realized that the right wing had broken. He glimpsed the hilltop before more plumes of dust closed around it and saw clusters of troops there. Someone making a last desperate stand? Or Tirsun's men, seizing the high ground?

The sunlit air was hideous with the roar and stink of slaughter. Only moments had passed since he hurtled out of the dust. Surely he still had more men than the twenty he could see near him. But fighting on was hopeless. Even if most of his troopers had survived and he could rally them, they couldn't snatch victory from this defeat.

Did Auvas split our line on purpose? Did Tirsun get him to betray Elyssa? Or was Auvas merely a fool?

Never mind that. He had to get his troopers together, look for Elyssa, escort her away to Dymie. A few of his men had seen him and were galloping in his direction. Among them, to his relief, was one of his signalers.

Out of the dust cloud cantered a figure in a green-and-white helmet. Elyssa, fifty yards away. No Halicar, no Larth. She was leaning across her saddlebow and his stomach turned over. He spurred toward her, saw that her helmet plume was half–sheared away and she'd lost her sword. She looked up and saw him, her eyes stunned with despair, as her mount slowed to a trot.

"Protectress!" Suddenly he was at her horse's head, seized the reins. "Are you hurt?"

Elyssa was still bent over as if her stomach hurt her. She gasped something, hard to hear in the cacophony. He thought it was "Hazannu mace." Blood threaded the corner of her mouth.

"Halicar?" he yelled through the din. "Larth?"

"Don't—know. Couldn't see—"

Ruin, catastrophe, at the hands of a fool or traitor. With no warning at all the rage erupted in him, searing all thought to ashes, scalding in his blood, turning his will to a white-hot flame of savagery. He would hurl himself at the enemy, kill and kill until he himself was killed, kill until he lay in his blood in the furrows, with an enemy blade in his throat.

He was already pulling on the reins when the thought rose, somehow, through the crimson haze of madness:

You were Tirsun's slave. Will you now be a slave to your fury? If so, you will be in bondage always, even if you live. And if you die, you will die a slave, though you call no one master.

The madness slipped, cracked, fell away from him. He still raged, but the rage was his to control. He held it, checked it, set it aside, and his sight cleared, leaving him sick and cold with reaction. No more than five heartbeats had passed.

Elyssa. His men. He must act.

"Can you gallop?" he shouted to her through the uproar of the battle.

She nodded. The signalman was only yards away. "Stesen!" Ilarion yelled at the man. "Sound the rally! Now!"

Stesen grabbed for his horn, put it to his lips, blew. The shrill notes pierced the din. A dozen riders pounded out of the dust, armor hacked, half of them without lances, arms and faces bloody, slashed.

"Keep sounding it, Stesen! Form wedge on me, shield the Protectress, everyone, canter, go!"

Stesen blew and blew again. The roar of the battle was deafening, and Ilarion knew not all of his men would hear the recall as the lancers withdrew. But he had no choice, and started his men moving quickly southwest toward the road. The army had broken in earnest, and streams of Dymie's panicked men were fleeing the battlefield with Tirsun's cavalry and hordes of Hazannu in deadly pursuit. Preferring the easier victims, the enemy light horse avoided the lancers; by the time Ilarion reached the road he'd collected over a hundred of his men. Elyssa's face was now white and bloodless, and she held her reins with one hand and kept the other across her belly. The pandemonium was dying down a little, to a many-voiced chorus of howls and wails and screams.

He took Elyssa's reins and guided their sweating horses onto the road. "Halicar?" he asked, dreading the answer.

Between clenched teeth, she said, "I don't know. We lost each other."

"He's inviolate," Ilarion said. "He'll come soon." For a moment he peered back at the hill. Though dust hazed its summit, he saw half a dozen figures standing there. Bodies lay on the grass around them. A battle standard pricked at the sky. Tirsun was up there, the victor.

We lost, he thought in sudden, racking anguish. *We lost. Elyssa has lost. Great Lord Allfather, Our Lady Mother, protect her, protect us. What's going to happen to us now?*

As they withdrew westward a few of Tirsun's horsemen rode after them, but these broke off after a few minutes. With tears of fury and despair streaking the dust that caked his cheeks, Ilarion led the Protectress and his men toward Dymie. It was the end, and he knew it.

Theatana stood on the hilltop and surveyed the battlefield. The fighting was over, and the dust had settled onto the bodies of men and horses. It wasn't quiet, though; the shrieks and howls of the wounded carried clearly through the sunlit air. Theatana had enjoyed the noise at first, but after a while it was merely irritating. She hadn't seen much of the actual battle; knowing there was a chance that Tirsun would lose and wanting time to escape if he did, she'd stayed back with the baggage train. She'd only arrived on the hilltop a short time ago.

Looters were busy among the bodies down on the plain, but the junior officers and the cavalry were slowly getting the First Levy battalions and most of the Hazannu mercenaries reorganized. Tirsun was a few yards away, his battle standard swaying over his head, conferring with his senior officers as they decided on their next move.

Growing bored, Theatana sauntered around the hilltop. A few of Elyssa's troops had made a last stand there, and a scattering of their corpses and Hazannu bodies lay on the salt grass. The fighting had been desperate and brutal; she smelled offal, excrement, blood, viscera.

"Ah, Theatana."

She turned around. Tirsun had come up to her, his eyes bright and his face cheerful. He'd won his war, or most of it, and for the moment he thought he owned the world. But she'd soon remind him that if he did, it was on her sufferance.

"Yes?" she said. A man she didn't know was standing a little behind Tirsun. A high-ranking prisoner? He was still armed, but perhaps this was some battlefield nicety extended to captives of noble status.

"You haven't met Larth Tetnias, former pronoyar of Dymie." Tirsun gestured the man forward. "Larth, please pay your respects to my honored companion, Theatana of House Dascaris. You've perhaps heard of her—the Gift-bearer's heir and my colleague in the restoration."

"Yes, Protector," Larth said. He made an obeisance. "My lady."

Why was Tirsun dispensing this peculiar courtesy? She said, "Tirsun, I presume you'll kill him once these introductions are completed. We don't need the nuisance of aristocratic prisoners."

Larth opened his mouth, then closed it. Tirsun was grinning widely, as if at a huge and secret joke. "My love, I should perhaps complete the introduction. Larth and I have agreed for some time that the future glory of the Rasenna does not lie with my sister." The grin widened. "Hence his order to the commander of Dymie's left wing for that premature and impetuous attack this afternoon. It wasn't as impetuous as it seemed."

Theatana looked from one man to the other. Tirsun's grin faded, and he took on the expression of a child caught in some significant misdemeanor.

She said, "This was *planned*? You've been plotting with Elyssa's pronoyar, and you didn't tell me?"

"Ah, well." He gave a nervous laugh. "I felt that the fewer people knew, the better. But you were very important in the matter. Like many others, Larth has come to believe that you're the Giftbearer of the new age of the Rasenna. And that you and I are the legitimate restorers of the Garden, and not my poor inept sister. Auvas, the commander of Larth's left wing, believed it, too. Larth and he hatched this little egg at my suggestion. Unfortunately, Auvas fell afoul of a Hazannu spear before he could reach my protection." He laughed again, more uneasily still. "Ah, the hazards of battle."

"I see." She was furious. Tirsun would think this victory was his alone, brought about by his cunning. He would not even have been there if it weren't for her. "I see."

The Protector hurried on. "Elyssa's defeat will be known in Dymie in hours, and Larth believes the garrison commander will open the gates to him as soon as we appear in force. So I'm going to rest the men until dusk, then go on. We'll be at Dymie's gates by dawn. How would you like to eat breakfast in the palace?"

Through her teeth, Theatana said, "And Elyssa?" It was time to show him how he'd erred in deceiving her, but what to do? She could use the mask to draw a sister-thing from her being, then kill a prisoner. Then she could make Larth disembowel himself. But the man might be more useful alive than dead. They still had to get into Dymie.

"It looks as if she got away, unfortunately," Tirsun acknowledged. "But she's lost her army, and you and I are here with ours. She won't control Dymie for long. Auvas's kin will see to that."

Larth said, "My lord, you undertook that the Protectress will be allowed to leave the city and go into exile in Ushnana. I did what I did only on that understanding."

"Of course you did," Tirsun said soothingly. "And so she will. I would never harm my sister. She's the only kin I have, and I value family very highly."

Theatana made a noise in her throat, but said nothing. She would make sure, even if Tirsun didn't, that Elyssa never left Dymie alive.

A minor commotion had broken out near the group of officers behind Tirsun. He turned to look and so did Larth and Theatana. Theatana saw a pair of horsemen by the group, and heard someone say, "Go back to your unit. I'll take him to the Protector."

A moment late an officer was leading a prisoner forward, holding the man's arm, but somewhat gingerly. Putting her anger aside for the moment, Theatana scrutinized the captive. He was obviously neither Rasennan nor Hazannu, for he was dark and slight, with brown eyes and slender hands. He was a handsome man, in spite of the dirt and bruises and the smear of dried blood on his chin.

"Well, well, well," Tirsun said. "I suppose, Larth, that this is the one who inflamed so many aristocratic rages in Dymie. There can't be many Antecessors in the neighborhood."

"My lord Protector," the prisoner said. His voice was weary and grieving, but his gesture of respect was precise.

"I see the battlefield doesn't erode your courtesy," Tirsun observed. "You're Halicar, my sister's Antecessor singer, aren't you? I suppose you were here to record the glory of my enemies' victory."

"My lord is correct on both counts." The bard's dark eyes went to Larth, then to the sword still hanging at Larth's belt. "We lost, Pronoyar," he said. "Yet here you stand. Was it your doing?"

Larth turned away. Halicar said, "Ah. I thought as much. The Protectress couldn't promise what you and the others dreamed, so you destroyed her. But the Green Lady has seen what you've done. *She* will remember it."

"Enough of that, Antecessor," Tirsun said in a voice of warning. "But now I think of it, since you *have* lost, how will you manage to sing about the heroism and the glory of my sister's army?"

"It will be a lament, my lord."

Tirsun laughed. "Singers! Always ready to make anything out of anything. Why aren't you on your way back to Dymie?"

"I would be, my lord, but one of your cavalrymen speared my horse. It threw me, and I was stunned, and here I am."

"Ah, what bad luck," Tirsun observed. He paused, then added thoughtfully, "I know you're Elyssa's lover. Still, fortunes change. Would you and your sister be interested in joining my household once everything is, ah, settled?"

Halicar closed his eyes, then opened them. "I think not," he answered in a slightly shaking voice. "I think I speak for my sister in this also."

"Very loyal of you . . . well, I suppose you'd better be on your way. But compose your laments quickly if you're going to. I'll be in Dymie soon, and then I suppose you'll want to leave."

"You're letting him *go*?" Theatana burst out. "He's your sister's *lover*. He's an enemy and a living insult!"

"I know that," Tirsun said. "But I can't harm him. Even a Hazannu wouldn't. Antecessor Master-Singers are inviolate. You must have learned that by now, my dear. I'd be cursed if I ordered someone to slit his throat, and the person likely wouldn't obey me, anyway. Then I'd have to slit *his* throat."

"I care nothing for curses," Theatana said, her voice thick and hot with fury.

"We can't risk it," said Tirsun, sounding a little desperate. "We have to let him go, Theatana. It's wiser."

"I'll show you wisdom," she snarled. She took two swift steps forward, drawing her long dagger. Tirsun's arm instinctively rose to stop her, and he yelled wordlessly.

She slipped past his arm. The dagger swung back. Halicar looked astonished. He put his hands up to ward her off, too late.

Theatana plunged the knife between his ribs, steel ripping past bone, shearing through flesh. She felt the knife's cross guard slam against his skin, the blade now home inside him, splitting his heart. He groaned, eyes widening in shock. Blood spurted against her fist on the dagger's hilt. She thought, *I should make him a wraith, then draw out a sister-thing—*

Larth and Tirsun, astonished into paralysis, were staring at her aghast. Halicar's eyes rolled in their sockets, and he began to fall. She tried to hold him up with the knife, struggled to summon her mind to the point she needed before he slipped away on her. She quelled her rage, almost had it—

He died still standing. She wasn't quite ready, try anyway, draw him in, his breath burned in her throat, it *seared* her. This wasn't right, she'd never felt this before, did something protect him? She spat him out, though her mind still called on the Black Craft.

Make of him what I made of the others.

A blur hung in the air for an instant and vanished. It might have been her imagination. The body folded at knees and waist, twisted the dagger from her fist, and dropped to the salt grass at her feet.

Her throat seemed burned raw. She hadn't been ready, and he'd escaped her. She must not make that error again. And the pain . . . it was fading, but it had been very bad indeed. Maybe there was something about Antecessor singers, after all. She'd be more careful from now on. But perhaps she could practice on the sister.

Tirsun and Larth had backed away from her. The officers' faces were stark with apprehension.

"I *told* you, Theatana," Tirsun said in a furious, tight voice. "I *told* you he wasn't to be harmed. You've broken—"

She turned her rage on him and Larth. It kindled her, burned in her, and she thrust her awareness at them with all the power of her wrath. She touched them as she'd never touched anyone before: perceived Larth, frightened both of her and of what he'd done, yet still yearning for the dream of Rasennan glory. And Tirsun himself, violent, ridden by appetites barely controlled, playful, capricious, cruel. And in return they glimpsed her, and for an instant she saw that glimpse reflected: her seething hatred, her cunning, the Other's reptilian coils in her flesh and in her ferocious will.

The moment of connection passed and her normal sight returned. Larth's face was working in spasms; spittle flecked his lips. Tirsun had gone so pale she saw the ghosts of freckles in his skin. His mouth gaped as if to cry out.

"Never tell me what to do, Tirsun," she said in a thin, cold voice. Their terror was already soothing her fury, but she did not let them see that; their dread delighted her. "Do you think I've suffered what I have to be at your beck and call? *Do* you?"

Tirsun managed to close his mouth. Then he opened it, and said, "No." From somewhere he dragged a gaunt, wavering smile, and continued, stammering, "No, my love, of course not. Never that. We're partners. Partners in all."

"Remember it," she told him softly. She was tempted to strike him across the mouth, but she had to leave him some dignity in front of his officers. The time was near when they'd obey her directly, but it hadn't quite arrived. "And if someday you think of cutting me down by surprise, don't. I'll see you coming. Can you understand what might happen to you then?"

Tirsun swallowed convulsively. "Yes," he croaked.

"Very wise of you." She glanced down and kicked the Antecessor's body in the mouth. "Sing about that," she told it, then stooped to retrieve her dagger. It pulled out with no resistance. For the first time she noticed that blood was drying stickily on her hands, not an unpleasant sensation.

She straightened. The men were still staring at her. "Don't you have an army to see to?" she asked. "Go and get on with it, or we'll be here for a month."

28

ILARION, ELYSSA, AND THE FIRST LEVY'S EXHAUSTED HORSE-men reached the capital as the dying glare of sunset flooded the sky. Some fifty light cavalry, whose officers had vanished in the battle, had joined Ilarion's hundred troopers in their retreat. But Ilarion had seen no infantry since withdrawing from Demacda. Those who hadn't been captured or killed were stragglers now, probably fled inland to the hills. Except for the cavalry remnants behind him, the destruction of Elyssa's army was complete. He realized that the Protectress herself was badly hurt; she'd wiped the blood away from her mouth, but a scarlet trickle kept seeping through her armor, low on her right side. Nevertheless, she had refused to stop so he could attempt to help her. He knew why she was forcing herself to endure her torment; as long as she appeared well enough to lead them, her men would follow her, and she had a slim chance of holding Dymie. But if she faltered, she was lost. So she rode beside him at a trot, sitting as straight in the saddle as she could, barely able to speak, her face white with pain. She'd told him a little, through clenched teeth; in the murk, she and Halicar were separated, and after that she'd been unable to find either him or Larth. Then a Hazannu got her solidly with his mace, and she rode dazed and half-blind with pain until Ilarion found her.

For Ilarion, the only good thing that had happened since noon was that he had defeated the furies of his Dascarid heritage. Had he managed it before this day of ruin, he would have been beside himself with joy. Now his victory, in the midst of such utter defeat, was no consolation at all.

At least, he thought grimly as they approached the Sunrise Gate, *if I die soon, it won't be as a slave to my temper.*

The gate sentries must have seen their dust cloud well down the road and sounded an alarm, for hundreds of Dymie's citizens watched from the battlements as the column neared the walls. The gates were closed, and Ilarion felt a jab of anxiety when they didn't open at his men's approach. But someone must have seen Elyssa's insignia on their shields. When they were a hundred yards away the gates finally swung wide.

The crowds on the battlements were muttering uneasily. They watched Elyssa and the horsemen ride into the city in the rusty light of sunset, and as Ilarion and the Protectress clattered from beneath the arch of the gate into Middle Street, the mutter turned to apprehensive silence.

A single, frightened shout broke the stillness. "Where's the army? Did we win?"

Foreboding swept through Ilarion as he realized that Halicar could not yet have returned to the city; if he'd done so, they'd already know what had happened.

Elyssa looked up at the crowds. "Tirsun won this time," she called back. "But only this battle. There'll be another—"

The crowd's wail drowned her words. Immediately, men and women began to stream down from the walls and towers, hurrying homeward to barricade their doors and hide their valuables. Many of the women wept with fear; everyone had known for days that Tirsun had Hazannu troops with him, and Hazannu troops raped. Even the slaves in the throng looked frightened.

"The garrison commander," Elyssa gasped, giving up any hope of controlling the crowd. She reined in her mount, and the horsemen milled to a halt behind them. "Find him, Ilarion. I have to get off this horse, and soon."

As luck would have it, the man had been watching their approach. He came hurrying down from the wall-walk, wearing civilian tunic and cloak, and from the wine stain on the tunic he had come from an interrupted dinner. Ilarion had met him several times; his name was Gethash and he commanded the retired First Levy veterans who served as the city garrison. He was thin, verging on elderly, with a small mouth pursed between flat cheeks.

"What's happened?" Gethash asked, shock and apprehension clear in his face. "Where's the pronoyar? The infantry?"

"Auvas Seitithi advanced the left wing too soon," Ilarion said wearily, to spare Elyssa the pain of speaking. "It opened a gap, and the enemy broke our line. The army's smashed. Dead or captured, most of it. The pronoyar, too, probably."

Gethash opened his mouth, closed it. "We *lost*?" he said in a disbelieving voice.

"Yes, we did. And badly. Keep the gates closed, but watch for any of our stragglers coming in. There may be a few. Even with your veterans, we'll need all the men we can get to hold the outer walls."

Elyssa said, in a halting, strained voice, "And we'll see enemy troops tomorrow, Gethash. The fighting was at Demacda."

"Firebringer help us! So close?" Gethash stared at her. There was fresh blood at the corner of her mouth and more on the skirt of her mail, but she didn't seem aware of it. "Protectress," he faltered, "are you hurt?"

Elyssa managed a white-lipped smile. "A bruise and scrapes, no more. I'm going to the palace now, to organize our preparations for the siege. Put all your garrison troops on the walls during the night."

"Yes, Protectress." Gethash swept his gaze over the exhausted horsemen. "But there're more than this to come, surely? This is fewer than two hundred."

Elyssa swayed a little in her saddle. Ilarion said, "That's all we have, unless we get stragglers. We'll be under siege by this time tomorrow." *If you stay loyal, that is,* he thought, for the man's alarm and fear were palpable.

Gethash managed to collect himself. "Close the gates, stragglers, yes. I'll see to it. Protectress, can you leave these men with me? I'll need reinforcements."

She shook her head. "No. They come with me to the palace. They need food and rest. Tomorrow you may have them, when Tirsun comes." She hesitated, drawing a pain-filled breath, and then said, "Has the bard Halicar returned?"

Gethash looked aside. "I've not heard. As far as I know, you're the first back, Protectress. But . . . there was an omen. People are worried about it. And you're a priestess, my lady, if you could tell us—"

"What omen?" Ilarion demanded. "What are you talking about?"

"The earth shook. It was only for a heartbeat, but it shook, just a little. Most of us felt it here. Some didn't. Didn't you?"

He tried to remember. "No. When did it happen?"

"After midday. Perhaps the second hour."

"We were in a cavalry charge about then. The earth was already shaking for us."

"It was the Green Lady threatening Tirsun," Elyssa said. "For sacrilege and for breaking the peace. Tell everyone that was why." She kicked her horse gently, and it started up the street toward Beacon Hill and the palace.

Gethash, looking after her, muttered, "Yes, Protectress," though there was no conviction in his voice.

Ilarion put his mount into a trot and led his men after her. He dreaded what he had to do when they reached the palace: tell Mereth not only of defeat but also that Halicar was missing. The Master-Singer might not be dead, though. He had a better chance of survival than a soldier did. Maybe he'd been captured. That would be good enough to ensure that he lived; even Tirsun wouldn't murder an Antecessor bard.

But Theatana would, he thought, and his misery deepened. Mereth wouldn't be safe from his aunt, either. He had to get both her and Elyssa away from the city as soon as possible. The Protectress was nearing the end of her strength, and the city would not withstand a siege for long if she could not lead it. Someone like Gethash would open the gates, hoping for reward or—at the least—mercy.

Nenattu, guided perhaps by some premonition, was waiting in the Lower Court. The sight of the Protectress leaning over her saddlebow in agony shocked him into paralysis for a moment, but then he recollected himself and began shouting for a litter and attendants.

As slaves scurried and the cavalry troopers wearily dismounted, Ilarion helped Nenattu ease Elyssa off her mare. For the first time, he could see something of the extent and nature of her wound. A Hazannu spiked mace had crashed into her right side at the lower edge of her rib cage and a spike had penetrated the armor. The barbarian weapons were massive, and the blow must have nearly knocked her off her horse.

"How bad is it, Ilarion?" she whispered, as they eased her onto the litter.

"Not bad. Broken ribs. A gash. You'll heal soon, my lady." Privately he was not so sure. He'd seen wounds like these, outwardly serious but not fatal, but which nevertheless killed their victims within a day or two. The real injuries were deep, and the person slowly bled to death within. Even if that wasn't so, the blood at her mouth suggested a punctured lung. The pain must be appalling; how she had even talked to Gethash, let alone ridden hard for twelve miles, was more than he could understand.

"Liar," she whispered. Her eyes rolled up in their sockets, and the lids closed. She had fainted.

He looked up and met Nenattu's worried gaze; the Grand Domestic had guessed the truth behind his comforting words. "I'll take her inside," Nenattu said. "See to the palace defenses and our men, my lord Ilarion."

"Where's Mereth?" Ilarion asked. "Halicar's missing."

"Lady be good to us," Nenattu said desolately. "When you came here without him I was afraid he might be—but he's safe, he's inviolate. I think the lady Mereth might be in the Protectress's aviary. You know how she likes the birds."

Ilarion, belatedly, ordered the citadel gates closed and barred, then left his men in the Lower Court to tend their horses with the help of the palace grooms. Then he hurried through the inner gate and up the Grand Staircase to the Middle Court. Above him, the windows of the High Palace glowed dimly with yellow lamplight. The sky in the east was velvety indigo and the southern stars, soft and hazed by high cloud, were coming out. The sunset was a vermilion slash on the horizon. He smelled lamp oil on the damp and cooling air.

He climbed onward and reached the Upper Court. It was deserted, the slaves all inside at their evening duties. Pausing for breath, he pulled off his helmet and scrubbed fingers through his sweat-caked hair. Then he hurried through the door that led to the aviary courtyard.

Mereth was there, feeding a sunbird through the bronze mesh. The golden creature was taking seed delicately from her fingertips. She looked composed; the news had not yet reached her. Ilarion knew it was best that he bring it, though he dreaded doing so.

"Mereth?"

She looked around at him and put a hand to her mouth. "*Ilarion?*"

"Yes, it's me." He hurried to her as she turned from the cage. Birds fluttered and chirped, disturbed at his abrupt entry.

"What's happened? Why are you here so soon?" Her voice was sharp with surprise, and even in the dusk he saw her face filling with alarm at the sight of him: dirty, bruised, cuirass-slashed, and spattered with dried blood. "Dear Mother of All, are you hurt? Where's Halicar? Where's Elyssa?"

He could barely find words but made himself do so. "I'm not hurt. And I'm sure Halicar's safe, Mereth. He stayed out of the fighting." Suddenly he wanted to weep. In his nostrils was his own stink, the stink of battle: blood, sweat, fear, and death.

"But he didn't come back with you—oh, Ilarion, sweet Mother, we *lost*? We *lost*?"

"Yes," he said miserably. "We lost. Auvas Seitithi attacked without orders. Tirsun's men broke our line, and it was all over. It might have been treachery, I don't know."

She seemed about to fall and he caught her arm. "Elyssa," she gasped. "You didn't say about Elyssa."

"She's here in the palace. We came just now. But she's hurt."

Mereth closed her eyes and spoke in her own tongue. It sounded like a prayer. She opened them again, and said faintly, "Is it bad?"

"Yes. I hope she won't die. But she may."

Straightening, she pulled free of his grip. "I'm all right. I have to go to her."

"I'll come with you," he said. If Elyssa had regained consciousness, he should find out what she wanted him to do.

They left the aviary, hurrying along the maze of corridors. Mereth walked stiffly, still clearly uncomfortable from the kick in the ribs the horse had given her, but she kept up the pace. As they passed a light well, she said, "Larth. What happened to Larth?"

"I don't know. He vanished on the battlefield. Elyssa couldn't find him."

"And our army?" she asked wretchedly. "Is it *all* gone?"

"All of it, except a few horsemen I brought back."

"But you didn't see Halicar . . ."

"No. He rode with Elyssa into the fighting, when she tried to rally the men, and she lost sight of him. He's likely been captured. Tirsun will let him go."

"Dear Lady Mother, he must. He must."

They continued toward Elyssa's private apartments. Slaves flitted past in the gloom, faces drawn.

"So few lamps?" Ilarion asked.

"Nenattu ordered it this afternoon. A minor precaution, he said. To save oil in case of a siege."

A single guard, the man named Orinnu, stood sentry at the entrance to Elyssa's quarters. He looked distraught. "She's here?" Ilarion asked him.

"Yes, my lord. With the Grand Domestic and Utea the healing woman."

They brushed past him and into the Blue Swallow Room, then into the antechamber. Beyond was Elyssa's bedroom, where Ilarion had never been. Unlike the rest of the palace, this was well lit. The Protectress lay on a plain narrow bed, a blue-and-white-striped coverlet drawn to her neck. Her eyes were closed. A cushion was under her head, and her hair lay in a flood of gold over its crimson-and-black embroidery. She looked worse than when Ilarion had left her; her skin was almost as white as the white stripes of the coverlet, and there were shadows like bruises under her eyes.

Nenattu sat on a stool by the bed, watching her. On another stool was Utea, the slave woman who served Elyssa as her personal healer.

"Is she awake, Nenattu?" Mereth asked softly.

"Yes," Elyssa answered. The weakness of her voice was shocking. Her eyelids fluttered open. "I'm awake, Mereth. Ilarion, you're here, too? Is Halicar home yet?"

Ilarion sank to his knees beside the bed, and she turned her head a little to look at him. Her eyes were green as spring grass in sunlight.

"Not yet," he said, with a constricted throat. "But he'll come. At the worst, he's captured. It might take a day."

"And Larth? He hasn't come back yet?"

"No, Protectress."

Elyssa blinked several times and teardrops inched slowly over her cheekbones. "Auvas betrayed us," she whispered. "I should have known. What a terrible mistake I've made. So many dead because of my foolishness." She fell silent, but when she spoke again her voice was a little firmer. "Nenattu, you will take command of the city's defenses until I can do it. Work with Ilarion and Gethash. But you're in charge unless Larth reaches us, if he does. We'll hold till Ushnana sends help. Then we'll join forces with them and drive my brother out."

"Yes, Protectress," Nenattu murmured.

"I'm very tired all of a sudden," Elyssa murmured. "I'd like to sleep now. I must be stronger when my brother and his army come."

Ilarion gestured to Nenattu and slipped out of the room. Mereth joined them just beyond the door.

"Tirsun will be here tomorrow," Ilarion said. "We don't have enough men to hold the city for long. We've got to take the Protectress somewhere safe—if he captures her, he'll kill her, and if he doesn't, Theatana will. I think we should take ship for Ushnana at first light."

Nenattu grimaced in despair. "Utea says she's too weak to be moved. Riding like that from Demacda, with her wound . . . it made her much worse. I think if we move her, she'll die."

Mereth said in a low voice, "Can't we hold out for a few days at least, until she's stronger? Even under siege we still control the harbor."

"I don't trust the garrison commander," Ilarion told her. "He may open the gates when Tirsun gets here. We've probably got till morning, maybe tomorrow afternoon at the latest. If that's enough time for her to recover a little—"

"I don't know if it will be," Nenattu said. "She can't even drink, let alone eat."

"Curse it. Then we'll have to wait and see. Maybe we can hold out in the citadel till Ushnana gets here, or she recovers a little."

"Maybe," Nenattu said. He sighed. "Right now, though, we have to look to our defenses. My lord, would you be so good as to go down to the city, and make sure the gates are sealed and garrisoned."

Ilarion woke suddenly and found himself staring into the near darkness of his sleeping cubicle. All was silent. In the reception chamber outside, the night lamp burned a subdued yellow.

He stirred restlessly, then got out of bed, felt his way to the window, and pushed it open. The rain was still holding off; Little Summer was not quite at an end. In the eastern sky was a band of pale gray. Dawn was coming. He had slept far longer than he'd expected.

He knew he wouldn't get back to sleep. He splashed water over his face, dressed, and buckled on his sword and dagger. His slave Bres appeared, rubbing his eyes, but Ilarion sent him back to bed. Then he left his quarters and made his way outside to the Middle Court.

The dawnlight was stronger now. He climbed the stairway to the Upper Court, intending to find Mereth and ask if Elyssa showed any improvement. Even if she didn't, they must risk getting her to a ship, anyway. Last night, Nenattu had announced publicly that the Protectress was slightly wounded but would recover soon; he'd had to do so to suppress the rumors that she'd already died. But the news had done nothing for the city garrison's resolve, or for that of

Gethash its commander. Like Ilarion, Nenattu didn't think either would resist Tirsun for long. Fearing as much, the Grand Domestic had taken Ilarion's suggestion, gone down to the harbor, and ordered Elyssa's senior naval captain to have a galley ready to sail at first light.

How close *was* the Protector? Instead of entering the building to find Mereth, Ilarion went along the palace's east arcade and followed it to the gardens of the Harbor Terrace. At the far end of the terrace rose Dristra's Light, the beacon of oil-soaked wood still blazing in its cresset. With the approach of morning, the slaves were allowing it to burn down, and the flames had turned smoky. The dawn's gray light made the shrubs and ornamental trees look luminous. He walked across the marble flagstones to the balustrade that guarded the sheer drop from the hill's summit to the city's rooftops. The eastern horizon was pink and gold.

Sandals whispered on stone behind him. He turned around and saw Mereth approaching. She wore a loose white skirt, a russet bodice, and a golden brown overmantle. Though she didn't look as desolate as she had last night, her face was wan and tired. It hurt him.

"Dawn's here," he said, as she reached him, as if she couldn't see it for herself. "Have you been with Elyssa?"

"About half the night, I think. I slept for a while and got up and then came out here. I needed to clear my head."

"There's no sign of Halicar?"

"No. But he'll come, as you said. I'm sure he'll come."

"How is she?"

She winced. "Worse. Much worse. She's very weak."

"We should have moved her yesterday."

"Perhaps." She sighed. "But she might be dead by now if we had."

There was a silence. "She's dying, isn't she?" he said.

"Yes, I think she is." Mereth crossed her arms on the balustrade and leaned on them. "I'm glad she met my brother. She didn't stay lonely all her life. She had at least a little time of happiness with someone who loved her."

"I'm glad of that," he said. "I should have killed Tirsun when I had the chance. My parents should have killed Theatana when *they* had the chance. She's mostly to blame for all this. An old evil. And we were so sure we were rid of her."

"Old evils cast long shadows," Mereth said. "But I'm glad you didn't kill him. If you had, you'd be dead, too."

"I know."

A silence followed. White seabirds wheeled over the harbor below. Then Mereth said, "I was so angry, in the beginning, that they loved each other and I was left outside. Now I'd give anything to see them together again. But I don't think I will, will I? Halicar will come, but too late. I'm losing my good friend, and he's losing the one he loves."

"I still have hope, Mereth."

"I feel the grieving in my bones," she said, and shivered. "And something worse. Will Theatana be with Tirsun when he gets here?"

"Probably," he said. "I can't imagine her missing something like this." He looked down at her. "When we get away from here, if Elyssa . . . isn't with us, will you and Halicar come to the Ascendancy with me?"

"I think we must. We would never stay on Haidra with Tirsun ruling it. And the mainland . . . there's nothing there for us after Haidra. But there's so much still to go through before that's possible."

"Yes, but we'll get there. Eventually."

Suddenly she put her face in her hands. "Oh, Ilarion, if only everything around us wasn't so dreadful." Her shoulders shook; then she straightened and let her arms fall. "Elyssa . . . I have to go back to her."

"I'll come."

They hurried along the east arcade and into the Upper Court. Nenattu was opening the double doors of the banquet hall. He was weeping silently. Ilarion's stomach turned over, and Mereth gave a sharp cry of distress. Then they saw that the guard Orinnu and three male slaves were following him, carrying Elyssa on her bed. As they brought the bed into the light, Ilarion realized that Elyssa's eyes were open; she still lived. She saw him and raised her hand a little.

"She wants to see the sun again," Nenattu said in a choked

voice. "We're taking her to the Harbor Terrace. I did send to
your quarters for you."

"I'll help carry her now," Ilarion said, his eyes scalding.
"Not you, Mereth, you've got those bruised ribs."

He took one corner of the bed and Nenattu, a slave, and
Orinnu the other three. Together they carried her to the ter-
race and set the bed on the flagstones near the balustrade.
The sun's rim blazed on the horizon.

Ilarion looked down at the Protectress. Elyssa seemed almost transparent, as though her substance were slowly
draining away. He knelt by her head, Mereth at her other
side.

"Ilarion, my friend," she murmured. "I wanted to know
you for much longer, but it seems I must leave you sooner
than I wished." She swallowed, closed her eyes, and opened
them. "And you, Mereth, your music brought me great peace
and joy. Tell Halicar so when you see him."

"I will," Mereth whispered. "I will."

"Oh, please don't cry, dear Mereth. I'm going to the arms
of the Lady. Where I really belong. To my true home."

Mereth bowed her head, tears running down her cheeks.

"Nenattu," Elyssa murmured, "my old and faithful friend,
when I'm gone, you'd better leave, too. My brother may not
kill you, but Entash likely will, if he can. Keep yourself safe.
Go with Ilarion."

"I will," Nenattu quavered. "I'll go to Ushnana. They'll
welcome me there, I think.

"Orinnu," she continued faintly, "you were a faithful soldier. But now I release you from my service. You may leave
me now, if you wish."

The man nodded, weeping.

"Let my birds go from the aviary," Elyssa whispered.
"Tirsun wouldn't know how to look after them. Nenattu,
send someone . . . Orinnu will do it."

The Grand Domestic nodded at the man, who hurried
away, eyes wet.

She was quiet for a while as if asleep, though the shadow
of death lay upon her eyelids. Orinnu returned and told her
the birds were free, but she only nodded a little without

opening her eyes. Then they waited with her as the sun rose and larks sang in the trees of the terrace garden.

At length, she murmured, "Those are dew larks. Do you hear them? Spring is coming."

There was another span of stillness, and then she opened her eyes, and whispered, "My love, I'm so sorry. I tried to wait for you. I did my best, truly I did. Oh Halicar, I'm sorry, I tried."

The dew larks sang in the spring heliotrope. There was no other sound.

"She's gone," Nenattu said in a soft broken voice, and Mereth leaned over and closed her eyes.

29

SHE WAS GONE. STILL KNEELING BY HER, ILARION TOOK THE blue-and-white coverlet and drew it up to cover her face. His eyes were dry; he was beyond tears, in a kind of disbelieving daze. So, it seemed, was Mereth, whose face was still and white.

He still had duties. Tirsun was approaching; Mereth had to be protected. He got to his feet and stumbled to the balustrade.

What he saw to the east shocked him from his stupor. "He's here," he said, voice rasping.

"*Already?*" Mereth was suddenly beside him, gazing into the morning light. Just beyond the city walls to the east, snaking toward the Sunrise Gate, was a long column of marching men. Cavalry preceded it. Standards glinted. Among them would be Tirsun's.

"He must have marched all night," Ilarion said. This was the end. With Elyssa dead, the garrison would have no reason to resist the Protector. His men would be within the walls only minutes after the news spread.

"We won't get away by sea now," Nenattu said at Ilarion's left elbow. He did not sound frightened or sad, merely resigned and very tired. "We left it too late. The galley captain won't take us, not with Elyssa dead and with Tirsun already here. We might be able to bribe a merchantman if we can get to the harbor fast enough. But I doubt it."

Ilarion knew he was right. What could they do? Fight to the end, defending the palace? It couldn't happen. Elyssa was gone, and her guardsmen and the cavalry troopers camped in the Lower Court would see no reason to die pointlessly for her memory.

He said to Mereth, "Nenattu and I have to try to get away. I think you'd better come with us. Your inviolate status will likely protect you from Tirsun, but my aunt respects nothing. I don't think you'd be safe with her here."

Mereth shuddered. "But Tirsun might have Halicar with him or know where he is . . . but you're right. Your aunt frightens me. I'll take my chances with you and Nenattu."

"Good." He saw that she was still holding herself stiffly, from the horse's kick to her ribs. "Can you run if you have to, with your side?"

"Yes, if need be, for a little way. If I have to stop, you must go on without me."

"No," he said flatly, and squinted into the morning sunlight. A cavalry squadron had split off from the main column and was heading west. Ilarion lost sight of them behind the city walls, but he knew they were riding to blockade the Sunset Gate.

"What's that?" Nenattu blurted suddenly. "Look, there!"

Ilarion's gaze followed his outstretched arm. From the southwest, still distant but winging into Monument Bay on vast slanted sails, came a ship. Not a galley, not a fat merchantman, but a ship like *Statira*.

He thought for a heartbeat that it was one of Tirsun's, sweeping in to land more troops. But then she turned a little and he saw the helmeted head painted on her mainsail in black and red and gold.

"It's Rook!" he yelled. "It's Rook and *Statira*!"

Mereth clutched his arm. "What? Are you sure?"

"That's his emblem, the helmeted man." Ilarion squinted, calculating speed and distance. "She'll be off the harbor breakwater soon. We have to get down there and signal him. He'll send a boat in for us. I hope."

"We can't go to the harbor," Nenattu said urgently. "That's one of the first places Tirsun will send men. We must get out by the Bayward Gate and signal from the foreshore there."

"All right." Ilarion turned and saw Orinnu the guardsman

looking distraught. "My lord Nenattu," the soldier said, "I know the Protectress released me from her service. But if you need me to come with you, I will."

Nenattu put up his hand. "Orinnu, I know you have a wife and children. Go to them and keep them safe."

"Thank you, my lord. Thank you." The guard made an obeisance and hurried away.

Mereth looked down at Elyssa's still form beneath its coverlet. "It seems so terrible to leave her lying here," she murmured. "So alone. She was our friend, and we're just leaving her."

"She'd want us to go," Nenattu said. "Someone has to keep her memory green. Tirsun will try to destroy it."

"I know. But it's still dreadful."

"Mereth," Ilarion told her, "I don't want to leave her, either. But we have to. We don't have much time."

"Yes. We must." Her eyes widened in sudden alarm. "Halicar's harp! My pipe doesn't matter, but I can't leave his harp behind."

"Run and get it. We'll meet you in the Middle Court."

She hurried away. Ilarion thought of going for helmet and armor, but there was no time. His sword and knife would have to do.

If I have to fight, we're lost anyway.

He and Nenattu went through the east arcade and down the staircase to the Middle Court. He looked around, but Mereth wasn't there yet. Indeed, no one but them was in sight, though normally the palace should be awake and alive at this time of the morning.

Suddenly she came through a doorway, the harp on its strap bumping at her hip, and ran to them. "I have it," she said.

"Give it to me," Ilarion told her. "It will slow you down."

He slung the instrument over his shoulder. It was heavier than he'd expected, and he remembered with a prickle at his nape that it was made of the bones of a Master-Singer.

"Should we get horses from the Lower Court?" Mereth asked. Even with Tirsun and Theatana at the gates she sounded reluctant.

"Saddling and bridling will take too much time. We'll reach the foreshore just as quickly on foot. We couldn't escape by riding, anyway—Tirsun's cavalry would cut us off to the west. It's *Statira* or nothing."

"Yes, you're right. Let's go."

They hurried down the Grand Staircase to the Lower Court. A dozen of Ilarion's troopers were on the citadel battlements, peering down at the city. Among them was the signalman Stesen, who saw them approaching across the courtyard and came down from the wall-walk. Ilarion put his hand on his sword hilt, but the young soldier was merely looking worried.

"First-Captain, someone has opened the gates to the Protector. Is the Protectress coming? We need to see her."

"She's dead, Stesen. Let Tirsun into the citadel when he comes. It's his palace, now. But help me open the gate. The Grand Domestic and I and the Mistress-Singer must leave."

Shocked into obedience, Stesen did so. In moments Ilarion and the others had left him standing miserably in the open gateway and were on the ramp, hurrying down the flank of Beacon Hill. Shouts and the blare of horns rose from the direction of the Sunrise Gate. The sounds came from within the walls. Stesen was right; the Protector's men had entered the city.

At the foot of the ramp they turned left, away from the harbor and into Old Market Street, which led to Bayward Gate and the beaches west of the harbor breakwater. This was the dyers' and tanners' district and at this hour of the morning the narrow street should have been bustling and noisy. But it was deserted; only the stink of curing hides and fullers' vats suggested that people lived and worked behind these blank, plaster-peeling walls.

"Are you all right?" Ilarion asked Mereth, who was hurrying along beside him.

"I'm fine," she managed, though she sounded strained and out of breath. Ilarion cocked his head; he kept hearing faint harmonies like distant music. Now he realized it was the harp, its strings resounding to his motion and the morning breeze. He laughed.

"What?" Mereth asked breathlessly.

"The harp. It's singing."

"Yes, I hear it. Maybe Halicar's thinking of us, wherever he is."

"Maybe."

"The gate's open," Nenattu wheezed from behind them. "Look, no one's there."

He was right. The sentries must have thrown it open, then run for the safety of their homes. Through the opening Ilarion could see the azure of Monument Bay glittering in the early sunlight.

They broke into a run, pelting under the gate's lintel onto the broad sandy foreshore. No one was there. They made their way down the beach, the coarse brown sand dragging at their steps. It seemed a long way, for the tide was at the ebb. Small waves broke gently on the gravel at the water's edge.

Statira was only half a mile out in Monument Bay. She'd taken in much of her sail and was picking her way through the shallows. Ilarion ran knee-deep into the water and began waving. He could make out heads at *Statira*'s rail. They could certainly see him, too, but no one returned his frantic gestures.

He backed onto dry land and waved again. Mereth came up beside him, and said, "Surely they can see us?"

"Yes, but they can't tell it's us at this distance. Rook's being careful. If Lashgar reached him with our news, he knows Dymie's at war. But he can't tell from out there who holds the city." He squinted. "Wait. Ah, look, they're starting to swing out a boat. He's sending a shore party, thank the Allfather. If they just get close enough to recognize us—"

"Curse it," Nenattu gasped. "I hear horses inside the gate."

"The Lady have mercy on us," Mereth said. "They're coming."

Statira's crew was only now swinging the boat over the ship's side. How soon could they reach shore, even if they rowed straight in? But they wouldn't come straight in. As soon as they saw cavalry on the shore they'd sheer off, wait

until they could find out if the horsemen were friend or
enemy. Even if they realized he and Mereth needed help,
landing would be suicidal with cavalry awaiting them.

"Who can swim?" he asked. It was a faint hope.

"I can't," Nenattu said, and Mereth added, "I can't, either."

Despair swept through Ilarion. Safety lay almost within
reach, and they would never reach it.

He unslung the harp and set it on the sand. Its strings
hummed in the wind. It was a good, fair wind. *Statira* would
flit out of Monument Bay in no time at all, once she turned
and set course for home. They wouldn't be aboard her.

"We're not going to escape, are we?" Mereth said.

"No."

"You know him. What will he do to us?"

"Me and Nenattu he will kill. He'll likely spare you if
Theatana leaves it up to him. But I don't know if she'll do
that."

Mereth said, "Lady Mother, then let it be quick for all of
us."

He couldn't bring himself to tell her it probably wouldn't
be. Theatana was no fool, and she would ferret out soon
enough that he was close to Mereth. Then Mereth would suffer a hideous death; that would be part of Theatana's revenge
on Ilarion and the House Tessaris.

Nausea flooded him, and he moved his hand to his sword
hilt. Mereth wouldn't be alarmed if he drew. He could step
behind her, make it so fast she'd never know it was coming.

"No, Ilarion," she said quietly, looking up at him. "We
mustn't give up yet. There's still hope."

His hand relaxed a little. "It would be far cleaner than
what she may do."

"No. I won't let her win so easily."

Horses appeared in the gateway. Tirsun rode through it.
The Protector had clearly expected no resistance from
Dymie's few defenders, for his flimsy parade armor flashed
gold in the morning sun.

And with him was not Auvas Seitithi, the traitor. Riding
through the gate, instead, came Larth. Larth, unharmed, in

bright armor. Elyssa's own pronoyar, his face expressionless, but his eyes haunted.

Nenattu swore, a stream of curses. Staring in disbelief,
Ilarion barely heard him. He had suspected Larth of a little
disaffection, but never this.

"It was Larth," Mereth whispered in a broken voice.
"*Larth*. And she trusted him."

Between Larth and the Protector, Theatana rode on a pale
gray horse. She wore a gray robe and where her face should
have been, bronze glittered, for she also wore the mask. Her
long black hair gleamed even blacker against its metallic
brilliance.

Ilarion watched her approach across the sand, barely
noticing the score of Kaneshite cavalry that trotted behind.
Theatana filled his vision. Even Tirsun seemed petty beside her, a frivolous man of small sordid lusts and trifling
ambitions.

When they were only twenty feet away, Tirsun put up a
hand. The cavalcade stopped.

"Hello, Ilarion," he said. "I know you'd like to kill me, so
leave your sword in its scabbard, or my men will slaughter
you and all your friends." He gazed out at the bay and
grinned. "This must be quite hard for you—so close to
safety, a ship out there all set to pluck you from my fingers,
and no luck at the end. You almost got away, you and your
little brood. But *almost* isn't the mark, is it? And my sister
is dead, the rumor goes. I imagine it's true, or she'd be with
you. *Is* it true?"

"Yes, she is," Ilarion said. He stared at the pronoyar. Larth
would not meet his eyes, but gazed stolidly out to sea.

"Larth Tetnias," Ilarion said, "you're forsworn. You broke
your oath. She trusted you, when she trusted no one else of
your rank. And you brought her this."

The pronoyar made an angry gesture. "She wouldn't even
try to give our realm back us," he said harshly. "She turned
her back on the heritage of the Rasenna. But the Protector
will restore us. With the sorcery of the Giftbearer's Heiress,
we'll take our old lands back and be great again."

"And you think she's told you the truth?" Ilarion said.

Even allowing for Larth's ignorance of Theatana, he could hardly believe it. "She lies. I know what she is and where she came from, and she's no heir of any Giftbearer. She's death and worse. Kill her while you have a chance."

"This is all very interesting," Tirsun interrupted, "but we have a great deal to attend to this morning. To begin with—"

"Let the Mistress-Singer leave us," Ilarion said, "before you do anything else. Give her a cavalry escort for wherever she wants to go. And remind them that she's inviolate. And do you know where her brother is?"

"Ah, as to that," Tirsun said, looking confused and taken aback for a moment, "well—" He smiled, but the smile was anxious, and he glanced aside at Theatana's still and silent form. "I won't harm the Mistress-Singer, but I don't think we'll let her go just yet. And as for Halicar . . . well, in fact, Theatana doesn't seem constrained by custom. If you see what I mean, Mistress-Singer."

"*Where is my brother?*" Mereth cried out. "What have you *done*, you monstrosity?"

"She—" Larth began, but broke off as Theatana turned the mask's eyes on him. Then she swung its gaze back to Mereth, and said, "Your chirping brother is dead, girl. I killed him myself. I stabbed him through the heart. It was quicker than I liked."

"No," Mereth groaned, sagging against Ilarion. "Halicar. Oh, no."

"You see?" Tirsun said. His false cheer had evaporated, though he struggled to maintain his nonchalance. "She's quite beyond my control when she's annoyed. I just have to indulge her."

"Mereth," said Theatana, "don't be so appalled at your brother's death. He had a quick one, which is more than you will. My nephew has tried to protect you, and he, and you, will pay bitterly for that. Your death will be slow. You'll shriek and wriggle."

"Leave her alone, Theatana," Ilarion shouted at her. "Take your revenge on me. She's nothing to you!"

"But she's your friend, isn't she? I thought as much. She's

a lovely young woman, but we'll change that. But I won't
use the knife and the hooks and the fire on her. *You* will."

Mereth swayed and almost fell. Ilarion's lips and face
went numb. Theatana watched him, amused, as he tried to
find words. At last he croaked, "Nothing you do to me can
make me hurt her."

She chuckled, hollow within the mask. "Ah, but there
you're wrong. I have recently made a man kill himself when
he wanted to live. You're fond of Mereth, I'm sure, though I
don't believe you're her lover, but you *will* hurt her. And
isn't she beautiful? But once you've been busy with her for
a day or two, she won't be beautiful at all. She'll be quite
disgusting—people will shriek at the sight of her. I don't
think you'll care for her by then, and Mereth certainly won't
like you, not after what you've been doing to her." Again the
chuckle. "And then it will be your turn. You'll likely have
gone mad by then, of course. But it will still hurt."

He should instantly release Mereth from the death that
hung over her. But even now he couldn't bring himself to do
it. "Tirsun," he said, "if you value anything at all, kill the
creature. I don't know if it's still possible, but *try*."

"Yes," Mereth said, her voice cracking with grief and
anger. "Kill her, Tirsun. She's killed my brother. She's
cursed. It will fall on you, too."

"Oh, but he's afraid to kill me," Theatana said. "*And* he
likes my bed too much. I rule here, Ilarion. In a few years I'll
rule in the Ascendancy, too."

Her confidence filled him with dread. "How?" he demanded. "With the army of Kanesh? The Paladine Guard
alone could flatten it."

"I meant it when I said I'd restore the power of the
Rasenna, Ilarion. With the mask I can do exactly that. And
on the mainland there are a myriad myriads of Hazannu, all
fit to be soldiers in the new Great Garden, and the Rasenna
know how to build ships that can reach the Ascendancy.
There will be a war. The War of the Chain will be a cross-
roads skirmish beside it." She laughed. "As for that, I may
not even need to defeat your armies at all. I have my mask.
Give me a half turn of the hourglass in the Fountain Palace

and your mother and father will speak with my voice. They won't like what I make them say and neither will the Ascendancy, but it won't matter. I'll do what I please, and they'll suffer the consequences. So will everyone . . . But now it's time to begin amusing ourselves. First, I need a death. Perhaps the dodderer with you. You, old man! Come here."

Nenattu stood as if rooted to the sand. Larth was staring past Theatana at Tirsun. In a strangled voice, he blurted, "Protector, didn't you hear what she just said? *Does* she rule here? Or do you?"

Tirsun looked sideways at Theatana and opened his mouth as if to speak. Then the mask turned on him, and he said nothing.

"Larth," Theatana murmured, shifting her gaze back to the pronoyar, "you never quite understood how it was to be, did you? But how convenient you've become."

She sat very still. So did Larth and Tirsun. It seemed to Ilarion that the morning had frozen into a single instant. The waves on Monument Bay hung poised and motionless, the horses' manes ceased blowing in the wind.

A spectral blur exuded from the mouth of the mask, formed into a shape. He saw Theatana in it, or a wraith of Theatana, eye sockets opening on an abyss. It contracted to a faintly glowing ball the size of a fist and slid through the air to hang over Larth's head. The pronoyar, face stark with fear, gazed up at it.

Theatana's hand darted. The dagger blade buried itself in Larth's throat, came out, flickered wetly, stabbed again. Blood spewed in pulses over his horse's withers, spattered his armor, drenched Theatana's forearm. He toppled from his horse, gurgling, and fell on his back on the sand. Theatana dismounted, knelt by Larth as he twitched and foamed. She bent over him as if to kiss him on the mouth. The cavalrymen watched, struck motionless with fear. Tirsun's face was white, his nostrils pinched. All eyes were fixed on Theatana and the blur hanging over her and the writhing pronoyar. No one watched Ilarion.

Kill her even though you die. In three strides he covered

the ground between them, his dagger drawn and swinging
back for a fatal blow. She half rose to meet him, but he
knocked her off her feet and she sprawled with a shriek of
fury to the sand. In an instant the javelins would pierce
him—

His dagger struck her over the heart. Skidded harmlessly.
She wore armor under her robe. She twisted under him, and
he saw the mask a handspan from his face. Tirsun yelled, but
still no javelin blade sliced into his back.

Pull it off her.

But at his first touch on the bronze the world ebbed,
shrank to a pinpoint. The mask swelled into him, became a
whirlpool, drew him down to its black eye where Theatana
lurked in its labyrinths.

"Come in," she whispered from its coils and spirals. "I
have a place for you here, forever. I am what you feared
most, you and your mother and father. I am Erkai's seed
grown tall. I am the scion of a thanaturge. I am the hand of
the Adversary."

His own voice, a whisper, reminding him. *I wore the mask
in Charunna. I found memories. I must look there.*

For a timeless instant he searched himself, found at last
what he sought: the moments when he lay in his mother's
womb as she and his father fought Erkai the twice-born. He
saw as if through her eyes; there was a green hill, and from
the hill's summit soared a colossal obelisk of black stone. At
the obelisk's foot stood his mother and father, hand in hand,
and before them roared a black whirlwind. In the wind's evil
the hill shook, and the obelisk cracked, and he knew what
his mother had not told him. Erkai the Chain had killed them
all. She and his father had given their lives, and their child's
life, to destroy him.

And then he saw that they were in a garden, and with
them was a woman. She filled a cup and gave it to them, and
said: *This is the water of life. Take, and drink.*

He'd heard her words in Charunna when he wore the
mask, but now he knew their meaning. For his mother's and
father's sacrifice they were allowed to come back from
death. As was he.

I died in my mother's womb, and returned into life before I took my first breath. I am twice-born, like Erkai the Chain. As he withstood the Ban, I can withstand even Theatana's sorcery. But how can I destroy her? I'm no Erkai, commanding the Deep Magic.

She killed Halicar. There is a curse.

The spiral heaved, broke into shards and vanished. Sunlight lay warm on his face. Rough hands dragged him along the sand, dropped him onto his back. He opened his eyes. Theatana stood a dozen feet away, still wearing the mask. Tirsun was next to her, holding a javelin poised and ready to strike. The soldiers who had thrown him to the sand were nearby. They looked frightened and kept glancing back at Theatana. Her phantom self roiled in the air at her side, a ravenous specter. Her silent stillness froze Ilarion's heart.

"I'd have spitted you already," Tirsun said, breathing fast, "but I know *she* wants the pleasure. What a stupid thing for you to do. Now she's *really* annoyed. I can tell."

Mereth was kneeling on the sand. Her eyes were closed, and she was rocking back and forth. Nenattu sat beyond her, elbows on knees, head sunk in hands. Halicar's harp lay by Ilarion's foot. The bones of the dead Master-Singer gleamed white in the sunlight. A gust of wind passed over it, and the bones hummed.

I have been among the dead. I must call upon my brethren.

He reached out and struck the strings.

Their chime rang out softly, strengthened, and without warning pealed into thunder. Harmonies blossomed in the sunlight. Color spilled from the air, floods of azure, crimson, gold, emerald. Vast chords of music poured through seething rainbows. Tirsun screamed, dropped the javelin, clapped hands over his ears.

"*Halicar!*" Mereth cried, her voice resounding with joy and terror.

The peal of harmonies faded and from the swirling light, from the music, from the bones of the harp, burst talons and scales and pinions, the golden-beaked head, the plumed serpent, the pandragore. Wings vast as sails, it hurtled skyward.

Ilarion struck the harp again, summoning, summoning. The
light became harmony, and the harmony became light, torrents of light, the wings of the pandragore sweeping Ilarion
into it, Halicar's face in the radiance, the dead not dead but
living, song without end. And this was Halicar transformed;
he was the Hidden Singer, the pandragore, the song at the
roots of Creation.

*Halicar, my brother. Theatana did not know what she
struck down.*

*I was Halicar then. Now I am her fate, as you are, be-
cause you called me, and we are together. We are the curse
she raised by my death.*

Now they *were* the pandragore, two in one in the plumed
serpent, the Transformed, the power outside eternity, and
Ilarion saw with its sight. They plunged on Theatana. She
shrieked and threw up her arms as the blazing creature fell
toward her, and her wraith fled into the mask's dark mouth.
They swept into the mask after her, riding its spiral. Fear
touched Ilarion, but they went on and plunged into its dark
eye, the coil where Theatana lurked.

She was there, and she fought. Pain speared Ilarion, shafts
of fury and hatred, but she fell back before their onslaught.
She fled them down the shafts and passages of her being as
they pursued her, the music burning her darkness away, until
in the depths they drove her to the yawning mouths of passages that led into realms beyond even the mask's vast
labyrinths. At last Theatana turned at bay, threw herself
against her pursuers. Even she would not plunge willingly
into those unknown gulfs, but in her last extremity she
screamed for help.

Ilarion heard her calling and heard the call answered.
From the abyss the Adversary boiled into the mask, a glacial
cold that withered hope, a freezing silence that rose before
the music and swallowed it. In that extinction, Creation died
and Theatana said, in a cold sweet voice like that of the one
she had summoned: *Now I have you both.*

Halicar laughed. The music burst forth again, in blazing
chords that seared the darkness, swept the Adversary from
the song of Creation, hurled it into the pit, and sealed it

there. Theatana shrieked, spun into unspeakable voids, eternities of silence, banished from all light, from all music. Dwindled, became a fleck, a mote. Winked into nonbeing. Ilarion spun with the pandragore out of the mask as its fabric frayed and strained. He saw the spiral from afar, watched it blur, fade, dissolve as the light of the music tore it apart. The music began to fade, and its radiance with it.

Halicar, is Elyssa with you?

Yes. We're well. Oh, well indeed. We'll meet again, you and I and Mereth.

Good-bye.

His essence remained for a moment, a winged light and piercing melody, and then he was gone.

Ilarion found himself on the beach, on his knees. The transition was so abrupt that he looked wildly around, dazed and blinking. But Mereth was leaning against him, warm and safe, and Nenattu was shaking his head as if to clear his sight. The cavalrymen had fled down the beach in a cloud of dust. Tirsun was galloping after them.

"I saw Halicar," Mereth said in a faint voice. "In the fireshta. I heard him. He's become . . . oh, Ilarion, he's become the Hidden Singer."

"Yes," Ilarion managed. "And Elyssa's with him. He told me."

"If only they could have stayed with us." Her voice broke a little. "Just for a while."

Words were useless, so he put his arm around her. The harp lay near them on the sand, humming faintly in the wind and looking as it had always looked. A few yards away, Theatana sprawled motionless on her back. She still wore the mask. Its bronze was dulled and streaked with green, as though some sorcerous life had drained out of it.

"Is she dead?" Nenattu asked in a halting voice. He seemed dazed.

"I'll look." Ilarion got to his feet and walked to Theatana. He did not want to touch the mask and so drew his sword to lift it from her face.

It would not come off. He tried again, with the same result. It was as though the thing had grown into her flesh. He peered at her. Within the shadowed eye sockets, her eyes appeared to be closed.

They opened, and his marrow went cold. They were not Theatana's eyes or any human's. He looked into a pit, a gulf, an abyss of annihilation.

In one motion he raised his sword and swung. The edge bit through skin and flesh, cartilage and bone, severed the slender golden neck, grated into the sand, stopped. Theatana's head rolled to one side and lay still. The mask cracked along a myriad of hidden seams, crumbled into fragments, the fragments shivered to fine dust and vanished like fog in sunlight. Theatana's face remained for a few instants as he had seen it in Charunna, cold and beautiful. Then her body, like the mask, dissolved, became a wraith, became thin smoke on the wind from the sea, and was gone.

30

ILARION STARED DOWN AT THE SAND. THE WIND WAS ALREADY smoothing out the shallow depression where Theatana's body had been. Not a trace remained to show that either she or the mask had ever existed.

From behind him Nenattu said shakily, "Would we be safe from her now, do you think?"

"Yes," Ilarion said, "I think so."

"The boat!" Mereth cried suddenly. "Ilarion, it's almost here!"

He'd utterly forgotten about *Statira*. He sheathed his sword and turned to look across the bay. The boat was close inshore now, Lashgar in the bow and waving. Ilarion waved back, then hurried to stand by Mereth.

The ground shuddered as he reached her. Like a drum struck in the earth's marrow, a long, thundering boom rumbled underfoot and resonated into the air. The sand twitched.

"Another tremor," Mereth said, alarm on her face. "I wish it wouldn't *do* that."

"So do I," Ilarion agreed. He scanned the horizon beyond the mouth of the bay, searching anxiously for a wall of water like the one that had surged ashore in Kanesh, but saw nothing out of the ordinary.

"What's the matter?" Nenattu asked. He still sounded shaken.

"I'm wondering if we'll get a wave, the way Kanesh did after the tremor last spring. But the water isn't falling, and it did then. Anyway, I don't see anything."

"It seemed to me the noise came from inland, not from the sea," Mereth said. "Maybe that's why there's no wave."

It seemed a good bet. He nodded and answered, "You're probably right." He returned his attention to *Statira*'s boat, which was almost at the shore. Lashgar was leaning over the bow, peering into the shallows for lurking rocks. Safety was at last at hand.

The boat surged into the low surf and Ilarion waded knee-deep into the waves to help ground her. Lashgar slid over-board on the other side of the bow, and together they skidded the craft securely into the sand at the water's edge. The crew hauled in their oars with a rumble and thump.

"Thank the Allfather you're all alive," Lashgar blurted as he followed Ilarion onto the beach. "I was sure it was you and Mereth here, but I saw cavalry and I think Tirsun and Theatana, too—then I saw lights, and Tirsun and the cavalry ran away, if it was Tirsun, and I *think* I saw Theatana go down." He looked around. "Where is she? *Was* that Tirsun? Who's winning?"

"I don't know who's winning right now," Ilarion said. "But yes, it was Tirsun. And you saw what you thought you saw. Theatana's dead. But her body vanished, with the mask."

"A sorceress to the end," Lashgar said angrily. "The poisonous bitch. You're *sure* she's dead?"

"As sure as I can be."

Lashgar looked anxiously at Mereth. "And you're all right, too?" he asked.

"No," she said. She seemed beyond tears. "No, Lashgar, I'm not. Halicar's dead. Theatana murdered him."

A brief silence fell, while the waves broke on the sand. Faintly, from within the city, came shouts and wails. Two helmeted heads appeared on the towers of Bayward Gate, but no one came out through the gate itself. Of Tirsun and his escort there was no sign.

"I'm sorry," Lashgar said at last. "He was my friend. He was one of the best men I ever met. Does Elyssa—"

He saw it on their faces. "No!" he burst out. "Not Elyssa, too. Not *both* of them."

Ilarion said, "It was a battle wound. There was nothing we could do. She died of it this morning."

"So her brother's won after all," Lashgar said furiously. Tears stood in his eyes. "She's dead, and Halicar's dead, and Tirsun gets everything. Where's the justice? *Where?*"

"There's more to it than that," Ilarion said. "But we'll tell you after we're off this beach. I—"

Sudden sharp exclamations from the boat's crew made him look around. They were staring inland. So was Nenattu. His mouth had dropped open in a dark O.

"Ilarion!" Mereth cried. "What's that?"

His gaze followed hers. A blue-black cloud was rising above the horizon to the northwest. It looked something like an inverted pine tree. Either it was fairly close and climbing slowly, or very far away and climbing very fast.

Suddenly he realized that it was indeed far away, and that meant it was rising at tremendous speed. And to appear so big at that distance . . . it was vast. Huger than mountains.

"Mereth," he asked urgently, "what's in that direction?"

Her brow furrowed. "Velchi. The hot springs."

"I don't like the looks of this. We'd better get out of here." He looked around for Halicar's harp, grabbed it up and slung it over his shoulder. "Lashgar, Nenattu, have you ever seen a cloud like that?"

"It might be from a burning mountain," the prince answered, shading his brow with a hand and staring at the cloud. "There are some in the eastern Havens that spit out smoke and melted stone. But nothing that *big*."

"Nenattu?"

The man shook his head. "I've never seen its like, my lord. But I think you're right. We'd better get out of here before—"

He broke off as a second cloud suddenly boiled from beneath the first. It was far larger. it swallowed the first cloud and sped skyward. In moments it was covering half the northwest horizon. People were shouting within the city.

The beach rumbled. Nenattu yelled, Mereth screamed. Ilarion staggered as the ground jerked, and without warning a great slab of Dymie's fortification wall leaned inward. The earth shuddered again; shaken beyond endurance, the wall abruptly toppled in a roaring welter of shattered stone. The towers of Bayward Gate swayed, then collapsed in thunder to their foundations; the massive oaken gates themselves burst from their hinges and crashed in splinters beneath tons of masonry.

But even that din was swallowed up in the bellow that rolled through the ground from the northwest. With it, as if the air itself had turned to iron, came a sound as solid as a hammerblow, a concussion that rattled teeth and bones, paralyzed thought and action. It drove Ilarion to his knees; around him, the others fell and sprawled on the shuddering earth.

How long it lasted he did not know; only a dozen heartbeats perhaps, but it seemed a dozen eons. Then the thunder lessened and the shaking stopped except for a slight, steady tremble underfoot. With the others he staggered to his feet and saw, through the huge breach in the wall, the ruin of Dymie. Half the city had fallen into its own streets.

"Merciful Lady," Nenattu wailed, "it's the end of everything." The boat crewmen were shouting to each other and calling for them to get aboard.

Ilarion found his wits. The cloud in the northwest was enormous, still rising and rapidly getting much, much larger.

"Quick, we have to be quick," he yelled. "The wind will bring it this way!"

They all splashed into the shallows. The crewmen were casting wild glances at the cloud and sliding their oars into the locks. Ilarion helped Mereth and Nenattu into the boat. Then he and Lashgar heaved the keel along the sand until the craft floated free, and scrambled aboard.

"What *is* that?" Lashgar asked apprehensively as he stared inland. The cloud was enormous, still rising and rapidly getting much, much larger. The men swung the boat around and began rowing furiously toward the ship.

"It's the end of Haidra," Ilarion said.

Dusk fell and the rain of Last Winter began to fall with it. Little Summer was over. *Statira* was many miles out in the Sleeve, tacking for Ushnana against a westerly wind.

The northern sky was black, but not with night. A mountain had spewed itself into the sky at Velchi, and the earth had shaken Haidra's cities down. Gray ash was falling from end to end of the great island, mixed with the rain, burying the winter rye, the vineyards, the fields plowed for the spring planting, the farms, the villages, the bodies of the dead. Charunna of the Roses, the city of tombs, was herself entombed. Kanesh lay dying under a deluge of cinders and sodden dust; the blue pavilion on the Citadel Stone had fallen in ruins.

In the darkness of the deluge of ash, Tirsun became separated from his men. He met a band of farm slaves whose overseer had run away. They knew he was a nobleman, and buried him under pumice in a cesspit, alive.

Elyssa lay alone on the Harbor Terrace of her palace. Soaked by the gray rain, ash gathered deep upon her. Like the dark mounds drifting now over the dead cities, this also would dry and harden in the warmth of the coming spring. Years would pass; mainlanders would tell stories of an island and a people turned to stone.

Then, slowly, the Green Lady would return. Ash would erode to soil and gather in sheltered hollows; grass would spring up, then bushes, and the roots of trees would knit the buried bones of cities. And tomb roses would grow on a quiet hilltop overlooking the sea, a place where a palace once stood, blooming white as summer cloud over the grave of the last Protectress of the Rasenna.

31

"If I'd known this was here," Rook said, staring at the colossal fortifications of Captala Nea as the ship glided from Chalice Bay into the mouth of the River Seferis, "I'd have been more respectful when I first visited the Blue Havens. And this is where you live. And it's your father and mother who rule"—he waved an arm expansively—"all this."

"They do," Ilarion said, in Rasennan; Rook hadn't learned much of the Logomenon on the voyage north, being both too busy with his ship and also somewhat inept with foreign languages. "That's Temple Mount," he went on, pointing ashore at the heights rising within the vast triple walls. "The building at its summit is the House of the Sacred Marriage. And over on its right, see there? That's Dynasts' Hill and the Fountain Palace. You used to be able to see the Obelisk on the Hill of Remembrance even from here, but it fell during the War of the Chain."

"It's a beautiful city," Mereth said, her lovely voice a little breathless with wonder. "I've never seen a place like it." In her excitement she also spoke in Rasennan instead of the Logomenon. She'd been learning Ilarion's tongue as fast as she could aboard ship, but was not yet entirely fluent. "And look at all the people on the walls. And all the boats coming out to meet us."

Ilarion's throat suddenly tightened. "I'm home, Mereth. I'm home."

"I know," she said, smiling up at him. He was glad to see that she could take so much delight in the splendor of his na-

448

tive city, for she was still grieving for Halicar. Though it was so quiet a grief that it was now almost invisible, he knew her sadness would never completely leave her. But she had begun to sing again.

"I wish Lashgar were here," he said, gazing at the banners and the crowds as *Statira* drew closer to the outer docks. "He loves celebrations."

"He's had enough travel for a while," Mereth reminded him. "Remember how happy he was to be back in Ammedara with his family? You must know how that feels."

"True. We'll see him next year, anyway. We were lucky, weren't we?" They'd had an easy voyage north, much better than expected. The actual sailing time between Ushnana and there had been just three months. They'd found the Meridians without trouble, and were very lucky with the weather. After the experience of his nightmare journey south on the first *Statira*, he had been worried by the prospect of the return voyage. Knowing that Kayonu had done it without extreme hardship had encouraged him only a little. But in the event the journey had been merely uncomfortable, not dire.

"We were very lucky indeed," Mereth agreed. She was staring up at Captala's towering ramparts. "I've never seen such strength in a city," she said. "Never."

"The walls were raised with the help of the Deep Magic," Ilarion said. "A long time ago, before the Ban was set."

Mereth shivered. "And that was the sorcery Theatana tried to grasp."

"Yes, it was."

"But she's dead now," Mereth said. "She can't hurt us anymore, can she?"

"No, she can't. She's gone forever."

"Are you sure your mother and father will welcome me?" Mereth asked, a little anxiously. "They won't think I've come as an uninvited guest?"

"Of course it will be all right. You know I wrote from Ammedara and told them everything."

"I can't help it. Suppose they didn't get the letters?"

"At least one must have reached them. Anyway, once they've heard you sing, you'll never have to leave the palace again unless you want to. There they are, look! That's Katheri with them."

His parents and his sister were on the dock. Two days ago he had sent a fast dispatch galley ahead, to warn of *Statira*'s imminent arrival, and he and Mereth were obviously expected.

Rook bellowed orders; the guide-sails dropped, *Statira* swung to the quay, ropes flew through the air, and the docking crew took the lines ashore. Windlasses turned, dragging the ship to her moorings. Ilarion waved furiously; his parents and Katheri waved just as furiously in answer.

The gangway went down. His father half ran to its foot, then raced up its planks, dragging his mother with him. Katheri was at their heels. Then for some time it was embraces, tears, kisses, slaps on the back. Suddenly his mother broke free, and exclaimed, "Key, for pity's sake, we're mannerless bumpkins. Ilarion, this must be Mereth?"

"Yes," he said, drawing her forward. "Mereth, this is my father, the Dynast Kienan of the House Tessaris. His friends call him Key. This is my mother, the Dynastessa Mandine of the House of the Dascarids. Here's my sister, who will talk you into distraction if you allow it, the Luminessa Katheri."

He took a deep breath, and went on, "And all of you, this is Mereth, daughter of Eranvel of the race of the Antecessors. As I wrote to you, she saved my life at great risk to herself, and then kept me alive when I was close to dying of fever." He grinned. "Perhaps more important, she's a musician of staggering talent. Wait till you hear her sing."

Mandine, smiling, took Mereth by her shoulders and embraced her. She said, "Welcome to Captala, Mereth. We thought for so long that we'd lost our son. And we would have, if it weren't for you. We can never repay that debt."

Mereth inclined her head. "Thank you, my lady Dynastessa." She spoke a little haltingly, in her lilting Antecessor accent. "But it's not any debt. I'm very glad I could help him."

"Please call me Mandine." Mandine was about to go on when Katheri broke in. "I play the flute, too," she said excitedly. "Not so well as you, Mereth, I'm sure, but we could find out how we sound together. And you're a singer, you *must* tell me what you think of my poetry—"

"Katheri, Katheri," Ilarion exclaimed, laughing. "Let us at least set foot on land before you begin." He looked past her at his father and made a despairing gesture. And he thought: *Tonight I can tell him that I'm fit to rule. I've been a Luminessos, and I've been a slave, and I've mastered the furies that my Dascarid blood passed down to me.*

Key grinned at him. "I'm glad you're back, my son," he said. "Welcome home, Ilarion."